To Madison for the inspiration.

And to Alex, who gave Madison
six more years of life —
allowing me to know her.

PART I

1

WINDOWS

February 2000

I T was like seeing someone again for the first time.
As Cara sat across from him at the coffee shop, she
looked into his comforting yet unfamiliar eyes that caressed
her unstable nerves into balance. Somehow all the chatter around
them faded, and he was the only thing in her focus. She wanted to
know everything about him but reveal nothing about herself. Two
and a half years ago, Cara wouldn't have been so closed off, but
the girl she used to be had died.

While they teased and flirted, she thought part of her old self
might resurrect, but as he gently pried, Cara couldn't allow herself
to open.

She raised her hot tea to her lips as she searched for the
words. "Look . . . I'm a pretty broken person with a past I'm not
ready to talk about yet. I've never been in a relationship, and now
would not be the time to start one."

He leaned forward, interested, but said nothing.

Cara swallowed hard. "I don't know if that's what's going on
here, and I'm sorry if I led you on . . . Please know I want to get
to know you, but you don't want to date me."

Her cheeks felt as hot as her tea, and she wanted to look down
but kept her gaze on him as he offered an empathetic expression.
"This is kinda perfect," he said. "There's something about me that

3

I'd rather keep hidden as well. It would be unfair for anyone to date me, so I don't want to get into a relationship either."

"Why did you ask me to come here, then?"

"Oh, I'm intrigued by you, Cara. But for now, let's not worry about each other's yesterdays or tomorrows. Let's get to know each other's todays."

Cara sat back in her chair. Her heart slowed, and all her senses relaxed.

So despite their mutual interest, they agreed to tell so many nothings, which slowly turned into all the everythings.

~

Fall 1988

"You're going to love this story!"

Eight-year-old Cara Ecrivain threw the dull pencil she had used to write her latest plot and ran into the living room. "Daddy, do you want to read my—"

She stopped, realizing the only response she'd receive was the deep wheezing sounds of her father who had already passed out in his recliner. Cara looked down at her words on the paper— ones she desperately wanted him to hear. She squeezed her eyes shut and let out a disappointed sigh.

The canned laughter from the neglected television unsettled the stillness of the room.

Cara saw the empty Scotch glass on the end table next to her father. Like so many other nights, she picked it up and shuffled into the kitchen. Her mother bent over the sink, washing dishes with extra care as if any little spot left on a plate would propel the rest of the house into disarray.

"Goodnight, Mommy," Cara said over the sound of running water.

It took her a moment to register that her daughter had spoken. "What?"

"I just said, 'Goodnight.'"

Her mother's gaze remained fixated on the dishes. "Oh, okay. Is your room clean?"

"Yeah."

"Did you make sure to say goodnight to your father?"

She looked over her shoulder at her father in the living room. "Yeah . . . I did."

Cara set the glass next to the sink and hurried to her bedroom. From the squeaky drawer of her nightstand, she grabbed her flashlight, clicked it on, and shone the beam from her window into the bedroom window of the house next door.

"Come on. *Please* still be up," she whispered.

The light of the other bedroom turned on, and there stood her best friend, Adam Aether, in plaid pajamas and thick pop-bottle glasses. Cara sighed. The sight of him immediately slowed her pulse.

"Hey, Cara," he half-whispered.

"Were you asleep?"

"Nope, just eating a Twinkie." His mouth still full.

They both began to giggle. Adam had the most infectious laugh, and they had to strain to keep themselves quiet.

Cara finally caught her breath. "Oh my gosh, you *know* you're going to get caught!"

"Eh, I'll blame it on Angela."

"Does your sister even like Twinkies?"

"She's a teenager. She'll eat anything."

This commenced more snickering.

"You got a new story for me tonight?" Adam asked as he polished off his stolen snack.

"I just finished one. It's called 'The Boy Who Rode the Wind.'"

Propping his elbows on the windowsill, Adam cradled his head in his hands as Cara began to read.

```
"There was once a boy who had a magical
kite that would take him away from home
whenever he wanted . . ."
```

The nightly ritual of reading stories through the window started when they were five. Even though they often played together after school, the daytime hours weren't enough for these best friends—they needed the nighttime, too.

```
". . . and as he watched his kite fly off
in the distance, he grabbed her hand and
knew he had made the right choice. And
they lived happily ever after. The end."
```

Adam's chin remained rested in his hands. He took a moment then said, "I think that's one of my new favorites."

"Really?"

"Yeah." He sat up, eyes bright. "It was about a boy this time."

"You only liked it because it was about a boy?"

He shrugged. "Well, kinda, I guess."

Cara rolled her eyes. "Remember, it's your turn to share a story next time."

"Oh, I've got a good one for ya."

"Why the hell did you wake me up?"

"You drove home drunk again, didn't you?"

Their conversation was broken by verbal punches thrown between her parents down the hall. Cara turned her eyes to the noise.

"Maybe next time, I just won't even come home!"

"Perfect! Then I could finally get rid of that hideous recliner you always pass out in!"

Cara placed her hands back on the window sill and faced Adam again. She could always tell when he could hear their fights from his room by his wincing face. He dropped his jaw, but Cara spoke first. "Have you ever snuck out of your window before?"

"No, why?"

"I think we should try it. Then we could talk right by each other instead of through the window."

"I don't know . . . I don't even know how to get out of the window. And what if I fall and break my ankles?"

"You're not going to break your ankles, Adam."

"But what if you get caught?"

Cara turned her head toward the door and listened to the vile insults and empty threats her parents hurled at each other. She wanted nothing more than to escape to somewhere else. Anywhere else. She looked at Adam and held him in her crestfallen eyes. "I don't think they would even notice I was gone."

Adam fidgeted with his glasses but finally puffed up his chest. He grabbed a blanket from his bed and lowered it onto the grass. Raising his window higher, he stuck out his right leg—holding onto the frame with white knuckles. With his chubby belly through, he dropped to the ground, walked over to Cara's window, and held up his hand to guide her as she crawled out.

There they were—eight-year-old fugitives.

The fall night in Canterville, Ohio, outside of Dayton, blew a warm wind between their small bodies. They stood on the dead grass that connected their ranch houses—his with white siding, hers with the brick façade—awkwardly staring at each other as they listened to their heavy breathing from the rush. Unsure of what to do next, the moment had become rather anticlimactic.

Finally, Adam grabbed his blanket and Cara's hand and led her to a portion of the back yard that was clear of the tall oaks. Dead leaves crunched under their feet.

"Here." He set the blanket on the cool ground and invited Cara to join him. They lay on their backs and looked at the sky full of diamonds. Their third grade class was in the middle of an astronomy unit, so they both felt like experts on the night sky. Taking turns, they each pointed out Venus, the North Star, the Big Dipper, Orion, and the Gemini Twins.

Then they sat wordlessly as they took in the night's beauty. In their silence, Cara noticed the steady rhythm of Adam's breath. Its cadence opposed the chaos inside her house, and it was so soothing that if she wasn't careful, it would lull her to sleep.

Something cut across the sky that interrupted her thoughts.

"Hey! A shooting star!" Adam whispered. "Now, you get to make a wish."

"Okay." Cara squeezed her eyes shut and gritted her teeth. She looked back up with desperate hope.

"What did you wish for?" Adam asked.

"I can't tell you. If I do, it won't come true."

"Actually, that doesn't happen if you only tell your very best friend, and if they don't tell anyone else."

"I don't know if I can take that risk," Cara said. "I really want this wish to come true."

"Come on, you can trust me."

"All right." Cara turned her eyes back up to the heavens, crossed her fingers, and rested them on her chest. "I wish your parents could be my parents."

2

PEN PAL

A buzzing noise continued after Cara turned off her alarm clock the next morning. It was the sound of the vacuum cleaner. Her mother always cleaned but not at this time of day.

After she dressed, Cara moved to the kitchen where breakfast usually waited for her. Today, however, the table was bare except for a small object the size of a candy bar in plain foil wrapping stamped: "Breakfast Bar."

This observation was interrupted when her father ambled in as he tied his tie.

"How about that episode of *Growing Pains* last night, Pen Pal?"

She cracked a small smile at his nickname for her.

"I didn't see it. I was in my room writing. I was going to read my story to you, but—"

"Ah, that's my little Pen Pal, always writing." He patted her head like a pet and finished tying his tie. "Maybe you'll read your latest story to me tonight?" He placed his half-full mug of black coffee next to the sink and walked out the door.

The vacuum now hummed from the office, and Cara followed the sound. There was her mother, mindlessly pushing the appliance back and forth—making perfect lines in the carpet. Not only was her timing unusual, but this morning, high heeled pumps and a tailored dress replaced her typical mom jeans and Keds.

"Mom? What are you doing?" Cara shouted.

Her mother shut off the vacuum just long enough to say, "I

8

have to vacuum before I head to my new job today. Did you make your bed?"

Cara tried to yell over the reverberations that quickly resumed. "Wha—? Yeah, I made my bed, but what are you talking about?"

Her mother let out a sigh and shut off the machine one more time. "What do you need, Cara? I can't stand here and have a whole conversation. I'm in a hurry."

"You never said anything about a job."

"Yes, I did. I'm going to start working part-time at Dr. Hall's optometry office. There's something for you to eat on the table. I won't have time to make you anything in the mornings now."

"But, Mom—"

"Cara, it's not a big deal. Besides, this will be extra money to put away for your college. You may not appreciate that now, but you will in ten years."

Cara grabbed the bar along with her backpack and walked to the bus with soft steps.

"What's that?" Adam asked.

Her face was expressionless as she slid into the seat next to him. "My breakfast, I guess."

"What do you mean? Your mom always makes you breakfast."

"I have to eat these from now on. My mom doesn't have time to make me anything because she's busy with her new job."

Adam furrowed his brow. "What? Moms aren't supposed to work!"

"Well, I plan to work when I'm a mom."

"You *do*? And be *what*?"

"Yeah, I do! I'm going to be a great author and publish a million books. Probably more. But I'd hire a housekeeper so I would have more time with my kids and not have to clean all the time."

"That doesn't count." Adam shook his head. "Authors just sit at home and write. They don't need to even leave the house. You could easily be a mom with that job."

Cara thought about his argument. Whenever she wrote, she *did* just sit at home. He must be right.

"I bet you sell millions of books, too," Adam continued. "Maybe you could sell some of my stories when you're famous, but under your name. People will buy it from you because you'll be famous-er than me."

"No way. You'll have to do that yourself."

Cara was always happily distracted when she was with Adam. They continued to joke as Cara bit into the Breakfast Bar. The synthetic taste made her gag.

"What's the matter?"

"This is horrible!"

"Let me try it." Adam ate anything, but when he took a bite, he struggled to force it down. "That's like eating . . . sadness! Did your mom give you that by mistake?"

"I don't know, but I'm so hungry. If I don't eat something, there's no way I can make it to lunch."

"Pretend it's a candy bar. Or maybe hold your nose while you eat it."

She didn't respond. Instead, a tear burned down her cheek that she quickly brushed away.

"Are you . . . crying?"

"No," she lied.

Cara pressed her lips together and looked down at her feet—Adam lowered his head too. Their morning ride to school was usually full of teasing and laughter, but today Cara turned away to gaze out the window. Adam didn't say anything more but gently took her wrist, turned her palm up, and unfolded her tiny fingers. Reaching into his backpack, he pulled out another stolen Twinkie and placed it in her hand.

3

ADVENTURES IN FOOD

"Cara, dinner's ready!"

Dinner meant it was time for Dad to be home. She couldn't wait to share her latest story as he had requested, so Cara grabbed her draft from her desk. The savory aroma of meatloaf hit her as she opened her bedroom door. When she entered the dining room, she sat at the table, perfectly set as usual.

Dad's chair was empty.

Cara's mother sat across from her with hands folded. "Your father must be running a little late. I'm sure he'll be here any minute."

They waited at the table in silence except for the ticking grandfather clock in the other room. Cara noticed the impeccable height of her mother's teased hair and the careful application of makeup. She embodied perfection in all aspects of life. If not for the frown on her face, she'd be the most beautiful woman in the world.

Through the window of the dining room, the darkness began eating away at the sun and still, no Dad.

Her mother finally broke the quietness through gritted teeth. "Of course your father is late again tonight."

Cara cocked her head. "We could start without him like we do sometimes."

"No, not tonight. I want him to see I can work and still keep house."

With each passing moment, the meal became colder, and with each drop in temperature, her mother's blood pressure seemed to rise. Once the meal passed the point of lukewarm, the garage door opened. Cara knew she wasn't supposed to leave the table without permission, but greeting her father at the door was usually an exception to the rule. She abandoned the dining room for the door. He stumbled in from the garage—his tie loosened around his neck, and his suit jacket draped over the same arm that held his briefcase.

"Hi, Daddy!"

It took him a moment, but then his gaze lowered to hers. "Hey, Pen Pal."

When he opened his mouth, whiskey overpowered the smell of dinner.

"Daddy, I finished that story you wanted me to read to you."

"Good. I'll read it after a while."

His steps were slow into the dining room.

"Hello, Charles." Her mother stood—her eyes glanced from him to the spread on the table and back.

"I'm not hungry quite yet. How about you pour me a glass of bourbon, Susan."

His wife's jaw tightened as she looked to the flawless meatloaf he didn't want to eat. Without a word, her heels clapped against the kitchen floor to the liquor cabinet. She poured a glass for her husband, who was already in his recliner and watching television.

Cara and her mother ate dinner with the sound of boxed laughter from the other room. When Cara got up to clear her plate, she noticed her father already asleep.

He didn't ask her mother about her first day of work.

He didn't eat dinner.

He didn't read her story.

~

WHEN CARA'S bedroom window caught the flashlight beam, she stopped writing and opened the window to see Adam and his pop-bottle glasses. A cool breeze entangled her long blonde hair as it wisped behind her.

"I think I have something that will cheer you up after this morning. As promised, my story is ready to share."

For the first time all day, a smile appeared on her face.

Adam grabbed a stack of notebook paper he stapled together like a book but held it out of sight until he announced the title like a circus ringmaster. "I present to you . . . *Adventures in Food* 'Volume One, Episode One.' Story and pictures by *the* Adam Aether."

Cara rolled her eyes and laughed. "Of course your story is about *food.*"

"Oh, and this is only the beginning. Did you hear me say it was Episode One? I have a whole series coming."

"Go on. I can't wait to hear it." This time, Cara's elbows mounted the windowsill, and her head rested in her hands.

"Okay, here goes." Adam took a long, dramatic breath.

```
"Once upon a time, there were two foods:
an orange and a Pop-Tart. They were the
best of friends. But one time they got
into a fight. Then it was a battle (with
full gear and weapons). Then it became a
war."
```

He held up the pages like a teacher reading a storybook to young students.

```
"BOOM! Now the Pop-Tart won. And that is
why Pop-Tarts are better than fruits and
vegetables. P.S. Nobody died. P.P.S.
Orange you glad I read this? The End."
```

Cara giggled and quietly clapped her hands. "I loved it! But I wish I could see the pictures better."

Adam scratched his head. "We've got to find a way to get the stories from my window to yours. Like with a conveyer belt or something!"

"I bet you could figure that out."

"I might have to take a break from *Adventures in Food* and work on an invention."

"Don't take a complete break. I really like your stories."

"Then I'll write *and* invent. I think my mom calls that double fisting."

"No, silly. You mean multitasking."

"Ooohhhh." Adam giggled.

Cara paused at the sound of a car driving down their street. "Adam?"

"Yeah?"

"Thank you for the Twinkie this morning."

Before Adam could respond, she pulled her blinds up and down four times, her secret code which stood for "Good-Night-A-Dam."

He repeated the same action. "Good-Night-Car-A."

4

FATHEAD

When Cara got off the bus, there was a note on the front door from her mother instructing her to go to Adam's house. Before she could read the last few words, she dropped her book bag on her porch and sprinted next door.

"Adam! I get to play today!"

"Yes! Let's go get a snack first." Adam opened the door and led Cara into the kitchen.

Inside was Mrs. Gloria Aether, Adam's mother, about a decade older than Cara's mom. Mrs. Aether wasn't necessarily stout, but she wasn't thin. Her hair was frizzy and glasses thick—not as thick as Adam's, though. She rarely wore makeup, and even though she was relatively plain, Cara thought she was beautiful.

Dirty dishes filled the sink and counter, and several pots were on top of the stove cooking that night's dinner. Mrs. Aether had an oven mitt on each hand as she bent over to check the food in the oven. She immediately stopped when she saw the children.

"Come here!" She gave them each a tight hug. "Cara, do you get to play?"

Cara stood with her hands behind her back, ankles rolled out. "Yeah, I do today."

A timer dinged on the kitchen counter. "Oh my goodness, I need to check the pasta!" Mrs. Aether ran back to the stove and grabbed a pair of tongs. "Do you know how to tell if your noodles are ready or not?"

Cara and Adam stood nearby on their tiptoes to watch. Mrs.

Aether took the pasta she captured in her tongs and threw them against the kitchen's tiled wall. To the kids' amazement, they all stuck.

"If your noodles stick to the backsplash, that means they're done! Pretty neat, huh? Do you want to try?" She handed Cara the tongs. Throwing food against the wall would never happen in her mother's immaculate kitchen. After letting it cool for a moment, she flung it at the wall. It stuck!

With all the noodle slinging, Adam snuck over to the pantry and unwrapped a Twinkie. He opened his mouth to take in the sweet golden bite when his mother snatched it out of his hands.

"I don't think so, little mister. I need to start hiding those." Adam winked at Cara after this comment. "Dinner will be ready in a little bit—you don't need to be eating all that sugar. How about some . . . celery?"

"Celery? Seriously, Mom?"

Someone snuck up behind Adam, pulled him into a headlock, and started rubbing his head with their fist. "Celery's good for ya, kid."

It was Angela, Adam's sister. She was tall and thin with shoulder-length hair that she teased to perfection. She always pulled half of it up, so she had a spunky ponytail on the top of her head that was held in place by a scrunchie. Being a freshman in high school, Angela held command over every subject, be it relationships, fashion, or politics.

She was the wisest person they knew.

"Speaking of Twinkies, a few more were missing than usual." Mrs. Aether put her hands on her hips.

"I didn't do it! Must have been Angela."

"Whatever! I wouldn't dare put that processed, prepackaged crap in my mouth."

Mrs. Aether shot her daughter a stern look. "Angela, don't say that word around eight-year-olds."

"Yeah, you would! You're a teenager—you'll eat anything!" Adam attempted.

"That's enough." A deep, gentle voice entered the room. It was Dr. Aether, Adam's father, a well-respected dentist in Canterville. "The real question is: did you brush all the sweaters off your teeth this morning?"

Cara scrunched her nose. "Sweaters?"

"Oh, Dad, come on! Not this story!" Adam begged.

Dr. Aether continued despite the plea, "Yes, sweaters! I have to tell my patients all the time about the Ivory Trolls who crawl into your mouth while you're sleeping and knit little sweaters for your teeth. They're so sneaky, you don't feel anything in the night. Then . . . WHAM! . . . you wake up with sweaters all over your teeth. Go on, feel them and check. They should feel slick if you brushed correctly."

Cara rubbed her fingers along her front teeth and felt confident in the results.

As she checked, Dr. Aether continued. "The sweaters are nearly impossible to see after just one night, but if you don't brush well, they'll start to be as wooly as a sheep! Oh, and they'll be yellow, so no one will ever want to kiss you."

"Good!" Adam yelled. "I don't want anyone kissing me anyway! Gross!"

Mrs. Aether interrupted. "Adam, why don't you go outside and play with Cara until dinner's ready?"

Adam jumped at the suggestion and grabbed a football before leading Cara out to the front yard. "Come on," he said, "let's play catch."

Outside, the September air was warm with occasional crisp breezes.

"Can you show me how to throw it?" Cara asked.

"What? Don't you ever play catch with your old man?"

Cara tucked a strand of hair behind her ear. "Um, no. My dad works late. And . . . he works so hard he has to take a nap when he gets home."

"Oh, well, you gotta put your fingers on the laces, so it's easy to grip. Then bend your elbow and launch it toward me."

Cara was no Joe Montana. She attempted to throw the ball, but it fluttered to the ground a few feet in front of her.

"Maybe I'll show you how to catch instead. You gotta put your hands together and make a diamond, like this." He touched his forefingers and thumbs together. "Just let the tip of the ball go right in the center of your hands, and you'll catch it."

"Okay!" Cara got back into position, and Adam threw her a perfect spiral. "Adam! I caught it! I didn't know you were so good at this!"

Adam grinned at the compliment. "Someday, I'm going to play in the NFL. I know you want to write books, but maybe you could be a sports reporter and write about me."

"What's the NFL?"

"National Football League. I want to be a professional football player."

"I bet you can do it, Adam. I could write about you *and* write my own books. Okay, let's do it again!"

"Try to throw it back to me like I showed you."

Right after he said that, Adam's tubby belly reverberated from a football thrown so hard that his thick glasses fell off.

But it wasn't thrown by Cara. It was thrown by Brandon Billings, a tall, athletic fourth-grader with flaming red hair. He stood with his four-man posse who laughed while Adam lay curled in the fetal position.

"Hey, Fatty Fatso! Surprised that hurt you at all with how fat your belly is!" Brandon's friends found this hilarious.

Cara didn't know what to do except run over and hand Adam his glasses.

Adam got to his feet and through attempted breaths, said, "I can't ... breathe ...."

More laughing and finger-pointing.

"Man. You're pathetic," Brandon said. He grabbed his football and rode off on his bike with his gang of nine-year-olds behind him.

Adam desperately tried to take some deep breaths. He grabbed the football and spiked it in the grass. "Man, I hate redheads!"

"Let's go inside," Cara prompted. She picked up the football for him as they walked back to his house.

They sneaked down to the basement to avoid his parents, but there was Angela sitting on the basement couch in the middle of blowing the world's biggest bubble. She had an algebra book in her lap, and she wore headphones plugged into a Walkman cassette player, playing U2's *Joshua Tree* album.

Adam and Cara froze. His sister would, no doubt, interrogate them. Before they had time to run back up the stairs, she swung around and caught a glance of her little brother with a grass stain on his pants and a face caked with dirt.

Her giant bubble popped. "What the heck happened to you?" She pressed stop on her cassette player and took off the headphones—resting the band around her neck.

"Nothing!" Adam shot back.

"Something happened. You can't get anything past me. I'm a

woman now, Adam. I now have what's called a 'Woman's Intuition.'"

Cara was intrigued. "A Woman's Whatta-Whatta?"

"A Woman's Intuition. It basically means I'm like . . . kinda psychic. I don't know exact details, but I get these . . . *feelings*, ya know? You'll get it too when you're older, Cara."

Cara squinted her eyes and nodded—taking in all the information.

"Anyway, kid. I know something happened. You gotta tell me. I'm your big sister." She got up and gave her brother a squeeze and then pulled him over to sit by her on the couch.

Cara took a seat on the floor in front of them. "Adam, maybe Angela could help. She *is* in high school."

A high schooler surely had all the answers. He took a seat with Cara on the floor. Angela remained on the couch and leaned forward as she rested her elbows on her knees and clasped her hands together. She vigorously chewed her gum—ready to offer her fifteen-year-old wisdom.

"Cara and I were playing by ourselves when Brandon Billings threw a football right at my stomach. I hit the ground, and I couldn't breathe. Then he called me . . . Fatty Fatso."

Angela leaned back in her seat with confidence stamped across her face. "Sounds like you got the wind knocked out of you, kid."

"What does that mean?" Cara asked.

"It pretty much means your lungs like . . . collapsed, or something. Truth is, Adam, you are *not* fat, but you *are* a little husky. That just means you're about to hit a growth spurt and thin out."

The kids exchanged bewildered expressions.

"Wanna know how to deal with boys like Brandon and his little crew?" Now it was Adam and Cara who leaned forward, ready to eat up some enlightenment. "You gotta turn the joke so they don't feel like they're getting to ya."

"How do you do that?"

"Okay, what was the stupid name he called you? Fatty Fathead or something?"

"No, Fatty Fatso," Adam corrected.

"All right, so you can't let him think his insults hurt you, so if he calls you that again, you say, 'Oh yeah? Well, I like being fat!'"

"Why would I ever say I like being fat!? Then he'll know I think I'm fat, and then everyone will know I think I'm fat. Wait! Do you think I'm fat? I thought you said I was just husky!"

Angela sighed. "Do you want my help or not?"

Adam crossed his arms and relented.

"You don't have to mean it. Brandon doesn't know that *you* know you don't mean it."

What was she talking about?

"What you're doing is causing his insult to backfire. He won't know how to respond if what he says doesn't have the effect he was going for." Adam looked to Cara who shrugged her shoulders back. "Just try it next time. Here, let's practice. Stand up." She grabbed Adam's hands, had him square up with her, and handed him a small ball. "Cara, you stand up and pretend you guys are playing. I'll be Brandon the Bully."

Cara and Adam looked at each other and giggled at doing a reenactment. They tossed the ball when Angela came by and shoved Adam in the shoulder. "Hey, Fatty-Fathead!"

"It's Fatty-Fatso!" Adam corrected.

"Yeesh, Adam! Fathead. Fatso. It doesn't matter! Just respond to whatever I say to you."

"Okay, okay. I got it, just . . . try it again."

Angela had the kids continue tossing the ball. She repeated her role with a shove to his shoulder. "Hey, Fatty-Fatso! Man, you're soooo fat!"

"Oh yeah? Well, I *like* being fat!" He seemed surprised at his own aggression.

"That's perfect!" Angela cried. "Now he won't be able to respond, and he'll probably leave you alone after that." She grabbed her little brother and rubbed his hair with her fist. "Okay, let me know how it goes."

Mrs. Aether hollered that dinner was ready, and Cara had to go home.

Adam walked her to the door. "Hey, thanks for staying by me while those jerk bullies were being . . . jerks."

"Of course. You're my best friend."

5

BLINDFOLD

The bus route from Adam and Cara's stop took twenty minutes to travel to John Patterson Elementary School. Cara noticed the neighborhood more today than she had before. How strange it was that all these houses had such similarities on the outside, but the families on the inside could be polar opposites. Why were her parents so different from Adam's? Cara continued to stare out the window and became lost in those thoughts until Adam's voice pulled her away from them.

"Cara, I think I have a new hidden talent."

This sounded intriguing. "Yeah? What is it?"

"We've ridden this bus so many times, I know every stop, every turn, every bump in the road. I think I can tell exactly where we are even with my eyes closed."

"No way! Prove it."

Adam closed his eyes, but that wasn't good enough for Cara. He cheated at games all the time. "Here, tie my jacket around your head so it covers your eyes."

"Fine." He looked ridiculous but didn't seem to care. Anything for a laugh. He lifted the jacket to get his bearings one last time and put it back down in front of his face. He felt the bus make a sharp left turn then he pointed to the right. "There's Washington Township Park."

"Too easy, you saw that before you covered your eyes," Cara protested.

"Hey, I just started! Let me keep going."

"I think you should take off your glasses, too, to make sure you really can't see."

He agreed and handed them over. He was legally blind without them, so this would surely be impressive. The bus hit a bump, and Adam pointed to the left. "That's Drew Parker's house there — Angela's boyfriend from seventh grade."

It was indeed Drew Parker's house. Cara was impressed and encouraged him to keep going.

A curve around a bend. "There's the fire station."

An abrupt stop. "There's Bill's Donuts."

A few consecutive bumps. "There's the Nazarene church."

Cara laughed hysterically. He was right on each one.

The bus came to a stop, and Adam exclaimed, "We're at John Patterson Elementary School!"

"Are you sure you couldn't see through my jacket?"

"I swear! I even took my glasses off, remember? I just have a special talent for recognizing things, I guess."

They hopped off the bus and weaved through the crowd of students toward the school.

"Hey! Fatty-Fatso!"

It was Brandon Billings and his posse standing a few yards behind them.

Out of instinct, Adam made fists with both hands and turned toward Brandon's voice. Cara yanked his arm to encourage him to keep walking into the school.

"Hey!" Brandon repeated. "I'm talkin' to *you*, Fatty!"

Adam stopped, and Cara noticed his voice sounded lower than usual when he responded. "What, Brandon?"

"How come I never see you hanging out with guys? You're always around this girl. You're too fat, so there's no way she's your girlfriend. You know what? I think you're a faggot!"

Cara wasn't sure what this meant, and by the blank stare on Adam's face, apparently, he didn't know either. But he must have remembered what Angela taught him because he yelled back, "Oh yeah? Well, I freakin' love faggots!"

Cara wanted to support her friend, so she added, "Yeah, and I love faggots too!"

Brandon and his gang stood, mouths agape, staring at the two who confidently turned around into the school.

〜

"*You* ask her."

"No, *you* ask her. She's *your* sister."

Angela was listening to her Walkman in her room while she stroked hot pink nail polish onto her fingernails. She hit the stop button and shook her head to make the earphones slide down to her neck so she wouldn't ruin her wet nails.

"Whataya need, kids?" she asked with a feigned sigh.

Cara nudged Adam to enter the bedroom. "Hey, um, well, first, I wanted to tell you that I used your advice today."

"Advice?"

"Yeah, with Brandon Billings and his friends. I turned the joke on him!"

"All right!" She leaned in to hear the story. "So, tell me about it."

"He started picking on me when we were walking into school. He called me Fatty-Fatso again, but I didn't respond to that. It was when he called me something else."

Angela raised her eyebrows. "Well, what did he call you?"

Adam looked at Cara. It was like he was so swollen with pride he could barely get it out. She smiled and nodded for him to continue. "He said, I was always around Cara, and she'd never like me because I was so fat and that he thought I was a faggot."

His sister sat up with wide eyes.

"So, I yelled back, 'Oh yeah? Well, I love faggots!'"

"Freakin'," Cara corrected. "You said you 'freakin' love faggots!'" She gave Adam a high five. "And then I said I loved faggots too. But, Angela, what's a faggot?"

Angela buried her head in her hands.

"What is it?" Cara asked.

"Oh my gosh, you guys. A faggot is when a dude likes other dudes and not girls. And it's very derogatory. This just proves what a jerk this Brandon kid is! How did they react when you said that, though?"

"Well, they shut up, and they left us alone."

"Perfect!" Angela clapped her hands together. "My strategy was still a success!"

Adam scrunched his nose. "How?"

"They left you alone, right? They were probably so shocked at your response they didn't know what to do. Plus, I bet they're super intimidated by you now."

"But what I said wasn't true," he reminded her.

She winked. "They don't have to know that."

6

WISHBOOK

Adam never invented the conveyer belt between their windows like they'd dreamed about, but they decided to spice up their nightly talks by utilizing the window in different ways. They tried paper airplanes, throwing a football with a note attached, a pulley system, and even Morse code.

They needed something more effective and efficient, especially since the air was becoming much colder in Ohio. Wintertime usually kept Adam and Cara's window antics to a minimum, but Cara needed to share her writings with him despite the cold.

Adam had an epiphany on the way home from school one day. "You know what would be awesome? What if we used walkie-talkies at night?"

"Why didn't we think of that sooner?"

They started brainstorming all the other situations where walkie-talkies would come in handy, but their excitement soon dissipated when they realized they had no means to go to the store and buy a pair themselves.

When the bus dropped them off that afternoon, Cara went straight to Adam's house. Mrs. Aether had baked chocolate chip cookies that were still warm on the kitchen table. Their noses led them right to the spot, and the warm treats were the perfect snack to fill their cold bodies.

That day's pile of mail lay next to the plate of cookies on the table. Adam rummaged through it, and suddenly his eyes widened.

The Aethers subscribed to the Sears catalog that was delivered twice a year. But today, the 1988 Sears *Wishbook* had arrived. This only came in the winter, and winter meant Christmas. It was over six hundred pages full of anything one's heart desired for the holidays from dustbusters to bathrobes to foosball tables. It was like Santa himself had listened to their conversation on the bus and dropped the solution on the table. Adam shoved the rest of his cookie into his mouth and wiped his hands on his pants to grab the catalog. He motioned for Cara to come to his room so they could look through the *Wishbook* in privacy.

Cara sat on Adam's bed as he locked the door behind him. "What's that?"

"Don't you get the Sears catalog in the mail?"

"No." She shrugged. "I've never heard of it."

Adam gasped. "This is basically everything from every store put into one magazine. You just call and order what you want, and they mail it to your house."

"Everything? So you can order, like, toilet paper from it?"

"No," he huffed, "not stuff like that. It has, like, toys and dishwashers and stuff. I bet there will be walkie-talkies in here!"

Cara raised her eyebrows. "Well, go ahead and open it!"

He quickly thumbed through the pages of appliances, jewelry, and clothes until he came across toys and electronics. "Come on! Where is it?" he mumbled.

Finally, on page 444, there they were in all their glory.

Fisher-Price Sky Talkers.

Adam read the description: "Four-transistor walkie-talkie set features Morse Code buttons and symbols on front. Flexible antenna and hook for belt . . . Set of two operate on 49.860 MHz fruh . . . fruh . . ."

"Frequency," Cara corrected.

"Yeah, frequency. Uses two nine-volt batteries—"

"Okay, okay, but how much is it?"

Adam looked up from the catalog and gritted his teeth. "Twenty-nine ninety-nine," he paused, "plus shipping and handling . . . plus taxes."

It might as well have been a thousand dollars. All Cara had was a desolate piggy bank. Adam received an allowance, though.

She asked if he would be willing to buy it, and she could pay him back someday.

"I don't have any money saved up."

"What? How?"

Adam dropped his eyes. "I spend my allowance at vending machines."

"Adam!" She threw her hands up. "Well, maybe you could ask for them for Christmas."

"I can't. I already begged my mom for a Nintendo. She said she'd get it for me, but I wasn't allowed to ask for anything else since it's so expensive."

Even though Dr. Aether made a lot of money as a dentist, he and his wife were frugal. There was no way they'd tack on another gift worth this much.

"Why don't *you* ask for them for Christmas?" Adam asked.

"I'm not allowed to ask for anything. My mom always picks out my gifts for me."

Adam lowered his head in defeat until he heard a ripping sound. Cara had torn out page 444 and held it up. "I'll see what I can do."

~

A BEEPING WENT off to signal that dinner was done. Cara's mother had succumbed to the convenience of microwave dinners on the daily. With her part-time job and her infatuation with house cleaning, elaborate meals were no longer a priority since her husband didn't appreciate them. She refused to serve dinner in their plastic trays, though—she wasn't a barbarian. Once the meals cooled, she meticulously scraped the contents onto a nice dish to serve at the table with the proper place settings.

As per usual, the ticking of the clock drowned their lack of words—her mother on edge since her husband was late once again, but this time they ate without him. Cara decided to cut the silence and bring up Christmas. Surely that subject would cheer her up.

"Mom? I was thinking about Christmas."

Her mother patted her lips with her cloth napkin and set her fork on the plate's edge. "What about it?"

"I wondered if I could ask for something this year." She took another bite of dinner.

"Why would you need to do that? Don't you appreciate what I buy you every year?"

"Of course!" She contrived an upbeat tone. "But there is something special I *really* want this time."

"And what is that?"

Cara stared at her food. "A walkie-talkie set." Then she raised her eyes to meet her mother's.

"A walkie-talkie set? Why in the blazes would you want one of those? You're an only child, Cara. It takes two people to use a walkie-talkie set."

Cara set both palms on the table and leaned forward. "I was going to use it with my friends. And I really, *really* want one! I wouldn't want anything else, as long as I could have that!"

"We'll see . . ."

Cara played with the edge of the tablecloth. "What would *you* like for Christmas, Mommy?"

A sadness took over her mother's countenance. "What I want for Christmas can't be bought with money, Cara."

And with that, her mother rose from the table and collected her dishes to clean. She took Cara's, too, for fear that everything wouldn't be placed in the sink just right.

Something that couldn't be bought with money? What a weird answer.

Cara grabbed her book bag and went to her room. She unzipped the side pocket to pull out the page from the catalog, unfolded it with care, and ran it against the edge of her desk to remove the creases. Maybe she could show it to her mom or leave it somewhere for her to find. She wasn't allowed in their bedroom, but the cleaning closet would be perfect. Cara headed that way when she heard the door shut that led to the garage. She turned to see her father but stopped when she heard her mother cut in.

"Where on earth have you been?"

Cara knew the tone. She usually shut the door to her room and started writing to block it out, but she was now in a position where her parents would notice if she moved from her spot. She leaned back against the wall in hopes to conceal herself.

"I don't need you questioning me, Susan. I had a long day at work." He loosened his tie and put down his briefcase.

"It would be nice if you'd at least make it home in time for dinner, Charles!"

"Why? So I can eat that microwaved shit you heat up?"

This shut her up. It wasn't so much that her husband insulted the food. It was the cussing. She loathed curse words and kept her own mouth as clean as her house.

There was a tightness in Cara's stomach as her parents fought, and she wished she could melt into the woodwork of the walls.

"I don't want anything to eat. Just grab me a glass of bourbon."

"Seriously? You already reek of beer! When is this going to stop? When are you going to stop drinking? That's all I ever want! I wouldn't want anything else for Christmas, as long as I could have that!"

She had echoed Cara's own words at dinner, like a child copying an adult. That's when she realized the gift her mother was talking about. She wanted her father to stop drinking . . . except Cara wasn't exactly sure what that meant.

Her father ignored his wife's plea, turned to his recliner, and sank into it. When he looked up, he saw Cara against the wall.

"Hey, Pen Pal," he said with a half-smile.

"Hi, Daddy." Cara held the page from the catalog behind her back.

"Did you write any stories today?"

"Not much today."

"I still need to read that one, ya know."

Cara nodded. She noticed her mother, who would have usually gone back to washing the dishes, was standing in the same spot—arms crossed—watching them.

"Hey, do your old man a favor and grab me a beer from the refrigerator." He knew Cara couldn't pour him a glass of bourbon, but she could bring him a can.

Cara looked at her mother, who stared back with a glare. She looked back at her father, whose eyes returned a desperate stare. No matter what she did, she was going to upset one of them. She remained frozen when suddenly her mom walked to the refrigerator herself and retrieved a beer. Wordlessly, she put it in her daughter's hands and returned to the sink. Cara looked down at the cold aluminum can then handed it to her father.

"Good girl."

INSTEAD OF A STORY THAT NIGHT, Cara decided to write her mother a note. With a bright red marker, she circled the Fisher-

Price Sky Talkers on the page from the catalog. Then she tore a page from her notebook, grabbed a pencil, and wrote:

Dear Mommy,
    Remember this is all I want for Christmas please. And I will see if I can help you get the present you want. The one that doesn't cost money.
    Love,
    Cara

She wrote "Mommy" on the other side of the notebook paper and started to fold it and the catalog page together but stopped. After what she witnessed tonight, she wondered if she should save the page to petition her father. Cara flipped her pencil over to the eraser and replaced the single word "this" in the note with "Fisher-Price Sky Talkers." It didn't quite fit, but she squished it in. She kept the page from the catalog for later, tiptoed out to the cleaning closet, and placed her note inside. Her father was already snoring in his recliner when she walked past him.

Back in her room, she grabbed her flashlight and shined it into the window next door.

7

TREE

Saturdays meant Cara's father was around the house to work on "honey-do" projects. This particular morning, he hung Christmas lights outside the house to prepare for the Ecrivains' Annual Neighborhood Christmas Party. This was her mother's chance to show off their immaculate house and her trim waistline in a swanky new cocktail dress. It was her father's chance to show off his sports car in the garage and brag about his insurance sales from the past year. It was their opportunity to prove to everyone they were not only "normal" but "better than normal."

Cara's father stood on a ladder wearing his tool belt low on his waist. It held everything he needed: hammer, nails, screwdrivers, pliers—and a flask. He stretched the lights to ensure there was no sagging. They had to look just right, or his wife would nag.

Cara wandered outside in a fluffy white coat. A light dusting of snow was on the ground, and she watched him struggle on the ladder when he noticed her.

"Hey, Pen Pal," he said through pursed lips with a nail hanging out of his mouth.

"Hi, Daddy." She observed him hammer. "Is there anything I can do?"

He grabbed his flask to take a swig. "Dammit, how is this already empty?" Then he looked at her. "I'm done out here for the morning. I need to do some other errands."

"Oh . . ." She purposefully didn't conceal her disappointment.

"You know what you can do, though, Pen Pal?"

She lit up before she knew what he was going to suggest.

He climbed down the ladder. "You can go with me to pick out the Christmas tree—just the two of us." He took his forefinger and tapped it on her nose like it was a button.

An incandescent smile came over her face that told him she wanted to go. Her mother usually picked out the tree and was particular about its height, thickness, and symmetry, so this would be a rare challenge for them to do it in her absence.

When her father came into the house for the keys to his truck, Cara ran to her room and grabbed the folded page from the Sears catalog. This time alone with him would be the perfect opportunity to mention the Sky Talkers. In the kitchen, her mother scrubbed the baseboards on her hands and knees, hair pulled up in a ponytail, and no makeup. Saturday mornings were deep cleaning days, and there was no use in looking nice when she was going to break a hard sweat.

"Susan, we're going to go pick out a Christmas tree."

His wife took her large sponge and dropped it into a bucket full of soapy water, hard enough to show her anger but light enough so it wouldn't splash everywhere. "I can't go out like this, Charles. We weren't supposed to go until this evening!"

"That's fine. You can stay home. Cara and I will go."

"You know I like to pick out the tree and—"

"We know what you like. We're perfectly capable of choosing a tree ourselves."

"Are you even okay to drive?"

"We'll see you in a bit." He put his hand on Cara's back, ushering her to the garage.

They hopped into his blue truck. Cara's dad put her hand on top of the gear shift lever then wrapped his hand on top of hers as they shifted through the gears together. Cara giggled as she felt him speed through the streets and swerve in and out of lanes to get around cars.

It was a thirty-minute drive out of town to the Christmas tree farm. They took back roads through several suburbs until they were surrounded by more cows than houses. Finally, a large sign appeared that read "TREES" with a red arrow pointing to the right.

The truck turned on to a long graveled road that spit rocks and built a cloud of dust behind them. Cara opened her mouth and made a monotone hum that involuntarily created a vibrato sound as they traveled the bumpy road. Her dad did it too, creating a staccatoed, accented harmony.

The tree farm consisted of what seemed like millions of evergreens. Some were small, waiting to be cut for future seasons, while others towered over the rest. In the middle of the field was a humble store. Cara's dad pulled in next to the building, turned off the ignition, and hid the small silver flask under the floor mat. The open air of the farm and the absence of her mother made Cara feel free. She couldn't recall many times she was just with her dad.

"I'm so excited, Daddy! I know I've been here before, but I've never realized how big and how wonderful it is. Wouldn't this be the best place to play tag or hide-and-seek?"

He nodded. "Too bad we're cooped up in that damn suburb where we're so close to all those neighbors. No privacy. We oughta move out to the country with the open sky like this where everyone leaves you alone."

Moving to the country sounded nice, but it would mean no Adam, and she couldn't imagine a world like that.

A worker approached. He was a middle-aged man with tight jeans, cowboy boots, and a baseball cap. "Hello there. The name's Brooks. What can I help you folks with today?"

Her father shook his hand. "Charles Ecrivain."

He told Brooks they were there for a tree, but he slyly turned the conversation to insurance. Cara watched her father in his element—a true gentleman talking numbers, selling himself, grooming a potential customer. Was this the real reason they came here today?

Brooks took the business card and shook his hand. Cara stood off to the side. Invisible.

"Thank you, Brooks. I think we will be quite all right finding a tree on our own, but I'll be sure to tell them you helped us anyway. Give me a call anytime." As he released his right hand from the worker, he turned to Cara with a grin. Suddenly, he tapped her right shoulder and yelled, "You're it!" and sprinted off into the trees.

It took Cara a second before her dad's actions resonated with her, and then she took off after him—ignoring the winter air squeezing her lungs. They ran through aisle after aisle of trees playing tag and hide-and-seek. Swerving, darting, turning. Sometimes running into other patrons without even offering an apology. It was just the two of them. Her dad was like another kid —a friend in this moment. He'd sprint at times, leaving Cara behind then he'd slow down on purpose so Cara could tag him. She'd never done anything like this with him before, and she loved every second of it.

With winter-stung tears down their faces, her dad gasped for breath. "Okay, Pen-Pal, we gotta go find us a tree."

The carefree-ness faded slightly. Even though Cara's mother wasn't with them, there was still pressure to choose one that would appease her. They examined each tree until her dad found a giant balsam fir that satisfied him.

"What do you think of this one?" he asked.

"I love it! But dontcha think it's kinda too big?" It was thick and mostly symmetrical but stood about nine feet tall.

"Ah, it'll be all right." Her dad swiped a hand through the air, dismissing her concern.

A worker loaded it onto his truck, and her dad slipped him a five-dollar tip before heading inside to pay. Cara noticed that he pulled out a small rectangular piece of plastic for the purchase.

"What is that, Daddy?"

"This is a credit card. It means I can buy things now but pay for them later."

The worker set the card on a small contraption, placed a strip of paper over it, and pulled a lever across both, which imprinted the card's numbers onto the paper. It was like magic! Maybe he could use that to pay for her walkie-talkies.

As he put his credit card back in his wallet, Cara noticed her father's mood change. His talk with the workers felt short and agitated. He continuously caressed the back of his neck and then over to his forehead in a nervous manner.

When they got back into the truck, he said, "Hey, how about we get some lunch?"

"Just the two of us?" She clasped her hands together.

"Yeah. But I've gotta stop somewhere first."

With the Goliath tree flopping around the back of the truck, her father made a hard turn and pulled into the parking lot of a building with bold letters spelling: LIQUOR.

"Liquor?" asked Cara, pronouncing it with a hard "qu" sound instead of a "k." Her father didn't correct her. Instead, he left the truck running with the heat on and told her to stay inside. When he returned, he carried a large silver and blue box in one hand

and a brown paper bag in the other. Plopping himself in the cab, he removed a large bottle.

Jack Daniels, Old No. 7.

She recognized it, but asked anyway: "What's that, Daddy?"

He offered no response. With his eyes fixated on the bottle, he unwrapped the plastic around the top—making a crackling noise that tore through the silence. His shaking hands unscrewed the lid, tipped it to his lips, and he took long, slow gulps. Then he pulled the silver flask from under the floor mat and filled it to the top. Letting out a huge sigh, he turned toward Cara again as if seeing her for the first time that day.

A wry smile came across his face. "Hey, Pen Pal."

Cara wasn't sure why he greeted her like that after they spent the morning together. "Hey, Daddy," she replied anyway.

"You ready for some lunch?"

"Can we still go to McDonald's? And get a Happy Meal?"

"You bet."

He kicked the truck into gear and spun out of the parking lot, just like he came in.

Her mother never permitted fast food, so Cara had only been inside a McDonald's a few times in her life. She wanted the Chicken McNugget Happy Meal with a Berenstain Bears toy inside and an orange pop to drink. Her father ordered a Quarter Pounder with cheese, French fries, and when he got a large Coca Cola, he pulled the silver bottle from his jacket and poured it into his cup.

After drinking "his Coke," he was talkative again. He told Cara how he didn't have a McDonald's in his hometown growing up; instead, he and his buddies went to a local burger joint where servers brought the food to their cars on roller skates. Cara enjoyed the story but wanted to steer the conversation to Christmas presents while she had his undivided attention.

"So . . . what do you want for Christmas, Daddy?" It was abrupt with no segue, but she didn't know how else to bring it up.

"I want to eat at McDonald's whenever I want."

They both laughed because they knew her mother would never allow that.

"I haven't thought about it much." He ate a few French fries and nursed his drink while he thought. "Probably some seat covers for my Mustang. Some tools. Maybe a new television.

They make them with these remotes now—you don't even have to get off the couch."

He thought some more, but Cara interrupted. "I know what *I* want."

"Well, don't tell *me*. Tell Santa."

"Daddy, I don't believe in Santa. I haven't believed in him since I was in my fives."

He looked caught that she had avoided his playful dodge. "Cara, your mother always picks out your gifts. She's probably already bought them all. You know she doesn't like you to ask."

"I know, but this is something I *really, really* want. I'd rather Mommy give away any other gift as long as I could have just this one!"

"Yeah? What is it?"

"Fisher-Price Sky Talkers," she said with confidence.

"What the hell is that?"

She paused. Even though he'd already done it several times that day, he wasn't supposed to curse in front of her. "They're walkie-talkies."

"I don't know that your mother would have the slightest idea where to even find those, Pen Pal."

Cara stuck her hand in her jeans' front pocket and pulled out the page from the Sears catalog. She unfolded it and handed it to her dad. He studied the page for a moment, seeming slightly amused that this was her heart's desire. In case he wasn't aware, she added, "It's from the Sears catalog. You can order from it, and it comes in the mail, right to your house."

"Where did you even get this?"

"Adam let me have it."

"That would be quite a gift," he admitted. He read the details on the page about all the functions. "I know I would have loved this as a kid. Hell, I would have fun with it now."

"Do you think you could talk to Mom? Convince her to get it for me? It's the only thing I want. I wouldn't want anything else for Christmas this year as long as I could have that!"

He used a tranquil tone to calm her excitement. "We'll see."

That was the same phrase her mother used.

Seeming to sense her defeat, he added. "I wouldn't count on it, but you never know." He followed that with a wink.

This made her feel better, and she continued her planned conversation. "Do you know what *Mommy* wants for Christmas?"

She took a sip of her orange pop to make it seem this was a standard everyday question.

He dipped a fry in some ketchup and shrugged. "Ah, I don't know. I usually give her some nice jewelry or something."

Cara imitated her dad with one of her fries—trying to think of how to word her next sentence. "*I* think I know what Mommy wants."

"Is that right?" He didn't seem amused, but continued with, "What do you think? Your mother is a hard one to read."

"It's something that can't be bought with money."

He chuckled. "That sounds complicated, just like her."

"I think . . ." She paused, unsure how her dad would react. "I think she wants you to stop drinking."

He stopped short of taking another bite. "She told you that?"

"No," Cara admitted, "but she told *you* that. I heard her—a few nights ago. Mommy told me that she only wanted something that couldn't be bought with money, and then I heard you guys fighting, and then she told you the only thing she wanted was for you to stop drinking."

In the awkward quietness, his face grew red, and he lowered his eyes to the floor. Cara started to regret that she brought it up. Maybe it was a mistake. Her dad continued the silence. He stopped eating, and instead, stared out the window as he shook his foot crossed over the other leg. His eyes slowly came back to Cara. "Do *you* want me to stop drinking?"

"I don't really know what that means, Daddy." She cocked her head and shot him an innocent smile.

He raised an eyebrow. "What?"

"To stop drinking. What exactly does that mean? Surely Mom doesn't mean *all* drinking. Is it that stuff you bought today? That you hide in that silver bottle?"

He looked back down. "Yes. That's what your mother means."

"Well, that can't be too hard. You can still drink pop . . . and . . . this gift doesn't cost any money. I bet she'll get you what you want, too. New seat covers? A new TV? The kind with the remote?"

His eyes still stared at the floor. "That would be nice, Pen Pal." He nodded then looked up to meet her eyes. "If that's what she really wants, I can do that."

Cara smiled.

Her dad folded the rest of his uneaten food into his wrapper and threw it away as they walked toward the door. Outside, he stopped at the edge of the parking lot. "Why wait until Christmas?" He opened his flask and poured the contents on the cold asphalt.

Cara hugged him. Her plan was already working.

8

HAPPY

When Cara and her dad returned home that afternoon, he professed to his wife a promise to quit drinking. Cold turkey. Cara was confused when her mom started crying at the news. She also didn't even care that the Christmas tree was oversized and barely fit in their living room.

For the next week and a half, her dad came home at a decent time, and her mom started cooking again. The Ecrivains sat down to dinner as a family and had conversations. They looked into each other's eyes and included Cara in the discourse. They laughed. They joked. They listened to Cara read her stories and even told old stories of their own.

"Susan, remember the time we bought Cara that metal tricycle when she turned three?"

Her mom clasped her hands together at the memory. "Yes! And she would ride around with the handlebars backward and scream, 'My ti-sickle! My ti-sickle!'"

Cara's face lit up. "I did that?"

"It was the cutest thing!"

Her parents couldn't stop laughing at the thought.

One night after dinner, her mom announced they were going to decorate the Christmas tree as a family. "Are you sure, Mommy?" Cara was never allowed to come close to the tree before. "You usually decorate the tree."

"Sure! It will be something fun to do together. You're eight now and need to learn how to do this yourself soon anyway." She gave her daughter a whimsical smile and then shot the same look over to her husband who'd just returned to the room.

He popped a piece of gum in his mouth and patted Cara on the back. "Come on. It'll be fun!"

Her mom brought out a tub full of glass ornaments wrapped in old cloth and placed ever so strategically as not to break. She handed each one to her husband and daughter with caution. Although she still commanded where each should go, she allowed them to do the actual work. She even brought out a step stool so Cara could reach the higher branches. Her dad struggled to place the star on top, which would have usually angered his wife since the tree was much bigger than her liking. Instead, they laughed at the incident.

Cara went up to her room later than usual for bed that night. Before she even put on her pajamas, she noticed the light shining into her window.

Adam.

She hurried over. The cold December wind rushed into her room as she opened it.

"Hang on," she whispered.

Cara grabbed a throw blanket from her bed, rolled it up, and put it at the base of her bedroom door to keep the cold from escaping into the hallway and alerting her parents.

When she reappeared in the window, Adam asked, "Where have you been? I've been waiting on you for like thirty minutes!"

"I was decorating the Christmas tree with my parents."

Adam looked puzzled. This was never an excuse before. "Do you have a new story to share tonight?"

"Actually, I haven't had a chance to write lately. I've been with my parents a lot."

"Oh," was all he let out, followed by an uncertain smile.

"Adam," Cara whispered back. He lifted his eyes and met hers again through his pop bottle glasses. "I think our chances of getting that walkie-talkie set are pretty good."

9

TOILET TABLETS

O n a bus ride to school, Cara told Adam her dad had stopped drinking and attempted to explain what that meant. She tried to put into words how this was an early Christmas present to her mom and the reason for the change in their house. For the first time, her eyes were genuinely bright and not weighed down.

"Oh, and guess what!" she exclaimed. "You know how we have that huge neighborhood Christmas party each year? It's usually no-kids-allowed, but my mom said you and your sister could come over this year and be helpers!"

"Really? Things *must* be different. I've never even been inside your house before."

Cara's mom didn't allow other kids to come over. They were a potential threat to her immaculate house.

"I know. I may not be able to play after school for the next couple of days because my mom said I get to help her clean the house for the party."

"You *get* to? Why would you be excited about that?"

"I don't know. I like helping my mom."

"More than playing with me?"

She paused. Cara wasn't sure how to answer that question. All she knew was she loved the change that had happened in her home.

41

CLEANING WAS a serious matter at the Ecrivain house, especially when they expected company. Cara's mom gave her a speech about how being eight was old enough to pitch in with some of the family duties. Cara already made her bed, folded her clothes, and could adequately pick up her room, but today her mom taught her to add white vinegar to the cleaning cloth in addition to the dusting spray, how to sweep everything into a dustpan, and how to scrub the toilets.

Each day leading up to the Christmas party became more intense. Cara's mom lamented not having as much time to run her errands since this was the first year she also held a job. At dinner that Thursday night, her husband told her not to stress—he would help out more.

While they cleaned their plates, she asked her husband, "Before I go to the store, I've been struggling with something. What should I do about alcohol for the party?"

"What do you mean?"

"I feel like I shouldn't buy any since you've stopped drinking, but our guests will expect it."

He put down the plate and wrapped his hands around her waist. "Buy what you'd usually buy. Most people bring a bottle of something themselves anyway."

"Won't that be tempting for you?"

"Nah! I'll be fine. It's my Christmas present to you, remember?" He pulled her in and kissed his wife on the forehead. "I'll finish the dishes. You get a head start on the shopping."

She looked at him like she was dreaming—like she was living the life she'd always wanted. Before leaving, she didn't even remind him how to dry the dishes properly.

～

THE DAY BEFORE THE PARTY, Cara did the new chores she recently learned. Cara's mom made sure the exterior of the house was in tip-top shape with sharp landscaping and Christmas décor. She scrubbed the baseboards, vacuumed the curtains, and dusted the tops of the ceiling fans.

While Cara swept one of the bathrooms, her mom rushed in and handed her three packages that contained what looked like giant blue Tums tablets. "I need you to put one of these in the tank of each toilet in the house."

"What is it?"

"Toilet tablets. They turn the water blue and make the toilet look extra clean and smell fresh. Just read the back to see what you need to do." She ran out of the room to get to her next chore.

The directions said to remove the lid of the toilet tank and drop one tablet inside. Seemed simple enough. There were three bathrooms in their house, so Cara started on the main floor. She had never lifted a toilet tank lid before, and they were heavier than expected. With the first one, Cara examined the inside and played with the float and chain. She finally dropped the tablet in and watched it slowly turn the water blue. When she flushed, the bowl refilled with the blue water and would stay looking clean for "One hundred flushes," according to the back of the package.

She made her way to the bathroom in the basement that the family seldom used. When she lifted the lid of the tank, she went to drop in the tablet, but something caught her eye. Hiding in the tank was a bottle like the one her father bought the day they got the Christmas tree.

She pulled it out to discover that half of the amber-colored liquid inside was gone.

Dad's been lying to us?

Everything had been so happy in her home for the past couple of weeks. If she said something, would that ruin it all? Maybe it was an old bottle. But if it was, why was it in the toilet tank?

Before she could ponder anything else, her mom hollered from upstairs. Cara carefully placed the bottle back into the tank and put the heavy lid back on top. Suddenly, her mom was in the bathroom.

"How's everything going?"

Cara stood up straight. "Fine! I like cleaning the toilets."

"What on earth's been taking you so long?" Her tone felt stressed.

"I just want to make sure I'm doing it right. I got them all done, though."

"Then why is that tablet in your hand?"

Cara looked down. Sure enough, the last blue tablet was still in her palm. She was so distracted she forgot to drop it in.

"Is the lid too heavy? Here, let me do this one." Her mom started moving toward the toilet.

"No!"

A shocked look came over her mom's face.

43

"Sorry, it's just that . . . you're already so busy . . . and I like doing this by myself."

Her mom held her stare.

She had to get her out before she discovered the bottle, which would ruin Christmas—would ruin everything. "Go on, mom!" Cara smiled to cover her fear. "What are you waiting for? The house isn't going to clean itself—that's what you always say." She grabbed her mom's hand and guided her out of the bathroom.

"Okay, but you need to be snappy with that. I've got more dusting for you to do upstairs."

"Of course." With that, her mom left.

It took Cara a moment to recover. She snapped back and knew she needed to finish quickly before her mom became more suspicious. After struggling with the lid, she placed the last tablet into the tank. The bottle remained as the water slowly turned a bright blue around it.

∽

THE CLOCK STRUCK 6:00 P.M. Cara's mom took a break from cleaning to finish dinner. Cara continued to dust in the living room when she heard the sound of the garage door. Her father entered with his briefcase and coat in hand—slightly later than he should have been.

Cara wiped clean the last Christmas decoration when he greeted her.

He slipped a piece of gum in his mouth then said, "Hey, Pen Pal! Your mother let you clean the house some more today?"

A tsunami of emotions overwhelmed Cara, but "Yes," was all she said—not making eye contact with him.

He tried to engage her in more dialogue. "What did Mom have you do?"

Cara continued to dust the decoration over and over even though it was done. "I'm finishing the dusting now, but I also swept, and cleaned the toilets." She paused. "I put cleaning tablets in the toilet tanks . . . even the one in the basement." With that, she raised her eyes to meet her father's with a hard frown on her face. By his reaction, it was clear he understood.

She didn't say anything more. Neither did he. Her eyes welled with tears as she continued to stare. She set the ornament down, then ran to her room before her mom could notice.

10

DEWAR'S 30

E very inch of the Ecrivain house was decorated, and every inch was clean enough to eat off any surface. The fireplace crackled, soft Christmas music played throughout the house, and a massive spread of finger food covered the table—it felt like entering a page from *Good Housekeeping*.

Cara had her own special dress for the evening. It was black and red with a big bow in back. Her hair was curled and pulled halfway back with an equally large bow holding it in place. This was the first year she wasn't banished to her room or shipped off with someone else for the night. Even though she was only there this year as "hired help," she was excited.

She practiced walking elegantly in the living room when her mom entered wearing a puffy-sleeved red cocktail dress that hugged her trim figure, black tights, pumps, and not a teased strand of hair out of place. She bought a new dress every year for this party that she never wore again. Cara couldn't turn her eyes away—she was stunning.

Usually, her mom ran around like a maniac before the party, but this year she seemed at ease. Cara worried if that would all vanish if she found out the truth.

She stood still to bask in the loveliness of her home before the guests arrived.

"You look really pretty, Mommy."

"Not as pretty as you, sweetie." She never handed out

compliments, and even though Cara appreciated it, it still felt odd to hear her say it.

Before she could thank her, her father entered the room in his tuxedo.

"Susan, help me with this bow tie, would ya? Every year it gives me so much damn trouble. I can never get it just right."

His wife let out an amused huff. "Come here." As she carefully folded and looped the fabric, her eyes shifted to the countless bottles of champagne, beer, and whiskey on the counter lined up like soldiers waiting to attack. "You sure you're going to be okay with all this alcohol?"

"I'll be fine," he said. Cara caught his eye, but he quickly looked away and leaned in to his wife for a kiss.

She pulled back. "I just put on my lipstick. You'll ruin it."

He let out a sigh. "Right." Then he squeezed her shoulders instead.

The doorbell rang, and Cara ran to answer it.

"Merry Christmas!" the Aethers shouted when the door opened, all four dressed handsomely with Dr. Aether holding a bottle of champagne.

Cara's worry released when she saw them, and she couldn't stop staring at Adam in a suit and tie.

"Don't just stand there, Cara. Do what we practiced—take their coats," her mom barked, but she quickly covered her tone with a smile.

"Oh, yeah. May I take your coats, please?"

"Before she does that, I'll take that bottle of champagne," Cara's mom interjected. She turned to Adam's sister. "Angela, that will be your job at the beginning of the night, and these two munchkins will collect the coats . . ."

While her mom continued talking with the Aethers, Cara whispered, "I think you look very handsome in your suit."

"Thank you. Did you know these suit jackets have pockets on the inside? Perfect for hiding Twinkies." They giggled, then he added, "You look very nice, too."

"Cool it, Romeo," Angela said. Cara wasn't sure who Romeo was, but she saw Adam's cheeks turn red. Luckily, the doorbell broke up the awkward moment. They had guests to attend to.

∾

THE HOUSE FILLED UP QUICKLY—EACH guest with a coat and bottle of alcohol, keeping the children busy. There were nearly four dozen people crowded in the house. It was a cacophony of music, conversations, and laughter.

Cara's parents played the role of the perfect hosts as they did every year—doting on each guest, refilling drinks, engaging in conversations of nail colors, sports cars, cleaning products, and investments. Her mom, who refused to drink alcohol, carried around grape juice in a wine glass. This year, her husband did something similar with a scotch glass full of Coke.

After excusing herself from a conversation with a guest, Cara's mom made her way to the children. "Since all of the guests should be here now, you're going to change your job from coat collectors to glass collectors. Don't get in the way of the guests, but whenever you see an empty glass laying around, pick it up and take it to the kitchen."

Adam and Cara headed to the dining room where most people left their glasses. This job proved to be more exciting—even though they weren't supposed to be in the way, they were closer to the action. They overheard boring conversations like how one of the neighbor's dogs needed cataract surgery, but they also heard some interesting neighborhood gossip, so it balanced out.

Without realizing it, they had migrated close to Cara's father and his yuppie buddies. The conversation started about his latest insurance sale but quickly shifted to what he was holding in his hand.

"Say, what are you drinking there, Ecrivain?" It was Mr. Guile who lived on the other end of the block.

After a nervous laugh, he replied, "Ah, just some Coke right now. I'm trying to take it easy tonight."

"You? That's bull," another neighbor laughed.

"Charlie, you gotta try some of this scotch—it's a bottle of Dewar's 30 that I got on a business trip in Canada. Bought it just for this party tonight." Mr. Alcott held the bottle in his hand and placed it on one of the tables set up for mingling.

Cara froze. She grabbed Adam's hand and led him behind the Christmas tree to conceal themselves.

"What's going on?" Adam asked.

She shook her head to signal for him to be quiet. Her breathing sounded louder than the noise from the party.

"That's okay, you just enjoy it tonight," she heard her father say. "I'm fine."

Cara scanned the crowd and spotted her mom across the room, busy in conversation.

"Charlie, c'mon. You're telling me I bought this scotch for nothing? I got it just for you," Mr. Alcott pressed. "You gotta try it. It goes down so smooth."

"Hey, don't waste time waiting on Ecrivain, let the rest of us enjoy it," Mr. Guile joked.

Cara's father saw her beyond the tree, and he motioned for her to come over. As she neared, he wrapped his arm around her shoulders. "Hey, Pen Pal. Go fetch me an empty glass."

Cara froze. Her eyes darted back to her mom across the room, who made contact back with her.

"Go on, Pen Pal," he repeated. His tone was casual, as if nothing was wrong with his request.

She finally obeyed. On her walk to the kitchen, she felt the burn of her mom's stare as she retrieved a glass and walked it to her father. Cara watched his every move as he poured.

And drank.

And poured.

And drank.

11

WHITE CHRISTMAS

A beam of light bounced off Cara's bedroom mirror. Adam had never signaled for her at this time before. They both should have been asleep hours ago, but the party ended late, and Cara couldn't stop replaying what had happened in her mind.

She tiptoed to the window, threw the latch, and lifted it to see Adam's chubby face and glasses on the other side. "I can't believe you're still up."

"I . . . I wanted to make sure you were okay. You seemed really sad at the end of the party tonight. Do you think you're not going to get the walkie-talkies anymore?"

"I don't know if I was ever getting those . . ." She trailed off. "And I don't think my family is going to be happy anymore."

"Why?"

Cara bit at the skin around her fingernail then looked up.

"My dad broke a really big promise."

~

IT WAS A WHITE CHRISTMAS, but the beauty of its light opposed the thickening darkness inside the Ecrivain home.

Cara's father hadn't only resumed drinking since the party a few days prior, it was heavier than ever. Late nights, slurred speech, passing out. He acted like nothing was wrong.

Her mother hadn't said a word. There was no pestering or

interrogation on where he'd been. She moved about the house doing her usual cleaning routine with no more help from Cara.

Usually, Cara woke before the sun to rush to the family room on Christmas morning. But this time, she stayed in her bed with a book under her nose, avoiding the unknown interactions between her family. Hours went by, and she began to write at her desk. No one bothered to interact with her until her mother finally knocked on her bedroom door around 8:00 P.M. Christmas dinner was finally ready. Cara's stomach had been so tangled, she didn't even realize she hadn't eaten the entire day.

Her father moved slowly to the table, eyes distant, but mood pleasant. The smell of whiskey oozed from his pores. Her mother tried to put on a happy face, but it was obviously fake.

They got through dinner around the time Cara typically went to bed. Despite her father's stupor, he put on an air of excitement about opening presents. There were almost double under the tree than what they had in the past.

Her parents opened their gifts. They were typical and emotionless—seat covers for the Mustang and new dishes. Cara opened boxes full of sweaters, an elaborate play kitchen, board games that her parents would never play with her. She smiled and tried to cover her disappointment when each gift wasn't the walkie-talkie set she so desperately desired.

The Ecrivains always saved the best gifts for last. First, her father opened his—a new television with a remote controller— just like he had talked about.

Then he looked at Cara. "Hey, Pen-Pal, why don't you go next?"

"Shouldn't I go last? It looks like Mom has a little gift right there, under the tree."

"No, I want your mother to open last this year. I have something extra special for her."

A stoic expression replaced the forced amiable one on her mother's face. Cara couldn't help feeling her disappointment. The only gift she wanted for Christmas was one that couldn't be wrapped, and her husband had taken that back with his broken promise.

Her thoughts were interrupted by a large package placed on her lap.

"Open it," her father urged.

It was a gift Cara hadn't noticed under the tree. The wrapped box appeared to be the perfect size for walkie-talkies. Cara's stomach untangled. She so badly wanted the Fisher-Price Sky Talkers but also felt selfish getting what she wanted when her mom wasn't. *Please . . . please*, she thought as she tore the wrapping paper. It felt like it was wrapped ten-fold before she unveiled what lay beneath.

Bold letters on the box read "Molly McIntire." Behind the clear cellophane cut-out of the box stood an eighteen-inch doll with auburn hair in pigtail braids and wearing a plaid jumper.

"It's an American Girl Doll," her mother explained as she joined Cara on the floor. "All the other moms of girls in your class said their daughters begged for them. Some people think they'll be collectible and worth lots of money someday."

Cara never played with dolls. This gift made no sense to her, but her mother now smiled a genuine smile for the first time all day. "Thank you, Mommy and Daddy. I love it," she lied.

"Not so fast." Her father took a drink out of his favorite scotch glass. "There's one more." He pulled out another wrapped box and handed it to her. Cara looked at both of her parents with squinted eyes. She'd already gotten more presents than she'd ever received before. "Go on, rip it open!"

She hesitated and looked at her mother, who nodded for her to continue. She ripped the wrapping back and screamed. "Fisher-Price Sky Talkers! Oh, thank you, thank you, thank you!"

Floods of visions stormed her head about how she could use these with Adam—nighttime talks, walks around the neighborhood, storytelling, detective work. She couldn't wait to give him his half of the pair. She opened the box and pulled out the dark grey radios with the orange tips on the antennas. "How do they turn on, Daddy?"

"We will figure all that out in a minute," her father said, moving toward his wife where she sat on the floor. "But now, it's Mom's turn to open her last, special gift." The look of pride could not be slapped off his face. In his hand was an intricately wrapped small rectangular box with a silver bow.

Cara's mother had no discernible expression as she held the gift in her lap. She slowly tore away the paper, and underneath was a light blue box that read: "Tiffany's." Eyes awe-struck, she lifted the lid, and a diamond necklace sparkled at her. The lights from the tree hit it so brightly that it cast a glow over her face.

Cara had never seen so many diamonds in her life. She left the walkie-talkies on the floor and crouched down to see the necklace. "That's the sparkliest thing I've ever seen. Are those real diamonds, Daddy?"

"Yes, ma'am," her father said, leaning against the wall next to the fireplace. "Specially cut and placed with 14-karat gold from the most famous jeweler in New York City. Nothing but the best for your mom."

His wife sat on the floor, staring at the necklace. Not a word exited her mouth. Her husband gave her a moment to let this sink in. It's not every day a woman receives jewelry more expensive than an average car.

Cara's father pulled out the bottle of Dewar's 30, the gift from Mr. Alcott at the party, and he poured more into his glass right in front of his family. He sniffed it and took a long drink. "Susan, don't you like it?"

"Charles," she started, "you shouldn't have bought . . . I can't believe you did this." Her voice was almost inaudible.

"You deserve it, dear." He took another drink. "Don't worry about the cost, because I wanted something as special as you are to—"

"No!" she stopped him with a thundering yell as if all of her energy was waiting to explode in this particular moment.

It startled her husband so much, he spilled some of his drink on his pants. "What . . . what the hell is wrong with you?"

"No! I wasn't complementing your gift. I was commenting on what an ass-move you just made."

It was the first time Cara ever heard her mother swear. She dug her fingers into the thick fibers of the carpet and watched everything unfold.

"Oh, you're cussing now?"

"Don't try to spin this!"

"I'm not trying to spin anything! Seriously, what the hell is wrong with you, Susan?" He attempted to brush away the drink from his pants. "Do you know how much money I spent on that necklace? What I went through to have it custom made and shipped in time for Christmas for your ungrateful self?"

Cara's mother stayed on the ground, sitting on her feet. "Don't you see what you're trying to do?"

"What? What the hell is it that you think I'm trying to do?"

"You—you're trying to win me over with a gaudy necklace you probably had to take a second mortgage out to buy." She stood up and threw the box at his feet. "Well, I don't want your stupid necklace! I only wanted you to keep your promise to stop drinking!"

Her screams were splitting, and Cara was sure every person in the neighborhood could hear them. Her volume fed her husband's temper—enraging him.

"Bullshit!" He kicked the coffee table, skidding it across the floor. "You're just trying to control me!" Then he threw his half-full glass of scotch at the wall. Shards of glass flew everywhere.

Cara was too petrified to retreat. Instead, she stood there motionless, eyes wide—the room closing in on her, and everything looked red.

"I bust my ass so I can get you this necklace, and this is how you treat me?"

The Christmas tree was his next victim. He grabbed glass ornaments off the branches and smashed them against the floor and the wall.

"Charles! What are you doing? Stop!"

Ignoring his wife's pleas, he continued to shout between ornaments, "All of this!" *Crash!* "I work so you can have all of this!" *Crash!* "This huge house in this nice neighborhood," *Crash!* "is for you and your little show for all your friends!" *Crash!* "All of this is for you!"

He kicked the tree—knocking it over. Whatever ornaments he didn't rip off and destroy were now crushed under the weight of the enormous evergreen.

"You think you're so easy to live with, Susan?" He went on, punching holes in the wall. "Ever wonder why I drink? Maybe it's because of *you*! You don't have time for my wants and needs! You and your obsessive-compulsiveness that makes you care more about Pine-Sol than people!"

He was so deep in a belligerent rage there was no stopping him. He grabbed anything in sight to throw—eventually coming to the Fisher-Price Sky Talkers.

Cara finally unfroze and reached out her hands. "No, Daddy! Please! Please stop!"

But he didn't hear her. The alcohol had complete control. Nothing mattered in this moment but to destroy. He took one of the walkie-talkies and chucked it into the fire.

"No! Not my Sky Talkers!" Cara cried.

He grabbed the other one and threw it as hard as he could—

crashing it into the center of their family portrait hanging on the wall. The glass shattered, and the frame fell to the ground.

"Daddy!" Cara screamed.

He remained deaf to her cries, and the rage progressed.

Cara finally ran to her room, shoving the pages from her latest story out of the way to shut the door and locked it. The shouting continued on the other side as she breathed heavily, her back against the door, thinking of what to do.

Through her window, she noticed how dark it was outside and that Adam's bedroom light was already out.

She didn't bother with the flashlight tonight. Shaking, she opened her window and crawled out. The icy snow crunched and cracked beneath her feet. It was then she realized she hadn't put on shoes in her need to escape. Her tiny hands knocked lightly against Adam's bedroom window—hard enough in hopes to wake him, but not his parents.

The snow came down in layers without a wind as she waited for an answer on the other side of the glass. Her socks now completely soaked through from the ground. Her face stained with tears that felt like icicles.

She knocked again.

"Adam?" She loudly whispered.

Finally, Adam's face appeared—practically asleep on his feet. "Cara?" he asked before opening his window. His thick glasses weren't on as he fumbled with the lock and slid up the glass. "Cara, you're crying. Are you okay?"

She couldn't respond—her heart felt like it was stuck in her throat and choking her. Instead, she held up her hands, signaling for Adam to help her in.

He did, and there she stood before him, just breathing, inside his bedroom.

Adam brushed the thick snowflakes out of her blonde hair. "Come here." He walked her over to his bed where he got in and raised the warm comforter for her. She crawled in beside him, and he reached his right arm over her thin frame and held onto her left hand. It was so little and cold.

Neither of them said another word. The rhythmic inhales and exhales of his breath calmed her down. Soon the weight of her emotional fatigue faded, and her hand fell limp in his.

PART II

12

POLAROID

Fall 1994

"Hang on!" Mrs. Aether shouted. "I want to take a picture of you two before you leave."

"Aw, Mom, we're gonna be late for the bus!" Adam protested.

"No, you're not. You still have over five minutes."

"Fine, but do it inside, please. I don't want Brandon Billings to see."

It was the first day of school. Adam and Cara were about to enter Canterville High as freshmen.

Mrs. Aether fumbled with her new Polaroid camera. "Now, let's see…"

"Right there. You push that button right there, Mom."

Snap.

A square Polaroid picture slowly slid out of the camera, which would take a couple of minutes to develop. Mrs. Aether grabbed a black Sharpie and wrote on the white space at the bottom:

Adam + Cara, First Day of 9th Grade - 1994.

"Here, Cara. You can hold onto it if you'd like to see the developed picture. Just please make sure to bring it back to me after school."

Cara reached out her hand. "I'll be careful with it."

"Okay, Mom, we gotta go!"

"All right, all right. But first, give me a big hug."

Adam rolled his eyes but smiled as he opened his arms wide. His mother squeezed him, and in that moment, Cara noticed that Adam was now the same height as his mom.

Mrs. Aether moved her hands to both sides of his face and put her forehead against his. "I can't believe my baby boy is already in high school!"

Adam let his mother indulge for a moment, and then said, "Mom, we're seriously going to miss the bus."

"Oh, okay," she relented. "But Cara, let me give you a quick hug too." She squeezed her just as hard. "You two have the best first day of high school."

"Yep! See ya!" Adam bolted out the door.

Cara followed but smiled and turned back with patience. "Thanks, Mrs. Aether. We will."

The Aethers and Ecrivains still lived side-by-side on Paddington Road. While the interiors of each house had minor changes of décor to keep up with fashionable trends, the exteriors remained the same. The Aethers with the white painted siding, the Ecrivains with the brick façade.

Her father's promise to his wife remained broken. Still married, they rarely talked, and when they did, it was to fight. Cara longed for those two weeks back from six years ago—the only time her family ever truly seemed happy. But those two weeks in 1988 were never spoken of. Her mother never wore her diamond necklace, and Cara never asked for a new set of walkie-talkies. She and Adam kept their late-night talks through the window as he continued to be a loyal ear for her stories and poems.

"I'm nervous." Adam fidgeted with the strap of his book bag while they waited for the bus.

"Yeah, me too."

Canterville High School enrolled about two thousand students. It was a massive step up from junior high, which had about one-fourth of the population. Adam's older sister Angela had already graduated and started her junior year of college at the University of North Carolina Wilmington, so any security from someone older looking out for them was gone.

Adam pulled out a Twinkie from his bag. His hands shook as he unwrapped the plastic cover and shoved a bite in his mouth.

"Adam!" Cara scolded. "What are you doing? The bus is going to be here any minute. Mr. Becket really cracked down on having food on the bus last year."

"I can't take it any longer," he managed to say with his mouth stuffed. "I need it to calm my nerves."

"Hey, Lard-Ass!"

A black Camaro pulled up. It was Brandon Billings, now a sophomore who could drive. His hair still red, he was tall, good looking, and a safety for the football team.

"Oh no . . ." Adam mumbled. Of course Brandon would pull up when he had a mouth full of Twinkie.

"Well, look at that. Little Fatty finally made it into high school. I hope you're not too fat to fit in a desk!"

"Shut up, Brandon," Cara said. She'd let Adam say it, but his mouth was still stuffed.

"You need a girl to stand up for you? Still fat *and* a faggot. Have fun riding the bus, little freshies!" With that, he drove off— leaving skid marks on the road.

Adam swallowed the huge bite and threw the rest of Twinkie into the street. "Man, I hate redheads! What a way to start high school!"

"Just ignore him. The school's so big, I bet you'll never see him around."

As the bus pulled up, Cara looked down at the Polaroid that finally developed. She saw herself in white Keds, high-waisted jeans, an oversized green top, and a lacy vest. No makeup and hair pulled half up with a scrunchie. Next to her was her best friend. Adam, still husky with pop-bottle glasses, in baggy jeans with a plaid flannel tucked in with no belt.

She noticed what Mrs. Aether had written at the bottom and realized she not only took time to take the picture, but she also labeled it with this important date.

In that instant, she realized that neither her own mother nor father had even said goodbye to her on her first day of high school.

~

STUDENTS SWARMED the hallways at Canterville High. Lockers slammed, people shoved, and the air smelled of too much cologne to mask potent body odor. Adam and Cara fumbled with their locker combinations and read over their schedules to make out a route to their classes.

An announcement blared over the intercom. It was the principal who monotonously said, "Welcome back from summer vacation. At this time, would all students please make their way to the gymnasium. Again, all students should report to the gymnasium at this time."

The first day was on an alternative schedule allowing for the Clubs and Activities Fair in the morning. Every student organization, sport, club, and committee had a booth set up in the gymnasium in an attempt to coax other students to join them—often offering free candy to passersby as a form of persuasion.

Adam and Cara stuck together as they made their way past each booth: Glee Club, Student Council, Chess Club, Volleyball, Yearbook, Baseball, and dozens more—each one shoved a flyer in their faces and had a representative who said something along the lines of, "Hi there, would you like to hear more about the Scholars Bowl Club? Here's a piece of candy."

For the first time ever, Cara watched Adam resist free sweets. She couldn't tell if it was first-day jitters or the effect of his interaction with Brandon Billings earlier. Either way, he was off. Nevertheless, he still forced jokes.

"Wait, Cara, don't you want to stay longer and hear about how you could join the Chess Club?"

She gave him a shove.

"No, seriously. I'm thinking there's a potential future boyfriend for you in that group."

"Shut up!"

The teasing stopped when someone shoved another flyer in Cara's face. "Do you like writing? Would you like to hear more about our journalism program? Here's a piece of candy while you—"

"Did you say journalism?" Cara asked.

"Yeah, we write articles and take pictures for the school newspaper, along with other stuff . . . so did you want that piece of candy? Most people don't want to hear me explain . . . they just want the candy."

"Actually," Adam interrupted, "I don't think she'll have time for that because she just signed up for the Chess Club. She has a crush on a couple of the guys."

The journalism girl looked back and forth at them, not sure if he was serious or not.

"He's joking." Cara rolled her eyes. "First, I'd love that piece of candy, and I love writing. Could you tell me more about the club?"

Journalism girl, whose name turned out to be Sarah, went into depth about the ins and outs with her first captive audience member.

After a minute, Adam leaned over and whispered, "I'm going to check out a couple other booths while you chat."

Cara barely nodded as she remained engaged with the pitch.

~

THE BELL finally rang at three o'clock to release the students from what felt like the longest day of their lives. Adam and Cara planned to meet by the front doors so they could walk to the bus together. They had a couple of the same classes and lunch, but the day was so busy, they hadn't had a chance to talk.

Scores of buses lined up, and after Adam and Cara wove through the mass of students, they jumped on theirs before it left. Freshmen were expected to sit toward the front, a similar hierarchy to their grade school days. Both backpacks dropped to the floor in unison as their bodies flopped into the seat like two soldiers back at the barracks after a day of combat.

After taking a moment to breathe, Adam looked at Cara. "So . . . how was your day?"

"Exhausting."

"I feel ya, sister."

"I got lost three times, knew no one in my third period math class, and almost fell down the stairs. Could have been worse, I guess."

"I got lost *four* times, a volleyball player spilled potato soup down the front of my pants at lunch, and Brandon Billings saw me across the hall between sixth and seventh periods and shouted, 'Hey! It's Fatty-Fatso!' as loud as he could. So, yeah . . . your day could have been worse . . . it could have been my day."

"Sorry." Cara tried to think of something to change the subject, but he beat her to it.

"That school is so big, we're like . . . two clocks in a clock store."

Cara raised her eyebrows. "Um, what's that supposed to mean?"

"I mean that we just blend in. We each need to find our niche. Make a name for ourselves." Cara liked his zeal. "Speaking of, did you decide to join the Chess Club?" He gave her a wink.

"Ha, no! I decided to join the Journalism Club—I'm really looking forward to it! It's actually a class, so I need to talk to my counselor about changing my schedule. I guess this first year they go over all the fundamental stuff like how to interview and write like a journalist, how to arrange articles so they fit perfectly on the page, how to take photographs, and even how to develop your film—how cool is that?"

"Pretty spiff-y . . ."

"Oh, come on. I've always thought developing film in a darkroom would be so cool. And that's just a perk. Next year, I'll be able to start writing for the school newspaper! And by my senior year, my goal is to be editor-in-chief."

"Okay, for real, that's honestly pretty cool. I'm happy for you."

"So, I don't know where you wandered off to during the fair. Did you find anything to join? You know, to make a name for yourself?"

"Does the school newspaper have a sports section?"

"I don't know. Probably. Why?"

"Well, maybe you could write about me in a couple of years. I've decided I'm going to pursue my childhood dream. I'm going to join the football team."

13

THE TRICYCLE

"Football?"

Mrs. Aether's response was identical to Cara's on the bus. "But you've never played football. I didn't think you even liked it anymore. And haven't practices already started?"

The house filled with the aroma of chocolate chip cookies that his mom made for the return from their first day of high school. Adam didn't touch any of them.

"I already talked to the coach," he assured her. "He said he could always use more guys and that I could start practicing tomorrow after school. So, could you pick me up around 5:30?"

"Wait," Cara said, "this means we won't be able to ride the bus home together anymore."

"Maybe you could stay after and work on homework or your journalism stuff. Then you could ride home with my mom."

"Hey, I never said I would pick you up!" His mother glared. "Honey, I sure admire that you want to pursue something new, but I'm worried about you doing . . . *this*. Football's kind of dangerous—"

"Mom, I'll be fine."

"I'm curious what sparked such a desire of something you haven't shown interest in since you were a kid."

"I was impressed by what the football guys said at the fair this morning." His mother didn't look like she bought that. "I don't want to be known as Fatty-Fatso for the rest of high school, okay? I thought this could be a way for me to lose some weight and show I can be tough. Maybe make a new name for myself."

Mrs. Aether nodded. "We'll talk about this over dinner when your father gets home."

~

CARA EVENTUALLY HEADED BACK to her home for dinner. The August humidity cloaked her skin when she stepped outside, but when she took her shoes off in the entryway, the marbled floor sent a chill from her feet to her forehead. And instead of the smell of lasagna, the smell of Lysol hit her nose. Her mother had just returned from work and immediately began disinfecting corners no one ever came near. Cara wasn't met with a hug or even a "hello."

Her heart was as hungry as her stomach, but she didn't want to bother her mother during, what was most likely, the happiest part of her day—cleaning.

Cara dragged her book bag, carrying roughly forty pounds of new textbooks, to her room. She distracted herself by pulling out her *Intro to Journalism* textbook and studied the pages. Cara learned to write soon after she learned to talk, but journalism was a whole new medium she'd never considered before. Newspapers didn't really interest her. In fact, she wasn't sure of the last time she'd read one. But writing with a purpose, writing something that thousands of eyes would read, felt exhilarating.

After devouring chapters of her book, her stomach couldn't take it anymore. There was still no food on the table or in the oven. Cara's mother now dusted the office that had been dusted just two days prior.

"Mom?" she asked. "Did you have anything to eat for supper?"

"Oh, hi. I never heard you come in. I'm not hungry, so I didn't even think about it. What time is it?"

"Eight o'clock."

"Oh, heavens. I won't have time to make anything, and I think we're out of microwaved dinners. How about you make yourself a sandwich?" She lifted some books and generously sprayed the shelf with Endust and was clearly finished with any potential conversation.

Cara rummaged for bread in the kitchen to make herself a PB&J. As she spread the last bit of grape jelly onto the right corner, in staggered her father from the garage. She didn't run to greet him like she used to.

He moved straight to his recliner, flipped back the lever to prop up his feet, and clicked the remote to turn on the television. Cara had to walk past him to get back to her room.

"Whatcha got there, Pen Pal?"

"Oh, just a peanut butter and jelly sandwich."

"Did your mother not make any damn supper again?"

"I think she's busy cleaning . . . it must have been a rough day at work."

"I'm the one who had a rough day."

Cara let out a huff. "I don't think it's a competition, Dad."

He dismissed her comment. "Make me one of those, would you? Oh, and make me a high ball while you're at it."

Cara desperately wanted to roll her eyes but turned back to the kitchen. She knew the liquor cabinet well and exactly how her father liked his drinks. Over the years, she'd become his own personal bartender.

She brought him the sandwich and the drink, and despite the buzz of the television in the background, she asked, "Do you have a newspaper subscription?"

"I do, why?" He took a slow drink and savored the burn down his throat.

"Oh, I never see the paper around here, so I didn't realize."

"I usually take it with me to work. Again, why do you ask?"

"Well," she couldn't contain her excitement, "I joined the Journalism Club at school today. I wanted to start reading the paper to get a feel for the voice and word-choice journalists use, plus camera angles, text layout, all that. Do you think you could bring it home each day after work instead of throwing it away?"

He swallowed a bite of his sandwich and kept his eyes fixated on the television.

"I didn't know you started school today."

~

CARA PRESSED her pillow against her face and screamed into it. Then she grabbed her notebook and started writing — breaking the lead of her mechanical pencil numerous times. All of her hurt and anger came out in small lines of metaphorical words that shaped a poem.

When she felt it was done, she clutched her trusty flashlight and shined it into Adam's bedroom. Talking through the window was one of the few comforting constants in her life.

He slid up the glass. "Hey, what's up?"

Focus on him first so you don't come across like a needy basket case.

"Hey, what did your dad say about football?"

"He was excited! He wants me to go for it."

A breeze flew into her window, brushing her hair in front of Cara's eyes. She tucked it behind her ears. "That's great! So you start tomorrow?"

"Right after school. We actually went out tonight and bought cleats and some other gear."

"That's awesome. My schedule is going to switch tomorrow so that I'll have that journalism class. Looks like both of our lives are going to look a bit different after today, huh?"

Adam adjusted his glasses. "I guess so. My mom said you're welcome to ride home with us after practice if you don't want to ride on the bus alone."

"Yeah . . . yeah, that would be great. I'll do what you suggested and work on homework or something while you're at practice. Umm . . ." She tapped her fingers on the window sill and fumbled for a segue. "Speaking of homework, did you already get any?"

"I'm finishing up on algebra right now. Why do math teachers always seem to dive right in on day one?"

"I know! Other teachers at least try to get to know you on the first day."

"What about you? Much homework tonight?"

"Not really, but I read about a quarter of my *Intro to Journalism* textbook . . . I also just wrote a poem. I had to get some feelings out. Can I share it with you?"

Adam's hand cradled his head. "Of course!"

"This was inspired by something that happened at home tonight." She cleared her throat. "I titled this 'the tricycle.'"

metal melted
formed with a purpose

Breathtaking

becoming the handlebars
seat
and frame
of a tricycle
whose only desire is to give joy

but you stayed inside
warmed by pale fire
with figures dancing
in your head
while she
was left out
year after year
in the cruel weather
with too much rain
from the heavens
eroding her
as though she was soil
and the snow covering her
like she was someone
all wrapped
from scalp to toenail
in gauze

she just wanted care
and hands to warm
her handlebars
and to make you happy
but you didn't notice

now oxidation has set in
and the metal of the tricycle
becoming fragile, rusted
can no longer
hold herself together
and will crumble to the ground
from which she came

and as she falls
she wants to scream
"Why didn't you try?"

I wanted you to try so hard

Cara closed the notebook and saw Adam brush a tear from his eye.

14

AEGGERS

The second day of school proved just as nerve-wracking as the first with the changes in their schedules. The excitement in the hallways had died down a bit, and students walked more purposefully to their destinations. Cara's Intro to Journalism class was now first period. She struggled to find it, causing her to be late. Luckily, Ms. Turner was forgiving.

A raspy voice called out, "You must be the new student. Welcome!"

Ms. Turner didn't wear makeup, had her mousy brown hair pulled up in a claw clip, wore thin gold-rimmed glasses, and a pencil behind her ear. Despite her petite stature, she was intimidating. Still, Cara felt a genuine warmth about her. The classroom was full of oblong tables, not desks, and she covered the walls with laminated newspaper clippings. Some were the works of her students, some were major stories Ms. Turner had written from her days as a writer for the *Dayton Daily News*.

"Remind me of your name, hon. I knew a new student was coming, but I don't have my new roster yet. The first week of school is pretty hectic."

"Cara Ecrivain." Her voice shook a little.

"Ecrivain—is that E-C-R-I-V-A-I-N?"

Cara nodded.

"Your last name is French, no?" Ms. Turner asked as she added her name to the roster.

"Yeah, it is. I'm French on both sides of my family."

"Oh intéressant. Comme c'est amusant d'avoir une fille française. Vous devriez rechercher la signification de votre nom. On dirait que vous êtes destiné à ce cours."

What in the world?

Cara shrugged and said, "Um . . . oui? Am I in the right class?"

The rest of the students laughed.

"Sorry, I studied abroad in France and like to have a little fun speaking the language." Ms. Turner pointed Cara toward an empty chair. "Yesterday, we introduced ourselves and discussed why everyone decided to take this class. Why don't you go ahead?"

Cara stood beside her seat. "Hi, I'm Cara. I'm a freshman here. Honestly, I never considered journalism before—that is until I met Sarah at the Activities Fair yesterday. But I've always wanted to be a writer. Scribing with a crayon is one of my first memories. I'm looking forward to learning more about this type of writing and having my words meet the eyes of hundreds, even thousands of readers."

Ms. Turner raised her eyebrows. "Thank you, Cara. I look forward to working with you." She then turned to the rest of the class. "Yesterday, we mainly took it easy. Today, we're going to get down to business. I'm not going to bore you with all the ins and outs on the syllabus yet, but you need to understand that this is the introductory class, and you won't be doing any writing for the *Tiger Tribune* this year. Instead, you're going to learn how to write like a journalist, how to interview, how to take photos with professional cameras, how to develop your own film, how to make your articles fit into the right size of the newspaper page, how to write an eye-catching title, and more."

Cara shifted in her seat.

Ms. Turner's body language and tone changed. "But first," she went on, "what is journalism? I want you to take five minutes and do a quick-write on your thoughts. Quick-writes don't have to be grammatically correct—don't worry about spelling, grammar, punctuation—for the *only* time in this class." That gave everyone a giggle. "Quick-writes should be an overflow of your initial thoughts. There are no right or wrong answers, just write what first comes to mind. Go."

They did.

When they finished, Ms. Turner called on several students to share. Most of them mentioned writing for newspapers, which put a satisfied, yet annoyed look on the teacher's face like she had heard these basic responses a thousand times. Once the hands went down, so did Ms. Turner's eyes.

"You're all only partially right." Gathering her thoughts, she paused before looking up. "Journalism isn't just writing—it's listening, lots of listening. And when you listen, you have to decipher what's newsworthy, what's important, what's true. Journalism isn't just writing, it's researching. Your stories must be accurate and credible to gain respect and trust from your readers."

The class clung to every word.

She slowly paced the front of the room and looked each student in the eye as she talked—pausing for emphasis. "You will, however, write, which is what most think of when they hear the word 'journalism.' But you won't just slap words on a page—your writing will become a craft—a powerful craft. You will agonize over using just the right word choice to tug at the readers' emotions without manipulating them. An effective journalist can change the minds of their readers, and maybe . . . just maybe even change the minds of the world."

Cara fought the urge to stand up and clap for this woman.

◦∿◦

LUNCHTIME WAS the first opportunity Cara had to talk with Adam. The day before, they had lost each other, but today the long lines ran a little more smoothly, and they found a place to sit in the corner. They simultaneously set down their lunch trays full of turkey, mashed potatoes, peas, and a carton of milk.

"Oh my gosh! I am ecstatic for my journalism class!" Cara leaned forward. "Ms. Turner is *so* cool. Did you know she used to write for the *Dayton Daily News*?"

Adam was chewing a mouthful of peas. "Nope, sure didn't."

Cara went on. "Yeah, award-winning, even. That makes her so legit! She's like, not just a teacher. She's lived the writer's life before, and now I'll be learning from the best. And get this. She gave this inspirational speech about what journalism *really* is. She ended by saying, 'An effective journalist can change the minds of their readers, and maybe . . . just maybe even change the minds of the world.' Isn't that super empowering?"

Cara had been talking without taking a breath and didn't even notice that Adam wasn't the least bit enthralled. She took some bites of her food and stared into the distance—basking in the excitement of it all for a moment.

"That's awesome, Cara. Looks like you've found your niche. You're already a great writer, so I bet you will end up being a star for the newspaper."

"Hey, actually, I was going to ask you—we have to practice interviewing people and writing their responses in shorthand. It's not due until the middle of September, but I wanted to get a head start on it. Would you be willing to be my practice interviewee?" It was in that moment she realized Adam had barely touched his food. "Why aren't you eating?"

"*That's* your first interview question for me?" Adam joked.

Cara rolled her eyes. "Are you nervous about starting football this afternoon?"

"No, I was just listening to you." He shoved a heaping spoonful of mashed potatoes into his mouth. "See? I'm fine."

"Are you sure you're okay?"

He shrugged. "How bad could it be?"

∼

WHAM!

Adam soared through the air and landed on his back. Brandon Billings had just jacked him within the first ten minutes of practice.

The wind was obviously knocked out of him. It was like third grade in the neighborhood all over again.

It looked like Brandon whispered something in his ear before he smacked Adam's helmet and ran off.

The head coach saw him lying there and started screaming. "Aeggers! What the hell are you still doing on the ground? Get your ass up! This is football, not patty-cake! Aeggers? *Aeggers?* Can you hear me?"

Adam, now on all fours, finally responded. "It's Aether, sir."

"I don't give a damn what your actual name is, kid! I just want you to get the hell up!"

"Yes, sir." Adam managed to stand, still hunched over and grabbing his stomach. The sweltering afternoon of August's heat wasn't doing him any favors.

Cara sat in the stands, attempting to do algebra, but she couldn't keep her eyes off her friend on the field. It was like a horror scene in a movie—painful to watch but impossible to turn away.

Coach Sampson's whistle blew three times. All the boys headed to the end zone. Adam looked around and followed the mass. Suicides. The boys had to form several lines and run up and down the field, adding ten yards each time. Adam's pudgy physique had never done much running before. He tried to keep up with the others but lagged far behind.

"Pick it up, Aeggers!" Coach yelled.

Adam finally completed the sprints and then headed to the sidelines . . . and puked.

As the team headed to the locker room, Cara packed up her partially completed math homework and waited for Adam at the gate of the stadium. She was sure that he would insist on quitting after being brutally tackled, cussed out, and humiliated. When Adam turned the corner from the locker room, he limped toward Cara. Mrs. Aether pulled up in her minivan, and he hobbled over to get in.

"So?" His mom asked. "How was your first practice?" She sounded so hopeful.

Cara braced herself because she knew his answer would be a disappointment. She was ready to help explain how savage and ruthless the practice was so his mother could understand. And then Adam interrupted her thoughts—

"I loved it."

Cara's jaw dropped.

"I can't wait for tomorrow."

~

WHEN CARA'S father came home from work, she approached him with hope. "Did you bring the newspaper home from the office?"

He hadn't.

Through the window that night, Cara asked Adam how he could love football even though it looked so brutal.

"I can't really explain it. But, I mean . . . look at me. I'm certainly not built for cross country or basketball. If I've got a chance to play any sport and make a name for myself, it's gotta be football."

Cara nodded in half-hearted agreement and changed the subject.

"Hey, do you think your dad would let me keep his morning paper after he's done reading it each day?"

~

THE NEXT SEVERAL weeks were different for Adam and Cara. Dr. Aether started leaving his newspaper for Cara after breakfast. She studied every aspect of it: what made a headline catchy, the stylistic wording, the captions for pictures. She pictured her name on the byline of future school newspapers.

Adam began his own studying. He checked out books on football, watched every televised game, and ran and lifted weights on his own to get into better shape. His eating had returned, but he wasn't sneaking Twinkies anymore. He forced protein upon himself. When Adam asked his mother if he could start drinking raw eggs for breakfast, Mrs. Aether looked at him as if he had horns growing out of his nostrils. She suggested a protein shake instead. He wasn't the best on the team, by far, but he worked the hardest. He told Cara he was sure Coach Sampson would start to notice his efforts and possibly even learn his real name soon.

The day of the first game arrived. Since the Friday night lights belonged to the varsity team, junior varsity played their games on Thursday afternoons. Cara stayed in the journalism room to work on homework while she waited on the game. Ms. Turner always stayed late when students worked on the newspaper or just wanted to hang out.

Cara glanced at her watch. Five o'clock—thirty minutes before the game. "Oh, no!" She gathered her belongings and shoved them in her book bag. "I've gotta go!" She was supposed to meet Adam's parents early so they could watch the team run in together.

"Where are you headed to in such a hurry?" Ms. Turner asked.

"Oh, the JV football game."

"The JV football game? That's not a hot ticket event. Are you a lover of the sport? Or do you have a boyfriend who plays?"

Cara was caught off guard by the question. She wasn't used to a teacher being so personable. "Boyfriend?" Cara laughed. "Yeah, right. No, my really good friend is on the team. My best friend, actually. He went out for the first time, so I wanted to support him." She tucked a loose strand of hair behind her ear.

Ms. Turner raised her eyebrows and pursed her lips. "That's very sweet of you. Maybe you could photograph some of the games in the future. Then you'd be close to all the action."

"Sure. That'd be great. Okay, I better get down there. Thanks for letting me work late in your room."

The early autumn sun beat down on her face while a crisp breeze cooled her at the same time. The junior varsity pep band set up in the stands, and the smell of the popcorn hit her nose. From a distance, she saw Dr. and Mrs. Aether and waved while she moved toward them. Mrs. Aether went all out, wearing a button pinned on her sweater that was a picture of Adam in his football uniform. They got seats along the fifty-yard line where other football parents sat.

"Are you nervous at all?" Cara asked Mrs. Aether.

"Oh, I've had butterflies all day!" She noticed the football team assemble outside the locker room and scanned the players. "What number is Adam?"

"Sixty-eight. I see him!" Cara pointed and then waved. "He's on the far left!"

The loudspeaker came on, and the announcer blasted, "And now, ladies and gentlemen, please welcome your junior varsity Canterville Tigers!"

The football team ran onto the field and broke through the paper sign the cheerleaders made while the JV pep band started to play "Eye of the Tiger"—their go-to song for the entrance of all their sports teams.

After the warm-ups, Adam stood with the rest of the team in the huddle. He turned several times, seemingly trying to spot his parents and Cara in the crowd. When he finally found them, he had a huge smile and waved.

"Hey! Adam's waving!" Cara said. She and the Aethers enthusiastically waved back. One of his teammates gave him a little shove as if to say he couldn't break the "fourth wall" between the field and the stands.

Ms. Turner was right. The JV football game was no hot ticket. The stands were mainly filled with parents of players, the pep band was sub-par, and the cheerleaders seemed to only know three chants, which they continuously repeated. But there was still an exciting surge about the game Cara didn't expect, and she knew it would intensify once Adam got in the game.

During the second quarter, Cara's stomach growled so loudly that Mrs. Aether heard it over the cheerleaders shouting their only defense cheer (while their team was actually on offense).

"Was that your stomach?" Mrs. Aether asked.

"Yikes, I think so." She glanced at her watch. "I guess my mom usually does have dinner made by now," she lied.

"Let's get a hot dog at the concession stand." Mrs. Aether started to rise.

"No, no. That's okay. Let's wait until half time. I'd hate to miss it if Adam gets in for the first time."

The game was tied fourteen to fourteen when the horn sounded at the half, and Adam still hadn't seen the field. Cara looked over at Mrs. Aether, who let out a deep sigh, then smiled and said, "How about that hot dog?"

After waiting in line, Cara drenched hers in mustard and relish and couldn't wait to scarf it down. "Thank you so much! My mom meant to give me some money for tonight, but I think she forgot. Her job's been pretty hectic lately."

"Don't even mention it, Cara."

The pep band started playing again, and they headed toward their seats. Adam sent up a little wave one more time, but the smile on his face was more of a slight grin. The second half continued, and before they knew it, another horn sounded indicating the end of the game.

Adam never set foot on the field.

15

THIRTY POUNDS

Cara attended six more JV football games, which were six more games Adam didn't play in.

She wondered if he was embarrassed by this, but he continued to ask her if she was coming. Instead of complaining about his playing time, he began running in the mornings before school, drinking more protein shakes, cutting carbs, and lifting weights on the weekends. All this was in addition to working his butt off at practice each day. It didn't hurt that he also grew about three inches from the start of the school year.

Autumn was ripe with crisp winds that detached the dead colored leaves from their trees and with the sun trading places with the moon earlier and earlier each night. A chilly October breeze swept into Cara's room when she opened her window to respond to Adam.

"Thirty pounds!" Adam said in a loud whisper. "Can you believe it? I've lost thirty pounds since the beginning of school."

Cara had known Adam her entire life and couldn't remember a time when he wasn't chubby. So much had melted away from him—he even had some definition in his arms now. If it weren't for his pop-bottle glasses, he might not be recognizable. "That's amazing," she said. "I'm so impressed with your dedication."

"My mom has to take me to the mall this weekend to get new clothes. Nothing fits anymore. I'm getting a little nervous about my football uniform too."

"Can't you just get a new one?"

"Cara, the coach doesn't even know my last name. He *still* calls me Aeggers!" They both laughed. "I think if I told him I needed new pants, he would just cuss me out."

"What else is new?" Cara joked. "Hey, but think about it. He wouldn't be cussing *you* out. He'd be cussing out Aeggers."

"You're still coming to the game tomorrow night, right? It's the last one, and we're playing Huber Heights. They're our biggest rivals."

Cara smiled. "You know I wouldn't miss it."

He smiled back then pulled his blinds up and down four times before turning off his light.

~

It was the day of the final JV football game. Thursdays now involved several traditions. Cara met Dr. and Mrs. Aether behind the bench on the fifty-yard line. Mrs. Aether wore her button of Adam's picture, and they cheered for Adam when he ran out with the team as if he was the starting quarterback. Adam always looked back to find them in the crowd and would give a little wave or nod. Mrs. Aether waited until halftime to buy Cara a hot dog and chips for dinner, just in case Adam happened to get in.

The sun went down as the fourth quarter began, and the game was a blowout. They hoped this meant Adam would get to play, but the second string players got in while Adam remained on the sideline. Cara and the Aethers were only partially watching the game and made small talk instead.

"So, Cara," Dr. Aether asked, "are my morning newspapers coming in helpful to you and your future writing career?"

"Oh, for sure. I've been studying them a lot and have a much better sense of how a journalist writes."

Cara munched on her bag of chips from halftime when she noticed something odd about Adam's pants. "Is that . . . duct tape around the waist of Adam's uniform?"

"Oh my goodness," said his mother. "He was complaining about how loose his football pants were, so I suggested using duct tape as a belt, but that was a joke! Oh, that looks so ridiculous."

"Aeggers!" Coach Sampson shouted. "Get in there!"

Adam looked shocked and took a moment before he put on his helmet.

Cara dropped her bag of chips as she grabbed Mrs. Aether's arm. "Look! Adam! Adam's going in!"

Adam held onto the waist of his pants as he sprinted to his position on the field. When the play started, he reached out and grabbed the ball carrier with his right arm, allowing the running back to gain three yards before finally pulling him down.

"Aeggers!" Coach Sampson screamed. "What the hell are you doing? Get your damn hands out of your pants and play!"

Adam obeyed and put both of his hands out for the next play as he got down in his stance. Just as Huber Heights snapped the ball, Adam's pants began to fall down below his waist, and he started to pull them up.

Coach Sampson yelled, "Go, Aeggers! Get in there!"

Adam attempted to fight through the blockers to get to the running back headed his way, but his pants dropped lower and lower until they were finally around his ankles!

The running back from Huber Heights was just out of reach as Adam lunged to tackle him. The pants shackled his movements as Adam fell to the ground, allowing the running back to break free for a big gain.

Cara covered her mouth and closed her eyes. Adam must have been mortified. This would be something the football players, and many of the students attending, would talk about for years. Not quite the impression Adam was trying to make, but he finally had made a name for himself, even if it was "Aeggers."

16

CONTACTS

Fall 1995

"It's perfect," Cara said to the worker at Things Remembered as she held the leather bracelet in her hands. Inscribed on the outside was the word "AEGGERS," a little gift for Adam to start his second football season.

Even though Adam had experienced one of the most humiliating moments of his life, the few minutes he got on the football field sparked a desire in him to improve. After football season, he continued to run in the mornings and lift weights after school for the rest of his freshman year. In the summer, he attended a football camp, and a few weeks before school, the football team began two-a-day practices. Adam had slimmed down considerably and gained a ton of muscle. Not only that, he was improving every day as a player.

It was the first day of Adam and Cara's sophomore year. Cara was anxious for this year because, for her, it meant she could be an official writer for the *Tiger Tribune*. She hadn't worked out all summer like Adam, but she was physically different herself. Curvier, with a better sense of how to do her hair. She started to wear makeup, but not much—just a little mascara and blush to enhance her natural beauty. On the first day of school, she wore a cute brown corduroy skirt, a white mini-tee, and a green sweater vest with an orange stripe across the chest. It was the first time she'd put much consideration into her outfit. She even bothered to put a headband in her hair.

Cara headed to the Aethers' for breakfast—something she began doing shortly after her mother started her part-time job. It was a little earlier than usual because they both volunteered to help with the Clubs and Activities Fair. They wanted to prove to their sponsors that they were zealous about the programs and willing to recruit the freshmen. One bummer to start the year was that they were still fifteen and couldn't drive yet, so they had to take the bus for the first few months of school. But on this first day, they got to catch a ride with Adam's mom. Not cool, but *"less not cool"* than the bus.

Cara still knocked even though they expected her. On the other side of the door stood her best friend—a tall, fit young man. But something was different this morning.

Instead of greeting him, "Where are your glasses?" came out of her mouth as she continued to stand on the porch.

A wry grin came over Adam's face. "I got contacts!"

Cara felt like she needed some corrective lenses herself. She barely recognized Adam without his pop-bottle glasses. In fact, she could scarcely remember a time she hadn't seen him wearing them. "I thought you had an astigmatism or something and couldn't wear contacts."

"The eye doctor said my astigmatism went away. I guess it's rare for that to happen, but it did. So I really wanted to get contacts for the start of the school year. Plus, it will be much better for football."

Cara didn't like this change, but she still told him, "You look nice."

"Thanks! Except it took me like thirty minutes to put them in this morning."

"That's more time than it takes *me* to get ready."

He saw the small box in her hand. "What's that?"

"Oh, this is just a little something I got for you. It's kind of a good luck present for football season."

"You didn't have to do that." Adam opened the box and pulled out the leather bracelet. "AEGGERS?"

"Do you hate it?"

"No, I love it! Thank you so much! I'll wear it for every football game."

"Are you sure? I didn't know if you could wear it during a game or not."

"If not, I'll just put some athletic tape around it or something."

He started to put the bracelet on when Mrs. Aether greeted Cara with her usual morning hug, remarking how she couldn't believe they were already in tenth grade. And like every first day of school for the past six years, she made them French toast.

As she filled their plates, Adam reminded her, "Mom, don't forget that we have to leave by seven."

"Oh, I forgot to tell you. I have a meeting this morning with some of the women in my book club and can't take you today."

"But we have to be there early for the Clubs and Activities Fair!"

"I know, sweetie, don't worry. I talked to Mrs. Billings down the street. She said her son could take you."

"Brandon Billings?" Cara and Adam exclaimed in unison.

"Yeah. He's a nice kid. Plus, he drives a sporty car. Surely that'll be way cooler than having your mom drop you off in a minivan, right?"

"Mom, we might die in that ride to school! I can't take that level of risk when I've got a whole new football season ahead of me! Trust me, I've never wanted to be seen with my mom taking me to school in a minivan more than this moment right now."

His mom just laughed and returned to her bedroom to finish getting ready.

Adam dropped his fork onto his plate and covered his face with this hands. "How could she do this to her only son? I seriously can't eat now."

A loud engine revved outside the house that followed with a couple aggressive blasts of a horn. Adam's eyes grew wide. "He's already here."

They gathered their belongings and hollered their potential last goodbyes to Mrs. Aether.

Cara tried to assuage Adam as they walked out the door. "Maybe Brandon's matured some."

Brandon rolled down his window. "Hurry up, faggot!"

"Or maybe not," Cara mumbled.

Adam and Cara went to the passenger side and fumbled with the handle so they could sit in the back together.

Brandon spoke up before Cara got in. "Whoa, now! I'm not a chauffeur. Ladies sit in the front."

Cara looked at Adam for guidance.

Adam nodded but mouthed, *Put on your seatbelt.*

Just as Cara snapped herself in, Brandon reversed out of the driveway and onto the street—leaving skid marks on Paddington Road while Metallica bled through the speakers. After going what felt like ninety in a thirty-five and speeding through yellow lights, Brandon's only attempt at a conversation was, "Where the hell are the specks?"

"Contacts," Adam replied without hesitation.

"Umph," was all Brandon grunted back.

He sped into the school parking lot and slammed the brakes as he pulled into a spot. It took Cara a second to recover. She grabbed her book bag and stepped out of the black Camaro. As she tried to release the lever to her seat so Adam could exit, Brandon surprisingly walked over to assist her. "Sorry, it has a little catch to it." He finagled with it for a moment then got it to slide up. "The next time you ride with me, you just need to do this." He showed her the special maneuver while Adam waited patiently in the back seat.

"I'll make sure to keep that in mind in the future. Thanks . . ." Cara said.

As Brandon walked away, he turned back to her. "By the way, Ecrivain, you look really nice today."

Adam crawled out and grabbed onto Cara's arm and whispered, "Dear God, we made it." He hyperbolically gasped as if finally able to breathe.

～

AFTER SETTING up for the Clubs and Activities Fair, Adam and Cara braved the hallways to find their new lockers and double-check their schedules. The first day as a sophomore was considerably different than as a freshman. Tenth graders weren't upperclassmen who ruled the school, but at least they weren't the scum of the earth.

As the warning bell sounded, the principal came over the loudspeaker and announced that everyone needed to go to the gymnasium.

The football and cheerleading booths were both across from

the journalism booth. Cara noticed the football players joking with Adam by pretending not to know who he was without his glasses. At the same time, she saw some cheerleaders glancing at him who would have never paid attention to him before. Cara and her fellow journalism representatives desperately tried to attract students to their booth, while swarms of kids crowded the football players and cheerleaders.

"Hi! Do you like writing? Would you like some candy?" they perpetually asked. Most students took the candy and walked away.

After some time, Adam careened his way over to Cara with a sympathetic look.

"Hi! Do you like writing? Would you like some candy?" Cara joked.

"Hi. I *kinda* like writing. I would *not* like any candy. And I do *not* want to join journalism." He winked at her. "Actually, I do want a small piece of chocolate," he added as he stuck his hand into their bowl.

"You're just like the rest." She rolled her eyes. "But you *do* like to write. I'm going to need your help in case I'm assigned to the sports section this year. You just can't be biased and make all the articles about you."

Over Adam's shoulder, she saw the same few girls staring at him.

Adam glanced at his watch. "The bell's about to ring for first period. You have second lunch, right?"

"Yeah, and I think we have biology together with Mr. Boggs fourth period."

"Great. I'll see you then."

∿

THE LUNCHROOM on the first day of school was more chaotic than usual. Kids tried to figure out which friends were in the same lunch as them, while freshmen weren't sure how the lines worked. Through the masses, Adam and Cara found each other.

After discussing their schedules and favorite morning classes, Adam got up to buy an additional carton of chocolate milk—for the extra calcium and protein, of course. While he was gone, Cara poked around at the canned fruit on her tray when a perky blonde sat next to her. It was Jenny Andrews, one of the cheerleaders who'd been eyeing Adam during the Clubs and Activities Fair.

"Hello?" Cara couldn't hide her confused tone. A popular cheerleader had never voluntarily been seen in public with her before.

"Hey! Who is that boy you've been sitting with?"

"That boy? That's Adam Aether."

"Oh, is he new here? I've never seen him before."

"Uh, no, he's been in this school district since kindergarten. In fact, you sat by him in algebra all last year."

"I swear I've never seen him before in my life."

"Well, he—" Cara decided not to waste her breath. "Yeah, you probably haven't."

"He's cute!"

Cute? Cara scrunched her eyebrows.

Adam returned with his carton of milk.

"Hey, Adam," Jenny said with a wink, then walked back to her group before he could respond.

He turned slowly back to Cara. "That was random."

"I think someone might have an admirer."

"No way. Jenny Andrews? I didn't think she even knew I existed."

"She didn't."

Adam stared off into space for a moment, then broke into a grin. "Dang. Never underestimate the power of contacts, I guess. Who knew I might be dating a cheerleader someday."

"Wait, you're not interested in *her*, are you?"

"What's wrong with Jenny Andrews?"

"I just didn't think she was your type," Cara said.

"Oh. Well, what *is* my type?"

Cara didn't like where this was going. "Never mind."

Adam didn't drop it. "No, tell me."

Cara wanted to scream that Jenny Andrews may be cute, but that's all she had going for her. She was an absolute ditz who wouldn't be able to carry on a deep conversation and only cared about popularity. But after a deep breath, Cara chose her words more carefully. "I think your type would be, at the very least, someone who cared about who you were *before* you wore contacts."

∾

THEIR AFTER SCHOOL routine was similar to last fall. Adam had football practice until 5:30, and since Cara didn't want to ride the bus without him, she waited to catch a ride with his mom. Because she finally got to write for the school newspaper this year, she was bound to have plenty of projects after school anyway. And as usual, she wasn't in any hurry to return home.

She stayed in Ms. Turner's class for a while to avoid the heat of the August sun but made sure to catch a few minutes of Adam's practice before it ended. She didn't know much about sports, but Adam seemed like a completely different player from last season. He looked coordinated and fast. Not only that, but he was unrecognizable from just a year ago. No longer a chubby kid, he was a young man with defined arms and legs, as tall—if not taller —than the rest of the team.

Cara noticed two more oddities. It appeared that Adam was no longer practicing as a defensive lineman but someone who caught the ball. The second was the cheerleading squad. They held practice close to the football field, which they had done before, and Cara tried to block out their chants. But this time they stopped practice and sat, staring at the football players. And Jenny Andrews's eyes seemed focused on her best friend.

Then a third oddity happened. As the players removed their helmets and headed for the locker room, Brandon Billings stopped on the field, made eye contact with Cara, and smiled.

17

DRIVING AND SKATING

B eing fifteen and a half in the state of Ohio usually included a particular evening activity for nine weeks.

Driver's Ed.

Adam and Cara couldn't wait to start, vowing to never ride with Brandon Billings again. They welcomed the extra work in the evenings and made a deal with their parents that they'd pay for a portion of the class if they could start right away.

The first class commenced a few weeks after school started. It began at 6:30 P.M., giving Adam barely enough time to shower and inhale some food after football practice. Dr. Aether dropped them off in front of a sign that read "B Safe Driving School" attached to a sketchy-looking small square cinder block building.

When they entered, a lady with a bad perm sitting behind a desk asked, "May I help you?"

"We're here for the Driver's Ed. class," Cara answered.

She made them sign paperwork then gave them each a handbook. "Be sure you bring that every night. You'll be in Mr. Fritz's class straight ahead."

They entered a room already full with a couple dozen other teenagers. Some read magazines, some etched cuss words into the table, and one was already sleeping. Only two seats remained open across from two guys wearing beanies. They were also chewing tobacco and discreetly spitting it into an open Coke can.

When they sat down, Adam decided to make the situation less

awkward and introduce himself to the chewers. "Hey," he said. "I'm Adam, and this is my friend Cara. What's your name?"

After spitting in the can, one of the boys said, "Jordan."

Adam made eye contact with the other one and waited for him to answer. "Name's also Jordan."

"Well, Jordans . . . where do you guys go to school?"

"Kettering Fairmont," the first Jordan answered.

"Ah, one of our rivals. We go to Canterville."

"We hate Canterville. It's full of preppy pricks," the other Jordan said.

Without hesitation, Adam said, "Yeah . . . well, awesome meeting you guys . . ." Cara grabbed his arm and desperately tried not to laugh at the awkward situation.

A tall, lanky man entered the room. He had dark hair to match his dark mustache. His mustard yellow shirt was tucked into his grey slacks, and he wore navy tennis shoes with Velcro. "Good evening, class," he said with a nasally voice. "Welcome to B Safe Driving School. I am your instructor, Mr. Fritz. While in class, no eating, drinking, or sleeping. You must be on time each night, or you will have to make up for that class. If you lose your handbook, you will have to buy a new one for twelve ninety-nine. If you have to use the restroom . . ."

The rest of the night consisted of reading dry instructions on driving laws out loud as a class, viewing cheesy instructional videos, and watching Mr. Fritz explain the rules of left-hand turns with an illustrated road map and magnetic cars.

"This is so lame," one of the Jordans mumbled and brought the Coke can to his mouth to spit out more chew.

Mr. Fritz looked like he was about to scold him for the comment, but the bright red can must have distracted him, and he shifted his reproof. "Excuse me, young man. Young man? With the stocking cap?" The Jordans both looked at him. "I see you're drinking a Coca-Cola Classic there. Maybe you didn't hear me when I said absolutely no food or drink."

The Jordan with the visible evidence just shrugged.

"Well, you're lucky that this is the first class. Instead of kicking you out for the evening, and since it's already an open container, my policy is that you have to chug it and then throw it away."

"Nah, I'm good," the Jordan said.

"I don't think you understand, son. You either chug your

drink, or you're out of here. I doubt you want to waste your parents' money after the first night." Mr. Fritz crossed his arms. "I'm being very reasonable by allowing you to enjoy your beverage instead of wasting it."

Adam intensified the situation by acting like the two were best pals in a fraternity and stood up to shout. "He's right, Jordan! Do it! Chug! Chug! Chug! Chug!" He started to clap to the beat of his chant. Soon the entire class joined in, including the other Jordan.

"Chug! Chug! Chug! Chug!"

Mr. Fritz basked in the atmosphere created by his rule.

To save face, that Jordan finally tipped back his can. The students watched his throat rise and fall as he swallowed. Then he darted for the trash can by the door and pulled it out of the room.

Mr. Fritz firmly but calmly said to the class, "Drinking carbonated beverages at rapid speed can have dire effects on some. Let that be a warning to you all to never bring a drink to class again in the future."

The Jordans didn't return the next week.

～

"THAT WAS PROBABLY the most disgusting yet hilarious thing I've ever witnessed in my entire life!" Adam said to Cara through the window that night.

They laughed the best kind of laugh—the kind that is so hard no noise comes out and tears start to trickle down the face.

"I feel so inspired tonight as a writer," Cara finally managed to get out. "Should my next newspaper article be about the risk of embarrassment in Driver's Ed. class? Or the hidden consequences of drinking chewing tobacco?"

"I can see it now." Adam extended his arm at the sky as if pointing to a major headline flashing across Times Square: "'Beyond Mouth Cancer, The Deceptive Dangers of Dipping.' Alliteration always adds a nice touch, you know."

"Are you sure you don't secretly want to join journalism?"

"Football takes up too much time, but I could ghostwrite for you every once in a while." He winked. "Speaking of football, you're coming to the game Friday, right?"

"You know I'd never miss a game."

"I just wanted to be sure since I've never had a game on a Friday night before. I told you I get to suit up for varsity, right?"

"I think you reminded me about a dozen times." She smiled. "Hey, there's a skating party for the school going on after the game. My first article in the newspaper was about it. Did you read it? It was in the 'Student Life' section." Cara found the irony comical that she was assigned to that section since she'd never been a social butterfly.

"You know I'd never miss an article." He smiled back.

"We should go. I bet I'll smoke you in the limbo!"

"Can you still do the splits like in grade school? You used to win the limbo every stinkin' time!"

Cara threw her head back. "Um, I don't think I'm nearly as flexible anymore. I'll have to beat you with a classic bend-of-the-knees and duck-of-the-head."

Down the hall, Cara could hear her parents shouting. She turned toward the noise then looked at Adam with weighted eyes —knowing he could hear it and that he knew the sound all too well. Their fights were becoming more and more common. She tried to block out the noise and bring the focus back to their conversation. "You didn't answer my question. You up for the skating party?"

Adam ran his hand through his light brown hair. "Yeah. Yeah, that sounds like fun. I'm just nervous whenever I think about the game. It's a big deal since I'm only a sophomore, and I don't want to screw it up, ya know?"

"I don't think anything could top your pants dropping to your ankles," she said. "So you have nothing to worry about!"

Adam talked to her until the shouting in the background ceased. Then he raised and lowered his blinds four times.

∾

IT WAS the night of the varsity football game. Cara put a little extra effort into her hair and outfit before leaving since she would be attending a social event after the game. Dr. and Mrs. Aether dropped her off at the gate as they parked. The sun painted the sky red before its final descent, and the air was crisp, but only required a light jacket. Juxtaposed against the calm was an uproar of cheers, music, and blinding artificial lights. Cara had been to plenty of JV games, but never a varsity one. Everything felt bigger, better, and brighter. The varsity band had over one hundred musicians ripping through their pre-game music. Dozens of customers lined up for concessions, middle school kids ran around the open area near the entrance, and hundreds of teenagers crowded the stands, cheering on the team as they warmed up on the field. It was electrifying.

She decided to brave the student section instead of sitting with Adam's parents. She spotted Sarah from journalism with a few other classmates toward the top of the bleachers and tried to maneuver her way to them. It was so crowded and rowdy that she was sure one of her toes would be broken and she would find at least three foreign objects in her hair before the game was over.

For nearly three hours, she endured blaring music, loud chants, and obnoxious students—all while standing on a narrow metal bench. The action on the field reminded her of football season last year because Adam hadn't moved from the sidelines except to follow the other players into the locker room at halftime.

The Tigers were trailing by four points with less than two minutes on the clock when it happened. A Canterville player was lying on the field, holding his ankle and writhing in pain. Players on both teams took a knee as trainers tended to the athlete.

All of the players except one.

Adam stood next to Coach Sampson. It was obvious to even the most casual fan that the coach was speaking words of encouragement, and Adam was about to enter the game. It was rare for any sophomore to get playing time on varsity—especially one who had changed positions.

As the injured player hobbled off the field, Adam jogged to the huddle.

Cara grabbed Sarah's arm. "I can't believe it. Adam's going in!" Without another word, she weaved through the crowd and shot down the stairs to get as close as she could to the field.

On Adam's first varsity play, they lost four yards.

"Time out!" Coach Sampson screamed.

The entire offense jogged to the sideline. The coach gathered the boys around him, showed them the clipboard with the next play, and sent them back onto the field.

Adam was positioned on the far side of the line as the center snapped the ball and the quarterback threw a perfect spiral to Pete Resner for a fifteen-yard gain. By the time he was tackled, the clock was at 1:09 and counting down. The team scrambled to line up for another play, which fell incomplete with 1:03 left on the clock.

Coach Sampson motioned to the quarterback a series of hand gestures, sending in a play.

The quarterback looked down at a band on his wrist. "Twins 491 Y Razor!"

The play started. Adam waited two seconds, then released his man and sprinted through his route.

Adam turned his head in time to see the ball soaring directly at him. Both the middle linebacker and strong safety hit him at the same time. The jarring blow stopped Adam momentarily, but he kept his legs churning and found himself pulling free of both defenders.

He didn't have the speed to go out of bounds to stop the clock, so he raced toward the end zone. The free safety stood in his way, but Pete sprinted toward the free safety screaming, "Run, Aeggers!"

As Pete blocked the free safety, Adam ran behind him and off to the right. Another defender was closing quickly at the five-yard-line. He caught Adam and jumped on his back to tackle him. Lumbering, struggling, and straining—Adam stretched the ball out in front of him with both hands as he hit the ground.

The sound of the crowd erupting brought Adam to his senses as his offensive teammates swarmed him.

Pete was on top, screaming in his face. "You did it, Aeggers! You did it!"

"Touchdown Tigers!" was the call over the PA System. "Pass completed to number eighty-eight, Adam Aether, for sixty-one yards and a Tiger touchdown!"

～

STUDENTS WERE HYPED about the winning play by the new sophomore star and headed to the skating rink to celebrate. The lights dimmed, the disco ball spun, and dozens of hot pizzas waited to be devoured by hungry teenagers.

Adam and Cara arrived together, and when they walked through the door, hundreds of voices shouted, "Aeggers! Aeggers! Aeggers! Aeggers!" Older members of the football team ran over and started tousling his hair and patting him on the shoulder.

When the chants died down, Adam finally looked at Cara. "Let's get some pizza. I'm starving."

"I'll Be There for You" by the Rembrandts blared overhead as they walked to the concession area. At least ten people stopped Adam to say, "Man, that was an awesome catch!" or "Great play!" or "You're the man, Aeggers!"

Adam and Cara finally got their pizza and sat at the only empty table they could find. They endured several more interruptions of congratulations while they ate. As Cara finished the last bite of her crust, she clapped her hands and said, "Okay, let's go get our skates!"

Adam hesitated.

"What is it?"

"I don't think I'm going to skate tonight."

"What? Why? Isn't that the whole reason we came? I'm supposed to beat you in the limbo like old times, remember?"

"I've been thinking—there's just too big of a risk of getting injured. I don't want to jeopardize the rest of the season, you know?"

Don't ruin his night. He did just make the winning play of the game. Try to be understanding.

"Okay. I get it," was all she said before leaving for the skate rental line by herself.

She had some time to contemplate while in line.

Why did his response bother me so much? It's just roller skating. Does he not want to be seen with me? Would he rather hang out with the more popular kids?

Before she could ask herself another question, someone grabbed her arm. "Oh my gosh!"

Cara whirled around to see Blair Easton, one of the most popular girls in the junior class. "May I help you?" Cara asked.

"I saw you sitting with Adam Aether. Is he your boyfriend?"

Cara rapidly blinked as if making sure this wasn't a dream. Blair was inches from her face, anxiously awaiting Cara's answer. "Uh, no. He's not. We've just been best friends for a long time."

Blair gave a relieved look and a quick, "Thanks," then walked away.

"What a bizarre night," Cara mumbled. She proceeded to check out a pair of size seven skates and headed to a bench to squeeze them on. She noticed that Adam had migrated to a table with some other football players. Blair and a couple of her friends approached. She couldn't stop eyeing them as they started flirting with her friend.

As if the night couldn't get any more outlandish, someone skated up to her as she finished tying her laces.

It was Brandon Billings.

"Hey, Cara. Wanna skate?"

Her eyes darted back to Adam, and she saw Blair Easton touch his shoulder as she threw her head back to laugh. Then she looked back at Brandon.

She didn't say no.

18

DONATION

"**M**ake sure you come to a complete stop at the stop sign. You have to actually stop, not roll through. You'll get a ticket if you don't."

"I've got it, Mom."

"That was questionable. You might get a ticket for that if a cop . . . Okay, you're going a little too fast . . . Make sure to use your blinker . . . Did you check your blind spot?"

It took everything in Cara to stay calm while driving with her mother to B Safe Driving School. She would have ridden with the Aethers, but she had to get in her fifty hours of driving with a parent to complete the requirements for her license, and Driver's Ed. class was one of the few places she had to go when one of her parents could come along.

"You'll be back at 8:30 to pick me up, right?"

"Ooh, couldn't you get a ride home with Dr. or Mrs. Aether? I have to scrub the showers tonight, and I highly doubt I'll be done by 8:30."

"But I have to get my driving hours in."

"Maybe we could do some driving tomorrow."

Adam had already driven nearly twenty-five of his fifty hours, while Cara only had four. At this rate, she was going to be eighty-six by the time she got her license. Her mother always had excuses; her father was always drinking. She unbuckled herself and headed into the cinder block building as her mother walked around to the driver's seat. "See you at home then," Cara mumbled.

She slipped into the seat where she and Adam usually sat, now sans the Jordans. Adam barely made it before class started and joined her.

"Football ran long," he said. "But, hey! I clocked fifteen more driving minutes! After driving home tonight, I'll be at twenty-six driving hours."

"Over halfway there." Cara forced a smile. "Speaking of that, could I catch a ride home tonight?"

"I thought you were driving with your mom."

"Well, I was supposed to, but apparently the showers aren't shiny enough."

A nasally voice stopped Adam's response.

"Mr. Aether, Ms. Ecrivain. It's time to stop chatting. Class is starting at this precise moment. Class, turn to page twenty-four in your workbooks."

As they were supposed to be taking notes, Adam wrote in the margin of his workbook and slid it over for Cara to read.

Sorry about your mom.
Of course you can ride home with us.

Seeing that simple note made her feel better.

They endured a riveting thirty-minute lecture by Mr. Fritz on the conundrum of what to do when four drivers approach a four-way stop at the exact same time. Cara already knew the rules, so she started making notes on a separate sheet of paper about her next article to be featured in the "Student Life" section of the *Tiger Tribune*: Homecoming.

The dance was coming up soon.

Adam spotted her scribbles and reached over to write a note:

When is Homecoming?

Cara slid the note back:

October 28

After several more videos, lectures, and practice questions, Mr. Fritz announced, "Our last topic this evening is a serious one

I want you to ponder between now and when you get your driver's license. Organ donation. When you pass your driver's test and fill out the paperwork for your license, you'll be asked if you want to be an organ donor. If you do, you will have a symbol of a heart at the bottom of your ID. If you were to be in a fatal accident, let's say, the medical personnel would know you're willing to donate your organs, and they will need to harvest them immediately."

Hands shot up in the air.

One kid asked, "What organs would they take from you?"

"Almost anything. Doctors can use most people's kidneys, lungs, heart, eyes, liver, intestines — even skin."

Another hand. "What are the benefits of being an organ donor?"

"Well, you wouldn't personally benefit because you'd be dead." The class burst into a nervous laughter.

"But, on a serious note, this matter is personal for me. I had a niece with cystic fibrosis, which is a disease that affects the lungs. She was on a waiting list for a lung transplant for over a year but never received one." A blanket of silence covered the room while Mr. Fritz paused after that last sentence.

"If you donate your organs, you will certainly enhance someone's life, and most likely, you will save someone's life."

～

ON THE BUS the next morning, Adam leaned his head against the back of the seat in front of him. "I am so ready to stop riding this thing. I can't wait to get my license."

"Yeah, but when you start driving, you can't cover your eyes and point out where everything is on the way to school. You haven't done that in a long time. You should do it again."

Adam ignored the request and looked out the window. "What did you think about that organ donation talk last night?"

"What about it?"

"I just . . . I think it's kind of weird. Someone else walking around with my intestines? I've had a lot of crap go through those things. Why would someone else want them in their body?"

"I don't think you'd care if you needed it to save your life."

Adam finally turned toward her. "Or, like, your eyeballs! Can you imagine someone else walking around with your eyeballs in their face?"

"Adam, organ donation is noble. Didn't you hear what Mr. Fritz said about his niece last night?"

"Yeah, I just don't know. What do you plan to do when you get your license?"

"Mark 'Yes.'"

"Really?"

"I'm shocked you're weirded out by this," Cara said. "It's not that big of a deal. Besides, when I die, I won't need those organs where I'm going anyway."

19

TAKE MY BREATH AWAY

Cara decided she was going to ask Adam to the Homecoming dance with her. Just as friends, of course.

She didn't go the year before—it hadn't even crossed her mind. Plus, no boy would have asked her anyway. But since she was in charge of the Social Life section of the paper this year, she had to write a huge article on Homecoming, so she needed to attend.

Even if they didn't dance, she and Adam could sit off to the side and observe. He'd crack jokes about every person and have her in tears all night. The thought of that alone made her excited to try out a high school dance for the first time. It would be nice to have rare quality time with her best friend that didn't involve the bus, Driver's Ed., or their bedroom windows.

She outlined notes for the article while she waited for Adam at lunch. He was caught by a group of football players and cheerleaders for a moment, which was typical as he was quite the hot commodity these days. He usually seemed comfortable with that group, but she noticed his face flushed when an older girl approached him. Cara laughed and contemplated how to bring up the dance when he came to sit with her.

"Hey, friend," she greeted.

"What are you working on?"

She let out a deep, stressed sigh. "My Homecoming article. I've got to make it really good, but I'm at a loss since I didn't go to the dance last year. I've gotta go this year for sure."

"I'm sure the article will be great because everything you write is great."

"Speaking of the dance," she attempted to transition, "what if we went together? I just figured we'd have the most fun with each other."

"Oh, no . . ." Adam closed his eyes.

Cara's heart cracked. Maybe she shouldn't have said anything —she didn't want to give him the wrong impression.

"Stephanie Cartwright literally just asked me to go to the dance with her."

Her heart cracked some more. "Who's Stephanie Cartwright?"

"She's the captain of the dance team and one of the Homecoming candidates."

Captain of the dance team . . . and Homecoming candidate?

That also meant she was a senior—a popular senior—who asked Adam, a sophomore.

"She sounds like a big deal."

"Trust me, I'd much rather go with you. I don't even know how to dance. I'll look like a total dweeb next to her. Maybe I should tell her I changed my mind."

She reached across the table to grab his arm.

"No, are you kidding me? I won't let you do that. It's fine. I'll probably just be taking notes and pictures for the newspaper anyway."

"You sure?"

"Yeah, yeah. I'd be a super lame date since I'd practically be there as a reporter and not a participant." There was an awkward stillness between them. "Hey, I could help you with your dance moves, though."

"Since when do you know how to dance?"

"I mean . . . I watch MTV sometimes." She smiled through her disappointment.

"Ha! Well, I could use any help I could get." He started poking at his food. "Hey, Stephanie also asked if I wanted to start sitting with her and her friends at lunch."

Cara's chest tightened.

"Do you want to sit with us?"

She shifted in her seat. "Oh, actually, I've been meaning to tell you, I need to eat lunch in the journalism room for a while," she lied. "I'm swamped with this article and all the other side projects

I have going on. This one is a huge spread, so I'll need some extra time doing the layout and everything."

Adam scrunched his forehead. "Oh, okay. Will I see you after football practice?"

"I think I need to ride the bus home," she lied again. "I've got to try to complete those driving hours with my mom."

"Okay," his tone softened. "Maybe through the window, then?"

"We will always have the window, Aeggers."

～

NEARLY TWO WEEKS PASSED, and Cara hoped Adam would forget about her promise to help him dance because it would practically be the blind leading the blind. She'd been to a few dances in junior high, which technically didn't count, but she had a basic understanding of what it should look like.

She saw Adam less frequently since she stopped eating in the cafeteria or waiting for him after football practice. They still had Driver's Ed. once a week. And, of course, the window, but even those interactions became less frequent. With Driver's Ed. almost over, they would each have their licenses soon, which meant no more bus rides. She wondered if she was avoiding him on purpose to get out of the dancing situation. Or maybe it was because he was simply in a different circle of people in high school now. At any rate, she was able to focus more on her writing, which got her mind off of Adam, her parents, everything.

The Thursday before Homecoming, Cara was up late completing a geometry assignment she'd neglected in favor of her article. Just as she was figuring out the Supplement Theorem, a light shone through her window.

Adam.

She went over and saw him peering out his bedroom with his flashlight.

"Hey, you're still up," he said. "Would you happen to be working on geometry?"

It was just a math question. Phew.

"Yeah, actually, I am."

"What did you get for number sixteen?"

She explained the process to him, and he scribbled it down on his paper.

"That was the only one I couldn't figure out." He paused for a moment, "Hey, Homecoming is this weekend, you know. And you never fulfilled your promise."

"You want me to teach you how to dance . . . *now*?"

"I don't see why not."

"Adam, it's almost 11:00 o'clock. Your parents would freak out if I came over there, and you know there's no way in hell you're coming through this door."

"You're right." He opened his window wider and crawled out. When he touched the ground, he reached back into his room and pulled out a portable radio and set it next to him. He walked over to Cara and extended his hand. "Please?"

She stared at him for a moment. "All right." She took his hand and crawled out of her own window. They faced each other, equally aware of the awkwardness.

Then Adam bent over and fiddled with the dial. "So, what radio station should I put this on? Which one would play songs that would be at the dance?"

"Um, try MIX 107.7," Cara suggested. "But make sure it's quiet."

Adam turned the dial as it caught glimpses of other stations until it got to the far right channel whose tagline was "Playing hits from the '70s, '80s, and today." The current song playing was "We Are the World" from 1985.

Cara laughed. "This isn't really a song a DJ would play at a dance, but it's got a good rhythm to show you the basics." She stepped closer to him. "First, you'll take your right hand and put it on the small of her back." She grabbed his hand and placed it behind her. "Then take her right hand with your left hand and hold it up like so. Now, use your hand on her back to pull her toward you."

Adam attempted but pulled her in way too abruptly. Cara pulled away and grabbed her stomach, laughing.

"What?" he asked. "What'd I do?"

"You're not tackling a football player, Adam, you're dancing with a girl! Okay, let's try again. Pull her in gently until you're chest to chest."

He slowly pulled Cara close. "All right, then what?"

"You sway side to side in slow circles to the beat of the music. You have to lead, though, so slightly lean the way you're both supposed to go, and she'll follow."

She demonstrated, and they danced to "We Are the World."

"She might put her head on your shoulder, or look longingly into your eyes," she said as she cheesily exaggerated the action. "You could also put both hands around her waist, but make sure they're not too low because . . . that could be awkward."

"Okay, can they be too high, though?"

"I mean, you don't want them around her neck or anything because that's what she'll do to you, but a hand higher on her back, sure. And it's perfectly fine to stay silent, or you can make small talk."

"Okay, let's practice making small talk," Adam said. "How about that weather?"

"Oh my gosh, Adam, you're fifteen, not fifty!"

"What? That's a go-to small talk topic!" Cara rolled her eyes. "Fine," he said, "you lead the small talk then."

"Let's keep dancing, and I'll let it come up naturally."

They danced.

Cara could feel his defined muscles under his shirt and noticed the rhythm of his breath began to match the music.

"We Are the World" ended, and the DJ came on. "Thank you for joining MIX 107.7 on this lovely Thursday night. We're playing some '80s favorites, and here's one from the hit movie *Top Gun*—'Take My Breath Away.'"

The iconic opening of the song started. It had been one of Cara's favorites since she was a little girl. She didn't know if it was the beautifully haunting music itself, the movie it was connected to, or maybe her desire to have that kind of effect on someone someday, but nonetheless, her heart flittered a little whenever she heard it.

"I love this song," she whispered.

"I know you do. You've said so since we were kids." Adam smiled. They swayed to the music, his hand on her back, holding her close.

"We're going to get our licenses soon. That's going to be life-changing. No more bus rides, or Driver's Ed., or waiting for your mom to take us places."

"It's going to be great," Adam said, "but I hope it doesn't pull us apart."

She looked up at him. "I feel like so much has already pulled us apart."

Adam sighed. "I know. But no matter what, you'll always be my best friend."

"And no matter what, we'll always have the window, right?"

"We'll always have the window," Adam repeated.

Cara laid her head on Adam's shoulder and took in the cadence of his breath as they continued to sway to the music.

❧

WHILE JUST ABOUT every other girl in the high school was off to hair and nail appointments on the day of the Homecoming dance, Cara agonized over what to wear. She wouldn't be in a semi-formal gown like everyone else—she was going to be on the sidelines taking pictures and writing details in her pocket-sized notebook. What could she wear that indicated she was there on business?

She settled on all black—black pants, black top, black shoes. Hopefully, that would make her blend into the dimly lit background. When she arrived at the school gym that had been transformed into a dance hall for the evening, she put the camera strap around her neck and a lanyard with a badge that read "Canterville Journalism." This screamed that she was only there for work, and if anything, at least it would guarantee she got in for free.

Students entered in droves. Most girls wore knee-length dresses with their hair pulled back into a French twist. The boys wore their dad's borrowed suit, dress shoes, and a tie either too long or too short. Couples headed to the picture station to have their portrait taken against the faux velvet backdrop. There was a punch table, a DJ table, and of course, the dance floor. The place was electric as it filled up and the music blasted. Cara emerged from the corner and took pictures of couples dancing. She even worked up the nerve to approach groups of friends. "Could I take your picture for the school newspaper?" was all she had to say, and they willingly posed for her. One group consisted of Brandon Billings with his buddies. It took him a moment to realize it was her behind the camera.

"Ecrivain! What are you doing? Did you forget your dress?"

"I'm strictly here on business," she shot back.

"Well, you're too good-looking to come to the Homecoming

dance without a date. If you don't have one next year, I'll take you myself."

Cara paused at the suggestion—she wasn't used to boys flirting with her. "We'll see," was all she managed to squeeze out as she walked off to take more pictures.

She finally spotted Adam with his date. Stephanie had a sash that read "Queen Candidate" and looked gorgeous. Tall, thin, tan. Adam looked right standing next to her, even though he was two years her junior. Cara watched as he followed what she instructed him to do just two nights ago. He took Stephanie's hand in his and put his other hand on the small of her back. She rested her head on his shoulder as they swayed. He looked like a natural.

A minute into the song, Adam met Cara's eyes through the crowd. She smiled and gave a "thumbs-up" sign and a wink. He winked and shot her an "okay" sign in return.

She had taken pictures of lots of couples throughout the night, but she didn't take one shot of them.

It was time to announce the Homecoming King and Queen, with three candidates for each. The DJ stopped the music and read off the names and credentials of each candidate as they made their way onto the makeshift stage. Students moved to face the action and anxiously listened to the DJ. Cara made sure she was in the perfect position for just the right shot for the announcement of the winner.

"Our first Queen Candidate is Stephanie Cartwright!" the DJ announced, and the crowd hollered for her.

Cara watched the football players pat Adam on the back.

"Stephanie was nominated by the Dance Team," the DJ went on. "Stephanie is a member of Student Council, National Honor Society, Scholars Bowl, French Club, and captain of the Dance Team."

A "Whoooooo!" went up from the dance team members.

"When she's not involved with her school obligations, Stephanie volunteers at the Canterville Animal Shelter and the Miami Valley Hospital. She plans on attending *The* Ohio State University in the fall on a scholarship to study sociology."

"I didn't know she could be more perfect than she looked," Cara said under her breath as she took the obligatory photos.

"Ladies and gentlemen . . . Stephanie Cartwright."

The gymnasium erupted at the repeated mention of her name.

After announcing the other candidates, the DJ said, "All right,

Canterville High School, your 1995 Homecoming King is . . . Matt Dillingham!"

Cara got a great shot as last year's Homecoming Queen crowned the new King. Matt was a surprise. He was a soccer player, which made it the first time in years that a football player didn't win.

"And now, the moment you've been waiting for. Your 1995 Homecoming Queen is . . . Stephanie Cartwright!"

Stephanie clasped her hands together and bent over as if she was lightheaded. When she came back up, she was crying like this moment meant the entire world to her. She waved to the crowd as she walked forward to be crowned by last year's King. Cara dutifully captured the quintessential moments of the new King and Queen together.

After the cheers died down, the DJ said, "And now, our Homecoming King and Queen will share their special dance. Please move to the edges of the dance floor to make room."

Cara squeezed her way to the front of the crowd, who seemed all too interested in watching them dance.

As Cara took pictures, she noticed how intimate this moment seemed for the royal couple—it felt like the first dance of a bride and groom. Matt held Stephanie close—*really* close—and she looked longingly at him. Next to her, she heard some a gawking junior girl say, "They are *so* cute! I wonder if they'll get back together after this."

"I sure hope so! They're so perfect," another one responded.

Cara didn't realize they had been a couple. Right after that comment, Matt leaned in and gave Stephanie a long kiss on the forehead in front of everyone. Stephanie's grin took over her entire face. She tilted her face and kissed Matt back on the mouth.

"Oh my gosh, this is sooooo romantic!" the group of girls gasped.

Poor Adam. Even if he didn't like Stephanie, it must be awkward for him. She tried to spot him in the crowd but couldn't find him anywhere.

After their song ended, the DJ started playing "Celebration" by Kool and the Gang, and the rest of the students joined in. Cara witnessed Stephanie dance song after song with Matt.

By 10:30 P.M., Cara had all the shots she needed but wasn't getting picked up until the dance ended at midnight. She made her way back to a secluded corner where she kept her camera bags and tried to blend in with the dark shadows until the dance was over. Next to her bag, Cara saw Adam sitting alone. She walked over and sat. "Sorry about Stephanie."

He looked down with his elbows resting on his knees. "I should have known. The only thing she talked about all evening was Matt. I guess I was just being used to make him jealous. It didn't make any sense that she would have really wanted to go with a sophomore."

"Well, you're not a typical sophomore. You're Aeggers, remember?" He let out an amused huff. "Why don't you go dance with Jenny Andrews or Blair Easton? They both seem rather infatuated with you."

Adam shook his head, "Nah. They've already got dates. I'm not feeling up to being social right now anyway."

They sat in the shadows, watching everyone else enjoy themselves.

"The worst part is . . . she was my ride."

Cara couldn't help herself and let out a muffled laugh.

Adam shot her a look, pretending to be offended, then grinned.

"Come on."

"What?" Cara asked.

"Let's go home. We'll walk."

"You sure you can make the four-mile trek in dress shoes?"

"If I can dance in these things, I can do anything."

Without saying a word to anyone else, they slipped out of the back door and into the expanse of the night. The door shut, and they could still hear the music and the chaos bleeding through. The clear sky allowed a dome of stars to shine over them against the chilly October night. Their breath was visible before them. Adam offered her his suit coat to cover her shivering shoulders. The sleeves hung way past her hands.

"Next year, we should just go to Homecoming together," Adam said. "I would have had a lot more fun with you."

Cara smiled back. "I think that's a great idea. It's a plan."

Before getting too far, the opening of "Take My Breath Away" echoed off the school walls.

Adam stopped. "Hey, it's your song."

Cara stopped too. "Aww, yeah. I love this song."

Adam grabbed her hand and led her closer to the school

building to block the wind. "Miss Ecrivain, may I have this dance?" He put his hand on the small of her back and gently pulled her to him like they'd practiced.

Cara placed her head on his shoulder.

They swayed to the distant music and the rhythm of his breath before their long journey home.

20

SNOWED

Cara asked if she could see the new *Sense and Sensibility* movie with some of the other *Tiger Tribune* writers, but her mother said no. She was expected to attend their annual neighborhood Christmas party.

"What? Why?"

"I don't know. Ask your father. He said he wanted you there tonight."

"So the first year I have a chance to get out of the house, I have to stay for the party?"

"Maybe your father has something special planned. And I already bought you a dress. Don't be ungrateful, Cara." She turned away.

"Ugh!" Cara let out as she fell on her bed.

She hated that Christmas party. The thought of mingling with dozens of middle-aged drunks while watching her parents put on their perfect façades in full force made her insides churn.

Christmas lights perfectly lined the front of the Ecrivain house, a new tree sat in the front window for passersby to adore, intricate holiday décor filled the interior, and Cara was stuck inside.

She longed for that freedom to leave the house more often, but even though she had finally finished all her Driver's Ed. requirements, she couldn't drive alone for over a month until she turned sixteen. For now, the hunger in Cara's stomach forced her away from the pen that scribed the poem in her head, and she rummaged through the kitchen to appease her appetite before the party. As she opened her bedroom door, she noticed an eerie noise.

Silence.

The party was still three hours away, and usually the sound of vigorous scrubbing or vacuuming by her frazzled mother could be heard. But there was nothing.

Cara looked into the dining room, but only saw dishes set out waiting to cradle the gourmet food for the guests. And in the kitchen—rows and rows of alcohol—just about every kind imaginable next to dozens of wine, champagne, and scotch glasses.

Her mother still never touched the stuff—her father never stopped.

Cara's bare feet crept through the dining room, to the living room, down to the hallway. She peered into her parents' open bedroom door. There, she saw the back of her mother in her bathrobe, knees on floor and head nestled in her hands quietly crying. Then she clasped her hands as if in a manner of prayer.

Cara would normally abandon such a private moment, but she stayed there in the doorway watching her mother—not sure how to feel about her or this situation. She wanted to both berate her and hug her.

She did neither, and instead, went back to her room hungry.

∾

THAT EVENING THE ECRIVAINS' doorbell rang consistently, and the noise of guests grew louder as the neighborhood filled their house for the biggest party of the year.

In the black dress her mother had bought her, Cara lay on her bed and waited in her room, praying her parents would forget about her so she could avoid the whole thing, but then she heard a knock on her door.

It was her already-intoxicated father.

She couldn't remember the last time her father stepped foot inside her room. "Hey, Pen Pal. Why don't you come out to the party for a little bit?"

"You really want me to go mingle with all of those drunk adults? I'm only fifteen—that's so awkward."

"You're practically an adult yourself. I want to show you off a bit."

She followed her father into the sitting room where Dr. and Mrs. Aether waved her over.

"Oh, Cara." Mrs. Aether hugged her. "You look beautiful."

"Thank you. My parents wanted me to make an appearance for some reason, but I was hoping to go with some friends to see a movie."

"That's what Adam's doing tonight. If I had known you'd be here, I would've asked your parents if he could come as well."

"He went to the movies? I just talked to him last night, but he didn't mention that to me. Do you know—"

Before Cara could ask who Adam was with, her mother walked by holding a wine glass filled with her usual grape juice. No one could tell she had been crying earlier—she looked gorgeous and wore a stunning evening gown. The dress didn't compare to the glitter of her diamond necklace, though. It was the one from the Christmas of 1988 and the first time she'd worn it.

Her mother approached them. "There's my girl. I was wondering when you were going to come out here."

"Nice necklace," was all Cara said.

A forced smile appeared on her mother's face as Cara continued a confrontational stare.

Then someone clutched Cara's arm. It was her father with a full scotch glass in one hand as he pulled her with the other toward the crowd of men whose faces she recognized, but whose names she couldn't recall.

"Comrades, this here is my daughter, Cara."

They stopped their conversation and extended their hands to greet her—making remarks like, "Well, hello," "Fancy to meet you, Miss Cara," and "No way in hell that's your daughter, Charlie! She's too good looking to be related to you." This last remark sent the group in an uproar.

"She most certainly is," her father replied. "She's a genius, too, just like her old man. Only a sophomore, and she's editor-in-chief of the whole damn school newspaper!"

"Dad, I'm just one of the writers—"

"Well, you damn well should be editor-in-chief! You're the best writer in that school—been writing before you could even walk."

There was no sense arguing. This was the most interest her

father had ever shown in her newspaper position, and he didn't even know what she did.

Some of the men humored the situation and asked her questions about what she wrote, how long she'd been writing, and if she wanted to pursue it as a career. Cara knew how to engage with adults from all the other dinner parties and events she'd attended over the years with her parents. One man started talking with her who she'd never seen before. During their small talk, she said, "I'm sorry, I don't recognize you. Are you new to the neighborhood?"

Her father interjected. "He's not from the neighborhood. This is Robert Stiles, one of my clients." He pulled Cara close and firmly whispered in her ear. "And I've got a huge investment riding on him, so don't blow this for me." After giving her a hard pat on the back, he left to mingle with others.

As she continued to answer more of Mr. Stiles' questions, the Christmas music shut off. Her father stood on a chair in the middle of the living room as he dinged a knife against a champagne glass to gain everyone's attention.

"Excuse me, everyone. Could I have your attention, please?" When they all turned his direction, he continued. "Many of you have known my one and only daughter, Cara, since she was a small child. She is the pride and joy of our lives, and I brought her out tonight for something very special. I know it's cold outside, but if you'd all grab your coats, please come out and gather in our driveway."

The guests grabbed their coats from the foyer and headed outside—each of them somehow keeping a drink in one hand.

There hadn't been any snow yet this Ohio winter, something rare for December. Even though the weather was freezing, the wind wasn't blowing, which made it bearable, if not pleasant. The Christmas lights on the house reflected off of everyone's glass against their dark outfits.

Confused, Cara made her way to her father in front of the crowd. He put his arm around her as she approached.

"Cara," he shouted loud enough for everyone to hear, "you're my little Pen Pal, and I'm so proud of you." The crowd responded with an "Awww," and he went on. "Your mother and I wanted to do something extra special for your sixteenth birthday."

Cara spotted Mrs. Aether, who picked up on her apprehension and gave her a comforting nod. Then she looked at her mother, who was smiling with her mouth but not her eyes. "My birthday? My birthday isn't for another six weeks —"

Cara's father nudged her on the shoulder—signaling her to shut up and not ruin the moment. "We got you something that we've heard every girl your age wants."

At that moment, her father pushed a button, and the garage door slowly went up. Parked inside was a brand new blue 1996 Jeep Wrangler TJ with a giant red bow on top. The guests gasped and cheered. Cara didn't move except for her mouth dropping and eyes widening. It was gorgeous and must have cost a fortune, but Cara had never once mentioned wanting a Jeep.

She was in a daze. Her mind trying to make sense of this bizarre situation. The only thing that she felt fully aware of was a snowflake that landed on her brow.

In that instant, it began to snow.

This energized the crowd even more.

"Well, go on, Cara," her father said, holding out a set of keys. "Go get in the Jeep. Take her around the block!"

Cara looked at her father with an expressionless face and quietly said, "I don't even have my license yet, Dad."

This wasn't the reaction he expected and gave her a harsh squeeze on her elbow. "I think it's safe to say she's officially in shock, everyone."

He grabbed her arm and urged her toward the vehicle. The crowd watched as she took the driver's seat with her father sitting shotgun. She turned the key, and a cheer erupted. When her father looked at her, Cara turned the key back to shut off the engine. He stared at her a moment, then exited the Jeep.

"We'll take it for a spin when we don't have guests to entertain," he said. "Thanks for joining in to make this moment so special for our little girl. Let's go back inside where it's warm."

Dozens of people told Cara, "Happy birthday!" and she politely thanked all of them. She lagged behind as each guest made their way back inside the house—holding the new keys in her hand.

She paused before going in and stared at the brick façade on the front of their house, then down at the thick snow that now covered the ground.

21

PROPHECY

Fall 1996

Adam and Cara were juniors, sixteen, and driving. Cara, now on the school newspaper's editorial board, needed to be at school early most days to work on articles, so she stopped going over to the Aethers' for breakfast. Adam was the starting wide receiver on the varsity football team and was on track to break the school record in touchdowns. Several Division I universities started scouting him for college scholarships.

Each activity kept their lives busy and completely separated from each other.

The phone rang at the Ecrivain house while Cara studied in her bedroom. She had a phone in there but didn't budge off of her bed to answer it.

"Cara, it's for you!" Her mother shouted from the kitchen.

"Who is it?"

"It's Adam Aether."

"What in the world?" She picked up the phone and carried it back to her bed. "Hello?"

"Hey, Cara, it's Adam."

"Hi?"

"Hey, so my sister Angela just got a job in Dayton and moved back here from North Carolina. She's getting settled into an apartment downtown in the Oregon District and said she wants to see you. Would it work for me to take you over there, say, tomorrow night?"

"Uh, sure. I'd love to see Angela," she said, trying to straighten up her tone. "Tomorrow night should work."

"You okay? You sound weird."

"I guess I'm confused. You've never used a phone when you wanted to talk to me before."

"Oh, well, she wanted an answer as soon as possible," Adam said, "so I figured this would be the fastest way to contact you."

Not satisfied with his answer, Cara stumbled around and said, "Uh, yeah, okay. So . . . I guess I'll ride with you over there?"

"Yeah, that sounds good."

"Maybe I'll *call* you when I'm ready."

Apparently not catching her cynicism, Adam said, "Sounds great. Should be around 7:00. Bye."

Cara hung up her phone as she looked through her window into his. She could see his silhouette in his bedroom.

~

CARA DIDN'T CALL Adam when she was ready—she walked right over and knocked on the door.

Mrs. Aether answered with a warm and welcoming hug. "Come in, Cara! It's so good to see you. It feels like it's been forever."

"I feel the same. I miss your chocolate chip pancakes and French toast."

"Well, you know you can come over any time. I barely make those anymore since Adam just wants protein shakes in the morning now." She smiled and went on. "I'm so glad you two are headed over to hang out with Angela. I'm sure she's excited."

"Yeah, it's been almost a year since I've had a chance to see her."

Adam came around the corner into the foyer, eating a banana with one hand and holding a second in the other.

"Is that your dinner?" Cara asked.

"This is *post*-dinner. I'm doing a banana diet to help me gain healthy weight. You add a banana every day for ten days. By the tenth day, you're eating ten bananas, and by then, you're guaranteed to gain ten pounds."

Cara quickly did the math in her head. "So you're going to eat fifty-five bananas in the next ten days?"

Adam looked up as he thought. "Yeah, I guess so."

"That sounds . . . horrible. What day are you on?"

"This is day four."

Mrs. Aether laughed. "You two don't want Angela waiting on you."

Adam peeled the second banana and bit into it, grabbing his car keys with his free hand. "Let's go," he said with a full mouth.

They loaded themselves into his 1988 silver Saab 900. It was his dad's car that he had handed down when Adam got his license. Not every teenager's dream, but it was free and still nice.

Cara wanted to bring up the phone call and how it bothered her, but she also didn't want to ruin the night.

It was about a thirty-minute drive from their neighborhood in Canterville to the Oregon District in downtown Dayton—an eclectic, artsy area that resembled SOHO in New York City. They caught each other up on football and the newspaper with the radio quietly playing in the background.

Cara interrupted something Adam said when Alanis Morissette's song "Ironic" came on. "I love this song!" She reached for the dial and cranked up the volume.

"Ugh! Are you kidding me? It's so overplayed. And nothing she mentions is even ironic. It's just a coincidence or bad luck."

Cara rolled her eyes. "Fine." She hit the "seek" button several times until she came to MIX 107.7. "We Are the World" was playing.

Cara slapped her leg. "No way! Does this station play this song every night?" She swayed her hands and shoulders to the music. "Is this a sign that we need to pull over so I can teach you how to slow dance again?"

Adam made a sudden move to the right like he was about to stop the car.

"I was joking! I was joking!" Cara laughed. Then she sighed. "I think I might ask the DJ to play this song at Homecoming this year. Can you imagine everyone's horror? But you and I could just dance like everything was normal."

Adam refocused on the road.

"Speaking of Homecoming," Cara said, "I'm really glad we decided last year to go with each other. We're going to have so much fun. I need to pick out a dress soon, though, so you can find a tie to match. Not that you have to. That might imply that we're a couple, so maybe we shouldn't."

Cara realized two things. She was talking way too much, and Adam was strangely quiet—until he finally said, "Actually, Cara, there's something I need to talk to you about."

She looked at him, but he kept his eyes on the road even though they were at a stoplight.

"I know we talked about going to Homecoming together this year, but I'm kind of talking to someone. And I feel like going with you, even though we're just friends, would . . . complicate things, you know?"

Cara's heart cracked like it had the year before, but more acutely this time. She had hoped the dance might rekindle their friendship that had been nearly dormant for the last several months. So many thoughts consumed her it felt like hours before the light turned green. She tried to see from his perspective. If she were interested in someone, her friendship with Adam might be a burden and something that could make a boyfriend jealous. But she kept coming back to one thought—she would never have done this to him. She would always choose him.

She didn't say, "It's okay," because she didn't feel like it was. All she said was, "Who is it?"

His jaw tightened and his shoulders raised like he was uncomfortable even mentioning the name. After a hard swallow, he said, "Jenny Andrews."

"The cheerleader? The one who didn't know your name last year—even though we've gone to school with her since kindergarten?"

"Yeah," he didn't even address her observation. "She and some of the other cheerleaders have been hanging out with me and my football friends, so we've gotten to know each other better."

"I see," Cara said. There is no way that he would have uttered a sentence like that two years ago. It was like he had gone from her best friend to a stranger in less than two years.

"When we talked about going together last year, I never imagined I would be in a situation like this." He sighed. "I'm sure you think I'm a major jerk, and I don't blame you."

Cara didn't respond.

"I bet one of my football buddies would go with you, though. We could double."

None of his football buddies even realized she, the newspaper nerd, existed. Cara wanted to tell him she didn't want to go with any of them—she wanted to go with him.

"I don't want to talk about this right now. Let's just enjoy our time with your sister."

She peered out the window as Adam slowed the car and parked right in front of an old art studio with Angela's loft apartment directly above. After walking up a tall flight of stairs and awkwardly waiting to be let in, they heard someone inside fumble with the lock. The door swung open, and there was Angela with a new pixie haircut.

"Hey, you guys!" she shouted with a wine glass in her hand.

Angela was twenty-three and a college graduate. During college, she stopped eating meat, stopped wearing a bra, and stopped shaving her legs. Apparently, she had also stopped using electricity because there wasn't a single light on in her apartment. Instead, dozens of candles lit her living room.

Adam slid his hands in his pockets and scanned the room. "What's up with all the candles, Ang? You holding a séance or something?"

"Very funny . . . no, I like the aura they give off. So much better than fluorescent lights. Plus, they're all a lavender scent, which helps me center myself." She pretended to start meditating. "And, it cuts the electricity bill way down—you'll care about that when you're an adult."

Adam couldn't resist. "Excellent. Let's save thirty dollars a month by buying three thousand dollars' worth of candles."

Angela laughed way too hard at that and poured herself another glass of wine—emptying the bottle.

"So, are you glad to be back in the Dayton area?" Cara asked. "Or do you miss Wilmington?" Angela had attended the University of North Carolina Wilmington where Dr. and Mrs. Aether went to college.

"Oh, a little of both. Wilmington is so wonderful, but it's great being back here with family. Plus, I love the Oregon District and my little apartment. I mean, my address is five-eighteen-and-a-half. How cute is that?"

Sitting on the arm of her couch, Angela went on to talk more about college life, her new job in Dayton, why women should be liberated from removing body hair, and everything in between. "So, what's going on between you two? Are you dating yet?"

Adam and Cara looked at each other.

"Um, no!" Cara said. "Just friends. Still just friends like always."

"Oh." Angela sounded disappointed but gave them each a suspicious look.

"Adam is apparently talking to someone. A cheerleader."

"What?" Angela almost spilled more of her wine. "I haven't heard anything about this! Who is she?"

"Yeah, tell us all about her, Adam." Cara nudged him.

"Her name is Jenny," was all he said.

"Jenny?" Angela pretended to be disgusted by the sound of her name.

"Yeah, they're going to Homecoming together," Cara added with feigned excitement.

"What? I'm going to have to meet this girl first to give my approval," Angela said, winking at her brother. Her words came out more slowly as the amount of wine in her glass diminished. She took another sip. "Don't worry about this Jenny girl, Cara, because you know what I know? Adam is going to end up with . . ." she gave a dramatic pause and looked right at Cara, ". . . you."

Adam stood. "And you're now officially drunk. How about I help you back to your room."

"Stop it! I am perfectly fine! And anyway, I just *know* these things. Remember that Woman's Intuition I told you about when you were kids? This is that. It may not be in a 'normal' way you might think of, but trust me, you two are going to end up together —some way or another."

∾

THE FOLLOWING WEEK, Cara came to school early every day to work on an article. Whenever she pulled into her assigned parking spot in her blue Jeep Wrangler, she'd receive compliments from other students walking by who shot her a, "I love your Jeep!" or "I'm so jealous! I've always wanted a Wrangler." It was the most attention she'd gotten from her peers since starting high school, yet no one even bothered to go beyond their covetous observation and actually learn her name.

She hated that Jeep, and with every compliment, it reminded her what it really stood for. It was all for show—the only thing her parents cared about—looking perfect on the outside but never allowing anyone truly inside to see the real person. The Jeep only attracted fleeting, superficial interactions with others.

Cara removed the key from the ignition, but she didn't go to the journalism room like she intended. Instead, she thought back to the night of the Christmas party last year. When it was over, she had talked to Adam about the whole Jeep situation through the window . . .

. . . "Your dad bought you a brand new Jeep Wrangler? That's awesome! What color is it?"

Cara didn't respond.

"What's wrong?" Adam asked.

"Everything."

She went on to tell him how she was sure she sounded like a brat because it was a nice vehicle that any teenager would kill to have, but she was sick of the show and disingenuousness of it all. How her father ignored everything about her but used her to make himself look like Father of the Year in front of his friends.

"Then," she went on, "he chastised me after the party for not acting more excited in front of everyone. That just proves my point. He only cares about the outward appearance while our world crumbles inside. I'd rather he gave me an old beater car and actually pay attention to me than do what he did. Any day."

That was nine months ago but seemed much longer. Cara couldn't remember the last time she and Adam had a close conversation like that. She ached for his companionship.

Her thoughts were interrupted when she saw Adam walk into the school with Jenny Andrews. They weren't officially dating but were with each other a lot. Their lives made sense together. A good-looking football jock and a beautiful cheerleader. It couldn't be any more stereotypical. But Adam shouldn't be stereotypical. That wasn't who he truly was, and it made her stomach turn.

Then Cara thought back to the night they visited Angela about a week ago.

". . . you two are going to end up together—some way or another," Cara said out loud to herself—remembering those words of Angela's ridiculous prophecy.

Before Cara could dwell on the gravity of that, someone rapped on her driver's side window.

"Hey, Cara!"

It was Brandon Billings.

Cara rolled down the window and assumed he was going to just compliment her Jeep like the others.

"Can I walk you inside?"

22

SOCRATIC

Cara and Adam had one class together junior year—English, fifth period with Cara's favorite teacher, Ms. Turner. She taught journalism most of the day but had room in her schedule to teach one English class each year, and she chose to do English 11. She said she loved the age—they were more mature than underclassmen but not as cocky or apathetic as seniors.

Cara was elated to have her favorite teacher twice a day. Journalism required Ms. Turner to be more stringent with deadlines and page layouts. But the English class allowed her to put an unorthodox spin on lessons, challenging her students to think for themselves. She often sat on top of a vacant desk among her students instead of standing at the front of the room behind a podium.

"Class, we're going to start implementing a strategy throughout the year where you will actually teach each other and yourselves by using the Socratic method."

One kid blurted out, "Then what are they paying you for, Turner?"

"Glorified babysitting, I guess," she said with a shrug, and the class burst out in laughter. "I'll still facilitate, but you're old enough to find most of the answers yourselves through collective observations and discussions. That is the Socratic method, based on the practice of the father of western philosophy—Socrates. Did you know Socrates never wrote any of his teachings down?

He believed in dialoguing, asking questions, and gathering opinions from others who think differently than you to help open your own eyes."

Cara moved to the edge of her seat at the explanation.

Ms. Turner started facilitating Socratic seminars by splitting the class into two groups who each discussed a poem, article, or even song lyrics they had to annotate. The main goal was to figure out the major themes of the text, but by doing so, they also focused on word choice, symbolism, meter, and less obvious writing techniques that added to the message. The direction of the discussions was left up to the students. It was all part of the method—a collective effort to get to a more centralized idea.

This week, the class had to analyze the poem "My Father's Dance" by Virginia Chase Adams.

When she passed around copies, Ms. Turner explained, "I don't like to give you any ideas before you read a poem—I'd prefer you read it raw, but I do want you to be aware of duality as you analyze this poem tonight." She wanted to say more but stopped herself. "Let me read it out loud first so you can hear it." She cleared her throat and went on to read:

> The liquor on your lips
> Could make a small girl spin,
> But I held on with grit
> For our dancing to begin.
>
> The China on the wall
> Fell 'neath our rhythmic feet
> While mother's face would fall
> With every passing beat.
>
> And as you gripped my arm,
> With palms bruised, cut, and dirty,
> Missteps that didn't charm:
> My mind would soon go blurry.
>
> Time beating on my head
> With hands that never faltered,
> You danced me off to bed
> Still clasping to your collar.

The bell rang as she read the last line.

"All right. Mark this up and be ready to discuss it tomorrow."

∾

THE NEXT DAY the class set up for a Socratic seminar, which typically took the entire hour. The written portion of the exercise was worth half the grade, and Cara's paper was usually marked up so much that barely any margin was left on the page.

But today, it was blank except for the poem itself.

Like every week, Ms. Turner went over the basic rules. "Stay on topic. I'll only interject if I feel it's necessary. Your participation grade comes from deep, insightful comments, not filler comments. It's okay to disagree, as long as you back up your reasons. Oh, and while you're in the outer group, you're not allowed to communicate with anyone—only evaluate and observe. Some of you had a problem with that last week."

She called off the names for the first group. Adam left his seat to join the circle on the floor. Cara was supposed to evaluate the first group's conversation, but she doodled on her paper instead.

When it was time for the groups to trade places, Cara made her way to the circle on the floor. Adam caught Cara's eye and broke a rule by mouthing, *Are you okay?*

Cara shrugged and looked at her doodles.

A minute or so into the discussion, someone said, "The meter of the poem has a certain beat, which is similar to the rhythm of a waltz, hence the title."

Cara looked up. The voice was from Jenny Andrews.

She was inconveniently in the same class—the only time Cara got to see Adam throughout the day.

"That's an awesome observation, Jenny," one of the classmates in the inner circle complimented.

Someone started to comment on another aspect of the poem when Ms. Turner interjected. "Excuse me. That *is* a good observation, but Jenny, could you please elaborate on why that's important?"

Jenny squared her shoulders and sat a little higher in her seat as she attempted to answer the follow-up question. "It's important because the poem is about this cute little routine between a dad and his daughter where they dance before going to bed each night. The similarity between the rhythm of the poem and a waltz further symbolizes that this is about a dance." She smiled as if she was impressed with her explanation.

The same student in the inner circle said, "Wow, Jenny. I didn't even notice that part about the rhythm—"

"You can't be serious," someone cut in.

This time it was Cara.

The proud smile on Jenny's face dissipated and her jaw dropped. "Excuse me?"

"I'll agree it was a good observation about the meter, but you can't seriously think this is just about a dance."

"Well, what do you think it's about?" Jenny shot back. "You don't even have anything written on your paper except a few doodles."

"Why would Turner have us analyze a poem that is so straight forward and one-dimensional? It's clearly a metaphor for an abusive relationship between a daughter and her alcoholic father."

"Where are you getting that the father is an alcoholic?"

"It's implied in the first line!" Cara yelled.

"Just because the dad drinks doesn't mean he's an alcoholic. Lots of parents drink."

"Yeah, but it implies he's so drunk, the girl is basically getting a contact high. That's a problem. Abuse is also implied by the double meaning of the word 'beat' and the hand imagery."

"If the dad is abusing the child, why doesn't the mom help? Why would a small girl cling to the shirt of an abusive father?" Jenny challenged. "And why would something so negative be compared to something as elegant as a dance?"

The rest of the class was silenced by the confrontation, and their heads went back and forth as if watching a tennis match. Surprisingly, Ms. Turner didn't intervene.

Cara rubbed her temples in annoyance. "I'll address the latter part of your question first. Dances often symbolize the motions we go through in life. It's a process that takes dedication, practice, and partnership. The iambic trimeter—which is the term for the rhythm you attempted to reference earlier—is misleading to the true tone of the poem, hence the duality Ms. Turner brought up yesterday. It has a pleasant sound because, as the speaker, who is now a woman, reflects on her childhood, she wants so badly to have positive memories, but she doesn't. As far as the girl clasping onto her father, children have an unconditional love toward their parents. Even when they're abused or neglected, they still go back to them time and time again for reassurance that they're loved."

She paused for a second, thinking of her own mother with equal parts frustration and sympathy. "As far as the mother goes, often the spouse of an abuser or an alcoholic is exhausted. Their partner is likely never going to change, so standing up to them is a lost cause. And when they do stand up, the abuse usually turns to them."

"Oh, right. Like you would know anything about that, Ecrivain. You live in a huge house, with perfect parents, and drive a brand new Jeep that every teenager would love to have."

"Okay, ladies," Ms. Turner finally said.

Cara glanced at Adam, who gave her a helpless look since he couldn't talk. "How would *you* know, Jenny? You don't even know me," Cara shot back.

"Ladies!" said Ms. Turner.

"Oh please. I'm by your house all the time when I go over to Adam's."

"Clearly, you're not looking hard enough. You of all people should know that the outside of something, no matter how pretty, is almost never like the inside."

23

WALKABOUT

Ms. Turner pulled Cara aside after class. Before she could say anything, Cara apologized for her behavior, but Ms. Turner cut her off. "I'm not concerned about that. I didn't appreciate your approach, but I admired your analysis and the passion behind it. You just need to channel it better. I'm more concerned about what got you so fired up. And this was the first time your paper was blank except for some doodles on it. Is everything all right?"

Cara wanted to scream and tell her everything. How she was losing her best friend—the only person who made her feel loved when her father was either gone or drunk while her mom constantly cleaned. How this poem hit too close to home. How her parents cared more about image than their daughter. How Jenny Andrews was an idiot. And how her best friend would rather go to Homecoming with that idiot than her.

"I'm fine."

❧

CARA WENT on with life as usual. Life, as usual, meant keeping herself busy with the *Tiger Tribune*. The only bright spots in her day were her two classes with Ms. Turner, even if English was a little uncomfortable with Jenny and Adam there.

The focus of Ms. Turner's class shifted from analyzing poetry to writing it.

She assigned unique projects for the students to practice their writing and ways to be inspired. One class, Ms. Turner stood on top of her desk. "Why do I stand up here?"

"Because you love *Dead Poet's Society*?" a smart alec asked.

"You're exactly right!"

Dead Poet's Society was, in fact, Ms. Turner's favorite movie. She played a VHS tape of it for class at the beginning of the year and referenced it at least once a week. She started dramatically quoting the line from Robin Williams' character philosophizing why he stood on his desk.

"Do we all get to stand on our desks now?" another student asked.

"No." Ms. Turner quickly answered. "One, because one of you will surely fall and break a rib or something, and I would be sued. And two, because I'm taking this in a different direction than the movie. In *Dead Poet's Society*, Mr. Keating has the students stand on his desk to gain a different view of the room from their seats. He did this to encourage students to look at life from a new perspective. I want you to consider something else. On a piece of paper, write down what you observe on my desk. Nobody get up. What do you see or even feel from where you're sitting? Five minutes. Write."

Everyone did as she said.

"It doesn't have to be poetic. Make sure you don't stop writing. Keep your hand moving the entire time and jot down observations."

After five minutes, students shared what they could see from their seats. As each spoke, they realized that what one student saw, others missed because someone or something obstructed their view.

Ms. Turner added how different her observations were by having a bird's eye view of her desk. "From up here, I see the pointed ends of my pencils in the jar staring up at me. I see dust on top of the picture frames and words on an essay that's on top of a stack I need to grade. I can feel the breeze from the air vent in the ceiling that is blasting in my face right now and drying out my contacts."

She hopped down from her desk.

"Why did I have you do this? What's the point?"

Cara didn't want to give Jenny a chance to spew some annoying response, so she answered first. "I think it's to show that even though we're in the same room, we all have different perspectives based on what's either available or hindering us. This can apply to real life because we often think we see the full picture when, in actuality, our view is limited, and there are various other perspectives out there."

"Very good," Ms. Turner complimented. "And I also want you to realize that your perspectives were different based on where you were sitting. Some of you may have had someone in your way, or you were in the back—both of which are out of your control. But think, did any of you crane your neck to get a better picture? That's something that *is* in your control. Consider how different your perspective is from your peers—even if just a little. Yours wasn't wrong, just different. But when you work together, you can gain a more complete view. It's things like these that make the Socratic method so valuable.

"Now, this next assignment is going to put this into practice in the real world. The objective is twofold. I paired you up with someone in the class. You and your partner need to go on what I like to call, a Walkabout. You are to walk deep into nature, far enough where you're not bombarded by noises or distractions of city life—just nature. Nature is always a great inspiration for poetry. While you're on your Walkabout, you're to jot down what you observe. Take in everything. After twenty minutes or so, I want you to compare your notes with your partner's and see how different your perspectives were. Then you'll write a poem on your experience. The poem can be in any style and can be about nature or even the person you'll be with, or both."

The students filled the room with murmurs, excited for the rare project.

"You'll have a whole week to complete this," she went on. "I wanted to make sure to give you enough time to coordinate with your partner. I also tried to pair you with the person who lives closest to you, so it should be easy to plan something together."

She scanned the list and announced all the partners.

"Adam Aether and Cara Ecrivain. Funny," she commented, "it appears that you two are next-door neighbors. I guess I never realized that before. This should be easy for you two to get together."

~

THE PHONE RANG AT THE ECRIVAINS' that evening. Cara's father wasn't home from work, and her mother was on a ladder dusting the tops of the ceiling fan in the living room.

"Cara, can you get that? I'm occupied!"

Cara rolled out of bed and grabbed the phone. "Ecrivain residence."

"Hey, is this Cara?"

"This is she."

"Hey, it's Adam."

Was this going to be his new way of communicating from now on?

"Hey," she responded—trying to sound neither excited nor put off.

"So, I guess we have to do this Walkabout thing together. I'm always out of football practice earlier on Thursdays, so I thought we could do it then."

"Um, sure, I could make Thursday work. What time?"

"I could be ready to go around 6:15, which should still give us enough light. I thought we could go to Alexander's Woods."

Alexander's Woods was a wooded area with a creek in their neighborhood. Adam and Cara spent hours there when they were in late grade school—old enough to go farther than just down the street, but not too far that the sound of Mrs. Aether's giant dinner bell couldn't reach them. Memories traveled through Cara's mind when he mentioned it.

"I think that sounds fine."

~

ON THURSDAY, Cara left her house to go next door so she and Adam could do their Walkabout. Before she even left her yard, Adam emerged from his home. There they were standing in their own yards facing each other. "Hey," Adam said with a smile like everything was normal. "I was just about to stop by to get you."

Why didn't you just call me? Cara wanted to yell. But she only asked if he brought a pen and notebook.

They headed in the direction of Alexander's Woods—both knowing exactly where to go, taking the shortcut through the Millers' backyard, onto Hugh Drive, and over to Druewood Lane. They held their composition books close to their chests to brace the nipping autumn breeze. Cara noticed that Adam was wearing the leather bracelet she bought him last year. She hadn't seen him without it since she gave it to him and wondered if Jenny knew it was from her.

Their brief trek was wordless until Adam finally asked, "Wanna go by the tree?"

Cara nodded.

Fallen leaves covered the ground near the creek and crunched under their feet. Tall, magnificent birch trees peppered the entire woods, but the tree he referenced was the biggest one in the park. It had a thicker trunk than a typical birch and towered over all the others. One day when they were ten, Adam had snagged his dad's pocket knife, and he and Cara carved their initials in its trunk. They had seen Kevin and Winnie do something similar on an episode of *The Wonder Years*. There wasn't a plus sign or a heart around their initials implying anything—just a simple *A.A.* and *C.E.* signifying that they had been there.

"There we are." Adam ran his hand over the letters in the bark.

Cara had so many negative memories of her childhood, but every good one had Adam in it. Going to the park and seeing their initials reminded her of the times that weren't so bad, and how she used to talk to Adam every day—several times a day. Her life felt wrong without him.

Cara noticed the bottom of the sun starting to hide behind the trees. "We better go ahead and start before it's dark."

They each took a seat on a fallen tree about ten feet apart. Close enough to have similar perspectives, but far enough away to prove the point of Ms. Turner's assignment. The peacefulness of the woods was undeniable. That's probably what drew Cara to it as a child. Other than going to the Aethers' house, it was the only place she could escape. Escape the fighting or the silence of neglect that was drowned by a buzzing television or a humming vacuum.

This silence was peace.

Cara opened her notebook and started writing what she observed. A single, weightless leaf slowly falling from the top of a birch, ants carrying twigs, the babbling sound of the creek washing over the rocks. The water inspired her the most. There were metaphors in there, like how the water isn't held back by the rocks—it adapts and goes around them—even smooths them. Water keeps moving, no matter what's in its way. That's how she felt her life had been going for the last ten years.

She felt such an inspiration that she had a strong urge to be *of* the water. She took off her shoes and socks, leaving her notebook on the tree.

This caught Adam's attention as he wrote his observations. "Uh . . . what are you doing?"

"Getting in. Come on, join me." Maybe sticking their feet in the creek together would break the tension.

"What for? The water will feel freezing."

"For inspiration. And it's not that cold. Come on."

She rolled up her jeans and went barefoot into the creek. With each careful step, she felt the current make its way past her—the water's energy felt empowering.

"Are you going to literally be a bump on that log? Come on."

Adam looked around and sighed. "Fine." He started taking off his socks and shoes and rolled up his jeans. Tiptoeing down the bank, he hesitantly stuck in his toes. He finally rested on the ground but kept his feet in the water to humor Cara. "I'm just going to stay right here."

Cara gave an annoyed smile as she leaned down to let the water run through her fingers. It was the first time in weeks she'd smiled in front of Adam. Without looking at him, she said, "Okay, so let's do the second half of our assignment, we're supposed to compare notes. What are some of the things you observed from your perspective?"

"How can you do that when you don't have your notebook with you?"

"Dude, I just wrote it like thirty seconds ago. I think I remember."

"Okay . . ." He flipped open his notebook. "I noted the bark of the tree, the breeze, and the shapes of the clouds. What about you?"

"The water," she said. "I noticed a lot of what you mentioned as well, but I couldn't stop coming back to the creek. Its distinct sound, the reflection of the autumn leaves like a mirror. And I'd never noticed before how it has this destination, and it won't let anything get in its way. It adapts and continues going. I hope I'm always able to be like that." She continued to stare into the current passing through her fingers. Then she tilted her head toward Adam. A strand of her hair came loose from her ponytail and dangled in front of her face. She reached her hand toward him and again said, "Come on." Not as a plea, but a confident request.

A smirk came over his face, and Adam made his way over to her. Most of the rocks at the bottom of the creek were smooth from the current.

"Remember when we used to skip rocks?" Cara asked, handing him a flat one. "We would do it for hours."

Adam side-armed the rock toward a deep section of water, and they watched it skip four times before sinking. Cara gave it a go herself as they both waded in the water, the ripples from the rocks creeping toward them.

"You seem better," Adam said. "Have you calmed down from that Socratic seminar yet? I don't know that I've ever seen you so heated before."

Cara's forehead wrinkled. The elation she had felt from the stream had vanished.

Why was he bringing that up weeks after it happened?

Just thinking back to that day made her blood pressure rise. "Nothing pisses me off more than ignorant people who make assumptions and think they're smarter than they actually are." She looked right into his eyes, her face hardening, then skipped another rock.

"I still don't understand why that would upset you so much."

Cara couldn't take it anymore, like there was an explosion inside her that she couldn't dismantle in time. "I cannot stand Jenny Andrews! She is an embarrassment and so one-dimensional. And the audacity she has! To claim in front of everyone that I have a perfect family? She has no clue. No freaking clue." She paused to regain herself. "I seriously don't know how you spend any time with her."

Adam stood wide-eyed. "Wow."

"I'm sorry. I don't mean to hurt your feelings or anything, but I just expected you to be attracted to someone better than . . . *that*."

"I mean, I guess I didn't expect you to be best friends with her or anything." He paused, then half-joked. "Does that mean you don't want to try to double with us?"

"No," she said. "I've got a date already anyway."

Adam's eyebrows raised. "Who?"

She hesitated to tell him, just like he had when he told her about Jenny. "Brandon Billings."

Adam had a rock in his hand to skip, but at the sound of that name, he chucked it at a tree instead. "Brandon Billings?" Then his face changed and he laughed. "Wait . . . okay. That was a good one. Who are you really going with? Or are you even going?"

"It wasn't a joke, Adam. I'm going with Brandon."

"Brandon Billings as in the Brandon Billings who almost killed us driving to school last year? The Brandon Billings who's relentlessly called me fat and a faggot since third grade? The Brandon Billings who's the biggest ass in the entire school?" He was screaming so heavily that a vein in his forehead looked like it was about to pop.

"The biggest ass in school?" Cara challenged. "He's not that bad anymore. In fact, he's pretty nice."

"Cara, you don't hear the kind of things he says in the locker room. I do! He's a major jerk and a pervert." He ran his hands through his light brown hair then shook his head in disbelief. "Plus . . . he's a redhead. I *hate* redheads!"

"Really, it's more of an auburn color now." She thought this might make him laugh, but it didn't. "I don't understand why you care anyway. You're going with Jenny Andrews!"

"Jenny Andrews hasn't bullied me since grade school, Cara!"

"You're right! That's because she was so consumed with herself that she didn't pay an ounce of attention to who you were. That is, until you lost weight, and got contacts, and became a star football player. She's fake, Adam—just like my parents. I'd take an ass over a fake any day."

Adam's face turned red, and he worked to steady his breathing.

"It's getting dark, Cara. We should head back home."

She splashed through the creek for her socks and shoes while Adam took baby steps toward the muddy bank like a fragile old man.

"Why are you taking so long?"

"I shouldn't have even gotten in here," he said. "I've got scouts from Ohio State coming to my game tomorrow. The last thing I need is a broken ankle."

"Seriously? All you ever care about is football anymore."

Adam's jaw tightened. "You're jealous!"

"You can't be serious," Cara huffed.

"That's right." Adam started counting on his fingers. "You're jealous that I'm popular, that I actually have friends, and for once in our lives, I'm more successful than you!"

Cara stood in silence while Adam returned to the bank. As he bent down to pick up his shoes, she pushed him into the water and walked home alone.

24

PELICANS

M s. Turner's class looked like a Beatnik coffee house the day the Walkabout poems were due. The overhead lights were off with just one lamp on in the front of the room to illuminate the poets as they presented. There was coffee for the other students to sip as they listened. And the audience was to snap, not clap, at the conclusion of each poem.

Each pair had to share their poems one after the other, so the class could compare and contrast the perspectives. When it was Adam and Cara's turn, Cara said she would go first and confidently took her place at the front of the room.

Before she started, Cara asked, "May I give a preface to the poem?"

"Of course," Ms. Turner answered.

"There were so many things from our Walkabout that I wanted to include, but I couldn't keep my eyes off of these two sparrows."

She raised her eyes to see Adam leaning forward in his seat. The expression on his face said he knew she was making this up. They hadn't seen any sparrows that night.

Cara went on. "Their interaction reminded me of strayed friendship. I titled this 'pelicans.'" With that, she cleared her throat and read.

> away from everything
> two sparrows cling to a birch's branch

Breathtaking

singing in the company of the other
neither noticing the initials
fading into the silver bark
of the solid trunk below

one's wing is clipped
disabling her flight
she watches with contentment
as a band of pelicans
crosses the homeless sky
and blocks the autumn sun

while her abled companion
watches with longing eyes
the flock to which he does not belong
and without consideration
spreads his wings
abandoning the woods; abandoning her

in the rarity of his returns
his face fades to unfamiliar

and in his absence
she learns to sing alone
attracting the attention of the raven
who offers solace to her solitude
another thing her abled friend doesn't notice—
too busy playing with the pelicans

As she read the last line, she held Adam's eyes in hers.
He locked with her eyes for a moment and then looked down.
The rest of the class started snapping.

25

___

LIGHTS OUT

Cara didn't go to the Homecoming game. It was the first one of Adam's that she'd missed, and they hadn't talked since the Walkabout.

She hoped going to the dance with Brandon would show Adam she had a life outside of him and had moved on since their friendship apparently meant more to her than him. She looked forward to spending the evening with Brandon anyway—he had a way of complimenting her that made her feel like she really mattered.

Brandon would be there in about forty-five minutes to pick her up in his black Camaro. She was already in her formal dress that accentuated her feminine features, and the light blue color nicely contrasted her tanned skin. As she put on her makeup, she noticed some strands of hair that weren't holding their curl.

"You've got to be kidding me." Cara went to the bathroom to turn on her curling iron, which would take twenty minutes to fully heat up while she finished applying her mascara. Her left eye was made up perfectly when the lights went out and the hum of her mother's vacuum ceased.

"You've got to be kidding me!" Her mother yelled from the other room.

Cara hated it when she realized she used the same phrases as her mother.

Curling iron still in hand, Cara came out to the living room while her mother marched to the garage where her husband always tinkered with his Mustang on Saturdays.

Not even bothering to shut the door behind her, she hollered, "Charles, I need you to reset the breaker. I think I blew a fuse."

He let out a deep sigh. "Did you have two vacuums going at once?"

His wife didn't laugh.

Cara's father grabbed a flashlight and flipped a switch on the breaker box, but nothing happened.

"Dad, can you please do whatever you need to do to turn the power back on? I need to finish my hair and makeup. Brandon's going to be here in less than thirty minutes!"

"The power's out in the bathroom too?"

"Yes! I was warming up my curling iron, and it's too dark to do my makeup."

"This isn't a fuse problem," he said. "It looks like a power outage."

Cara's mother walked out of the front door to observe the neighborhood. "Everyone else has lights on."

There was a long pause.

"I guess I could recheck the breaker box just to be sure."

But his wife stopped him. "Charles, when was the electric bill due?"

"Don't worry about it." He started walking back to the garage.

"I *will* worry about it! When was it due?"

Cara's father stood mute while his wife ran to the office. After rummaging through the mail pile, she came back with several unopened envelopes. Cara watched her mother storm toward her father. "You want to explain this to me? Why hasn't this been paid? You even received two notices!"

He ignored her and made his way to the liquor cabinet.

"Answer me!"

"Look, I'll take care of it."

He poured himself a drink.

"It's Saturday! The earliest you could take care of this is Monday! What are we supposed to do for the entire weekend? Why didn't you take care of this when you got the first notice? Or the second?"

He took a long sip of his bourbon. "I've been working a lot, Susan. I forgot."

His wife crossed her arms. "Forgot? You *forgot*? It takes

months of not paying for the lights to go out! How could you forget for months?"

He poured another drink without answering her.

"You were probably too drunk to remember! What are our neighbors going to think? They're going to notice we're the only house on the block with no lights!"

She continued to scream questions and accusations at her husband, and he began yelling threats and hatred back. Cara stood in the living room with her cold curling iron in her hand. Without thinking, she grabbed her makeup bag and went through the front door—heading for the only place that made sense.

The Aethers' home.

She prayed that Adam and Jenny had already left for the dance.

Barefoot, in her formal dress, and hands full, she knocked on the Aethers' front door. To her horror and his, Adam answered.

At the sight of her, his eyes widened. "Cara? You okay?"

"I'm really sorry. I . . . I figured you would already be gone. I . . . uh . . . was going to ask your mom . . . it's a long story, but our electricity's out, so I need to use Angela's old bathroom to finish my hair and makeup before Brandon comes to pick me up, and he should be here pretty soon."

Adam opened the door wider for her. "Uh, sure. Come on in."

"Thanks."

Before she took two steps in, she heard, "Adam, sweetie, who's at the door?" Walking toward her was Mrs. Aether . . . and Jenny Andrews, who, of course, looked flawless in a tight black dress with spaghetti straps. "Oh, Cara! We were just taking pictures. Are you doubling with Adam and Jenny, and they forgot to tell me? You look..."

Her hands still awkwardly full, Cara cut her off. "I know . . . Could I please use Angela's old bathroom real quick? It's a long story."

"Does that long story explain why only one of your eyes has makeup on it?" Jenny asked.

The only time Jenny Andrews could be observant was if something literally stared her right in the face. "Actually, it does, which is why I need the bathroom." Cara wanted to add a few choice words at the end of her sentence, but out of respect for Mrs. Aether, she restrained herself.

Without any more questions, Mrs. Aether said, "Sure, sweetie, you know where it is. Go ahead and plug in your curling iron."

Cara rushed to the bathroom and started on her makeup while the curling iron took its twenty minutes to heat up. As she applied mascara to her right eye, there was a knock on the bathroom door. Cara figured it was Mrs. Aether and contemplated if she should tell her the real reason she had to come over.

"Come in," she said, still looking in the mirror.

It was Adam.

"Jenny and I have dinner reservations at the Chop House, so we have to take off. But . . . I want to make sure you're okay. I can stay if you need some help."

Cara hesitated, wanting to tell him everything. "It really is a long story, Adam. I'm fine."

"Okay, I know how—you know . . . I just wanted to make sure." He started to walk away but stopped. "Also, I wanted to, uh . . . to tell you to please be careful with Brandon tonight, okay?"

She looked away from him and continued stroking the mascara brush against her eyelashes, even though they didn't need any more. "Thanks, but I can take care of myself."

Her tone was cutting. Adam turned to leave as Cara started curling her hair.

∽

CARA RUSHED barefoot through the lawn to her house where her parents still combated in the dark. After Cara gathered her shoes and purse, she stood on her front porch and waited for Brandon. This was awkward but less awkward than having to explain why her lights were off and her parents were fighting.

His black Camaro pulled into the driveway and parked without jerking to a stop like when she rode with him to school last year.

See? He'd totally changed.

He killed the engine and stepped out in a custom-tailored suit. Something looked different about his eyes, though, and he had an uncharacteristic grin on his face. "Hey, gorgeous! Damn, you look amazing. I mean, you always look great, but I've never seen you like this."

His compliments felt good to hear. "Thank you." She felt a sheepish grin crawl up her cheeks.

"Were you so excited to see me that you had to wait outside?"

She hadn't thought of a cover-up. "Oh, well, my parents are at a dinner party, and I thought I'd just enjoy the fresh air until you arrived. It's such a nice night."

"Aw, I was looking forward to seeing Ol' Charlie. So your parents aren't going to take a thousand pictures? Sounds good to me. I hate that stuff."

"I guess not," she shrugged, praying he wouldn't hear her parents' war inside.

He offered Cara his arm and opened her car door.

A true gentleman.

As they drove out of the neighborhood, he stayed within the speed limit and played soulful R&B music.

"You really do look stunning."

"Thanks. You look very handsome yourself." The exchange of compliments felt unnatural for her. "You know, I used to think you were a major jerk."

Brandon looked shocked at first and then laughed.

Cara slapped her forehead. "I'm sorry! That was an awkward thing to say. I'm a little nervous. I've never really been on a date before."

"You don't need to be nervous with me." He reached over and squeezed her knee, then went on to say, "You mean you never dated Aeggers?"

"Adam? No! We've just always been good friends."

"Well, he's an idiot for never taking a chance on you."

"Adam and *me*? I don't think that would ever work out anyway. We're too much like brother and sister."

"You know when you said you thought I was a jerk? Most people misunderstand me. But it's my fault. I don't think I channeled my energy too well when I tried to cover up my own insecurities. It's something I'm working on."

Cara was impressed by this response. "How metacognitive of you."

"Meta-what?"

She laughed. "Metacognitive. It means you're aware of your own thoughts and behaviors, realizing why you do what you do."

"Oh, yeah. I guess that's me."

They came to a stoplight, and he looked her in the eyes. Cara could feel that he was about to lean in for a kiss, but he picked up something off the floor of the driver's seat. It was a flask that looked identical to her father's.

"Would you like a drink?"

"What is it?" She didn't need to ask.

"Vodka and orange juice. No one can smell the vodka on your breath." He took a swig himself. "It'll make the evening extra fun."

"What are you doing? You're driving."

"It's okay. I know my limits. I would never do anything to hurt you, Cara. We've known each other since we were kids. I just want to have fun with you tonight." He handed the flask to her.

"I don't drink."

Brandon took another drink and slipped it inside his suit jacket. "I'll keep it in here in case you change your mind later."

Cara's knuckles turned white as she gripped the door handle. He didn't seem tipsy, but she wondered how long he had been drinking before he picked her up. That had to be why he was acting so mellow.

When they arrived at the dance, Brandon finished off what was in the flask, and then filled it with more vodka hidden under his seat. "Let's go. It's going to be a great night."

Cara suddenly wished she could go home, even with the lights out and the screaming. But she had to save face in front of Adam and look like she was having the best time with Brandon.

The Student Council members had transformed the Canterville gymnasium into a quasi-ballroom for the evening. Brandon and Cara did the usual Homecoming routine—got their picture taken, drank some punch, and danced.

It felt weird being with someone from a different class. Cara grew up with Brandon in the neighborhood, but she had never been in his "circle" before. Several of Brandon's friends approached at different times during the night and made comments like, "Whoa, who's the hot date?" "Does she go to a different school?" or "Is that the girl from yearbook?"

Close. Newspaper. At least someone somewhat recognized her.

The first slow song of the night played, and Brandon pulled Cara in. He put his hands around her waist; she draped hers around his neck and rested her head on his shoulder. For the first time that evening, she saw Adam and Jenny, dancing just how she instructed him last year. When Adam looked over and saw her, Cara turned her head away.

It was then she felt Brandon's hands slide down her back, past her waist, and forcibly squeeze.

Cara reached back with both hands and grabbed his wrists. "What the hell are you doing?"

"Oh, come on. I can't help myself."

"Well, stop."

"Cara, you need to loosen up. It's Homecoming. I had a great game last night. I just want to celebrate and have some fun. How about I get you a drink?"

"Fine."

Cara let him go and went to the chairs lined up along the wall and sat. She noticed Adam looking at her with concern, but she averted her eyes and tried to busy herself so she didn't look so out of place until Brandon returned.

"Here you go, gorgeous."

She took a sip of the drink Brandon handed her and spat it back into the cup. "You put vodka in my drink!"

"Cara, I'm just trying to help you have some fun tonight."

"I already told you, I don't drink."

He set down his cup. "I . . . I'm sorry. I shouldn't have done that. Come here."

He pulled her into him, which caused her to spill the red punch down the front of her light blue dress. She gasped and stood there in shock. Her dress was ruined. Brandon pulled her into him again, oblivious to her stained dress. "I'm sorry. Come here."

She couldn't get out from his grip as he leaned down and started kissing her neck.

"Get off of me!"

He grabbed her tighter. "It's okay, it's okay. I know you're probably not too experienced, but I'll take care of you."

"Brandon, I said let go!"

He put his hand over her mouth to stop her protest when another voice spoke.

"She said let her go."

It was Adam.

"Get out of here, faggot! Come on, Cara."

Brandon's grip was so tight, his fingernails pierced through the skin of Cara's arm as he tried to take her out the side door.

Adam grabbed the back of Brandon's suit and spun him around—holding onto his collar.

"First, you're going to stop using that word. And second, Cara said to let her go."

Then he launched a fist at Brandon's left eye.

Brandon recovered and lunged at Adam. Soon they were on the floor—fists flying and pummeling each other. Students gathered around, and chaperones ran to the scene to break up the fight.

Cara stood to the side, red-stained dress and red-scratched arm. With everyone else's rapt attention on the fight, she removed her silver heels and slipped out the back door.

She left the Homecoming dance the same way she left it the year before. But this time, she was barefoot, alone, and heading back to a miserable house that wouldn't have electricity until Monday. At best.

26

OFFERING

It was nearly midnight by the time Cara made it home. Physically and emotionally exhausted, she opened the door to her pitch-black house and waited for her eyes to adjust. Her father lay passed out in his recliner in front of a black TV— an empty scotch glass sat on the end table.

No one lit a candle to help guide her way. No one waited up to see if she made it home safely. Nothing.

Cara wondered if her mother was able to fall asleep after such a stress-induced evening and thought about checking on her, but she didn't have the energy to care anymore. She just needed some sleep.

Once in her bedroom, she took off her ruined dress, wadded it up, and threw it in her trash can. From inside her top drawer, she grabbed and put on the first garments that felt comfortable, and fell onto her bed.

~

CARA AWOKE TO A KNOCKING. She felt discombobulated in the darkness, but the moonlight hit a battery-powered clock on her wall just right so that she could tell it said 1:15, meaning she had only been asleep for an hour. She looked over at her window and saw a dark figure standing outside.

"Cara? Are you there? It's me."

Adam.

She rubbed her eyes to make sure she wasn't dreaming, then proceeded to the window. He was still in his dress shirt, hair disheveled, cuts and bruises on his face, and a bag of frozen peas wrapped around his right hand—the one that busted Brandon's face. But the first thing she noticed was that he had on his glasses. She hadn't seen him wearing them in over a year.

Cara opened the window.

He spoke first and sounded reserved. "Hey. I remembered that your electricity was out, so I couldn't tell if you were home yet or not. How did you get home anyway?"

Cara was reserved too. "I walked."

"All the way by yourself? Cara, I could've taken you home."

She didn't respond.

"Well, the main reason I stopped by was because you left your curling iron and makeup in Angela's bathroom." He handed them through the window with his unbandaged left hand. As she silently took them, he added, "Well, now that you have those, I can rest easy tonight. I'm glad you made it home okay." He turned toward his own house but waited before taking a step.

"You're wearing your glasses."

Adam turned back around. "Uh, yeah. I think one of my contacts flew out when Brandon punched me in the face. That can happen a lot with hard contacts. I really need to switch to soft ones. Luckily I have a backup pair I can wear."

"Did you get in trouble tonight?" She was almost too afraid to ask.

"Suspended. Three days. And benched from the next game."

"I'm so sorry." Cara knew that not playing was going to kill him. "What about Brandon?"

"Suspended. Ten days. And kicked off the football team for drinking at a school function." The grin on his face made it seem like his own consequence was worth it.

Cara smiled back.

"Well, I'm going to head home. I don't want to get in trouble on that front as well."

Her conflicting emotions took over her thoughts. She knew she should thank Adam, but as he left, the only words that came out were, "Adam, I really like the glasses."

∾

CARA MANAGED to shower in the dark on Monday morning. The water still worked without the electricity, but it was cold. She would usually blow dry her hair to straighten it, but if she put gel in it while it was damp, she could scrunch her hair in an acceptable way. Maybe this altered look would help conceal her identity after what had happened on Saturday. Normally, no one cared who she was, but people were bound to talk after this.

As she walked the halls of Canterville High, she heard snippets of the rumors. Many students lamented that the starting safety was out for the rest of the season and that the starting wide receiver was out for the next game against Kettering Fairmont— one of their rivals. Besides Brandon's stupid drunkenness, she heard all of this was over some girl whose name no one could recall. And no one noticed they were talking about that girl as she passed by.

Fifth period was English. It was the only time Cara usually got to see Adam, but he wouldn't be there for three more days because of his suspension. When she entered the room, she felt Jenny Andrews's glare follow her to her seat.

∼

THURSDAY. Most of Cara's life had gone back to how it used to be, which included having the lights back on at the Ecrivain house. Even though kids were wary about the football game on Friday without two of their starting players, talk of the fight had settled. Cara went back to putting her energy into her newspaper assignments, and she hadn't talked to Adam since their late window exchange after the dance.

He was supposed to be back at school today, and the closer fifth period approached, the greater her anxiety grew. She didn't know how he would act or how she should respond. Walking through the door of Ms. Turner's English class, she felt Jenny's glare again. Cara ambled to her seat and attempted to look busy by doodling in her notebook while waiting for the bell. Out of the corner of her eye, she saw Adam walk in. She dared to look up, and when she did, a smile involuntarily appeared on her face.

Adam was wearing his glasses.

∼

WHEN CARA GOT into her Jeep after school, she made a point to rummage through her purse. She only had five dollars in there, but it was just enough. She *had* to stop by the store after school to buy something.

~

10:00 P.M. Cara was reading on her bed when she noticed the light in Adam's bedroom. She opened her window, crawled out, then reached back in to grab a package. She walked over to Adam's window and gently knocked on the glass. He was already in pajamas and wore his pop-bottle glasses.

He slid the window up with a huge grin. "Hey, what are you doing out there?"

"I need to talk to you." She paused to steady her breath. "The past several weeks, I've felt an array of emotions and didn't really know what to think or how to act, but I've been able to clear my head some, and I know I need to say two things to you. I'm really sorry, and thank you." She kept it simple, knowing he would fill in the details on his own.

Small lines appeared in the corners of his soft eyes. "Thank you for saying that."

She held up the package and offered it to him. "Here's a little token of my appreciation. Sorry that it's in Christmas wrapping, though. It was all we had, and I didn't have enough money to buy any after I got this."

That made him laugh. "The only thing that matters is what's on the inside anyway, right? Do I open this later or right now?"

"Now, please." She bit her lip.

Adam ripped away the wrapping paper, and underneath was a twenty-four-pack box of Twinkies. His face lit up. "Oh my gosh!" He laughed, but then he winced. "Aww, Cara. Thank you, but you know I don't eat these anymore. Sugar gives me stitches when I run."

She grabbed his hand and looked in his eyes. "Adam, we've had too many changes over the last couple years. Please—give me this." She cocked her head a little. "Besides, you don't need to worry about stitches. You're benched from tomorrow's game, remember? You won't need to run again until Monday."

She had a point.

"Well, I don't want to eat them alone." He pulled away from

the window to grab something from his room. It was his blanket. "Let's have a picnic."

He crawled out his window and laid the blanket between their houses. They lay down and looked at the stars as they stuffed their faces with Twinkies.

"Oh man, I forgot how good these were," Adam said with a full mouth. He and Cara laughed so hard but tried to keep quiet so they wouldn't get caught, which only made them laugh harder.

They finally calmed down, and soon were both simply breathing as they looked up at the stars. The cadence of Adam's steady breath could put Cara to sleep if she wasn't careful. He smelled good, too. She couldn't place the exact scent, but it seemed to be a combination of his cologne and shampoo. The chill of the night increased, so she pulled up the corners of the blanket to cover Adam and herself.

"Can you still find Orion?" Cara asked, trying to stay awake.

Adam looked around for a bit. "Yeah, right there. And over there's the Gemini Twins . . . and over there is the Big Dipper."

"I've always loved finding the constellations," Cara said. "For a while in third grade, I thought about giving up my dreams of being a writer to be an astronomer."

"Well, I'm glad you stuck to writing. You have good things to say."

Adam hadn't complimented her writing in a long time. "You think so?"

"I've always thought that. Even when you used to read me all those stories through the window when we were kids. And when I hear the writing you share in English and the things you write for the newspaper . . . it's really good."

"Even the poem I read in class that was directed to you?"

"Especially stuff like that. I'm not the only one who deserved an apology tonight. I owe you one, too. I let my ego get in the way and was a real ass. Here you've had these problems with your parents, and I just kinda ditched you."

This was the conversation Cara had longed for.

Adam grabbed another Twinkie. "I think Jenny Andrews and I are over."

"Really? Why?"

"She can't stand my glasses."

Cara frowned. "What? That's really the reason?"

Adam laughed. "Yeah. You were totally right about her. So superficial."

"Well, you were right about Brandon too. I should have listened to you." She turned toward him. "Really, I'm super thankful you looked out for me."

He looked right back. "Of course. You're my best friend."

27

TWENTY-SIX AND A HALF

Fall 1997

D ishes clinked, cooks shouted at each other in the kitchen, and servers nearly sprinted past tables at the Spaghetti Warehouse on Fifth Street in downtown Dayton.

Adam and Cara ate in the trolley that garishly sat in the middle of the dining area. Cara ordered the classic spaghetti and meatballs while Adam ordered the 15-Layer Lasagna, breadsticks, and a side salad.

It was the last day of summer before their senior year of high school, which wasn't spent as glamorously as they'd hoped. Adam had football conditioning that morning, and he and Cara helped Angela paint the living room of her apartment that afternoon.

Adam insisted they end the night with something positive to finish their last day of freedom. The Spaghetti Warehouse was a favorite restaurant of theirs and only a few blocks from Angela's apartment in the Oregon District. Adam needed to load up on carbs anyway. Tomorrow's practice was sure to entail an excruciating amount of running.

"What if we *do* end up together?"

Cara was chewing a meatball but swallowed immediately to respond. "What are you talking about?"

"Like what Angela predicted. When was that? Last year? She said she knew we were going to end up together somehow."

"Yeah, and she was also super drunk when she said that."

They both laughed. "Besides, I don't know. That would be weird. You're like my brother."

"True. And you're like my sister. I think it's different when you know someone your entire life like we have." He took an enormous bite of his lasagna. "What if we made a deal, though?"

"Oh, geez, what do you mean?"

"I say if we don't get married to someone else by the time we're like . . . thirty, we marry each other."

"Thirty?" Cara almost choked. "That's *so* old! I want to have kids, you know. I don't want to be the same age as their friends' grandparents when they graduate high school."

"Who, our age, do you know with a *grandparent* who is forty-eight?"

"Okay, still, thirty is too old."

"Is that your way of saying you agree to this deal, at least?"

Cara rolled her eyes. "Sure. But I always wanted to marry young, like right after college. How old are most people when they graduate college? Twenty-two? Just think. If they both lived to be ninety-two, they would celebrate a seventieth wedding anniversary. That's so freaking cute. That can't happen if you marry old."

"Whoa! Wait. Twenty-two? Hold your horses there, zippy! That's *way* too young! What if you don't meet anyone in college?"

"Isn't that the point of this deal? If we don't meet someone by a certain age, we end up together?"

"Yeah, but right out of college? Lots could happen after that. Look at Angela. She didn't meet her boyfriend until she moved back to Dayton."

"Let's compromise then. How about...twenty-five?"

"Twenty-six and a half, no younger, and no hard feelings if one of us gets engaged before that," he countered.

Cara wanted to throw one of her meatballs at him. "This is stupid."

"Do we have a deal?" Adam held out his hand. "A handshake makes it official."

"Only if we spit on it like when we were kids."

"At a dinner table? In public?" he faked a pretentious sneer.

Cara spat on her palm. "Yeah, in public. Make it official, Aeggers."

Adam spat, too, and clasped her hand.

"Deal."

⌒

CARA HAD her first-day-of school-outfit picked out for weeks. She had on a khaki jumper dress that fell a few inches above her knees, a white and blue floral baby tee underneath, and wedged sandals. She recently cut her hair like Rachel from *Friends* and spent way too long in the bathroom that morning trying to style all of her layers with a blow dryer and round brush. After applying a little mascara and blush, she walked to the Aethers' house.

Adam answered the door in an oversized Polo button-up shirt and loose-fitting jeans. Most importantly to Cara, he wore his glasses. He'd worn them ever since Homecoming last year—except during football practices and games.

Instead of greeting her, he said, "Serious question. Do I tuck in the shirt? Or leave it out? In? Out?" He demonstrated both.

Cara assessed the situation. "Do you plan to wear a belt?"

"Absolutely not."

"Then leave it out. You should always wear a belt if you tuck in your shirt."

"I'm so glad I invited you over for breakfast now!" He gave her a wink.

Once she walked through the front door, the sweet smell of chocolate chip pancakes hit her nose. Cara closed her eyes and breathed in the nostalgia.

"Is that Cara?" Mrs. Aether said from the kitchen. She left the stove and came to the foyer, her frizzy hair pulled back into a casual French twist with a claw clip and wearing her favorite apron. She looked at Cara in admiration. "Oh my goodness, you look adorable in that jumper. I can't believe this is your last year of high school."

Cara and Adam moved to the breakfast nook where Dr. Aether sat with his morning newspaper. A tall plate of warm pancakes waited on the table.

"Good morning," Dr. Aether greeted. "Hard to believe this is your last year of high school."

Cara wondered how many people were going to say that same thing today.

"Do you know what your plans will be next fall?" he asked. Another question she was sure to hear a lot this school year, but she didn't expect it *before* she even walked through the halls as a senior.

She washed down her pancake with some orange juice. "I want to study English. I might do the journalism route or maybe be an English teacher."

"You'd be great at either," Adam said.

"I've actually been talking to Angela about UNC Wilmington," Cara continued. "It seems like my dream school. But if Adam ends up playing football at Ohio State, it would be great to go there so I could watch him play."

"Ahh, UNC Wilmington . . . our alma mater. Did you hear that, Gloria?"

"That's where we met," Mrs. Aether said. "We got married a month after graduation."

Cara shot Adam a look with raised brows. *See?* Cara inaudibly mouthed. He rolled his eyes but grinned.

Adam interjected. "Yeah, but you waited a long time to have kids, right? Weren't you like thirty when Angela was born?"

"Thirty-one," his mother answered. "Why?"

"Oh, I don't know. Just wondered." He shot the same look back at Cara and also mouthed, *See?*

"UNC Wilmington's a great school," Dr. Aether said. "That's where we hoped Adam would go. Been saving up since he was a baby, and now he could probably go wherever he wants for football. If you end up with a full-ride, we might cash in the money and take ourselves on a nice vacation."

"I like that idea!" Mrs. Aether hollered. "Let's see Paris or the Great Wall of China!"

"I wouldn't act too fast," Adam said. "You never know, I could fall down the stairs and rip my arm off or something, and you can kiss that scholarship goodbye. Then you can use that money the way it was intended."

Typical Adam. He was always concerned about getting injured.

"That's not going to happen, Adam," Cara said. "Even if you get injured, you're good enough that they'd let you redshirt and play the next year. I say start planning that vacation, Dr. and Mrs. Aether! My parents have told me they've been saving for college since I was a baby, too, but I doubt I'll be getting any full rides, so I guess no vacation for them. Don't say anything."

"I like that advice. Don't worry. We'll keep it a secret." Mrs. Aether winked. For a moment, she looked like she was about to burst into tears, and then she perked up. "Before I forget, I have something special to show you two real quick." She left the kitchen and hurried back with a Polaroid picture from their first day of freshman year.

Adam and Cara leaned in to see it. There they were—Cara in white Keds, high-waisted jeans, an oversized green top, and a lacy vest. She wore no makeup and her hair was pulled half up with a scrunchy. Adam had on baggy jeans with a plaid flannel tucked in, and of course, his pop-bottle glasses.

"Oh—my—goodness!" Cara squealed. "Look at us! I haven't seen this picture since that day. And look at you with your shirt tucked in with no belt. Oof!"

"Yikes! No wonder Brandon Billings called me Fatty-Fatso!"

"Here's another one." Mrs. Aether handed over a standard 4x6 picture.

"Is this from kindergarten?" Cara asked.

"It sure is."

Adam and Cara were five years old with oversized smiles and backpacks standing in front of the bus.

"Awwww, I don't think I've ever seen this picture before!" Cara said.

"Adam, look at your little glasses! We were pretty adorable."

"What do you mean 'were'?" he teased. Then he snapped his fingers. "Do you remember what time the bus comes?"

Cara shook her head. "I don't know, like 7:45?"

Adam looked at his watch. "We have three minutes. If we hurry, we can recreate the moment!"

"Oh, what a cute idea!" his mom said. "Let me get my camera."

Adam turned to Cara and grabbed her shoulders. "You know what else we're going to do?"

Cara was worried. "No . . . What?"

He looked uncharacteristically excited. "Let's ride the bus like we're kids again."

"What? We'll be the only seniors on there!"

Adam gave an assuring smile. "Come on, it'll be fun."

"Okay, but only if you do that thing where you're blindfolded and point out everything as we pass by."

"Of course I'm going to do that. That was the best part of riding the bus!"

Outside, Adam rushed to the corner of the street to wave down the bus driver. Even though they were on the route, they weren't expected to get picked up.

The doors opened and revealed Mr. Becket in the driver's seat. "Aren't you too old to be riding this bus?"

"No, sir, we're still in high school, Mr. Becket. Would you hold on one moment? My mom wants to take a picture."

"Make it quick."

Mrs. Aether had her Polaroid camera aimed and ready to go. Adam and Cara positioned themselves in the same spot in front of the school bus. "Say, 'cheese!'"

"Cheese!"

The camera made its mechanical whirring sound and spat out the picture. Mrs. Aether handed Cara the undeveloped Polaroid as well as the one from kindergarten. "Please take care of both and make sure to bring them back this evening."

"Sure thing," Cara said.

"I love you both. Have a great first day of school!"

Adam and Cara took a seat toward the back and giggled at themselves. Before wasting any time, Adam said, "All right, let's see if I've still got it. Do you want to wrap something around my eyes?"

"No, I trust you."

Adam was as accurate as ever, pointing out Drew Parker's house, the fire station, the Nazarene church, and Bill's Donuts.

Cara looked down at the pictures in her hand. The Polaroid was developed now, and she held it side by side with the one from kindergarten. So much life had happened between those pictures. It was like the dash between the birth and death years on a tombstone. Even with their ups and downs, she couldn't imagine a better friend to have by her side during the dash.

28

SKY TALKER

S enior year was better than expected for both Adam and Cara. Adam was captain of the football team and had offers from a dozen universities for a full-ride scholarship. Cara was appointed editor-in-chief of the *Tiger Tribune*. She was honored by the position, but she so badly wanted to write, so Ms. Turner allowed her to be a section writer, as well.

Even though Cara and Adam rekindled their friendship, they were each swamped with hectic schedules and barely saw each other. Cara went over for breakfast a few times a week, they occasionally grabbed a bite to eat together, and they saw each other in a couple classes—government and anatomy. And of course, they had the window.

Midterms were coming up around the same time an issue of the *Tiger Tribune* was due, which put additional stress on Cara. She often locked herself in the journalism room or her bedroom to get everything accomplished and hadn't seen Adam, outside of class, for over a week. Adam caught her after government one Monday morning.

"Hey, you okay?"

She leaned back against the lockers. "I'm just really stressed. Why?"

"I haven't seen you in a while, and you haven't been acting like yourself."

"Sorry, this first quarter has me feeling like I'm drowning. I thought senior year was supposed to be easy!"

"Why don't we get some Marion's Pizza after I clean up from football practice tonight?" Marion's was her favorite place to eat.

"I'd love to, but I don't have time for that with midterms coming up."

"Well, bring your books, and we can study together. We have most of the same classes." Cara was more studious than Adam, but he was definitely smart and was always a good study partner. "Come on," he encouraged, "it will be way more fun than just locking yourself in your room alone. Plus, you'll have delicious little squares of pizza heaven to make it a billion times better."

"You make an excellent argument. All right. What time?"

"Seven o'clock. Oh, and it's your turn to drive. Just honk when you're ready."

$\sim$

CARA PULLED INTO THE AETHERS' driveway and honked right at seven. It took a minute before Adam came out, and he appeared from the side of the house.

"Why were you already outside?" she asked as he got into her Jeep.

"It's a secret. Don't worry. You might find out later tonight."

"Oh, man. I'm already stressed about so many things. Now I'm going to be thinking all night about what you did. Can you just tell me?"

"Nope." Adam smiled. "And I'm ridiculously good at keeping my own secrets."

$\sim$

MARION'S PIZZA parlor had pictures all over the walls of famous people who had visited over the years and faux windows that made it look like sunlight was peeking in at all hours. That illusion made it a perfect place for studying. Adam and Cara sat in a back corner away from most distractions and split a large cheese pizza —extra cheese, extra sauce—and a pitcher of Coke in hopes the caffeine would be an added benefit.

After hours of studying the three branches of government, velocity, and the literary themes of *Beowulf*, Cara thought Adam was about to throw her a question about British literature, but instead asked, "What do you want to do with your life?"

She scrunched her face at the question. "What? Adam, we need to study."

He pushed their books aside. "I think we've studied enough for the night."

"That wasn't the deal."

"Okay, we don't have to be done for the evening, but we at least need a brain break. I've just been thinking about this a lot. We're seniors. In a few months, we're going to be out of here and making decisions that will affect the rest of our lives. And what are we going to do with the rest of our lives? Man, listen to me. I'm getting all deep—I sound like *you*."

Cara, still irritated he was getting off task, couldn't turn down a meaningful conversation. "To answer your initial question, I want to be an author. You already know that. What about you?" As close as she was to Adam, she realized she didn't know the answer to that question.

"I . . . don't have a flipping clue."

"Well . . . good talk. How about that Brit Lit?"

She tried to reach for the books, but Adam slid them even farther away and wagged his finger like she was breaking a rule.

"I know I really want to help people. I want to do something with my life that truly matters—I just don't know how."

His answer put a smile on Cara's face even though it didn't surprise her. He'd always looked for ways to take care of her.

"I have no doubt that you'll figure it out and do just that," she assured him. "Have you decided where you're going to go yet? For college? Don't you have to choose soon? The signing date is coming up."

Adam sighed. "I think I've narrowed it down to two. Either Ohio State or the University of North Carolina."

Cara arched her eyebrow. "UNC? That's the first I've heard you mention that one. Why are those your two choices?"

"Ohio State is close, and well . . . it's *The* Ohio State University. Their football games are like a religious experience. But I've been thinking a lot about North Carolina. They've been to a bowl game every year for the past five years with Mack Brown. I know my parents have always wanted me to go to UNC Wilmington, but they don't even have a football team. I could go somewhere close, though." He took another bite of pizza before going on. "Plus, I know you've been heavily thinking about Wilmington—what if we both went to North Carolina?"

Cara loved the idea but pointed out: "Wilmington and Chapel Hill are still like two hours apart."

"Yeah, but you could still come up for football games on the weekend, and in the off-season, I could come hang out with you. What do you think?"

"Wilmington is my dream school. It's not too big or too small, they have great journalism and English departments, and it's right by the beach. And best of all—it's almost ten hours away from my parents."

"Do you think your parents would be okay with you going there?"

"They only care that where I go and what I do makes them look good. I'm sure paying out of state tuition won't be cheap, but as I told your dad, my parents have told me they've been saving up for college since I was born, like your parents have. I wish they dished out writing scholarships as often as football scholarships. Then I wouldn't have to worry about anything."

"I know. It doesn't seem fair. You actually have a talent that requires brains. I just catch a leather ball and try to run a few yards without some other guys throwing me to the ground."

"Ms. Turner told me about a few writing scholarships, though. That's another thing that's been adding to my anxiety. The one worth the most money is due right before Thanksgiving, and I have no idea what I'm going to write. Even though my parents have saved up, I still want to do what I can to help out, you know?"

"Of course." Adam paused. "So, we're both going to North Carolina?"

"Yeah. North Carolina."

Neither of them moved or spoke for a moment.

"I'll talk to the coach and tell him I want to commit this week."

"Really? You're one hundred percent sure?"

"If you're going to Wilmington, yes."

"Okay, well, I guess it's another deal, Aeggers."

Time slowed for a moment as they took in the gravity of this decision that, at the same time, removed the weight of uncertainty from their shoulders.

Cara looked down at her watch. "It's almost ten o'clock. They're going to be closing soon. We need to go."

They finished the last couple squares of pizza and packed their books.

"I'm sorry," Adam said as they headed out to her Jeep. "I didn't realize how late it was, and that brain break took a little longer than anticipated."

"That's okay. Talking about next year helped ease my mind a little bit."

"Well, hey. You know that secret I told you about when you picked me up?"

"I told you I wouldn't stop thinking about it all night."

"Well, I know you've been stressed about all sorts of stuff, so I got you an early Christmas present."

"Adam, it's October."

"I know, but I couldn't wait."

Cara looked around. "Okay? Do you have it here? Do I open it now?"

"No, you'll get it when you get home tonight." Adam sat in the passenger seat and shut the door.

"How is that going to work?" Cara started the engine. "My mother isn't going to let you into her immaculate house, especially this late at night."

"Well, that's still part of the secret. You'll have to wait and see."

~

CARA DROPPED off Adam and rushed to her room as quietly as possible so she wouldn't wake her parents. As soon as she entered, she saw it.

Below her bedroom window was a shoebox-size package in white wrapping paper with blue letters that said **"It's a Boy!"** clearly intended for a baby shower. She laughed, knowing Adam was poking fun at the Christmas wrapping paper she used for the Twinkies she gave him last year.

Underneath the wrapping was a shoebox that once held his football cleats. Cara grabbed a pair of scissors from her desk and carefully cut the tape around the edges.

Inside was one Fisher-Price Sky Talker.

It was the exact version from the 1988 Sears catalog with the long antennae that she desperately longed for but never got to use. Cara clasped her hand over her mouth when she saw it. That was nine years ago, and she hadn't talked about them since.

He remembered.

She rolled the dial on the side and it clicked on. After letting out a deep breath, she pushed the large orange button and cautiously—yet hopefully—spoke. "Hello?"

When she released the button, Adam's voice broke through the static: "Breaker one-nine, I see you found your early Christmas present. Do you copy? Over."

"Oh my gosh, Adam!"

"Um, while using Fisher-Price Sky Talkers, one must use official walkie-talkie lingo. Over."

Cara giggled. "Um, okay . . . ten-four?"

"Roger that."

"First, how did you even remember these, and where on earth did you find the exact ones I wanted when we were eight?"

"When I was on a run one morning, someone in the neighborhood was having a garage sale, and there they were. I instantly recognized them from the Sears catalog and remembered how badly we wanted them. I asked the couple to hold them for me and ran back home to get the money. I knew I had to give it to you, and it had to be an early Christmas present because they would be perfect."

"Perfect for what?"

"To ask you to go to Homecoming with me . . . Over."

Goosebumps run up her arms. "Homecoming? With me? I figured you had another dancer or cheerleader to go with this year."

"As I stated at dinner, I've been doing a lot of reflecting lately since it's our senior year. And for our last Homecoming, I want to do it right. I know I would have the best time with my best friend by my side. We should have gone together last year," Adam said. "And the year before that, so I'm not going to miss the opportunity this time. So, Cara Ecrivain, would you please be my date to the Homecoming dance? . . . Over."

Cara couldn't stop smiling. She pressed the big orange button and brought the walkie-talkie close to her mouth.

"Affirmative."

29
___

WORTHLESS

C ara wanted to write an article for the student newspaper
about Adam's verbal commitment to play football at the
University of North Carolina. National signing day
wasn't until February, but this got the whole school and
community buzzing. It was the first time in decades that someone
from Canterville would be going Division I for a sport.

Cara was admiring the article that had just been printed for
tomorrow's release when Ms. Turner interrupted her. "I need you
to work photography at the Homecoming game tomorrow night."

"What happened to all the other photographers? I haven't
taken photos since I was a sophomore."

"Mono. All of them—plus a couple of writers. They must have
had a journalism group make-out session or something." Ms.
Turner smirked. "Tomorrow's the big Homecoming game, so it
absolutely must be covered. But, hey, it'll be the closest you'll ever
get to watch your friend Adam play. That will be a cool
experience."

Cara was initially put out by the request. It wasn't just going
to entail taking pictures. She would then have to develop the film
next week, figure out which shots to use, and keep track of
everything during the game so she could have a good caption for
the photos once it was printed in the newspaper. But Ms. Turner
had a point. This would be an up-close-and-personal experience,
and she could watch the game without the crowd of high school
students suffocating her in the stands.

164

"Yeah, no problem, I can do that."

~

CARA TOOK a break from her homework that night to heat up a microwave dinner. She swore to herself that she would never eat another one of these after she moved out.

As the microwave dinged, her mother entered the kitchen, and her father came in from the garage. She rarely saw her parents simultaneously, and when she did, it was usually because they were fighting. This semi-pleasant encounter was like some weird planetary alignment.

Her father staggered in with his briefcase. He had clearly been drinking but appeared to at least be more coherent than usual. "I heard about Adam on the radio station tonight," he announced to the room. "That's really something. He's going to be a Tar Heel."

Cara stirred the gravy into her mashed potatoes. "Yeah, I'm really proud of him. He worked so hard for this, and it all paid off."

"I bet his parents are proud too," her mother chimed in. "That reflects well on them just as much as him."

"A full ride," Cara's father went on in awe. "And at a Division I school."

Cara could think of dozens of other things she'd rather do than talk to her parents together, but this reminded her that she had some obligatory collegiate discussions to have with them. Since they were all in the same room, she figured this was as good a time as any. "That reminds me. I wondered if we could do a few college visits soon."

Her father momentarily recoiled at the words but responded with, "Well, sure. Of course—of course. Where do you want to visit?"

"Well, I guess Ohio State, but my top choice of as now, I'd say, is UNC Wilmington."

"Wilmington? You're following Adam to North Carolina?"

"No, I had actually been thinking about going there before he said he was going to commit to North Carolina. I talked to Angela quite a bit, and it seems perfect. I know it will be expensive since it's out-of-state tuition, and I wish I could get a full ride like Adam, but there are opportunities for other scholarships with writing competitions and things like that. I'll enter as many of those as I need and—"

Her father cut her off. "I don't see much need for that. I've told you before that we've been socking away money for your college since you were a baby, Pen Pal. Plus, your mom has been working, too."

Her mother looked up and cracked the tiniest of smiles.

Cara felt a sense of relief. "Are you sure?"

"Of course. You should be able to go wherever you please."

"Okay, then I'll start working on the application process, and we can figure out a time to visit."

That conversation went surprisingly better than expected. Cara actually felt a little guilty. She could go to any college she wanted? No wonder people like Jenny Andrews assumed she had the perfect life.

～

"BREAKER ONE-NINE. This is Adam Aether. Do you read me? Over."

Cara put down her calculus book and grabbed the walkie-talkie. "Who else would this be?"

After a long pause, Adam said, "Are you done talking? Because you didn't say 'Over.' Over."

"Stop." She tried not to laugh. "I'm not doing that. I have a huge calc test tomorrow and an essay to finish."

"Okay, fine," he conceded. "I wanted to let you know that I'm headed to bed early tonight. Tomorrow's the big game, and I need to get some rest. Plus, there's the dance Saturday night."

"I know! My dress is looking at me right now. It's so pretty—I can't wait to wear it."

"It's going to be a blast."

Before he could say goodnight, Cara said, "Hey, I found out today that I was assigned to take pictures of the game tomorrow. I'll be right down on the sideline with you."

"That's awesome! You'll be so close you'll be able to see the sweat drip off my face."

"Ewwww! Over!"

She started to turn off the walkie-talkie when Adam said, "Wait, look out your window."

Cara got out of bed to see Adam peering through his window

at her, walkie-talkie in hand. "Just because we have this fancy technology is no excuse to forget how we properly say goodnight to each other." He took the strings of his blinds and made them go up and down four times, which, of course, was their signal to say, "Good-night-Car-a."

She returned the gesture. "Good-night-A-dam."

◈

TWO HOURS LATER, Cara finished her essay but still had to study a little more for her calculus test. She was fading and needed a snack to give her a small boost of energy to make it through another thirty minutes or so.

She tiptoed down the hall—dreading having to pass through the living room to the kitchen. Cara heard the dull hum of the television that played for no one every night at this hour because her father had always passed out on his recliner. She went to turn it off—it was practically a nightly ritual—but this time, the glow from the screen illuminated her father's eyes and showed that they were barely open. Then they peered up at her.

"What the hell are you doing?" he slurred.

He had to have been drinking all night. How was he still awake?

"I was just getting a snack, Dad, and I was going to turn off the TV because I thought you were asleep."

"Why would I be asleep? Letterman's on." A burst of laughter roared from the audience behind the screen as he said this, which countered his contentious tone.

Cara just wanted to get out of there. She sighed and let out a soft, "I don't know."

"Wait." He looked up at her again with squinted eyes. "What are you doing?"

She started for the kitchen. "I'm just getting a snack."

"While you're in there, pour me a glass of bourbon."

"I think you've already had enough, Dad." She turned her back on him and walked away.

"What the hell did you say to me?"

Cara didn't have time for this—she needed to finish studying. He was sure to pass out any second and would forget all of this by morning, so she ignored him and rummaged the pantry to find anything to spike her blood sugar a little.

Then she felt his presence behind her.

Her father had never hit her, but for the first time since the Christmas of 1988, she felt afraid of him. She slowly turned around to see him just inches from her.

She remembered the line from "My Father's Dance":

The liquor on your lips / could make a small girl spin . . .

"When I ask you a damn question, you better answer me. Now, I want to know what the hell you said to me." He seemed more cognizant now—his speech less slurred.

Cara considered just making the drink to pacify him so she could move on, but something in her resisted. "I said, 'I think you've already had enough, Dad,'" she spoke through gritted teeth.

He got even closer. "I said to get me a drink."

"No."

It was the first time she had blatantly defied a request from him. She swallowed hard, expecting a blow to the face. Her eyes scanned the kitchen for anything she could use to defend herself in case he tried to physically harm her in his drunkenness.

What followed was worse.

He looked her in the eyes but seemed to be staring at nothing. Then he moved even closer to her face. "You're a real bitch, just like your mother."

Cara clenched her jaw and commanded her eyes not to well up.

"I work my ass off every day to provide you with a nice house, a brand new Jeep, and now you want me to pay for you to go to some damn out-of-state college . . . and you refuse to get your old man a drink? Adam got his parents a full ride, and you can't do nothing. You think you can get some measly writing scholarship when you can't write worth shit. You spend all your time locked up in your damn room like you're too good for us."

He paused.

"You're completely worthless to me."

She closed her eyes and took in a jagged breath, continuing to will herself not to cry—not to let him win her outward emotions. At least not in front of him. She tried to convince herself that he didn't mean what he was saying when he was so blasted. But the numbness Cara usually felt from years of neglect and fakeness was replaced with a sharp sting in the heart and a stab in the gut. She opened her eyes, uncertain of what she might say or express, but he had already walked back to his chair.

She didn't get a snack. She didn't look to see if he was watching the show or passed out. Instead, she ran to her room and locked the door. Hidden from him, she started sobbing uncontrollably. Those first and last words tore through her head, over and over.

You're a real bitch, just like your mother.

You're completely worthless to me.

The sobs turned into hyperventilations. She had to get away—out of the house.

As if by second nature, she opened her window and crawled out—not even bothering to close it behind her. In a few short steps with the cold autumn ground and the crunchy leaves under her feet, she was at the one place she always felt safe.

She tapped against Adam's window, praying he would hear. The blustery wind outside felt like it was stirring all the emotions trapped inside her—all the quiet chaos. Her blonde hair flew in front of her tear-flooded eyes. She didn't see Adam approach the window as she kept tapping.

He opened it.

Without asking a single question, he held out his hands and pulled Cara inside of his room.

Her sobs mixed with dry heaves subsided as soon as her feet touched his floor, and the window shut behind her. Now it was just tears. The only other time Adam had seen Cara cry was the last time she sneaked into his room.

The faint moonlight that came through the window was the only thing that allowed them to see each other in the otherwise pitch-black bedroom.

Adam wiped a tear from her face. "Come here," he whispered and pulled her in. "Was it your dad again? Was he drinking?"

Cara knew she wouldn't be able to control the volume of her voice if she spoke and feared waking up his parents. She looked at the dark ceiling and nodded. Adam squeezed her tightly. She turned her head so that her ear rested against his chest. The cadence of his steady inhales and exhales soothed her, and soon she was breathing in sync with him.

"Come here," he whispered again. He held her hand as he crawled into his bed and left enough room for her. She lay close to him as he reached over her body and held her left hand with his. She could feel the leather bracelet around his wrist.

"I love you," Adam whispered.

169

It was the first time Cara remembered hearing those words since she was very young. They made her father's words sting a little less.

As before, she knew she couldn't control her voice to audibly respond. So she squeezed Adam's hand that held hers four times as if to say, "I love you, too."

She closed her eyes, and the rhythm of Adam's breathing lulled her to sleep.

30

LADYBUG

Cara's swollen eyes were evidence that exhaustion had taken over her the next morning. On days like this, she wished she had thick glasses like Adam's to cover the puffiness, but even more, she longed for a way to cover her emotional fatigue. She probably shouldn't have gone to school, but she had to leave that house—it was the last place she wanted to be.

There was also Homecoming. Canterville High had a strict attendance policy. If a student didn't attend five out of the seven class periods that school day, they couldn't participate in any social events that evening or weekend. If she had called in sick, that would mean no football game and no dance—something she was genuinely looking forward to that might brighten the darkness from last night.

If anything, it would get her out of the house.

Cara got to school at the end of second period. She tried to sleep in to rest up for the calculus test, but it didn't make much difference. She had missed government class with Adam, so the first time she saw him all day was in anatomy. Both glad and nervous to see him, she prayed he wouldn't ask for details about what happened for fear that she might burst into tears in the middle of the main hallway.

Adam gave a sympathetic smile when he saw her that also said he was happy she was there. They took their seats before the bell —Adam sat right in front of Cara.

He turned around and said, "Hey, did you make it home okay? What time did you leave?"

"Probably around four in the morning," she whispered.

"I was worried you weren't coming at all today. Are you still going to the game tonight?"

"Yeah, I got here by third period, so I'll still have the 'best seat' in the house — right on the field."

Adam gave her a relieved look. "Hey, I know we didn't get to talk about what happened last night, and we won't have much of a chance today at all. And I'm not sure you ever even want to talk about it, but — "

The bell cut him off, and Mr. Porter was ready to start class right away.

"Class," Mr. Porter said, "today we're going to talk about the function of the lungs." He let in a deep inhale . . . and then exhale for dramatic effect. "Breathing. It's something we do without even thinking about it. It's actually a very simple process . . . or is it?"

Adam attempted to finish what he wanted to say to Cara. He turned around and whispered, "Since I don't think we'll have time to talk, I wrote you something instead." He handed her a folded-up note. He even folded it the fancy way like they used to always do in junior high, with the little corner tucked in at the top where he wrote: "lift here." It made her smile.

Right as she took it from Adam, Mr. Porter interrupted his speech on respiratory functions and yelled, "Excuse me! Mr. Aether, that wouldn't be a note that you just passed, would it?"

Cara shoved it into a pocket of her jacket. If Mr. Porter ever intercepted a note passed in class, he read it out loud in front of everyone. Cara couldn't risk that. She knew this would be way too personal.

"No, sir," Adam answered. "I was only giving Miss Ecrivain a pencil. She left hers in calculus." Adam had hidden a pencil up his sleeve, which he slid out as he turned to Cara's desk. He winked at her and then held up the pencil like he just recently set it there.

"I see," Mr. Porter said. "Sorry for the accusation." With that, he returned to the lung lesson.

When Mr. Porter wasn't looking, Cara double-checked her pocket to make sure the note was still there. She quietly zipped up the pocket to ensure it wouldn't fall out.

CANTERVILLE FOOTBALL GAMES were full of vivacity, but the Homecoming game was several notches above par. Student council members made sure to schedule the festivities for a week they played a rival school so a victory would feel even sweeter. In addition to the regular attendees, alumni traveled back for class reunions and gathered in clusters throughout the stadium. It felt like the entire town was there.

Cara wore her photographer badge to enter the game for free and made her way to the field. She immediately noticed the energy felt different down there—no more or less than being in the stands, but there was something electrifying about being under the Friday night lights and seeing the masses in the bleachers.

The band entered in a formal parade that was almost militant, and the crowd clapped and sang along to the fight song. As the football team gathered to run onto the field, the cheerleaders lined up to make a sort of tunnel for the players to run through. The crowd knew the cheer and shouted the ending with them, "You're messing with the best, we're C-H-S!" Four cheerleaders held a huge paper banner that read "Canterville Tigers Homecoming 1997," and the football team burst through. At this, the marching band blasted "Eye of the Tiger."

Cara fidgeted with the cameras, ensuring she had the right lens and F-stop settings for the game. She grabbed an extra roll of film from her camera bag to put in her pocket in case she needed it fast. Unzipping the left pocket of her jacket, she slipped the film in and felt a folded piece of paper.

Adam's note.

She had forgotten to read it. She couldn't look at it now but made a mental reminder to open it after the game.

She took a few practice shots on the sidelines. Scanning the stands, she spotted Dr. and Mrs. Aether and Angela toward the front of the parents' section. It was the first time she hadn't sat with them for at least some of the game and waved to get their attention. They finally saw her, and she took a picture of them in the crowd. She shouldn't have done something so personal on a school camera, but she thought it would be a cool gift to give Adam for Christmas or graduation. It would be a reminder of how blessed he was to have supportive parents who never missed a game—especially when he didn't play a single minute his freshman year.

She took a few more practice shots while the football players lined up for the national anthem. Adam stood near her, removed his helmet, covered his heart with his hand, and sang along to the band's accompaniment. When the song ended, the crowd erupted.

Adam turned to Cara. "Make sure you get my good side." Then he gave her a wink and ran out on the field.

As the sun went down, the temperature dropped, but since there was no wind, the pleasantly crisp evening only required a light sweatshirt or jacket—unusual for early November in Ohio. At halftime, Canterville was beating Wayne High from Huber Heights twenty-one to fourteen.

Cara casually watched the second half of the game for a while near the end zone. She let the camera hang around her neck and enjoyed the night as a fan for a bit. Even though she wasn't that into sports, she was going to miss these nights. It wouldn't be the same watching Adam play at UNC. Plus, she was just so proud of how hard he'd worked. She gave him grief for always being so cautious because he was afraid of injuring himself and being out for a season. But now he was the one with a full-ride scholarship to play the sport he loved.

She realized that she hadn't taken many shots of Adam. As the star player, she wanted an awesome blown-up picture of him in the sports section. She would see to it that he had a special write up about the game.

Cara started to take some close-up shots of him but stopped when she saw something resting on the shutter release.

It was a bright red ladybug.

Cara found this pleasantly odd. She wasn't sure if they were in season at the beginning of November, but she didn't remember seeing one this late in the year before. He, or she, was just relaxing right on the camera, not knowing or caring if it was in the way. Cara stuck her finger out as if to pet it and said, "Hey there, little guy." The ladybug didn't move. Cara got lost in metaphorical thoughts about the little creature. How it was so beautiful but also had a hard shell to help it withstand adverse conditions—all while being a valuable asset to nature.

Her thoughts were interrupted by an uproar from the fans.

She ran to the football team's trainer and asked what happened.

"Adam Aether just caught an incredible pass! Looks like we're about to score again."

Frustrated, Cara mumbled, "Of course I missed that."

Readying her camera, the ladybug hadn't moved. Cara gently picked it up and set it on her shoulder. She was sure it would fly away immediately, but it stayed.

It was the fourth quarter with four minutes left in the game. She moved down the sideline closer to the action, then adjusted the settings and spotted Adam—determined to take a perfect shot of him. The Canterville's quarterback called the play and yelled, "Hike!" Cara followed Adam through her lens as he darted to catch another pass. The quarterback found him, and Adam leaped into the air to catch the ball.

There was a simultaneous loud crack as Cara pushed the button to snap the shot.

The all-league safety from Wayne High School had collided into Adam head-on so forcibly, it flattened him on the ground.

Adam was on his back. One of his teammates ran over and reached his arm down to help him up, but Adam didn't move. He was playing a joke. He did stuff like that all the time. Cara expected him to pop up any second and say, "Haha! Gotcha! I'm fine." And then limp off the field to rest.

She waited to see him do that.

Still no movement.

Several teammates now huddled around him while all the players from both teams took a knee. The head coach and trainer ran out on the field toward him. Without thinking, Cara ran out onto the field right after them. Each step she took pounded in her ears.

"Don't move him! Don't even touch him!" the trainer yelled. "Back off, back off!"

Cara stood near the small huddle of players around Adam and took a step back when demanded. Luckily, no one seemed to notice her amid the chaos. She could see through his helmet that his eyes were open and saw his chest move up and down.

He was breathing. He looked okay.

Coach Sampson spoke in a calm manner. "Aeggers, do you know where you are?"

"I'm dancing at the Homecoming dance."

The coach's eyes now full of panic.

"Aw, coach, I'm just teasing," Adam said. "I just caught a beautiful pass."

Relief settled back on Coach Sampson's face, and he let out a good chuckle. "Yes, you did, son. That was a hell of a catch. Can you tell me where you're hurt?"

"Not really. I can't feel too much."

The trainer held out his hand to hold Adam's. "Aeggers, I want you to squeeze my hand."

Nothing happened.

"Are you trying to squeeze?"

"It doesn't feel like I can move my fingers."

Concern covered Coach Sampson's face.

The trainer continued. "Does it feel like you can move anything? Can you feel anything?"

"Um, I think I can feel the tops of my thighs. Yeah, I can feel that."

The trainer locked eyes with the coach again and gave him a nod. The coach got up and signaled for the ambulance, then told an assistant coach to find Adam's parents.

"Wait, what's going on? Is Adam going to be okay?" Cara asked the trainer.

"What the hell are you doing down here? Get off the field!"

"Cara, is that you?" Adam asked, straining his eyes toward the sound of her voice.

Cara ignored the trainer and kneeled next to Adam.

"Hey!" the trainer yelled again, "You can't be down here, and don't you dare touch him!"

"It's okay. It's okay. She's my sister," Adam lied.

With that, the trainer was assuaged and stopped his interrogation. Cara made sure not to touch him but leaned in close so he could see her. "Adam, I'm here. I'm here."

"I know you are. You've always been here for me."

Her eyes struggled to see him through her tears—looking at his still body on the field. In the distance, she could hear some of the football players crying. "Adam, I'm scared."

"Hey, everything's going to be okay. Don't be scared. Everything's going to be fine, Cara."

"What do you want me to do? I'll do anything you need." It was all she could think to say to try to comfort him.

"Well, my nose is itching, and since I can't seem to move my arms at the moment, I could sure use some help." Cara let out a sigh and smiled. Only Adam would be able to make a lighthearted comment in a moment like this.

"You want me to scratch your nose?"

"Yes, ma'am. That would sure help me out."

She looked back over at the trainer who nodded. She reached out her hand—making sure not to touch any other part of his body and gently scratched his nose. "Right here? Is that okay?"

"Perfect," he said. "Thank you." His eyes expressed deep sincerity. "Everything's going to be okay, Cara."

She wasn't supposed to touch him, but she discreetly squeezed his hand. Not knowing if he could even feel it.

Then Cara saw the leather bracelet she gave him sophomore year that he was wearing under a sweatband. When the trainer turned his head, she quickly untied the string, slipped it off his wrist, and put it on her own. She didn't want anything to happen to it when they took him to the hospital.

Adam's parents and Angela approached as paramedics started to remove his helmet to put on a neck brace. They rolled him to his side and slid a flat board under his body.

Mrs. Aether was hysterical. "What's going on with my son?"

The trainer pulled them aside. "I'm not going to sugarcoat anything. This isn't good. Adam is conscious and talking, but," he took a long pause, "he appears to have lost all feeling from the neck down."

Angela wrapped her arms around her mom, who shook her head. Dr. Aether stood in shock.

"It could just be a stinger," the trainer said.

"A stinger? What's that?" Angela asked.

"A bruised spinal cord that causes temporary numbness. If that's not it then—" He couldn't finish, and the Aethers didn't wait for him to anyway.

The paramedics placed Adam on a stretcher and prepared to load him into the ambulance. Dr. and Mrs. Aether rushed over to him.

"Adam, Momma's here, sweetie." She leaned over her son. She sounded like she was talking to a small child. The combination of that sight and sound was hard for Cara to process. This was Adam, who was almost an adult, strong, and able.

At the sight of his mom, Adam feigned the same encouragement. "Mom, don't be scared. I'm going to be all right. Everything's going to be okay."

"I love you so much!" His mother struggled through tears.

"I love you, son," his dad said.

Angela squeezed between them. "I love you, bud."

"I love you all, too."

Cara stayed back a step to give them space but was close enough to hear.

"Mom?" Adam said. "I am a little scared."

"That's okay, baby, I'm scared too, but we're going to get through this. We'll see you at the hospital, okay? We're going straight there." She tried to sound calm.

"And, Mom? Please tell Cara that everything's going to be okay."

With that, they loaded him into the ambulance and shut the door.

It was then that Cara noticed the ladybug still on her shoulder.

31

BREATHTAKING

ara arrived at the hospital just moments after Adam's family, and Mrs. Aether scooped her into a tight embrace as soon as she walked through the door. No words were said as they held each other—Mrs. Aether's tears dripped onto Cara's shirt. They filled the moment this way as they stood inside the bare walls of the Emergency Room. Waiting the unknown.

"Where is he?" Cara finally asked. "What's going on right now?"

Mrs. Aether could barely talk, so Angela responded for her. "He's getting a CT scan to see exactly what the injury is."

The silence resumed until the neurosurgeon came out in her blue scrubs, white coat, and a nametag that read "Dr. Reuhland."

"Lisa," Dr. Aether said. "Thank God you're the one on call tonight." Though Dr. Aether was a dentist, he was familiar with many medical doctors in the area. He and Dr. Reuhland shared many friends.

"Bruce. Gloria." She nodded to both of them, shook their hands, and spoke pleasantly but with concern in her eyes. "Let's go back into the conference room to talk about Adam. Family only."

Mrs. Aether looked at Cara and motioned her to come with them.

Dr. Reuhland frowned, knowing Adam had only one sister.

"She's family too," Mrs. Aether said, and they continued walking.

Cara and Angela linked arms and pulled each other close.

Dr. Reuhland shut the door behind her and waited for everyone to have a seat. "The paramedics said Adam was talking to you before they rushed him here, is that right?"

"Uh, yeah. Yes, he was talking to all of us until he took off in the ambulance," Dr. Aether answered.

Dr. Reuhland took a deep breath before she continued. "What you experienced was a true miracle then." She paused. "We're going to do surgery here very soon and will know more after that, but according to the CT scan, it looks like Adam has a burst fracture to his C5 vertebrae."

Mrs. Aether closed her eyes.

"Damage around this area affects the diaphragm and restricts people from being able to breathe. They usually can't talk, and sometimes it results in immediate death."

"Can you please explain what this means for Adam?" Mrs. Aether asked. "You just said the word death."

"There are many possible outcomes. The most likely is that he will become a quadriplegic . . ."

She continued to talk, but Cara couldn't process any more information. She felt her blood pressure dropping, the bare walls closing in on her, and everything sounded muffled. She made out certain words Dr. Reuhland said—*emergency surgery, spinal injury, quadriplegic*. But Cara couldn't get out of her head some of the other words she had heard so far that night—*miracle, death, stinger*—and couldn't piece all of this together. She thought of the last thing Adam said to his mom—*Please tell Cara that everything's going to be okay.*

He had to be okay, right? He said so himself. God, she wanted to see him. To talk to him. She wished she could just press the button to her walkie-talkie and hear his voice on the other end. With every thought, Cara's breath sped up. She noticed Dr. Reuhland left the room. Cara grasped the armrests of her chair and focused on a cigarette burn on the ugly brown leather of the seat she was in. It was the only thing that seemed to stop the room from spinning out of control.

～

CARA DIDN'T HEAR Dr. Reuhland tell the Aethers she would give them access to see Adam before he went in for his spinal surgery.

She was still staring at the cigarette burn when Angela pulled at her arm and asked, "Hey, you coming?"

They were escorted into a small, white-washed room. Adam lay on a hospital bed with the thick brace around his neck and a hospital gown that had replaced his football uniform. He was staring at the ceiling, but his eyelids looked as if they were fighting to close. His breathing was labored. The four of them approached his bedside, and his eyes slowly shifted their way.

"Hey, buddy," Mrs. Aether said, putting her hand on his arm. "We're all right here. Dad, Angela, Cara, and me."

Adam's tired eyes moved to look at each of them, and the corner of his mouth pulled into a slight smile.

Cara smiled back at him. She so badly wanted to hear his voice—maybe one of his stories, his laugh (man, he had the best laugh). She would even settle for a simple "hello" at the moment.

Adam's mouth started to open. Cara leaned in to hear what he had to say.

But it wasn't to talk.

It was to vomit.

The noise was awful, like a clogged drain trying to empty itself.

"He's choking!" Angela screamed.

Adam helplessly lay there as the vomit had nowhere to go, and with his neck injury, they didn't know what to do.

Mrs. Aether pushed the emergency button, and Dr. Aether ran out of the room for help. Within seconds, three nurses rushed in, followed by Dr. Reuhland.

"We have to roll him! Stabilize the neck!"

They went into position like it was a drill they'd practiced many times. Cara and the Aethers backed themselves to the wall. Dr. Reuhland held Adam's head while one nurse slid her hands under his back, another under his hips, and another under his knees. Together they rolled him onto his side, and the vomit ran down the corner of his mouth, soaking his sheets and dripping onto the floor.

No one thought to grab a pan to catch it.

Adam's face started to turn blue—a nurse pushed a long suction tube into his mouth.

"He's starting to aspirate!" Dr. Reuhland yelled. "We need to intubate immediately and get him to surgery."

They began to roll his hospital bed out of the room.

"Adam!" Cara cried.

"Aether family," Dr. Reuhland said, "we're going to take good care of him. Head to the waiting room—I'll meet with you as soon as he's out of surgery."

The four of them stood frozen for a moment. Before they left, Cara noticed the puddle of vomit still in the middle of the floor.

※

WHEN THE AETHERS and Cara returned to the waiting room, it was full of students, teachers, and coaches. Everyone took turns comforting the family and then each other. More visitors steadily arrived despite the night growing late.

A few people approached Cara with a hug. She knew words were coming from their mouths and that their arms were embracing her, but she only heard noise and felt pressure. Her vision was like a vignette, with darkness closing in on the peripherals of her sight. Most of the time, she tried to stay by Angela to avoid the crowd—leaning her head on her shoulder while most people approached Dr. and Mrs. Aether.

Angela asked her if she wanted to go home or at least call her parents. Cara simply said, "No."

To remove herself from the mass, Cara left the room to find a vending machine. She dug into her purse to retrieve fifty cents for a Snickers bar. She tore the corner of the wrapping but couldn't eat it.

Those words kept spinning around in her head again: *emergency surgery, spinal injury, quadriplegic, miracle, death, stinger.* And then the last words she heard Adam speak: *Please tell Cara that everything's going to be okay.* She saw herself scratching his nose as he lay on the football field under the lights, the neck brace, the vomit on the floor, and then she heard the crack of helmets against the sound of her camera's click.

She didn't notice the chocolate from the candy bar melting from her tight grip, nor did she realize she walked back to the waiting room. Through the small circle in the center of her vision, she saw someone approach with a black bag in their hands.

It was Jenny Andrews in her cheerleading uniform.

"Cara?"

Cara didn't respond. She just looked at her—the dark

perimeters of her vision closing in as the voice sounded like it was in a tunnel.

Jenny went on anyway. "Hey, I saw this camera and bag kind of close to where I was cheering. It was on the side of the football field after everyone left. I thought it might be yours for the newspaper."

It was hers. Cara stared at the bag—thinking of the last shot she took with that camera and the undeveloped film inside—it was at the exact moment Adam got hit and broke his neck. She didn't even reach for it, but almost inaudibly said, "Thank you."

Jenny continued to hold the bag. "I'm really sorry about Adam." She started to cry and wrapped her arms around Cara, who continued to stare into the distance.

~

AROUND 11:30 P.M., Dr. Reuhland entered the waiting room with a slight smile on her face, her mask pulled down around her neck. Cara and the Aethers stood up anxiously at the sight of her.

"The surgery could not have gone any better. We were able to remove all the bone fragments, fuse his neck, and there was minimal blood loss. The spinal cord wasn't severed, which was critical."

"Oh, thank God." Mrs. Aether grabbed her heart. "Can we see him?"

"Yes, but I need to let you know some things first." She took a breath. "He's still sedated from the surgery. He might wake up in an hour or so, but it's also late, so he might just sleep through the night. Like I told you earlier, the area of the spinal cord around the C5 vertebrae controls the diaphragm. He started having trouble breathing before the surgery, so he's hooked up to a ventilator, which is typical for any surgery, but he may have to stay on it for longer. It's going to be a long road ahead—a lot of surgeries, therapies." She paused again, and her shoulders lowered. "He *is* most likely going to be a quadriplegic."

There was that word again.

Mrs. Aether buried her face in her husband's shoulder and began to sob.

"Is that certain, though?" Dr. Aether choked out the question.

"Since he didn't sever his spinal cord, there's a slight chance he might regain the ability to make some small movements in his upper torso, like shrugging his shoulders, but that's about it."

She led them to Adam's room in the Intensive Care Unit. It was past visiting hours, but she made another exception for them. Still sedated from the surgery, Adam lay there with his eyes closed —the same thick brace around his neck and a web of wires seemed to come out of every inch of his body. Part of his head was shaved. A heart monitor steadily beeped to declare the track of his heartbeat.

What Cara noticed first, though, was the rise and fall of his chest, which now required the help of a machine. It made him seem inhuman and powerless, but he breathed with the same steady movement that often soothed her when she needed it.

When they approached, Adam had drool coming out of the side of his mouth. Mrs. Aether quickly wiped it with her sleeve.

All of the words that were floating around in Cara's mind stopped on one word now: *quadriplegic*. She couldn't imagine a world where Adam wasn't playing football, driving, or sneaking out of the window. He was so strong but now looked so helpless. He couldn't move. He couldn't even breathe on his own. She refused to accept this. He was going to prove them wrong. She didn't care what the doctor said.

Dr. Reuhland waited until everyone had held his limp hand, whispered sweet greetings in his ear, and emotions started to level. "Technically, no one is allowed to stay the night in the ICU, but this is a special case I'll let slide. All I have are a couple of recliners and some sheets, though."

"That will be more than enough. Thank you so much," Dr. Aether said. He looked at Cara. "It's past midnight. Do you want to get some rest at home and come back in the morning?"

Cara shook her head. "No, I'm not leaving here. I want to see Adam when he wakes up. I'll sleep on the floor—I don't care."

And that's what she did. She used her purse as a pillow and her jacket as a blanket. She barely slept—partly because the floor was hard and cold, partly because nurses checked on Adam every fifteen minutes, but mainly because she kept getting up to see him. Cara hoped any second, he'd wake up so she could talk to him, comfort him.

Eventually, she gave up on the idea of sleep and quietly carried a chair to the side of his bed, careful not to wake the Aethers who all seemed to be asleep finally. She looked down at his hand that had a pulse oximeter attached to his left forefinger. Not wanting to disrupt the monitor, she held onto his left pinky.

She looked at the endotracheal tube that was down his throat to send oxygen into his lungs. Feeling a panic attack coming on, Cara tried to sync her breath with his. Long inhales, slow exhales. Then she leaned in and whispered in his ear an array of disjointed thoughts: "You're my best friend . . . I need you . . . You've always been there for me. Now I'm going to be here for you . . . No matter what happens . . . Please wake up . . ."

The beeping of the heart monitor almost became as soothing as his breath, and for the first time since she got to the hospital, her mind felt somewhat clear. Cara thought about how different life was going to be with Adam paralyzed. With no football scholarship, would he still go to North Carolina? Would he go to college at all? Would he have the same drive for life and want to help people if he couldn't even help himself?

Then she thought about their conversation a few months ago at the Spaghetti Warehouse—their marriage deal. If still single at twenty-six and a half, would she marry him as a quadriplegic? Her answer came without hesitation. Yes. Of course she would keep her end of the bargain. Had this happened to her instead, Adam would do the same. The more she thought about it, the more she realized she couldn't imagine a life without Adam, fully-abled or not.

Cara continued waiting—hoping he would open his eyes and talk to her again. She longed to have a conversation. Maybe she would recite one of her poems to him or tell him an old story from their childhood. But his eyes wouldn't open.

～

HOURS LATER, Dr. Reuhland came in to check on Adam. She had a worried look as she did a sternal rub, checked his pupils, and tested his reflexes.

Her movements woke the Aethers who were barely asleep anyway.

"I'm concerned that Adam hasn't woken up yet, so I'm going to take him back for another CT scan and possibly an MRI."

They were all exhausted, and as they were starting to get some rest, this new information felt like going to the top of the highest hill of a roller coaster again. Cara thought how she wanted this all to be over. But would it ever be over? The doctor had even said that there was a long road ahead full of many surgeries and procedures.

Adam was wheeled out on the hospital bed without discussion.

It was then that Cara gave the leather bracelet that had "AEGGERS" engraved on it to Mrs. Aether. "I wasn't supposed to touch Adam when he was on the field, but I took this off his wrist when the trainer wasn't looking. I didn't want anything to happen to it when he got here."

Mrs. Aether took it and thanked Cara. They all tried to comfort each other and collapsed into a few more moments of rest as they waited.

~

ANGELA GAVE Cara soft nudges to wake her. "Dr. Reuhland is back with an update."

The ICU room looked different when Cara opened her eyes. It took her a minute to realize it was from the sunlight forcing its way through the cracks of the window blinds. Cara's body was stiff from sleeping on the cold, hard linoleum, and she slowly rose to her feet. She looked up at the clock, which read a little after seven in the morning and wondered why Adam's hospital bed wasn't back in the room.

She thought Dr. Reuhland was going to return in about forty-five minutes, but she must have been gone for several hours. The CT shouldn't have taken that long. By the look of Dr. Reuhland's face, Cara's heart felt like it dropped into her gut as she was sure she was going to hear the answer to these questions.

Dr. Reuhland's voice was hesitant and shaky. "The second CT scan we ran showed that Adam had a massive brain stem stroke on the part of the brain that controls speech, blood pressure, and breathing . . .." She cleared her throat and took a deep breath. "Strokes often take a while to show up on CT scans, so that's why we weren't aware of this initially. There was a considerable amount of swelling on the brain, so we took him in for another emergency surgery and removed part of his skull to relieve some pressure, but . . . I'm afraid it was too late."

"What do you mean 'too late?'" Mrs. Aether cried.

Dr. Reuhland's eyes welled up. "Adam's not going to recover to the point where he can open his eyes, talk, or have any semblance of a normal life. There's a very low chance that he's going to have any sort of function, and he will be dependent on machines to survive. He's expected to be in a vegetative state pretty soon."

Silence covered the room.

After a moment, Dr. Reuhland added, "He most likely has what's called Locked In Syndrome at the moment—meaning he can hear and understand you but won't be able to respond. I'm not sure how much longer that will last since the swelling is expected to worsen and cause him to go brain dead. He's in Recovery right now, but you can go back and talk to him, and we will allow visitors once he's back in ICU. Think about what you would like to do. If you want to keep him on life support, we will need to get him on dialysis immediately because he's also in kidney failure, and then we'd need to insert a feeding tube . . ."

Even through her tears, Dr. Reuhland tried to regain a distant professionalism, but the knot in her throat was obvious when she said, "I'm so sorry."

∼

LOCKED In Syndrome sounded crueler than death. Having the ability to hear everyone but with no way to respond—not a wiggle of the finger, a nod, or even a blink. It seemed like a horrible trap. Cara thought about their lifelong friendship—so much of their relationship revolved around communication of so many types. And now that was gone.

The family asked Cara to step outside so they could make their decision about Adam. She quietly left the room, but through the shut door, the hysterics of Adam's mother bled through as she cursed God, and fate, and everything. Cara envisioned her punching the air at the cruel reality while her own body sank and lay face down on the cold floor—wishing, praying it would crack open and swallow her whole.

∼

THE ULTIMATE DECISION was based on the belief that it wouldn't be fair for Adam to rely on machines to survive with no quality of life.

For the remainder of the day, they would let friends and

family say their final goodbyes to Adam. In the meantime, the nurses kept him comfortable. And then, they were going to let him go.

The Aethers and Cara spent time with him—each of them took time to tell him everything they wanted to say. Memories, how much they loved him, how this wasn't fair, how much they were going to miss him. Each hoping they had him in the window of the Locked In Syndrome when he could understand their words.

∾

THE WAITING room was so full there weren't enough chairs. The ICU nurses let groups of five or six come back at a time to say their goodbyes. Cara and the Aethers stayed in the room while the visitors came back. Some people they didn't even know, and some they weren't sure even knew Adam. Many told him how much he meant to them. It was nice to hear, but Cara couldn't help thinking how much more Adam meant to her.

She kept looking at Dr. and Mrs. Aether, at the pain they were going through and wished she could trade places with Adam. He had parents who loved and cared about him. She thought of the most recent words her father had spoken to her: *You're absolutely worthless to me.* If she was about to die, she doubted her parents would care.

∾

IT WAS the early evening hours, and the visitors continued. One member of the football team entered the room wearing a sharp suit and had a girl on his arm in a formal dress. They were stopping by before heading to the Homecoming dance.

Homecoming.

Cara hadn't even remembered that the Homecoming dance was that night. The year she and Adam were finally going to go together, and now it wasn't able to happen.

∾

AFTER ANOTHER GROUP of people left, a single person came into the room. It was Cara's mother. At the sight of her, Cara realized she never let her parents know where she was and why she wasn't home. Wearing a green dress suit with her hair and makeup perfect, Cara knew her mother wasn't there to comfort her—she was there to keep her reputation secure.

This was "Christmas Party Susan."

The loud click of her heels against the hard floor made their way to the Aethers first. She gave them each a hug. "I'm so very sorry about your son."

Cara wasn't sure she'd ever seen her mother hug someone before.

She looked at Cara next and squeezed her shoulder. When she walked to Adam's bedside, Cara wondered what her mother would say. She had never made any effort to know Adam.

"Thank you for being a good friend to my daughter."

Then she left.

~

IT WAS midnight when Adam started to fade fast. Due to his brain stem stroke, malignant hyperthermia came on quickly, and he started developing diabetes insipidus. The Aethers requested no more visitors, wanting their final moments with Adam alone. They let Cara stay the entire time.

They each took turns to say their last goodbyes to him privately. When it was Cara's turn, the latch of the door behind her was deafening, and she slowly walked to the side of his bed. She and Adam were supposed to be ending that night dancing together at the Homecoming dance—instead, they were here.

There was more drool coming out the side of his mouth that she wiped with the sleeve of her jacket.

Whatever words she gave him now would most likely just vanish into the air, but there were so many to say. Words she wished she would have said a long time ago when she thought she had a lifetime to say them. Cara had to get them out anyway— there was a comfort in speaking them and simply being in his presence.

Before she spoke, she placed her head on his chest and listened to his breath. It would be the last time she'd hear it, and she wanted to remember.

This realization hit hard. With her head still against his body, Cara started sobbing—a deep gut-punching sob. She didn't only hurt emotionally; her entire body physically hurt from the pain of knowing this was her last time with her friend. A small area of his hospital gown was soaked by her tears as she clenched fistfuls of the fabric in her hands.

"Oh, God, Adam. I'm going to miss you so much! How am I going to manage without you here every day?" She struggled to breathe. "Your words made me laugh. Your words made me feel valued. I just wish you could communicate with me. In any way. One last time."

Cara put her hands in her jacket pockets, searching for a tissue to wipe her face. And there it was—the sharp edges of the craftily folded paper. The note Adam gave her in anatomy class yesterday that she hadn't read yet.

Her fingers shook as she unfolded each crease, fearful she might ruin the message. Her hands steadied after it was open. Before reading the words, she took in the entirety of the page. Adam's handwriting, immediately recognizable to her, was written in blue ink. And the paper. He had touched that paper. It was like a part of him was in her hands. Through the pooling of tears in her eyes, she read.

November 7th, 1997

Cara,

First, I'm always intimidated when writing you since you're clearly far more superior in this area, so please try not to judge. I wish I could tell you all of this in person, but I didn't think I'd have a chance today and wanted to make sure I wrote all this down for you because I know you need to hear these words now.

I want you to know that when I told you I loved you last night, I meant it. I know that I have failed you at times, and we've fought like brother and sister, but please know that (other than my family), you're the most important person in my life. You're my best friend, and I want the best for you.

I've been thinking even more recently about what Angela said to us in her apartment last year (even though she was pretty tipsy. Haha!). She said that some way or another, the two of us were going to end up together even though it may not be in a normal way.

I'm really sorry for whatever happened with your dad last night. But I'm glad you feel comfortable enough to come to me when you're hurt, stressed, or heartbroken. I don't know what will happen in the future, but I hope I am always able to take care of you and offer you the comfort that you need.

For now, remember to breathe.

Love,
*   Adam*

Cara pressed the letter against her chest. As she felt herself breathe, she thought about how Adam's last breath was just moments away.

"Thank you, Adam." And then she said the words she couldn't get out the other night, "I love you, too."

32

PLANTS

W hat followed felt like the cruelest hours Time could ever give. Cara couldn't bear to have her final memory with Adam be when they wheeled his body away, or pulled the plug, or whatever it is they do. She wanted her last memory to be their moment alone with his letter, so she needed to leave the hospital.

Sleep-deprived, food-deprived, and riddled with grief, she got into her Jeep close to one o'clock in the morning and drove aimlessly around Dayton in silence. Without intent, she found herself back in her neighborhood and drove past their side by side houses—his with the white siding and hers with the brick façade.

She couldn't go home. Not yet.

Instead, she drove down a few streets to Alexander's Woods. Her headlights shone into the birches but only revealed darkness. Cara stared into the shadows and waited in its stillness before killing the engine and slamming the door as she got out of the vehicle. It was the early hours of Sunday morning, and she still had on the same clothes from Friday night. The November air was cold, but she didn't even pull her jacket tight as she walked the path that led to the creek among the birch trees.

When she reached their spot with the carved initials in the tree, she stood for a few minutes listening to the water. Last year she was inspired by how it glided past any rocks in its way and liked to think she'd been like that adaptable water for so long, but not now. Adam's death was like a permanent dam that stopped everything, creating energy with nowhere to go. With this realization, she hunched over, hands on her knees, and started to violently heave. She hadn't eaten in nearly forty hours, so what little came up was just bile. Void of everything, her body collapsed—knees hitting first, then chest, then face against the damp earth. She was so numb, the fall barely hurt, but she wished it would have so the physical pain could mask the internal pain. That's when the whimpers came out. She lay there on the cold ground and let out long, deep cries as little pebbles protruded deeper and deeper into the left cheek of her grimaced face.

∿

AROUND FOUR IN THE MORNING, Cara returned to her house. She didn't want to go through the front door and risk running into her drunk father, so she sneaked in through her bedroom window. Similar to what happened in the woods, she collapsed again but on her soft bed.

Sleep only came in small spurts. Each time she woke up, Cara prayed that everything was a dream. When she realized it wasn't, she cried herself back to sleep.

Beams of morning sunlight gradually danced through her bedroom until it reached her eyelids. When she woke up this time, the first thing she saw was her Homecoming dress hanging on her closet door. Then she looked at the window, which felt so prominent in her room now. For the past thirteen years, she had Adam on the other side of that window. There would no longer be any flashlight beam shining through or blinds signaling a special message.

Cara reached for her journal and a pen. Writing always helped when she needed to release feelings. She held the pen tip against the blank page, but her hand wouldn't move. It felt stuck. Finally, she closed the journal and retrieved her Fisher Price Sky Talker— it felt heavy in her hand. She kept pushing in the orange button as if she was going to radio over to Adam, every fiber of her being wishing his voice would be on the other side. Stopping for a moment, she unzipped the pocket of her jacket that she still wore to make sure her most prized possession was still there.

Adam's note.

She opened it, and after reading it over a dozen times, she

grabbed a book from her nightstand—*Robert Frost's Anthology of Poems*—and tucked it between pages 241 and 242.

Being awake was too painful, so Cara let herself fall back asleep—hoping not to wake up for a very long time. But she did. And when she did, she reached for the walkie-talkie and clicked the orange button over and over until she cried herself to sleep again.

~

CARA STAYED in bed for the rest of that Sunday and three days that followed. The smallest of tasks required an immense amount of energy. Everything was exhausting. She hadn't showered or even changed out of her clothes from Friday night. She only got up to use the bathroom. Grease in her hair had built up so much it clumped in thick strands. Every waking moment reminded her that Adam was gone, so she slept instead.

Her mother left a Breakfast Bar on her nightstand each morning and a microwave dinner each night. Cara nibbled a few bites but could never finish.

On Wednesday night, her mother quietly knocked on Cara's bedroom door. This time she didn't have a microwave dinner—she held an envelope and a black dress on a hanger.

"I bought you a nice dress for the funeral. I got it from that new boutique in Oakwood."

The funeral was tomorrow morning. It was a nice gesture by her mother, but it was difficult to feel gratitude when the gift was for an occasion she wished she never had to attend. She watched her mother hang the black dress where her Homecoming gown used to be.

"I got your usual size, but you've barely eaten these past few days, so it might look a little baggy." Then she came over to the bedside without touching her daughter or even getting on her eye level. "You can't stay here forever. You need to go back to school. You really should just take the first step by taking a shower, Cara. Being clean will make you feel better." She started to leave and then remembered something. "Oh, and this came for you in the mail today." She set the envelope on her nightstand before walking out the door.

Cara mustered the energy to lift herself onto her elbow. The envelope was made out to Cara Ecrivain, and the return address said Turner. Cara sat up and opened the sympathy card from her favorite teacher. She told her that she was sorry, that they missed her at school, and that she could talk to her about anything. The words felt meaningless, and she let the card slip from her hands to land on her floor.

She tried to force herself out of bed to shower, but she couldn't do it. She knew it wouldn't make her feel better, just cleaner. The funeral wasn't until tomorrow. She would do it then. For now, she needed more sleep to escape the pain of being awake.

~

CARA HAD ONLY BEEN to one other funeral before—her paternal grandmother's in Wisconsin. She was six years old and had only met her a handful of times. She didn't even remember feeling sad. There were just a couple dozen people in the pews at that funeral. Apparently, the older someone is when they die, the fewer people come.

Adam's family invited Cara to ride in the limousine with them. It was the first time she'd seen them since the hospital. She wanted to comfort them, but it was hard when she felt so much grief of her own. Cara wore the black dress her mother bought her and had finally taken a long shower that morning. The shower didn't make her feel any better—it only seemed to have washed away the numbness as now she only felt intense pain in every fiber.

Adam's funeral was the opposite of her grandmother's. Patterson Park Church, where the Aethers attended, couldn't seat everyone. Canterville High still had classes, but any student who attended the funeral received an excused absence. Cara wondered how many of them were taking advantage of a skip day.

Adam's body in the casket, the football players crying, the eulogy—it all seemed like shadows and whispers.

She longed for more sleep.

~

CARA RODE with the Aethers back to their home. They had dozens of plants to carry in that people had sent in honor of Adam, and Cara helped bring them inside. If she was exhausted, she couldn't imagine what they were going through—losing their son and planning his funeral in less than a week.

When the last plant came through the door, they now had a living room covered in so much vegetation, it resembled a small jungle.

Cara wondered why people sent plants. It felt pointless, if not cruel. It showed the family someone was thinking of them, or was sorry for their loss . . . but now they had a room full of plants and still no son. And the plants will all eventually die . . . just like their son.

Cara noticed that nothing else in the house had changed. Adam's shoes and a pile of mail from North Carolina were in the same spots he'd left them on Friday.

"May I see his room?" Cara asked.

Mrs. Aether nodded.

Her steps were careful. Nothing had changed in his room, either, except the leather bracelet she retrieved from Adam's wrist was now on his dresser.

Cara looked through his window and saw hers peering back. She had never thought what their conversations had looked like from his perspective. Refocusing her eyes, the ghostly reflection on Adam's window had Cara staring at herself.

Stepping away, she saw the blanket on his bed—the one he brought outside and set on the grass so they could look at the stars. She held it to her nose. It smelled exactly like him.

When she returned to the living room, Cara cradled the blanket in her arms.

"I hope you don't mind, but I took this from his room."

Mrs. Aether gave Cara a gentle smile. "You can keep it out here if you'd like."

Cara crawled onto the couch, covered herself with Adam's blanket, and fell asleep to his scent.

～

THE SOUND of a blender woke Cara from the couch that evening. She walked into the kitchen to see Mrs. Aether making homemade spaghetti sauce for that night's dinner even though the fridge was full of casseroles made by little old ladies from their church. Cara leaned against the countertop and watched Adam's mom from behind. How could she even function when all Cara could do was sleep?

As Mrs. Aether boiled noodles, the lid to the blender blew off, and red sauce spewed out—splattering on the cabinets, the counters, the floor, and Mrs. Aether. She pounded on the machine to turn it off with no success, so she tried to unplug it, instead. But the sauce gloved her hands, and she couldn't get a grip.

"I can't stop it! I can't stop it!" she cried as her hands slid against the cord.

Cara ran over with her dry hands and pulled the plug.

The blender stopped.

Mrs. Aether cried.

Cara embraced Adam's mom, and for the first time was comforting her.

∾

CARA FORCED herself to go to school the next day, but only because Mrs. Aether encouraged her to. "Returning to a routine is supposed to be helpful for the grieving process," she said.

"But it's so hard," Cara said. "It's physically painful."

"I know, sweetie, but you've got to try."

So she tried.

It was not helpful. Not that day.

Fear of the unexpected caused nerves to bubble in her stomach. Would everyone stop her to offer condolences? Would everyone be so emotional that it was hard for them to go to class? Would teachers mention his death at the beginning of each class? Would there be a moment of silence? Would the football team do something special to recognize him?

There were a few things she observed immediately. The first was that football players all wore their jerseys with a little memorial ribbon pinned to their chests that said A.A. for that night's game. The second was that his locker resembled a memorial site, with flowers, cards, and stuffed animals either attached or placed on the ground in front of it. She heard a few students in passing mention something about his funeral, but for the most part, the entire school seemed to have moved on like everything was back to normal.

How? How could everyone be so . . . *fine*? One of their peers, who walked among them just a week ago, was gone. Forever. This could have happened to any one of them.

What Cara noticed next was slowly realized throughout the morning. Every turn contained a memory, a constant reminder that Adam wasn't there. She would pass a water fountain that was Adam's favorite because it was the coldest or the spot where he tripped in ninth grade. And of course, there was his locker — or rather, the memorial.

Cara wondered about the inside of the locker. Were all of his books still there? Had his parents already come to clean it out? Or would everything stay in there forever, and the school would retire the locker — never to be used again as a way to immortalize a student?

She wondered about other things that screamed of his absence. Would his name remain on the teachers' rosters? What would they do for a substitute? Leave his name, but have a note that read: "Absent for the rest of the year"? Or "Don't call on — he snapped his neck and was killed"? What about his desk in each class? Had the teachers already made new seating charts so his empty desk would seem less noticeable? Would they give it to a new student and just replace him like he was never there?

As Cara entered her government class third period, which was the first class she had with Adam throughout the day, she got an answer to some of her questions. Everyone went to their usual seats, and then there it was. It was as if it was shining in neon lights.

His empty chair.

And when Ms. Bower called roll, she started with Natalie Bell's name, whose was always second on the roster — right after Adam Aether's.

Ms. Bower began to lecture about the legislative branch, and while the other students took copious notes, Cara only sat there. She couldn't take her eyes off the empty chair. Suddenly, she stood up and began packing her bag.

"Miss Ecrivain, are you okay? May I ask what you're doing?"

Cara started to walk out of the room.

"Miss Ecrivain?" Ms. Bower asked again.

"I have to go."

She didn't stop by the counseling office to let them know she was having a rough go, nor did she stop by the attendance office to tell them she was leaving.

She just left.

Being in that school didn't help her grieve—it suffocated her. When she turned onto Paddington Road, it wasn't her house she went to, it was the Aethers'.

When Mrs. Aether answered the door, Cara attempted to hide her emotions, but couldn't. She shook her head at Adam's mom and pressed her lips together. Mrs. Aether wrapped Cara in her arms.

"I tried," Cara said through her tears. "I tried."

Mrs. Aether invited her in without using words. Inside their walls, Cara smelled him again. She went over to their couch in the living room—Adam's blanket folded and sitting on the edge. She grabbed it and fell asleep there for the rest of the day.

33

BROKEN

Psychologists say there are five stages of grief—Denial, Anger, Bargaining, Depression, and Acceptance.

These feelings don't occur on a linear timeline. They come and go like they're playing a perpetual five-way game of tug-of-war, and the one winning at the moment takes over all the other emotions.

In the months that followed, Cara hoped each day would get a little easier. In some ways, they did, but only fractions of fractions at a time. Some days she felt close to okay, and then a particular song would come on the radio, or she would drive by a memory, and an emotional storm from one of the stages would crash into her.

Thanksgiving break was a couple weeks after the accident, and winter break a few weeks after that. Those breaks gave Cara a chance to ease back into the school routine. She couldn't decide what was worse, though—continuing to attend school with constant reminders that Adam wasn't there, or coming home to her silent room that provided no distractions for her grief.

After many requests from the school, Cara finally started to see Mr. Atkinson, the school counselor. She didn't do much talking at these meetings—they usually consisted of Mr. Atkinson making sure Cara was doing okay and speaking in metaphors to help her see the situation in a different light.

"If your life were a sentence, Cara," he'd say, "this incident isn't a period. It's a dash or a comma. Make sure you finish the sentence."

Sayings like these usually resulted in crossed arms and blank expressions from Cara.

One time though, Mr. Atkinson said something that stuck. Cara had finally opened up a little about Adam and couldn't hide the emotion from her voice. Mr. Atkinson leaned in a little and asked, "Would you rather he was less loved, so you could all grieve less?"

Honestly, she wasn't quite sure.

~

CARA HAD several coping mechanisms she used to survive. She spent a lot of time at the Aethers', which comforted both her and Adam's parents. For Cara, it was the familiarity of the house, the smells, seeing Adam reflected in his parents, and his belongings in the same spots. Plus, Dr. and Mrs. Aether said it was nice to have her around. Cara went there almost every day, and while she interacted with his parents some, she spent most of her time there sleeping on their couch beneath Adam's blanket—sometimes spending the night.

When other stages of grief hit her, she did a lot of wandering in Alexander's Woods. It didn't matter that it was winter in Ohio with frost-covered trees and a frozen creek. She'd walk the same path they took as kids and rest among the birches. Sometimes she would just sit. Sometimes she'd cry. Sometimes she'd scream and curse God. And sometimes, she'd talk to Adam. She didn't believe he could actually hear her, but there was solace in letting the words out.

The one thing Cara didn't do to cope was write. This had always been her outlet for anything positive or negative. Pages that would have normally been overflowing with ink lay barren in her room. She often reached for her notebook and stared at the blank canvas with nothing to offer it. Then she'd slip it back into her drawer.

This matter of the writing, or lack thereof, was finally addressed after winter break when Cara received a pass during calculus to see Ms. Turner. As soon as she saw it, she knew what it was about—this was Ms. Turner's planning period, which meant a private conversation.

Cara walked slowly up the stairs to the second floor where the journalism class was. The longer she could avoid this conversation, the better. She stood in the hall for a long time before entering.

"Did you want to see me?" Cara asked as she walked through the door. She held up her pass with her sweaty palm.

"I hope this was an okay time to miss class."

"Any time's a good time to miss calc," Cara said as she forced a small laugh.

Ms. Turner forced a laugh too. "Hey, I needed to talk to you about the newspaper."

Cara could probably finish her thoughts for her, but she listened.

"You know the newspaper program works as a team. We have deadlines, and we rely on each other to meet those deadlines. I gave you some grace until winter break, but you haven't produced an article since November. I know it's been a hard time for you, but I need to know your status."

Cara stared at one of the computers in the lab—remembering how her fingers used to punch those keys with vigor. Now whenever she sat at a computer, her fingers froze—producing nothing.

"Since Adam's death," Cara said, "I . . . I can't . . . I . . . I haven't been able to write." She kept her eyes on the computer instead of her teacher.

"Cara, sometimes a person can use a difficult situation like this to express that pain. Let it out. Otherwise, it will tear you up inside. Maybe you could use your position with the newspaper to honor Adam in some way."

"No, you don't understand!" Cara tried to control the tone of her voice. She started to pace as she flailed her arms. "I . . . I have all these thoughts and ideas in my head, and I try to get them from my brain down to my fingers, but they won't come out. I physically cannot make them come out!"

She covered her face, and Ms. Turner scooped her into her arms.

"I'm so sorry, Cara. I'm sure that's so frustrating." It sounded like a canned comment, but it seemed genuine coming from her. After a moment, Ms. Turner went on, "I know you're hurting, but I also have to be fair . . ."

"Stop. You don't have to say it, Ms. Turner." Cara pulled her journalism badge out of her purse—the one that got her into every school event to cover the stories. She rubbed the corner with her thumb for a few seconds and then handed it over. "I'll have my counselor put me in a study hall during this hour instead."

~

FEBRUARY.

What an awful month. In Ohio, by the time February shows up, it feels like it's been winter for about seventeen months. Spring is so close on the calendar but never seems to arrive. Everything is cold, frozen, and dead.

Ironically, despite the gloomy weather, this particular February day was one Cara would categorize as "okay." She made it to all of her classes, the counselor didn't bother her, and she actually accomplished some work in study hall. During homeroom that day, the seniors had to meet in the auditorium where guidance counselors went over admissions reminders for college.

College.

Cara hadn't thought about college since Adam's accident. With graduation only three months away, she needed to finalize her plans, especially if she wanted to go to Wilmington. It was her ticket out of her house, and a chance at a fresh start. She had to bring it up at home that evening, but her father's last response about college was so hateful and ran deep. He was drunk, she had to remind herself. Plus, she should have nothing to worry about— they'd been saving for college since she was a baby.

When Cara got home, she went through her room and gathered all the pamphlets and information she had on UNCW. When she went down to heat up a microwave dinner that evening, her mother—in dress clothes—was washing dishes in the sink. She seemed to be in a good mood for once. What were the odds they would both feel better than usual in a month like February?

"You're all dressed up," Cara said. "Are you going somewhere?"

"Didn't I tell you? I joined a Bunco group with some ladies in the neighborhood. We meet on the second Monday of every month to play."

"Bunco? Uh . . . no, you didn't tell me about that."

"Well, it's a great time. There are twelve of us, and we each take turns hosting every month. My turn will be in May. You should get a group of friends together to play. It's real fun."

Friends? Cara didn't have any friends, and if she did, she wouldn't suggest they play a game associated with middle-aged women, not even as an excuse to leave the house. Her mother was so delusional, but she had to keep the conversation sweet to bring up college.

"Right . . ." Cara tried to sound convinced. "Hey, I need to talk to you about some stuff."

The two of them never had much of a conversational relationship, but it was nearly nonexistent since November. Her mother kept her eyes on the dishes instead of her daughter.

"Okay, what is it? But make it fast. I can't be late."

Cara moved a little closer to the sink, hoping to catch her mother's eye. "I need to get on the ball with college stuff. With everything that's happened, I know I haven't done much of anything in the last three months, but I think I'm in a place where I'm finally ready. I still want to go to Wilmington in North Carolina and hoped we could go for a visit soon . . . maybe make a mother/daughter trip out of it. What do you think?"

Cara's mother finished wiping the glass in her hand and set it on the drying rack. She then grasped the edge of the sink, eyes closed as if in pain, and took in a deep inhale.

"If you aren't up for the trip," Cara continued, "I could just go by myself. Or with Angela Aether or something." She paused for a moment to make sure she showed her appreciation. "I know it's a long way away—I'm just so grateful you guys are able to send me to college where I've dreamed of going—"

"There's no money for college, Cara." Still gripping the sink, her mother bent forward like she was about to be sick.

The words came out of her mother's mouth so abruptly that Cara was sure she didn't hear it correctly. She tried not to raise her voice. "What are you talking about?"

Cara's mother turned around and looked pointedly at her daughter. "There's no possible way we can send you to Wilmington, or just about anywhere for college. There's no money, no savings account. It's all gone."

"But Dad just said back in November that I could go wherever I wanted because you've been saving up since I was born. And you said that was part of the reason why you got this part-time job. So that was all a lie?"

For the first time, Cara could remember, her mother looked ashamed. "Not necessarily a lie, Cara."

"Then, where did all that money go, Mom?"

"Every time I got a paycheck, your father took it."

She didn't sound like she intended to finish this sentence with an explanation. Cara's entire being felt hollow, afraid to hear the answer, but she asked again anyway. "Where did all the money go?"

Her mother looked at the floor for a long time before she finally met Cara's eyes. "Your father drank it."

They stared at each other—their eyes exchanging feelings of hurt, embarrassment, and anger. And then, without another word, her mother left for Bunco.

Cara stood silent in the still, empty house.

This felt like another death. Not with the same severity of losing a person, but it was losing a dream. Cara knew she wasn't entitled to have her parents pay for anything. It was the false sense of hope, the betrayal, and despite what her mother claimed, the lies. Fake. All these material possessions they owned, the over-the-top parties, the country club memberships—all to impress people they didn't even like. She thought back to the lights going out right before the Homecoming dance last year.

Were they actually broke this whole time?

Four of the five stages of grief—Denial, Anger, Bargaining, and Depression—started to fill Cara at once, tugging at each other for which one got to dominate her feelings. The one emotion she didn't feel, the stage she knew she'd never feel, was Acceptance. How could she accept that her parents would lie for so long about something like this?

She looked at the liquor cabinet, and the only feeling to remain was intense anger. It was like she was a teapot that began to boil over, and she needed somewhere for the emotion to go.

Cara opened the liquor cabinet and pulled out a bottle of her father's favorite whiskey, Old Forester 1897, and stared at it for a long time in her hands. This bottle represented so many broken promises and false hopes in her life. The cost of this and the gallons that came before it could have paid for several college credit hours. She looked at all the top-shelf bottles of liquor—they would have covered at least a semester's worth of classes.

After taking in a deep breath, she screamed with every ounce of her core, then threw the bottle against the wall—shattering it to pieces. Cara grabbed and threw another bottle. And another bottle. She couldn't stop. Screams persisted with every throw, breaking the shot glasses, the wine glasses, the whiskey glasses.

She continued until every ounce of energy from her body was depleted, and all that remained were shards of glass and coat of alcohol on her mother's freshly mopped kitchen floor.

PART III

34

FROZEN SPOONS

November 9, 1999

"Y ou can do this."
Cara gave herself a pep talk as she lay on the living room floor of her bare apartment with frozen spoons over her eyelids. It was an attempt to reduce the swelling after all the crying she'd done the night before.

Today was the second anniversary of Adam's death.

Acceptance is the stage of grief that eventually sticks for most of the year. It doesn't mean being okay with the loss—it simply means a person finally realizes the situation is real and can begin functioning without that person they loved more than their whole existence.

Cara had carried on with her life. She moved out of her parents' house to an apartment above her landlord's garage. Working as a server at the Applebee's in Bellbrook made her realize she didn't want a career in the food industry, so her best solution to avoid that was college.

UNCW was no longer an option, and she refused to go into debt and live like her parents, so she enrolled herself at Sinclair Community College. It was cheap enough to pay cash for tuition. She didn't do much outside of work and school. Instead of going out with coworkers or classmates, Cara usually came home to her apartment—content with her face in one of the hundreds of books she owned.

On most days, she was fine. But these milestone dates caused the other stages of grief to creep back in.

Cara took the spoons from her eyes and turned toward the digital clock that rested atop a neatly stacked tower of books. It read 9:18 A.M.

She had a 9:00 A.M. class.

She turned her gaze back towards the popcorn ceiling and put the spoons back on her eyes.

"You can do this," she repeated.

~

THAT AFTERNOON, Adam's mother opened her front door to see Cara on the other side.

"I thought today would be easier than last year," Cara said, "but it's not."

Mrs. Aether pulled her into a tight embrace. "I know, sweetie. I know." Her hot tears burned Cara's cheek—neither of them in a hurry to pull away.

She eventually invited Cara in and poured her a cup of coffee. It had been a few months since Cara had gone over to the Aethers', and the way the light hit the countertops was different than she remembered.

"Will you tell me a memory you have of Adam? Maybe one of your favorite ones? Or something I wouldn't know?" Mrs. Aether asked.

Cara held on to the coffee mug and thought about what to share. There were so many memories. "When we were kids, we used to stay up way past our bedtimes and talk to each other through our bedroom windows."

Mrs. Aether smiled and took a sip from her mug.

"We even snuck out a few times. But we didn't go anywhere, just the yard between our houses."

"I knew you did," Mrs. Aether said.

"You did?"

"Sure." She enjoyed Cara's surprise. "But I never punished him or stopped it. I knew you needed him."

~

THEY SHARED MORE memories of Adam as the sun inched across the sky. Mrs. Aether told stories from when he was a baby, and Cara told of his shenanigans at school. It was healing for both of them. When the afternoon had become evening, Mrs. Aether abruptly changed the subject. "We never went on that vacation."

"What vacation?" Cara asked.

"The college money saved for Adam. Since he had a full ride to UNC, Bruce and I were going to take that money and travel . . . but we never did."

"Maybe you guys should start planning it—"

"No, it wouldn't feel right," Mrs. Aether interrupted. "We've talked about it a lot recently, and that money should be used for what it was intended—college."

Cara didn't understand.

"We have enough money in that account to send a student to just about any university in America. We feel one of the best ways to honor Adam is to take that money and send his best friend to her dream school in Wilmington."

Cara lost her breath. "What? No. I couldn't do that. I couldn't take away your dream vacation."

"Cara, nothing would make us happier than to do this. Besides, you'll be transferring as a sophomore. I'm sure we'll have enough left for a vacation." She paused and set down her mug. "Please let us do this. We need to do this for you. I know it's what Adam would want."

It was the kindest thing she'd known anyone to do, and they were doing it for her. Trying to process it all, she looked back at Adam's mom.

"When can we go?"

~

CARA HAD NEVER VISITED Wilmington before. She only knew about it through the Aethers' descriptions, pictures from Angela, and pamphlets she received in the mail. Angela and Mrs. Aether escorted her there on a last-minute flight on Thursday night right after her last class. Cara found someone to cover her shifts at work and ditched class again on Friday. She was worried about getting admitted to Wilmington on short notice, but the Aethers were well known within the university and called in some favors.

Wilmington was better than she had dreamed. The town had

a mixture of an east coast vibe and a southern charm. The campus featured colonial-style buildings with towering white pillars against red brick. The admissions counselors and professors were all so welcoming. Downtown was an adorable cluster of eclectic buildings with horse-drawn trolley rides and a beautiful river-walk along Cape Fear. A major bonus was its proximity to Wrightsville Beach, and Cara had never seen the ocean before.

That Friday afternoon, Cara met with an advisor. He looked over her transcript from Sinclair Community College and made suggestions for what she should sign up for at Wilmington.

"What's your major?" Dr. Kurtz asked.

Cara, who had planned to major in English since she was a young girl, responded with, "Undecided." She still hadn't been able to write since Adam's death.

"You're about to finish your sophomore year, and you're still undecided?"

"Yes, sir."

"Your transcripts look good, except you have no English or literature courses."

Cara didn't respond.

"You realize you have to take a minimum of nine language arts credits to earn a degree, no matter what your major, right?"

"Yes, sir." She paused. "I kind of struggle in that subject. I guess I've been avoiding it."

Dr. Kurtz leaned over and showed her a list of all the language arts classes available. "What's one you feel you could handle this next semester?"

She pondered the options:

> Composition I
> Creative Writing
> Foundations of Literary Analysis
> Intro to Journalism
> Intro to Literary Studies
> Intro to Professional Writing
> Poetry

"I think I could do poetry," she said with a slight quiver in her voice, trying to hide the fear of writing again.

"Poetry? Interesting choice," he said. "Most students avoid that class like the plague."

~

TRANSFERRING to Wilmington halfway through sophomore year, Cara didn't want to live on campus with the freshmen. Even though she was only a year older, the past two years forced her to mature in ways they'd never understand. Downtown was only five miles from campus, so she decided to live there and commute. The old buildings had been revitalized over the past decade. Many structures that had former obligations as auto parts stores or old ice houses were turned into charming apartments and restaurants.

Cara found a place on Dock Street called The Livery, which used to be just that—a livery stable constructed in 1914 that was converted into eleven studio apartments. Mrs. Aether encouraged her to rent something larger, but Cara didn't have enough possessions to fill a regular-sized apartment anyway, and she liked that a studio would keep her from collecting more than the essentials. She had lived her whole life in fake luxury and was ready to live minimally.

They signed the papers, and her new lease would start on January 1, 2000.

New state.

New college

New apartment.

New year.

New century.

New millennia.

New beginnings.

New Cara.

35

LAUNDROMAT

January 1, 2000

The world didn't come to an end as predicted when the clocks hit midnight on January 1, 2000.

New Year's Eve fell on a Friday night that year. When the Gregorian calendar was developed, did they do that on purpose? It couldn't have been better timing. Everyone would have the entire weekend to figure out how to survive like Neanderthals, keep the world from ending, and return to work by eight on Monday morning.

While everyone else partied like it was 1999—and it was— Cara said a brief goodbye to her parents, a heartfelt goodbye to the Aethers, and drove her blue Jeep through the Great Appalachian Valley of Ohio, West Virginia, and Virginia, until she came to the southern part of North Carolina. There was no one she cared to spend that evening with—she wanted to get to Wilmington as soon as she could.

The road trip took nearly ten hours. Cara had a stack of Dave Matthews CDs on the passenger seat that she popped in and out of her stereo for the duration of the trip, and she got to the point where she didn't even have to move her eyes from the road to make a change. She loved all of his albums, but her favorite was *Live at Luther College with Tim Reynolds*. She preferred live albums over studio perfection any day.

Somewhere in Virginia, her favorite song, "#41," began to

play. She turned up the volume to sing along when a few lines hit her like emotional shrapnel.

Cara shut off the music and pulled over to the side of the highway to collect herself as thoughts of turning around crept in. If she headed back now, she could probably make it to Charleston, West Virginia before she needed to get a hotel. She could be back to Ohio by late afternoon the next day.

Keep going, she told herself. *There's a new life for you in Wilmington . . . you have to go.*

The highway ahead, stretching over miles of hills, waited for her—called to her. It wanted to lead her to the rest of her life.

After a few deep breaths, she turned the key in the ignition and took her own advice.

∼

TWENTY MINUTES BEFORE MIDNIGHT, Cara exited the highway to get gas in the small town of Benson, North Carolina, an hour and a half away from Wilmington. No one was working, but there was a Coke machine outside the gas station, and she needed some caffeine to keep her awake. She stretched her legs, rested her aching back against the Jeep, and took long, slow gulps from the can as she waited for the tank to fill. The air was chilly but not bitter cold like she was used to in Ohio during that time of year— something she could get used to, for sure. In the distance, she noticed a brightly lit building. It was a twenty-four-hour coin laundromat and the only thing that appeared to be open other than the bars.

Through the windows, she could see whitewashed walls and a television playing for no one.

Cara got back into her Jeep and drove toward the light of the laundromat—the graveled parking lot crunched under her tires.

It was so bright on the inside, it felt like daytime against the dark night. Cara couldn't understand why it was even open. Did they expect anyone to actually do their laundry on a night like this?

But then again, there she was.

On the TV, Dick Clark spoke over the noise of hundreds of thousands in the elated crowd, which looked like a forest of people.

Cara crawled on top of a washing machine and held her knees

to her chest while she waited for the ball to drop. No one to kiss. Completely companionless.

She laughed at the future conversations she'd have:

So, where were you at the turn of the millennium?

Alone in a laundromat.

~

EVEN THOUGH IT WAS A HOLIDAY, the landlord of The Livery—her apartment complex—had arranged a time for Cara to pick up her keys. He lived a few apartments down and was heavily hungover when she knocked that late morning. He practically threw the keys at her, slammed the door, and yelled, "Come by later if you have questions."

Cara unloaded her Jeep that contained everything she owned —a few dishes, bedding, toiletries, clothes, books, and Adam's blanket, which the Aethers gave her when she left. The studio thankfully included all large appliances, a bed, and a couch, so she didn't have to haul or buy any of those. As she made her last trip from her vehicle, a petite redhead about her age with a bounce in her step moved toward Cara in the courtyard.

"Oh. My. Word. Are you my new neighbor?"

Her reaction was a stark contrast from her landlord's. Cara couldn't handle that level of enthusiasm after her long trek—or maybe ever.

"Uh, maybe. I'm in apartment six."

"Oh. My. Word. I'm in apartment five! What's your name? I'm Trenna. Where did you move from? Do you have any friends here? Do you need a job? My boss is hiring."

Cara waited for her to stop talking. "I'm Cara. I just moved here from Ohio to attend UNCW."

"College? That's so awesome. School was never my thing, but I wish I could go! And Iowa? What brings you all the way from Iowa?"

"Ohio," Cara corrected. "And that's not really a conversation to have with someone I've just met. I'll probably talk about it after I encounter you at least thirty-four more times." Trenna stared blankly at Cara's attempt to be funny. She changed the subject. "It's never too late to try school, by the way—you should enroll in a class sometime and see how it goes."

Trenna spewed more words, but Cara tuned her out as she

thought about everything she needed to accomplish that day—like finding a job. The Aethers were taking care of her tuition, books, and apartment, but she still needed her own money for living expenses. She had only saved a few hundred dollars before putting in her two weeks' notice at Applebee's, and after the gas for the trip, a large chunk of that was already gone. She wasn't sure she could handle much more of this girl, but she ended up asking, "Wait, did you say your boss was hiring?"

"Yes! I'm a server at the Dixie Grill! It's only a few blocks away."

"The Dixie Grill? What kind of place is that? Do you have an Applebee's around here?"

Dear goodness, have I already picked up the habit of asking multiple questions at once from this Trenna chick?

"Oh, there are hardly any chain restaurants in Wilmington. They like to keep everything local around here. The Dixie Grill is a dive, but it's probably the most famous place in the whole town. It's been used in movies. Some guy . . . Arthur something . . . wrote a play that became a movie and was filmed there. *Everybody Wins*, I think."

"Arthur? As in Arthur Miller who wrote *Death of a Salesman*? *The Crucible*? *All My Sons*?"

"Yeah . . . uh . . . I was never good at literature . . ."

"Well, I heard *Everybody Wins* was a pretty crappy film, but that's still cool, I guess."

"Oh, people go nuts about it. The Dixie Grill is always busy, so you'll make a ton of money. Come on, I'll introduce you to Nikoleta."

Before she could ask who Nikoleta was, Trenna grabbed her arm, and they were off.

∾

THE DIXIE GRILL had a traditional bar full of regulars and teal cushioned booths that screamed 1960s. Grease splatters stained the ceiling and crusted in the corners of the floor. It was the kind of place where customers felt like they might need a tetanus shot when they left, but they went anyway because the food was so good.

Nikoleta, she soon found out, was the matriarch of the Greek family who owned the restaurant. After Trenna introduced her,

Nikoleta spoke in short, direct sentences, which both intimidated and endeared her to Cara.

"You ever served before?"

"Yes, ma'am."

"You friends with 'Bouncy' here?"

"Yes, ma'am."

"You as hyper as her?"

"Definitely not, ma'am."

"Hmm, well, I do need some more servers. When can you start?"

Trenna had landed Cara a job within minutes of meeting her. Maybe she wasn't so bad after all.

36

PHOENIX

For the next two and a half weeks, Cara trained and worked over forty hours a week at The Dixie Grill before classes started after Martin Luther King Jr. Day. Because of this, she was too tired to explore Wilmington—she reverted to her habits of returning to her apartment alone where she would curl up with Adam's blanket and read until she fell asleep.

Cara was anxious for school to begin. She wanted to dig into deep conversations with like-minded people, but she also wanted to keep to herself. Interacting with others would likely lead to her having to open up about her past, and that was a door Cara wanted to remain closed. Maybe she could blend in and no one would notice her.

Her first class was Poetry 203 at 10:00 A.M. with Dr. Wilkes in Morton Hall, one of her favorite parts of campus. That building sat directly across from Leutze Hall, and between the two buildings were towering white pillars and a charming fountain where students congregated between classes.

She entered room 106. It was smaller than her high school classrooms.

Great, no place to hide.

She hadn't considered that since it was a 200 level, and since it was poetry, the class was bound to be small. It was evident that most of the students already knew each other—probably all English majors with similar schedules. They sat in clusters, catching up on each other's winter breaks. They could not have been more stereotypical. Cara felt like she was at a Woodstock-esque revival for stoned poets.

It was equal parts entertaining and irritating.

Their pretentious conversations became more heavily filled with grandiose words the longer the dialogue lasted as if they were trying to impress their classmates. And as they listened, they looked like their companion had suddenly told them their deepest, darkest secret, when really they were just describing the new flavored potato chips they ate at a Christmas party.

Hearing these conversations solidified her desire to be invisible, so she pulled out her notebook and started doodling. Maybe if she didn't make eye contact, people would leave her alone.

Then Cara sensed a body sit next to her. "You new here? I've never seen you before. Are you an English major? You must be a transfer. I'm Will—Lit. major."

Yeesh. Will was like a male version of Trenna with his consecutive questions. He had a bad bowl cut parted down the middle and dressed like a guy who wanted people to think he skateboarded but never actually had. His glazed over red eyes indicated he had smoked a joint right before class.

After his interrogation, Cara introduced herself and made small talk with Will out of politeness. But suddenly, she felt a strange magnetism and turned her eyes toward the door.

It was as if he entered in slow motion so Cara could take in every detail. Average height, thin but muscular build, and the lightest blue eyes she'd ever seen that contrasted his long thick eyelashes. His dark curly hair was pulled back into a thick ponytail—Cara didn't normally like ponytails on guys, but he pulled it off. He reeked of confidence and mystery.

The sight of him made Cara's breath stop for a moment. Her heart pumped faster, and flutters burst in her stomach. She looked down at her doodles so she wouldn't be caught staring and drooling over this dude. Never had she had such an instant attraction to someone before.

In the background, Will was still yapping about how much he loved *Walden* by Henry David Thoreau. She hated *Walden*—it was the most boring piece of literature she'd ever read, and Will's conversation was equally dull. She politely continued to smile and nod as she zoned out his words to listen to whatever conversation Mr. Mystery Man was about to have.

A small co-ed group greeted him. "Reid! How was your break?"

Reid, his name is Reid. Remember that.

She couldn't make out all the words of their conversation, but it sounded like he had gone on a cruise. His smile had adorable creases at the corners of his mouth, and there was an ageless handsome look about him.

Dr. Wilkes entered. She had a young face, but it looked like she had conducted a bad perm on her hair, which made her appear old. She was either forty or seventy. Her countenance suggested she would rather be in this poetry class more than anywhere else in the world. She gave no greeting or introduction; rather, she stood in front of the class until they quieted.

"What is a poet?" she asked.

At first, the class waited for her to go into a philosophical rant, but then it became clear this wasn't a rhetorical question. The class shared responses like:

"A poet is someone who writes songs without music."

"A poet is someone who sees the world and makes art out of words."

"A poet is someone who sees beauty in everything."

Dr. Wilkes nodded emphatically with each response.

Then a deep, buttery voice spoke. "I don't mean to be a downer, but I recently came across a great quote regarding this by the Danish philosopher, Søren Kierkegaard. Do you mind if I read it?"

It was Reid.

"By all means, please do," Dr. Wilkes said.

Reid pulled out a copy of *Either/Or* by Kierkegaard and thumbed through the pages until he found it. Then he read:

"What is a poet? An unhappy man who hides deep anguish in his heart, but whose lips are so formed that when the sigh and cry pass through them, it sounds like lovely music . . . And people flock around the poet and say: 'Sing again soon'—that is, 'May new sufferings torment your soul but your lips be fashioned as before, for the cry would only frighten us, but the music, that is blissful.'"

The air from Cara's breath left her lungs at his reading. It was so poignant. She had never heard that quote before and jotted down the book's title so she could check it out.

"Basically," Reid went on, "a poet is someone who endures anguish and suffering, but who can turn his pain into something pleasurable for the reader. Poems can be cute or about love, but I still think those are able to be light because they've come out of the dark. Not the most uplifting observation, but this quote definitely holds true for me."

As Dr. Wilkes complimented his insightful comments, Cara became lost in her intrigue with this Reid guy and also wondered why she took this class. Most of her old poems centered around suffering—exactly what she wanted to forget. She couldn't imagine pulling out anything but pain from deep inside her for any new poetry.

Eventually, the professor's words became audible to her again. "Before we go any further, I want to rearrange the desks." Everything she said was full of passion, adding dramatic gestures for emphasis. "Poetry is so personal, and it takes guts to share what has emerged from our souls—the hidden corners of our spirit. We need to develop a trust and community with each other, and that won't happen in rows. It happens in circles! Circles allow you to make eye contact with everyone. So take your desks and let's form a circle right now."

They rearranged the room, and Reid ended up right across from Cara. It was difficult for her to keep her eyes off of him.

"I like to call this the Circle of Comfort. Any and all observations are welcome and safe here." Dr. Wilkes sounded like a preschool teacher. "Our goal here is to practice analysis of poetry, write poetry, and—most importantly—gain a deeper appreciation for poetry."

She went over class policies, the grading scale, and what they were expected to produce. "Throughout the semester, you will write in a weekly journal, create a poetry portfolio, and read at least four original poems out loud. When you share your poems, you must provide some kind of visual so we can follow along because it's important to *see* the poem when we *hear* the poem. So much meaning can come from the typography." She closed her eyes and clenched her fists when she said that last part like she was reciting a charismatic prayer.

The realization of having to write and share her writings made Cara want to vomit. She tried to calm herself with deep breaths.

"To create this Circle of Comfort, let's go around and introduce ourselves and say why you're taking the class and something fun to let us know each other better. Why don't you share where you were at the turn of the millennium? Right when the clock struck midnight."

Nearly every student said they were at some New Year's Eve party, but their answers for why they enrolled in the class varied. More than half said they took this class because they were an English major and it was required, a few said they really enjoyed poetry, and one person said, in all seriousness, because they wanted to change the world. Cara squeezed her eyes shut instead of rolling them.

When it got to Reid's turn, he said, "Hey, I'm Reid Phoenix."

Reid Phoenix? What a sexy sounding name.

He went on: "I'm an English major. I'm not sure what I want to do with it yet, but I feel like English classes help you explore the world and yourself more than any other subject. I love poetry and would have taken this course even if it wasn't required for my major. Oh, and for New Year's Eve, I was in the hospital."

The hospital?

He didn't elaborate, and Cara couldn't tell if he was joking or not.

When it got to Cara, she said, "Hi, I'm Cara. I'm still undecided on my major, and I'm only taking this class because I need the English credit."

"And what about New Year's? How did you ring in the turn of the millennium?" Dr. Wilkes prompted.

Cara had to laugh on the inside, thinking about the scenario she had played in her head a few weeks prior. Not only had someone asked her the question, she had to answer in front of the entire class.

"I was actually alone in a coin laundromat in some tiny town upstate."

She didn't elaborate either.

37

ORANGES

That afternoon, a knock on Cara's door woke her from a nap.

"Hey! How was your first day of class? Did you get lost? Did you make any friends? Are the professors tough? Were there any cute guys? I bet college guys are sooooo cute!"

Cara wanted to slam the door in Trenna's face and go back to her nap, but she also kind of wanted to engage in this conversation. She had never really talked to another girl about boys before. So she widened the door to let Trenna in. She had learned to wait for Trenna to ask all of her questions first, and then Cara answered them in order.

"My first day was pretty good. Surprisingly, I only got lost once. I didn't make any friends, except one kinda annoying guy in my poetry class talked to me. The professors were about as tough as I expected. And there were zero cute guys."

"What? How is that possible?" Trenna was indignant.

"Well . . . there was this one cute guy . . ."

Trenna shrieked. "Oh. My. Word. Tell me all about him!"

Cara sat on her bed. "I don't know . . . I wouldn't say he's the hottest guy I've ever seen or anything, but as soon as I saw him, I felt this instant attraction to him. He just seems so . . . mysterious."

"So, love at first sight? That is so romantic!"

"Whoa, I never said anything about love. I only said I felt an attraction. It was weird. I've been attracted to guys at first glance before, but this was different. It was like this magnetism, and I literally sensed his presence as he walked through the door."

Trenna flung herself onto the bed, acting like she had passed out. "Nope. It's love. Love at first sight." She grabbed her head with both hands like she couldn't believe the information she'd just heard and wanted to keep it from seeping out. "What a best first day of school!"

Cara tried to calm the excitement. "I mean, I guess. All I did was see a guy."

"Wait." Trenna shot back up. "You didn't talk to him? You didn't give him your number?"

"What? No. Trenna, it was the first day of class. I'm not going to randomly go up to some guy, who didn't even notice me, by the way, start chatting him up and slip him my number. That would make the rest of the semester ridiculously awkward."

"Or ridiculously awesome because you would be dating the whole time! Cara, you can't blow your chance on this. It's love!" Trenna jumped up off the bed using large gestures as if her overly exclamatory sentences weren't enough.

Cara's first girl-talk about boys amped up way more than expected. She tried to change the subject. "Well, that's the last thing I need to worry about right now. I have to do a ton of writing for this class, and one of the requirements is to share our original poetry in front of everyone."

"Well, what's wrong with that? Oh, are you afraid of what's-his-name hearing your personal writings? Wait . . . what *is* his name?"

"His name is Reid. I'm pretty sure his last name is Phoenix."

"*Reid Phoenix*?" Trenna threw herself onto the bed again. "That is *such* a sexy name!"

Finally, something Cara agreed with.

"No, the issue is I can't write."

"Wait, what do you mean you can't write? Didn't you tell me you were part of the school newspaper in high school?"

Cara had forgotten she'd told Trenna that detail. She didn't want to go into what had changed—she wanted to start over in Wilmington and not relive the heartache and memories. She was still so broken. It seemed better to let the pieces stay where they lay.

$\sim$

STUDENTS SPENT the next several poetry classes analyzing poems instead of writing—similar to Ms. Turner's Socratic seminars. Cara appreciated that these discussions went beyond what her high school classmates were capable of, but sometimes these poetry students were a little too much for her. These people thought everything was deep about everything. They would say things like, "I think the poet used a plethora of lowercase i's to symbolize the precipitation he was referring to."

But Dr. Wilkes loved all comments, no matter how ludicrous, and the rest of the class nodded along as if it was the most profound suggestion they'd ever heard. It gave other students courage to come up with their own attempts at analysis.

"Yeah, and that makes me think the poet created a special typography with the last line, making all the words go across in a straight line—probably to symbolize the ground."

Don't most poems—and prose—have words arranged in a straight line? Cara wanted to say, but she refrained. She didn't have the energy or the guts to stand up to strangers who were perfectly nice people. Besides, it was entertaining to sit back and listen to them go.

She had no personal contact with Reid yet, but she made a point to observe him while in the Circle of Comfort. She discovered he didn't get sucked into the silly analyses. He chose his words carefully, saving his responses for when he had something insightful to say.

One of the poems Dr. Wilkes had them read was "Oranges" by Gary Soto.

> The first time I walked
> With a girl, I was twelve,
> Cold, and weighted down
> With two oranges in my jacket.
> December. Frost cracking
> Beneath my steps, my breath
> Before me, then gone,
> As I walked toward
> Her house, the one whose
> Porch light burned yellow
> Night and day, in any weather.
> A dog barked at me, until
> She came out pulling

Breathtaking

At her gloves, face bright
With rouge. I smiled,
Touched her shoulder, and led
Her down the street, across
A used car lot and a line
Of newly planted trees,
Until we were breathing
Before a drugstore. We
Entered, the tiny bell
Bringing a saleslady
Down a narrow aisle of goods.
I turned to the candies
Tiered like bleachers,
And asked what she wanted -
Light in her eyes, a smile
Starting at the corners
Of her mouth. I fingered
A nickel in my pocket,
And when she lifted a chocolate
That cost a dime,
I didn't say anything.
I took the nickel from
My pocket, then an orange,
And set them quietly on
The counter. When I looked up,
The lady's eyes met mine,
And held them, knowing
Very well what it was all
About.

Outside,
A few cars hissing past,
Fog hanging like old
Coats between the trees.
I took my girl's hand
In mine for two blocks,
Then released it to let
Her unwrap the chocolate.
I peeled my orange
That was so bright against
The gray of December

That, from some distance,
Someone might have thought
I was making a fire in my hands.

Students brought up obvious observations about the universal nervousness of a first date, the longing to not be embarrassed, and the imagery of color against the bleak winter.

Cara finally offered her first insight. "I think we're overlooking the importance of the breathing imagery in this poem."

Dr. Wilkes seemed surprised by the sound of Cara's voice. "Interesting, Cara. How so?"

"Well, he mentions it twice, which is a hint to its significance. The first time is to provide the imagery that it's cold outside when he describes 'My breath / Before me then gone.' The second time is a simple glimpse of their interaction. They're 'breathing / Before a drugstore.' There's no indication that any communication takes place on this walk. They're probably nervous, but I like to think that they're simply comfortable with each other. Just breathing with someone suffices at times."

She saw Dr. Wilkes smile in approval, but before she could comment, a deep, buttery voice chimed in.

"I had some notes similar to Cara's."

It was Reid. And he had said her name!

He continued. "The act of breathing is what I like to call 'simplexic.' It seems so simple because we don't have to think about it, but the function of the lungs is actually complex. Soto's mention of breathing is so subtle, but it's vital—it's like life. We don't recognize our own breath in the moment, but it's essential to our whole existence and what makes us take chances."

This time, Cara couldn't take her eyes off him, and she refused to turn away. When he finished speaking, he looked in her direction. For a moment, they were bound by their similar analyses. She stared into his piercing blue eyes that shot ice through her veins and gave him a warm smile.

He returned the expression.

38

HAIKU

C ara deeply hoped this class would help her pull out the words trapped inside her, but the approaching due date of sharing an original poem only caused anxiety to spread throughout her body.

The night before the first poem was due, Cara looked at her notebook that remained blank. Many times she sat and attempted to force the words to come through her hand and onto the page. But it never did. Sometimes she hid her notebook in her nightstand so she wouldn't have to think about it. She considered dropping the class but knew she couldn't do that—not when the Aethers had given her such a gift.

Her thoughts drifted to the Kierkegaard quote Reid had shared in class. The truth of it made her mad. Why should someone else enjoy the sweet music of her suffering?

Cara lay on her bed—pen in hand—and stared at the empty lines in front of her until she could keep her eyes open no longer.

∾

STUDENTS SHOWED up early the next day to make sure they had everything prepped to share their poetry. As Dr. Wilkes mentioned, everyone had to provide a visual so their classmates could read along as they listened. Students could write their poems on the board, bring handouts, or have it transferred on a transparency to show on the overhead projector.

One girl brought her own chalk and took up a considerable chunk of board space, writing words in different fonts, sizes, and colors. She even added pictures.

Dr. Wilkes handed out small squares of paper to each student. "These are Feedback Slips. After each poet shares their poem, you're to take a minute to write feedback on this paper. Tell them how it spoke to you, what you liked, what connections you might have with them, whatever you like. But keep it anonymous."

Cara found the task of writing valuable or even positive comments on the Feedback Slips excruciatingly difficult. Some of the poems were okay, but she expected more from a 200 level class. There was an overuse of clichés, lack of meter, and if she heard one more person use the word "abyss" in their poem, she was going to stab her ears with her dull pencil. If ever there was an overused word in poetry, it was that one.

Still, even though the slips were anonymous, she didn't want to be a jerk, so she succumbed to writing "Nice!" on each one.

She doodled in her notebook between presentations but stopped once Reid's smooth voice said, "I'll go next." When he placed a handout on Cara's desk, she realized it was the closest she'd been to him.

Reid stood at the front of the room. "I titled this poem 'The Chain.'" He cleared his throat and read:

> I cannot escape
> this chain on my chest,
> fastened through with an iron screw,
> holding tight the links
> to this chunk of granite,
> dragging the floor
> between my feet.
>
> I shuffle, bowlegged—
> the weight between my knees.
> I've stopped looking for the key.
>
> That is a lie.
> It is all I wander after—
> that and nothing else.

Cara was so sucked in by his words, it took her a moment to

come back to the reality of the room. She looked down at the Feedback Slip and finally felt words aching to come through her hand and wrote:

Wow! Beautifully cryptic metaphors.
You're quite the mystery.

She rose out of her seat to hand it to Reid and imagined a spark of electricity if their fingers were to touch.

As Cara was within reach of testing their conductivity, Dr. Wilkes said, "Cara, I believe you're the only one left to go today."

Anxiety now consumed her entire body and cut off her breath. She stood beside Reid's desk, the slip still in her hand, trying to think of some excuse as to why she hadn't done the assignment.

Dr. Wilkes interrupted Cara's panic. "On second thought, class is almost over for today. Would you mind starting the next class with your poem?"

Exhale.

"Yeah, sure," Cara said.

She quickly gave Reid the paper so she could get out of there. Their fingers never touched.

❧

THE NIGHT before the next poetry class, Cara toiled over the poem she had to present in the morning—the poem that remained unwritten. She'd kept Reid's poem in her notebook and pulled it out to read over several times—wondering at the metaphors, and then Reid, in general, consumed her thoughts.

She, of course, wanted to know if he had a girlfriend, his philosophical thoughts, and if he was really in the hospital on New Year's Eve. But she found herself wondering about the simple details of his life too. Like, did he prefer smooth or crunchy peanut butter? Did he let his toilet paper hang over or under? Did he love or hate Neil Diamond?

She scanned his poem again.

"I cannot escape / this chain on my chest . . ."

She reached for her notebook and a pen—and for the first

time in over two years, she squeezed out a few words onto the blank page.

~

THE NEXT MORNING, Cara passed out copies of her poem. She didn't have time to type it up and print it out, so she ran to the Xerox machine at the library to photocopy the page from her notebook — paying a nickel for each copy.

After each classmate received her handout, Cara took her spot at the front of the room and said, "I'm not much of a writer, so I just did a haiku."

quite the mystery
now my curiosity
i long to know you

She made no eye contact with anyone and walked back to her seat with a grin. That was possibly the ballsiest thing she'd ever done. Trenna was going to die when she told her about it. Cara's heart pounded so hard she was sure it showed in her temples. She wondered what the class thought — but more importantly, what Reid thought. The Feedback Slips started pouring in from her classmates. When Reid set his on her desk, she slid it to the side after he turned his back so she would know which was his.

Instead of paying attention to Dr. Wilkes's lecture, Cara caught her breath and turned Reid's slip over.

This says so much in so few words. I love it.
By the way, you're quite the mystery yourself.

She closed her eyes and tried to hide the smile that wanted to show on her face. The words from the lecture buzzed in the background.

~

WHEN CLASS ENDED, Cara tried to psych herself up to approach Reid. She had no idea what to say. Trenna suggested to give him her number. Was that all she needed to do? Should there be any small talk first? Should she bring up what he wrote on his Feedback Slip?

Students poured out of Morton Hall, and Cara stopped by the fountain, hoping to catch Reid. When he came out, they locked eyes, and she started to open her mouth—not sure of what might come out.

"Cara!"

She turned her head to see Will approach her from the left.

"Oh, no," she muttered.

And in no time, he was right by her side. "Hey! I really liked your poem, man. It reminds me of what Henry David Thoreau once wrote,

'Talk of mysteries! — Think of our life in nature, — daily to be shown matter, to come in contact with it, — rocks, trees, wind on our cheeks! The solid earth! The actual world! The common sense! Contact! Contact! Who are we? Where are we?'"

Cara was actually impressed by Will's ability to quote that on the spot, but she was more frustrated by his interruption. She looked to see if Reid had left. He hadn't—he was leaning against the building with a smirk as he looked at his feet. She wanted to end the conversation with Will as soon as possible without being rude. "Thanks," she said. "I recognize that quotation. That's from *The Maine Woods*, right?"

"Yeah! Not as good as *Walden*, but it's a close second. I take it you've read it? Do you think it's better than *Walden*? Did that happen to be the inspiration for your haiku?"

"Uhhh . . . sure," was all she could think to say to collectively answer all of Will's questions. She turned to look at Reid, who had started walking away.

"There's a get together at my apartment on Saturday," Will said. "If you want to come. I'm sure I could score you some free weed."

"Oh, sorry. I work all day Saturday. But I need to—"

"You have a job? I didn't know that. Is it on campus? What do you do?"

"I'm a server at the Dixie Grill."

Cara couldn't escape the grasp of all his questions. As she looked at Reid, his figure became smaller and smaller in the distance.

~

"OH! MY! WORD!" Trenna said that phrase over and over as she heard the story.

The Dixie Grill was slammed, so Cara had to patch bits and pieces of it to her whenever they had a spare moment brewing coffee or rolling silverware. She told her about Reid's poem, her response, her poem, his response. And Will, who ruined everything.

"Wait. Who is this other guy? Is he also in your class? Why did you keep talking to him?"

"His name is Will, and I couldn't stop talking to him because he asks questions in multiples just like you do all the time."

Trenna was oblivious to Cara's friendly jab. "And then this Reid guy just walked into the sunset? Never to be seen again? What are you going to do?"

"First of all, it was like eleven in the morning—no sunset. And I have no clue. I honestly don't know why I did that. I've never had a boyfriend before, and I certainly couldn't handle one right now."

Cara ended the conversation to take food to one of her tables. She then scanned her section—her eyes darting between customers to make sure she was caught up with everything. She remembered someone asked for a refill of decaf and went to the back to discover the decaf pot was empty, so she had to brew some herself.

While Cara filled the coffeepot with tap water, Trenna grabbed her arm. "Cara! Some guy with the most gorgeous eyes I've ever seen just walked through the door and asked to sit in your section!"

"What?" Cara couldn't register the words coming out of Trenna's mouth. She spun around to see Reid Phoenix saunter toward the bar.

"Oh! My! Word!" Cara had been around Trenna too much. She ducked down so she couldn't be seen. "That's him!"

Trenna ducked beside her. "Who?"

"That's Reid Phoenix!" She tried to whisper above the noise of the clanging dishes.

"That's him? You didn't tell me he had dark curls pulled back in a ponytail! That's as sexy as his name."

"Why is he going to the bar?"

"Your section's full!"

"So, what do I do?"

"Go over and say you heard he asked for you."

Cara tried to see her reflection against the coffee pot. She tucked the loose hairs from her ponytail behind her ears and pinched her cheeks to give them some color.

"Man, what you did is ballsy, but what he did is ballsier," Trenna said. "Now, make sure to act cool."

Cara grabbed the decaf coffee and stopped at her other table as not to appear in a rush to greet Reid.

What should I say to him?

Hey, you're Reid, right? You're in my poetry class. I'm so glad you're here because I've been dying to ask, do you let your toilet paper hang over or under? Oh, and while we're at it . . . Neil Diamond — love him or hate him?

She was hopeless.

Just talk to him like you would have talked to Adam, she finally told herself. And then she approached him.

"Hey, you. I heard you asked for me. What are you doing here?"

That sounded surprisingly normal.

Reid turned toward her and coolly rested his elbow on the bar. "Well, I don't have your number, and I was hoping to start the conversation we never got to have after class the other day. When do you get off work?"

Cara looked at the clock. "I'm working a double, so I'll probably be the first cut. I'd say in the next thirty minutes or so."

"There's a coffee shop that also serves ice cream a few blocks from here. It's open late if you'd like to join me when you're off."

Cara shivered on the inside. "Well, I probably smell like burnt toast and bacon grease, but my apartment's also just a few blocks from here. I can change and freshen up, then meet you there."

"Great. It's called Madison's. Head south a few blocks on Front Street. What do you drink? I'll order and get us a table."

"Okay. Hot tea with lemon and honey, please."

"Perfect. See you soon."

With that, he left. Cara turned her head slowly to look back at Trenna as her mouth dropped open.

Trenna exaggeratedly mouthed back, *Oh. My. Word.*

39

THE AGREEMENT

Cara rushed to her apartment after work and frantically tried on a dozen outfits—examining each in the full-length mirror. She settled on a slimming black turtleneck and flared jeans, applied more deodorant, splashed on some perfume, added silver hoops, and re-did her ponytail.

Conflicting thoughts of wanting to sprint there versus just crawling into a hole tugged at her mind.

She wanted to know everything about him but reveal nothing about herself. With each step she took toward the coffee shop, she convinced herself to turn around and stand him up. Cara stopped in the middle of the sidewalk to gather her feelings and breathe.

Then she saw it.

A ladybug landed on her shoulder.

Suddenly, Cara felt a sense of calm enter through every pore.

What was the point of coming to Wilmington if you're going to live the same, isolated life?

With every step, she now convinced herself to keep going until she arrived at Madison's Cafe.

When she opened the door, Reid's comforting, unfamiliar blue eyes were waiting for her in the back corner.

It was like seeing someone again for the first time.

She sat down across from him. Her hot tea was already on the table with lemon and honey on the side, and he had also gotten her a glass of ice water, which she sipped immediately after she said hello. She noticed that instead of a coffee or a tea, Reid had a large milkshake, but she was too distracted by his slight grin to ask him about it. The corners of his mouth were weakeningly adorable, and his eyes told her he was glad she was there. Everything about him balanced her unstable nerves, and she couldn't wait to hear the words he was about to speak as he opened his mouth.

"Excrement."

Cara almost spat out her water. "Excuse me?"

"That's what I think about the persona you try to give off in class—that you're not a good writer. That you're only taking the class for the English credit. I don't think any of that's true." He nonchalantly took a sip of his milkshake as he stared at her.

Cara was both impressed and annoyed. She took another drink of water to give her extra time to think of a response. "Okay . . . what makes you think that?"

"You're clearly well-read, you're prodigiously insightful, and you not only wrote a poignant poem in just seventeen syllables, you cryptically spoke directly to me within those syllables. You're also subconsciously dressed like a beatnik, which is a cute look, by the way."

"How do you know I'm well-read?" she tested.

"You recognized a quotation from *The Maine Woods* by Thoreau. No one's read that book. It's worse than *Walden*."

Cara was in awe of his observations. She poured the honey into her hot tea as she attempted to change the subject. "Well, it's good to hear we have something in common. I'm not a Thoreau fan either. That Will guy must think I am, though, because he talks to me about him constantly."

"It's pretty obvious he likes you."

"Will? Oh, no, no, no."

"What's wrong with Will?"

"For one, he's a major pothead, and I'm totally not into that. And, two . . . he's obsessed with Thoreau." She smiled.

"So liking authors from the Transcendentalism movement is a deal-breaker for you, huh?"

"Exactly. Except for Hawthorne. *The Scarlet Letter* is tolerable."

"See, you're proving my observations about being well-read the more you talk."

Cara looked down and laughed like she'd been caught. "Actually, even if Will weren't a Thoreau lover, I wouldn't date him." She hesitated to say what needed to come next. "Look, Reid, I'm a pretty broken person with a past I'm not ready to talk about yet. I've never been in a relationship, and now would not be the time to start one."

He leaned forward, interested, but said nothing.

Cara swallowed hard to say the rest. "I don't know if that's what's going on here, and I'm sorry if I led you on with my poem. I meant what I wrote. And please know I want to get to know you, but you don't want to date me."

Reid nodded. "This is kinda perfect."

What?

He had a way of making her feel at ease, but then he sure threw in some awkward statements.

"Excuse me again?"

"There's something about me that I'd rather keep hidden as well. It would be unfair for anyone to date me, so I don't want to get into a relationship either."

"Why did you ask me to come here, then?"

"Oh, I'm intrigued by you, Cara. But for now, let's not worry about each other's yesterdays or tomorrows. Let's get to know each other's todays. So why don't we agree to start a completely platonic, or even a shallow relationship, and we won't have to tell our pasts to each other. We'll rest assured that we can live in the present and not share our pain—unless we feel ready, of course."

This was an interesting proposition, and all of Cara's senses relaxed. "Okay. It's a deal. I guess we'll continue to be a mystery to each other."

"Honestly, that sounds alternatively appealing. We need to know at least some essentials about one other, though, right? Without getting too personal or giving anything away."

"Yeah, of course. What were you thinking?"

"Uh, I don't know . . . what's your favorite sandwich?"

"Yeah, that's way too personal."

He let out a deep belly laugh. Cara froze at the sound of it because his laugh was exactly like Adam's. Her reaction must have been awkward because Reid stopped to ask what was wrong.

She shook her head as if trying to wake from a trance. "Sorry, it's nothing. Your laugh . . . it just sounds identical to a friend of mine."

Reid leaned back.

She fought to bring herself back to the present. "Anyway, sorry. What am I supposed to answer? Sandwich? Yeah, I'd have to say a Reuben. Yours?"

"Good choice. I'd have to go with a classic club."

"Okay. Let's see . . . if you could change your name, what would you change it to?" Cara asked.

Reid had to think about this one for a moment. "Probably Jackson. You?"

"Either Katelyn or Danielle. I wouldn't mind being called Kate for short, but I wouldn't want to be called Dani."

"That's fair. Favorite novel?"

"Oh, boy. Too many. The first one that comes to mind though is *To Kill a Mockingbird*."

"Classic. Mine is definitely *Walden*."

Cara threw her head back and laughed. "Shut up. What is it really?"

"What if it was?"

"I think we've already established what would happen in that scenario earlier in this conversation."

Reid grinned. "Okay, so mine changes depending on my mood, but the one I've probably read the most is *On the Road* by Jack Kerouac, so I'll say that for today. Next question."

"Were you really in the hospital on New Year's Eve?"

Reid raised his eyebrow at her attempt with a personal question already. "I was. But I won't tell you why. Were *you* really alone in a laundromat?"

"Yes. But I won't tell you why, either."

He gave her a provocative smirk. "Fair enough. So, tell me. How accurate was I with my first observation? Without getting too personal, of course."

Cara circled her finger around the lip of her teacup as she thought of what to say and how to say it. "You were pretty accurate. I love language arts, and I used to write a lot. I was even the editor of the school newspaper. But like I said, something happened in my past, and it's like I've lost all ability to produce. The haiku for class was the first thing I've written in years, and it took every ounce of my energy. I enrolled in the poetry class in hopes to resurrect my writing again, but it's like I'm paralyzed."

She cringed at the sound of that word as a vision of Adam, motionless, on that football field entered her head.

Genuine sorrow filled his eyes as he saw her pain. "Wow . . .

I'm sorry. That must really suck." He looked down at his milkshake and fiddled with the straw. "So that's why you've put on a front, isn't it?"

Cara nodded.

"When's our next poem due?" he asked.

"In about two weeks."

He leaned in toward her. "Let me help you."

"Oh, Reid, no. I can't claim your work as my own. I would feel horrible."

"I didn't say I would write anything *for* you. I said I'd *help* you. Let me help you find your voice again." His eyes felt so genuine.

"Okay," she nearly whispered.

His grin came back. "You realize this means we have to spend a lot of time together, right?"

"That actually sounds great—but no personal stuff."

"Of course not." He took one last sip of his milkshake and sat back. "You know, there *are* a couple solid lines in *Walden*."

"That's not possible."

"No, seriously. Thoreau spent two years, two months, and two days of his life at Walden Pond because he wanted to live deliberately. He wrote, 'I wanted to live deep and suck out all the marrow of life.' That's how I try to live. And that's what we're going to do in the next two weeks."

He reached for her hand across the table.

"Starting now."

40

ABYSS

B efore she knew it, Cara was buckled into Reid's yellow SUV. As he turned the key in the ignition, he asked. "Is it okay to ask where you're from?"

She thought about it for a moment. "No."

"That's fair. Can you at least tell me if you're from Wilmington —or even North Carolina?"

"I'm from neither. I just moved to Wilmington New Year's Day and haven't had a chance to do or see hardly anything yet. When I'm not at school, I'm working."

"Then the first thing on your 'to-do list' is to cut back your hours. You need more time to experience life. Have you ever been to Britt's Donut Shop?"

As soon as she said, "No," his foot hit the gas for the thirty-minute drive to Carolina Beach. He explained on the way that he was more of a milkshake guy, but that experiencing these donuts was essential for the evening.

When they were a block away, the scent of vanilla glaze traveled through the air. Soon after, they encountered a line at least sixty people deep—*outside* the donut shop.

"This is insane! Are all these people waiting for the same donuts we are?"

"Don't worry. The trick is to sit at the bar. These people are waiting to get a bag to go. If you sit at the bar, you'll get served faster."

He was right. They sat at the bar and were waited on almost

immediately while the others still stood outside in the chilly air. "We'll take a bag of a half dozen donuts, please," Reid said.

"A half dozen? For just the two of us?"

"Trust me. You'll want more than one."

Cara saw a sign above the register: *Britt's Donut Shop — Since 1939.*

"So, what's so special about this place? They just serve glazed donuts, and they've been open for over sixty years?"

"They don't need to serve anything else. These are the best donuts you'll ever eat. You know the phrase 'melt in your mouth'? Well, whoever coined that phrase said it after they ate one of Britt's donuts."

They watched through the windowed walls as teenagers rolled, cut, fried, and glazed the donuts before their eyes. An older gentleman dropped a white paper bag in front of them. Reid grabbed it and stood up.

"We're leaving already?"

"Oh, we're not eating these here. One must eat Britt's donuts on the beach."

He grabbed her hand and led her to his favorite place on the boardwalk. There, he shut his eyes and inhaled deeply. "I came to UNCW so I could be close to this."

The wind off the waves was so strong that the smell of ocean water nearly replaced the scent of the donuts. The sea had already made itself a grave for the sun, and there was a deep, black vastness in front of them.

"You're not going to believe this, but I've never been to the ocean before," Cara said.

"Wait, so I get to be the one who introduced you to Britt's Donuts *and* the ocean? On the same night? You're really sucking the marrow out of life now."

He handed her a donut. It was still hot, and when she took a bite, that phrase "melt in your mouth" became a reality.

"Awh muh guash," she said, mouth stuffed with glazed dough, "awhmazhing!"

Reid watched her as she ate. "I don't mean to stare, but I will never get this moment back, and I don't want to forget it."

She shyly smiled back at him.

"You should take out your ponytail and let the wind run through it." Reid let his hair down. It was the first time she'd seen it that way. His tight, dark curls dropped right above his shoulder. She copied him by letting her own hair down.

"What do you think? About the ocean?" Reid asked.

Cara looked straight ahead, but there wasn't much to see except faint white ripples of surf hitting the sand in the darkness. "It's calming, but it's terrifying. Hearing its power, but not being able to see it, feels like staring into an abyss." Maybe that's why everyone in her poetry class used that word in their poems.

"Take off your shoes," he said.

"What?"

"Don't worry. Nothing's going to happen to them. Come on."

Without questioning further, she took off her shoes, and for the third time that night, Reid held her hand as he led her off the boardwalk and onto the beach—the bag of donuts still in his other hand.

The sand between her toes felt cold as they trudged through it for what felt like miles. Finally, they stopped at a spot far enough away from all the lights.

"Roll up your jeans," he said, "and stick your feet in the water."

"Reid, are you crazy? It must be freezing, and I can't get soaked."

"Do you trust me?"

"I honestly don't know yet."

He just smiled at her until she complied. They walked toward the water—it chilled her bones at the touch. Her toes rounded and tried to grasp the sand to keep her steady as the waves went back out.

"I want you to look out at the ocean," he said. "Can you find a metaphor in it?"

Cara stared ahead and thought for a long time. "It reminds me of grief."

"Okay, keep going," he invited.

She felt the words forming in her mind, collecting together, and forced them with all her might to come out. "It's so powerful. It could suck me right in and drown me if I let it. And it's so deep, and it's so wide that no matter how well I know how to swim, I would never reach the surface again. And it's so dark that even if I could come back up for air, I'd never find my way back."

She continued to look into the nothingness—hair flailing in the wind so wildly it lashed her face. Reid gently brushed her hair away with his hand, and when she looked at him, he pointed upward. Her eyes moved to see the entire sky peppered with thousands of the brightest stars she'd ever seen.

Then Reid recited:

> It is the dark
> and the distance
> that lets us see the stars.

In their silence against the crashing waves, he handed her another donut.

41

CHURCHES AND BIRCHES

There was a light knock on her door at 9:30 the next morning. When Reid walked Cara to her apartment at The Livery the night before, he told her he'd be picking her up in less than nine hours and to wear something nice—they were going to church.

Reid looked even more handsome in a white collared button-up shirt, khakis, and brown dress shoes. His hair pulled back gave a contradicting look to the dress clothes.

"Where exactly are we going?" she asked.

"The First Presbyterian Church on Third Street. You've seen it—it's the tallest church in town. And, fun fact, Woodrow Wilson's father was the pastor there in the 1800s."

"Then are we going for the history, or are you religious?"

"Are you?"

"Not really. I had a good friend who went to church, but my family only went on Christmas and Easter."

"I wouldn't consider myself religious, but I'd say I'm close with God. I go when I can out of reverence, but tend to church hop. I like to see their similarities, though they all think they're so different. They serve the same God with the same message. But going gives me a chance to reflect. I want you to come because it's important for you to know what you believe. Maybe you'll think it's a bunch of nonsense—well, at least you'll have that belief. That is usually an important inspiration for writing."

He held the door for her as they entered the church. The

vaulted ceilings made the sanctuary feel as vast as the dark ocean from the night before. Ornate stained glass windows left her eyes full as she tried to take in the beauty and sacredness of it all. They took a seat near the back, and Cara tried to focus on the sermon, but her mind continually wandered back to Adam and his beliefs.

Was he in heaven? What exactly did she believe?

The service ended with communion, and Cara felt as if she wasn't worthy to partake, but she broke the bread and dipped it in the wine anyway.

When they left the sanctuary, Reid asked, "Did you know it's a tradition for church-goers to go out for lunch after the service? It's kind of a competition to see who can arrive at the restaurants first. Will it be the Baptists? The Methodists? The Lutherans? Today we're Presbyterians, so we gotta win for them."

"Do we go to hell if we don't?" She winked.

"Maybe! That's why we have to hurry! How do you like seafood?"

"I don't really know," she said. She thought about home. On occasion, Cara joined her parents at the NCR Country Club to wine-and-dine her father's potential customers. Other than that, she didn't have a well-rounded palate as she mainly grew up on microwaved dinners.

"Well, part of sucking the marrow out of life is trying new things. Let's go."

They walked until they reached the Oyster Bar downtown on Dock Street.

Reid ordered a colossal sampler platter that included clams, mussels, crab legs, and of course, oysters. "You can't live by the ocean and not have seafood. This is caught fresh daily right here." He showed her how to crack crab legs and shuck oysters. "So, what did you think of the church service?"

"Three words that ran through my mind were peaceful, hallowed, and beautiful. It made me think a lot about the afterlife."

"What do *you* think happens after you die?" he asked.

"Are you sure that is an 'on-the-surface' level question?"

He leaned back in his seat. "That depends. Will your answer reveal what you want to keep secret?"

She considered that. "I guess not."

"Then it's a perfectly fair question," Reid said.

She struggled to crack a crab leg. "I don't know. I used to

think once you died, that was it. Your body just decayed in the ground. But then I thought about the people I love the most in this world. I can't imagine that happening to them, so I assume God wouldn't let that happen. What about you? Do you think about death and the afterlife?"

"I probably think about death more than the average person, but I try not to think about the afterlife too much. I mean, the thought of eternity isn't something our human minds can grasp. So I focus on the fact that God is loving, but he's also just."

"I like that." Cara pressed further. "Do you believe everything happens for a reason?" This was something she pondered a lot. It was such a common saying, but she couldn't think of any good reason why Adam should've died.

"Ugh, that hurts my brain as much as the concept of eternity. I guess it depends on if you think we humans actually have free will or not. If we do, then everything has happened by our own doing, and humans adapt and react accordingly. If we don't have free will, then we're just puppets to a greater being—and then, sure, everything happens for a reason because it's already premeditated. I'm a bigger fan of coincidences than fate."

Through more discussion, they agreed that theology was too overwhelming a topic to cover in one sitting, so they would spread it out over future meetings. Reid encouraged her to think about it more in between, though.

After they paid the bill, Cara asked, "What's on tap the rest of the day?"

Reid rubbed his chin as he thought of his response. "I'm not available in the afternoons—I actually have an obligation at a certain time every single day."

"Would telling me why break our on-the-surface rule?"

"Uh, yes. Very much so." He smiled. "But I can come by in the evening if you'd like."

It had been less than twenty-four hours since they'd started their first conversation, but knowing she wasn't going to have Reid to herself for the next few hours made her eager for more.

"Yes," she said. "I'd like that very much."

～

OVER THE NEXT WEEK, Cara and Reid spent every spare moment together that they could between classes, work, and his afternoon obligations. They went on horse and trolley rides, sang karaoke, strolled on the Cape Fear River Walk, toured antebellum mansions, and went on long drives to nowhere.

Trenna wanted details every time Cara returned home and asked the same questions: "Oh. My. Word. What did you guys do? Are you officially dating yet? Has he kissed you?"

Cara gave the same responses each time and considered recording herself on a cassette tape so she could just push play. "Trenna, we're not dating. We agreed that we both have some dark stuff from our past that we're still dealing with and don't want it to surface. Because of that, we agreed it wouldn't be fair to date. We just want to live life in the moment together with clean slates."

"Sorry, but that makes no sense," Trenna would always say back.

Cara would shrug and dismiss the criticism. It was a unique situation, and she didn't expect anyone else to understand.

~

THE NEXT SATURDAY, Cara was supposed to work a double but had someone cover the second half so she could spend time with Reid. She didn't really need the money—she'd saved enough from working so much before—and intended to have them cut her hours back for the future anyway. She needed more time to actually live.

"Where are we going today?" she asked when Reid came by her apartment.

"To my favorite place in the entire world."

They walked several blocks downtown until she saw a sign for Old Books on Front Street.

"Shut up. Is this a used book store?"

Reid smiled at her reaction and opened the door for her. There were shelves from floor-to-ceiling stuffed with dusty books and old chairs throughout the store so customers could curl up and read. As she walked in, Cara closed her eyes and inhaled deeply. "Ah. It smells so good in here!"

"It's the best smell there is—with ocean breeze as a close second. Come on, let me show you around."

He brought her to a jukebox in the middle of the store. "This doesn't play music. It's full of audiobooks on CD. He put in four quarters, and a narrator's voice came through speakers hidden throughout the store.

"Hey, this is *Fahrenheit 451.*" Cara ran her fingers over the machine. "I love Bradbury."

Reid's eyebrows raised. "Really? I never pegged you as a sci-fi fan."

"I'm not. I'm just a Ray Bradbury fan."

"Well, now you can 'read' Bradbury while you shop." As the narrator continued, Reid took Cara to the back of the store where an antique typewriter sat on a desk.

He sat down in the squeaky chair. "Okay, check this out. This is used to make a collaborative story. Someone types only one sentence and leaves it for the next person to add one more sentence, and so on. You're basically writing a story with dozens of strangers."

"That's super cute. What's the last line right now?" she asked.

Reid read it out loud.

```
"As he rowed into the darkness of the sea,
the  beams  from  the  lighthouse  faded  to
nothing."
```

Cara nodded. "That's a pretty line."

"Let's add to it," Reid suggested.

"Okay, but let's make the next line ridiculous and almost impossible for someone to continue."

Reid grabbed his heart. "You mean you want to practically sabotage the collective efforts of other used book lovers in the community?"

"Exactly."

"I love it."

They tossed around a few ideas, and then Reid finally typed:

```
"After  he  was  certain  he'd  made  the  right
decision,  the  itch  from  the  sand  fleas  was
almost more than he could handle."
```

Cara watched over his shoulder as he punched in the words. She had to bend over and grab her stomach she was laughing so hard. Reid had tears streaming down his face, and he held his finger to his lips as he tried to mouth *Shhhh!* but couldn't get it out through the laughter. They felt like kids who had broken a sacred rule on the playground.

Still laughing, and with *Fahrenheit 451* playing in the background, he brought her up to the cash register. "This is my favorite part of the store. It's a vend-a-quote." He pointed to an old gumball machine that didn't contain gumballs at all. Instead, it had small round containers with folded papers inside each one. Reid put in a quarter, and a container came out. "I buy one every time I come in here. These can be great inspiration for writing." He handed the container to Cara. "Here, this one can be yours. What does it say?"

Cara unfolded the tiny piece of paper. "You've got to be kidding me." She read it:

"Simplify, simplify."
~ Henry David Thoreau

She put a hand on her hip and gave Reid an annoyed look. "Really? Did you plan this?"

Reid held up his hands. "No, I swear."

Cara rolled her eyes. "He repeats the same word, and it's quotable? Gah! This makes me hate him even more."

"Whatever. I think you secretly love him." Reid laughed as he put in another quarter for another quote. He cleared his throat.

"You don't write because you want to say something,
you write because you have something to say."
~ F. Scott Fitzgerald

Reid folded the paper and handed it to Cara. "I think this one was meant for you."

They browsed the bookstore—inhaling the aroma of books, talking about the ones they'd read, and flipping through ones they hadn't. Without realizing it, they migrated to the poetry section.

"Who's your favorite poet?" Reid asked.

"I love Shakespeare, of course, Langston Hughes, Emily Dickinson, and E.E. Cummings . . . But Robert Frost has to be my favorite."

Reid foraged the shelves until he found a complete collection of Frost's poems and held it like he'd dug up a rare fossil.

"Oh, I already own that," Cara said.

"I'm getting this for *me*." He walked to the counter and paid for it. "Let's buy takeout and go back to your place to read some poetry."

~

THEY SAT on Cara's couch and stuffed their bellies with lo mein as they got drunk on Frost's words—each taking turns reading from the thick book.

"So, I know that Frost is your favorite poet, but you never told me if you had a favorite poem of his or not."

"'Birches,'" Cara said. "I haven't read it in years . . . it reminds me of this wooded park where I would go back home . . . usually when I needed to escape life."

Reid pulled her in so that her head rested on his chest—she'd never been so close to him before. She observed the rhythm of his inhales and exhales as he flipped through the pages to find the poem.

"'Birches' by Robert Frost," he said in his deep, silky voice, and started to read.

> When I see birches bend to left and right
> Across the lines of straighter darker trees,
> I like to think some boy's been swinging them.
> But swinging doesn't bend them down to stay
> As ice-storms do. Often you must have seen them
> Loaded with ice a sunny winter morning
> After a rain. They click upon themselves
> As the breeze rises, and turn many-colored
> As the stir cracks and crazes their enamel.
> Soon the sun's warmth makes them shed crystal shells
> Shattering and avalanching on the snow-crust—
> Such heaps of broken glass to sweep away
> You'd think the inner dome of heaven had fallen.
> They are dragged to the withered bracken by the load,
> And they seem not to break; though once they are bowed
> So low for long, they never right themselves:
> You may see their trunks arching in the woods
> Years afterwards, trailing their leaves on the ground
> Like girls on hands and knees that throw their hair
> Before them over their heads to dry in the sun.

But I was going to say when Truth broke in
With all her matter-of-fact about the ice-storm
I should prefer to have some boy bend them
As he went out and in to fetch the cows—
Some boy too far from town to learn baseball,
Whose only play was what he found himself,
Summer or winter, and could play alone.
One by one he subdued his father's trees
By riding them down over and over again
Until he took the stiffness out of them,
And not one but hung limp, not one was left
For him to conquer. He learned all there was
To learn about not launching out too soon
And so not carrying the tree away
Clear to the ground. He always kept his poise
To the top branches, climbing carefully
With the same pains you use to fill a cup
Up to the brim, and even above the brim.
Then he flung outward, feet first, with a swish,
Kicking his way down through the air to the ground.
So was I once myself a swinger of birches.
And so I dream of going back to be.
It's when I'm weary of considerations,
And life is too much like a pathless wood
Where your face burns and tickles with the cobwebs
Broken across it, and one eye is weeping
From a twig's having lashed across it open.
I'd like to get away from earth awhile
And then come back to it and begin over.
May no fate willfully misunderstand me
And half grant what I wish and snatch me away
Not to return. Earth's the right place for love:
I don't know where it's likely to go better.
I'd like to go by climbing a birch tree,
And climb black branches up a snow-white trunk
Toward heaven, till the tree could bear no more,
But dipped its top and set me down again.
That would be good both going and coming back.
One could do worse than be a swinger of birches.

While he read, it was as if everything else had gone dark in the surroundings. They sat in quietness for a moment as he digested the poem—re-reading it silently to figure out how it was part of her story. Cara pulled back to study him and thought of the last week they'd spent together—the ease of their conversations, the way he made her think, his mysteriousness. It was in that moment she realized that the haiku she wrote couldn't be more true. She longed to know Reid Phoenix—every part of him. She slid her head back down to relax on his chest.

"Reid?

"Uh huh?"

"Do you prefer creamy or crunchy peanut butter?"

Without hesitation: "Crunchy."

"Do you let your toilet paper hang over or under?"

"Over."

"Do you love or hate Neil Diamond?"

"Love."

She let another inhale and exhale go by.

"Perfect," she said.

42

THE GIFT OF WORDS

I t was an unseasonably warm day in late February. Cara had never worn shorts in that month before, and it felt bizarre to not only wear them but to see everyone else in shorts on the way to class.

She had philosophy at 9:00 A.M. The professor spoke in monotone about epistemology, and Cara struggled to concentrate or take notes. Out of the corner of her eye, she saw some movement through the small window of the door.

It was Reid.

He motioned for her to come out.

She shook her head, but he persisted. Finally, she left her stuff in her seat and pretended she needed to use the restroom.

When the door shut behind her, she asked, "What are you doing? Don't you have class right now, too?"

"Skip class with me."

"What?"

"It's beautiful out, and I've been itching to go surfing for months!"

"Surfing? I can't even ride a skateboard, let alone surf!"

"Come on. I'll teach you. It's just one class. Your poem is due in a couple days, so we need to get you all the inspiration possible to help you write it."

Cara looked back at her seat through the window. She felt badly about skipping a class the Aethers were paying for. But

Reid had a good point about inspiration, and his mouth looked so cute as he tried to convince her.

"Okay," she said. "Why not? Let me grab my things."

~

WHEN THEY ARRIVED at Wrightsville Beach, she noticed that Reid's eyes were the same color as the water. He took in a deep breath. "Ahhh! The ocean air is so good for the lungs."

Cara took a moment to breathe in the air herself. "It does feel different than anywhere else."

She removed her cover-up and wore a teal tankini that showed off her thin waist and curves. Reid was already in his swim trunks and wore a nylon shirt that he didn't take off. Through it, she could make out the definition of his trim muscles on his skinny frame.

"Why are you still wearing a shirt?"

"It's a rash guard shirt. Keeps me from getting a sunburn and chafing against the surfboard."

Cara didn't question it any further and followed him into the water. It was the first time she had fully submerged herself in the sea. She tried to take it all in—noticing the waves' power as they pushed her out and pulled her in, the salt in her mouth, the soft sand under her feet, how it went on forever. Then she thought about the creek back home in Alexander's Woods and how different the experience was with this water.

After she became used to the rhythm of the waves, Reid taught Cara beginner steps on the surfboard. She lay down on it and paddled in on her stomach. She never got up on her feet, but the command of the waves behind her was invigorating.

"I want to watch you do it," she told him. She walked back to shore and laid on her towel as Reid took to the waves. He stood on the board effortlessly and cut back and forth with ease, gliding under the wave's power.

When he came back to her on the sand, Reid had a horrible coughing fit. Hunched over with his hands on his knees, he couldn't seem to catch his breath.

"Reid, are you okay? Did you swallow some water?"

He shook his head no.

"No? No, what? No, you're not okay? Or no, you didn't swallow seawater? Do you need me to get you some help?" She started patting his back and looked around for the nearest person she could run to.

Is there a lifeguard? Or a payphone?

His coughing finally ceased and morphed into laughter. That deep, infectious laugh that sounded so much like Adam's.

Cara's eyebrows furrowed. "What's so funny?"

"You just asked me like five consecutive questions. You sounded just like your friend Trenna."

Cara could feel her cheeks turn red as his laughter continued against the sounds of the waves. Here she was, genuinely concerned, and he thought it was hilarious. She stood still and let him crack up a bit more. Then Cara charged toward Reid and tackled him to the sand. "You're such a jerk!" And they laughed during the skirmish—sand covering them and tangling their hair. Eventually, exhausted, they lay in silence, holding each other and soaking up everything the earth had to offer them in that moment.

Reid brushed sand from her cheek. "I hate to do this, but I need to take you home so I can go do my afternoon routine. I'll come by this evening, though, if that's okay."

"Of course." She didn't get up. Instead, she tucked a strand of Reid's curls behind his ear. "Hey, seriously. You sure you're okay? That cough was awful. You sounded like you were about to die."

He rolled over to face her. "We're all dying, Cara. Every day, it gets closer and closer. That's why we have to suck all the marrow out now before it's too late."

~

REID STOPPED by Cara's apartment that evening and brought pizza and milkshakes with him.

"How do you drink so many milkshakes and stay so thin?" She noticed that he drank one just about every day.

"It's a gift," he said—shrugging and changing the subject. "So, our next poem is due in just a couple of days. Have you started it yet?"

"No, but I have it all stewing in here." She pointed to her forehead.

"Do you mind me asking what's inspired you the past two weeks?" Reid asked as he nursed the rest of his milkshake.

"Honestly, everything. But I think the ocean had the strongest effect on me. Being in it and experiencing it in the sunlight instead of the shadow this time completed the whole experience for me. I'm so glad I skipped class with you today."

The corners of his mouth upturned, and he studied her face. "Will you share one of your old poems with me? From when you used to write all the time in high school?"

The request was unexpected. Cara hadn't even looked at her writings since Adam died. She wanted to tell Reid no, but his calming blue eyes made her feel safe. "Okay," she said with a slight tremor in her voice, "but no revealing ones. And no questions."

"Deal."

Cara knew right where her old notebooks were and retrieved them from her top dresser drawer. Often there were three or four pages of edits—words crossed out and replaced by others, arrows indicating words or lines to be switched. With each careful turn of the page, memories hit—reminding her of the painful past she wanted to forget of her parents and the present she longed for with Adam. The emotions she had locked in were overwhelming, but she refused to let them out. Instead, she sat shaking her head as she looked at the words on the page from years ago.

Reid seemed to sense her apprehension. "You okay? You don't have to read any if you don't want. I'm sorry I suggested it if you're not ready."

"No," she said, crossing her arms. "You were right in asking. I need to do this."

Finally, she came to one she thought was worthy of sharing.

"Okay. This is around the time I stopped titling my poems. I think I was a junior in high school when I wrote it." She stood as she read to Reid sitting on the couch.

> i will never be enough
> the bars of the iron gate cannot
> keep the squirrel from weaving her way in and out
> the wide leaves of the oak cannot
> block the sun from heating the forest floor
> the jagged boulders cannot
> with clenched fists
> rise up and dam this roaring river
> so neither will i ever be enough to
> silence the spilling of this blood
> from the tip of my pen

They were both so silent when she finished that the closing of her notebook felt jarring. Reid stared at her in awe. "Damn." He ran his fingers through his curls. "Cara . . . that was beautiful. You were meant to be a writer. Promise me, please, that you will start writing again . . . and never stop. The world needs your words."

~

IT WAS the day of the poetry reading. The typical stirring occurred before class with students scrambling to prepare their poems' visuals and practicing their deliveries in faint whispers.

Cara sat nervously as the others volunteered and shared pieces of their hearts through their words. She tried to give adequate comments on her Feedback Slips but found it hard to concentrate.

"Cara, why don't you go next?" Dr. Wilkes suggested.

Cara looked at Reid, who gave her an encouraging nod. She stood and apprehensively took the floor. She didn't make any Xeroxed copies of her poem or write it on the board—she was exhausted from forcing the near-scribbles onto the page and could barely read it through the tears that began to form in her eyes and her shaking hands.

She calmed herself by prefacing the poem. "I'm not from Wilmington, and I had never even seen the ocean until about two weeks ago, thanks to a friend. That's what inspired this poem."

is your infinite gravity not enough
that you must swallow me as well
your unending waves rising and falling around me
stretched out a thousand miles in every direction?

why, grief, have you submerged me in your depths
where i can neither see nor be seen
where i can neither feel nor be felt
where i am only consumed by your expanse?

should i let go of my breath
or keep grasping in the dark
uncertain if i am reaching for
the surface or the deep?

if i must be lost in this sea
at least let me see the distant horizon
if nothing else let me be lost
in the light of the dawning sun

She returned to her seat, drained from the exploring, the writing, the sharing. The Feedback Slips piled onto her desk. As she sat there, the fatigue began to fade and was replaced with exhilaration. It was therapeutic to get the words out onto the paper and into the ears of an audience.

She tuned out the next presenter and looked through the Feedback Slips. All the words were so kind and encouraging. Then she came to Reid's—she knew his handwriting after studying his last one so often:

Breathtakingly beautiful.
Thank you for the gift of your words, Cara.

She looked at Reid, sitting across from her in the Circle of Comfort. His blue eyes stared back at her, and the corners of his mouth made her feel weak. If she had been standing, she would have been knocked off her legs.

43

BLANKET

Spring came on so strongly it practically assaulted the residents of Wilmington. Buds forced themselves through the soil — blooming to the satisfaction of eager bees.

Cara's writing started to blossom too. It was slow, but there. She and Reid continued to spend as much time together as possible. The warm weather allowed them to be outside, wrapped in nature's embrace.

They went on walks, bike rides, and trips to the beach, but what they enjoyed most was to sit in a park shaded by maples and oaks. They talked about all the everythings from their favorite condiments to the nature of God — but between all those conversations, they still kept their secrets close to their chests. Sometimes they went to a park to read or write and share their creations. Sometimes they merely sat in silence and stillness — enjoying the simple presence of each other.

One April afternoon in the park, when the sunset made the sky look like it was set on fire, they lay on their backs with notebooks in tow.

"The most beautiful words came to me last night," Cara said. "But I couldn't keep my eyes open, and I didn't write them down before I fell asleep. Now I can't remember them."

"I think it's such a beautiful moment when that happens," Reid said.

"You think it's beautiful that I forgot a great line that will never come back to me?"

"Yeah, because now you realize how special that moment was —you experienced suffering their loss, so it's a reminder of how precious they were."

Cara rolled her eyes then smiled. "I guess."

They existed into the late afternoon when Cara saw that Reid appeared to be finished with something and stared at his writing. He interrupted their quietness and read the poem he'd just written.

> I want nothing more in this moment
> than to be able to see
> what is on the other side of those trees,
> making the sky so orange,
> and can only assume this is happening because
> distance is the womb of desire

"'Distance is the womb of desire'? I like that line . . . is that about us?"

"No, it's about the orange sky." He winked at her. "Okay, maybe your assumption is a little accurate."

Cara looked beyond the trees instead of him. "Do you think we'll ever tell each other our whole story?"

"If we're going to stay in each other's lives, I think eventually, we have to." He nudged her chin with this forefinger, inviting her to look his way. "I like this moment. Right now, until way in the future, I want you to forever remember me this way—*us* this way, okay?"

Cara nodded as she held his gaze—if she had an hourglass, she would block the sand from falling through so she could stay suspended in that moment with him forever.

∿

THE NEXT MORNING, Cara came down with an awful flu. She had chills, a high fever, and couldn't keep anything down. There was no way she would make any of her classes. She had no energy to do anything but take the few steps it took to reach her bathroom to vomit. Too weak to drive to a doctor or even make it back to her bed, Cara lay on the linoleum.

For the first time, she started to miss home. The only time her mother ever showed her any compassion or attention was when she was sick. She thought of Mrs. Aether, who would take such good care of her if she were there.

Then her mind traveled to Adam.

If he were still alive, he'd be at UNC—just two hours away from her. Cara knew he would drop everything if she needed him.

But no matter how much she missed him, nothing would bring him back.

Grief grabbed hold of her and added pain to the aches she already felt. She needed some sort of comfort and mustered enough energy to pull Adam's old blanket off her bed. She squeezed the fabric like a pillow and held it to her nose to take in its scent.

But there was no scent.

She cushioned her pounding head with it as she lay back down on the bathroom's linoleum. It reminded her of lying on the hospital floor when Adam lay paralyzed on the hospital bed.

Later, the phone rang, waking Cara from the floor. Every muscle in her body ached when she moved, but she slowly dragged herself over to answer it on the last ring before it went to the answering machine.

"Cara? Are you there?"

It was Reid.

"Yes," her voice barely let out.

"Why weren't you in class? Are you okay?"

"I think I have the flu."

"The flu? Oh, man. I'm so sorry."

"Can you take me to a doctor?"

There was a long pause.

"Reid?"

"Cara, I'm really sorry, but I can't. I can explain more later, but I'll figure something out, okay?"

Cara selfishly wanted to yell at him and ask why he couldn't take her. It felt like all the rejections of her past. But she was too weak to express herself.

"Okay," she whispered instead and hung up.

The insecurities and questions roamed through her mind in the moments of consciousness when she heard a knock at the door.

It was Trenna in her Dixie Grill uniform.

"Oh. My. Word. Cara, are you okay? You look awful. Do you

feel awful? What do you think you have? What doctor do you need me to take you to?"

Nearly comatose on her feet in the doorway, Cara said nothing but leaned in and gave her a weak hug. She'd never been so relieved to see Trenna before.

❧

TRENNA DROVE AS FAST as she could to the closest Urgent Care facility where they prescribed Tamiflu and told Cara to get lots of rest and fluids for the next few days. Trenna was sweet and kept her questions to a minimum as she brought Cara back home and helped her into bed.

Gaining more consciousness, Cara asked, "Why are you in your uniform?"

"Reid came by the restaurant late this morning and told me you needed help immediately. I was in the middle of my shift, but somehow he convinced Nikoleta to let me go."

"He did that?"

"Yeah, it was really sweet. I don't understand why he couldn't have taken you himself."

There was another knock.

Trenna told Cara to stay in bed and opened the door. No one was there, but she noticed a small tray on the doormat. It held a couple cans of chicken noodle soup, hot tea bags, honey, a freshly sliced lemon, a small bouquet of hand-picked wildflowers, and a note.

"Oh! My! Word! You won't believe this." Trenna carried the tray in and put it on her bed. Cara opened the card.

Cara,

I'm so sorry I couldn't help you today. I promise that someday I will explain why. For now, please get lots of rest, drink lots of hot tea with honey and lemon, and eat some chicken noodle soup. And of course, enjoy the flowers from our favorite park. Let me know when you're well because I can't wait to see you again.

And please tell Trenna thank you from the bottom of my heart for helping you for me. She's a good friend.

~ Reid

Trenna grabbed the note to read herself. "Oh. My. Word. That might be the most romantic thing I've ever witnessed in real life!"

~

TRENNA STAYED with Cara that entire night. She held her hair back when she vomited in the toilet, made her hot tea, and got her anything else she needed. She worked at the Dixie Grill the next morning but came back after her shift to help Cara that afternoon.

"How do you feel?"

"Slightly human again," Cara whispered. "Thank you. Being sick made me really homesick, but you helped. You're a good friend."

"Of course. That's what friends do. Do you think you can keep down some chicken noodle soup?"

Cara nodded. From the kitchen, Trenna shouted, "What Reid did last night was seriously so cute. Why do you think he couldn't come help you himself?"

"I assume it has something to do with his past that he's not ready to talk about yet."

"But not being around you while you're sick doesn't have to do with his past, that has to do with *now*."

For not always being the brightest, Trenna made an interesting assertion.

"I don't know," Cara said. "We promised we wouldn't pressure each other to talk about anything we weren't wanting to share yet. He'll tell me when he's ready."

"When are you going to tell him about *your* past?"

Cara's mind crept back to Adam. She missed him so strongly that she couldn't tell if her body hurt from that or the flu. Living a new life without the memories of her home and the pain of Adam's death was what she wanted, but now she felt like it was dishonoring him—like she was pretending he never existed. Cara couldn't imagine a future where that was the case. She thought about his blanket and feared her memories would fade like his scent. Maybe talking about it would make her feel better. Her head started to spin.

"I imagine it will be soon," she finally answered.

~

THE NEXT DAY, Cara stayed home again. She felt better, but not well enough for class. She thanked Trenna incessantly for taking care of her but said she could manage on her own now. Cara wanted to be alone so she could call Mrs. Aether. They had spoken regularly since she moved to Wilmington, but this conversation would be different.

Through both their tears, Cara told her about Reid, their agreement, her writing, the flu, and how much she missed Adam. And she was angry. Angry he wasn't there anymore.

"This friend of yours, Reid?" Mrs. Aether said. "He sounds like he's been a great friend. I know he doesn't know about Adam, but how do you think he would suggest you handle your grief right now?"

Cara tapped her fingers on the counter as she thought. "He'd tell me to write about it."

After ending the call, she pulled Adam's old blanket over her lap and opened her notebook to a blank page.

~

A WEEK after Cara got the flu and was finally well, Reid came by to pick her up for class. He wrapped Cara in his arms and held her tightly. "I'm so sorry you were sick and I couldn't help."

"You did, though. You helped me through Trenna, and you brought all that stuff by. It was very thoughtful."

He looked down, almost as if he was ashamed. He'd never avoided eye contact with her before.

"I'm not going to ask why you couldn't come near me, Reid, if that's what you're afraid of."

"Okay," he said and let out a breath. "Are you ready to share another poem in class today?"

"No." She sighed. "But I'm going to. I was able to write a bit when I was sick."

~

IN CLASS, Reid shared his poem first. "I titled this one 'The Weight of Me.'"

> I was born of something heavy,
> thick and abundant,

a burden I have carried
and into which I might finally fall.
That would bear the weight of me.

The class made audible sighs of approval at his last word and filled out their Feedback Slips. This reminded Cara of the first poem he shared in class and wrote:

Sometimes I feel like you're more of a mystery to me today
than you were three months ago.

"Cara, why don't you go next?" Dr. Wilkes asked as she set her Feedback Slip onto Reid's desk.

Her hands began to shake. Not because she cared what anyone would think, but because she knew she was about to spill pieces of her heart all over the room—pieces Reid had never seen. When she first took the floor, she concentrated on her breathing —convincing herself that it was good to write. It was good to share. Without giving an intro this time, she began.

the blanket on my bed no longer smells of you
like it once did
after we wrapped ourselves in it on chilly evenings
and you lay next to me
on the ground
and it breathed in your scent
the blend of which i could not decipher
the way i can no longer decipher
your thoughts about this particular
shade of blue morning light
emanating through the fog
or about this sip of tea
that i decided to try for the first time
or on the verse
those who want to save their life will lose it
or if the same things would still make you
weep or stew
or belly laugh
or the reason that you left
me with just this blanket
which exhales your aroma

wafting it to the ceiling
with all the other fading memories
like warm breath rising for the very last time

She bit her lower lip so hard it felt like it was going to split open, and she squeezed her eyes shut—willing back the tears. The silent reaction of the class screamed that they each felt the pieces of her heart that she dropped in their laps.

"Thank you very much for sharing that, Cara," Dr. Wilkes said.

Cara nodded and then walked out of the classroom.

Once in the hall, she pushed through the doors that led to the fountain between Morton Hall and Leutze Hall and gasped for fresh air.

She heard the door open behind her.

It was Reid.

He didn't ask if she was okay because she obviously wasn't. Instead, he approached her and said, "Hey, come here." He wrapped his arms around Cara. She stood limp in his embrace, her head resting against his chest. As he held Cara, the rhythm of his breaths calmed her. He ran his fingers through her hair then slid them along her jawline until reaching the bottom of her chin. He lifted her face toward his.

"I'm here," he said.

She pulled away from him. "I can't *not* talk about it anymore."

"That's okay. Do you want to talk to me now? You can tell me whatever you want. Whatever you need."

They sat by the fountain—Cara ready to share, and Reid ready to listen.

"My dad has been a functioning alcoholic since I can remember, and my mother was always distant—compulsively obsessed with cleaning. Looking back now, I think that was always her way of coping. He neglected her, and she, in turn, neglected me. They put on a great show, though. They made us look like the perfect little family. My way to escape was reading and writing . . . and Adam."

Reid reached for her hand.

"He was my next-door neighbor and my best friend before we even started school. Our bedroom windows faced each other, and we used to stay up late talking through them. I'd write him stories all the time when we were kids, and he was the best audience.

Sometimes we bickered like siblings and went through typical high school drama, but he was always there for me. He was my constant amid the chaos in my home." She paused, not ready to say the next part. "Then he was tackled in a football game and broke his neck. He died two days later. The most important person in my life was gone, leaving me with two parents who didn't care, and I didn't know how to function. I would go over to his house all the time afterward and just sleep. The smells of that house were the only thing that comforted me. That's my past," she said. "That's why I couldn't write."

Reid let the words settle and held her close for a long time against the sound of the fountain behind them.

"I'm so sorry, Cara. I'm glad you wrote about it and that you told me."

She turned to him and tried to steady her breathing.

"It's okay to cry," he said.

And she did.

44

HONEY

Not much changed after Cara shared Adam's story with Reid, except she felt lighter. She hadn't pressured Reid to share anything in return—she could tell he wasn't ready. The end of the semester was approaching quickly, and they continued spending what time they had together.

On a Friday evening, Reid came over to cook dinner with Cara at her apartment. Neither of them had much experience in the kitchen, so they made spaghetti, and, of course, milkshakes. She remembered how Mrs. Aether would throw the noodles against the tiled backsplash to see if it would stick—testing if the pasta was ready. She showed the trick to Reid, and he thought it was hilarious. Soon, half the noodles were on the wall because he did it so much.

With their bellies full, they sat on the couch, and Cara handed Reid a thick anthology of poetry.

"Read to me?" she asked with arched eyebrows.

"I will always read to you." He took the book from her and flipped through the Table of Contents. "Any particular poet tonight?"

"Hmmm. I think I'm in the mood for some Edna St. Vincent Millay."

"All right." He turned to that section. "All of them?"

"Please. I love her."

He read "Inert Perfection" and "Renascence" and "Sonnet IX"

and several others while Cara laid her head on his chest. Again, she was soothed by the rhythm of his breath in conjunction with his deep voice methodically reading Millay's words.

He turned the page to read the next poem to find a piece of paper with Cara's writing.

"What's this?"

She raised her shoulders to pretend she didn't know, but then admitted with a sheepish smile, "It's something I wrote for you."

"You wrote something for me?"

"Yeah, after our conversation the other night," Cara said, "when we talked about how everything on earth has a purpose and is beautiful if used how it's intended. How that means there has to be a Creator, and we were created to live and function with purpose and unity. The evidence is all around us, but we—*I*— tend to focus on the negative parts of life instead of the beauty."

"Will you read it to me?" Reid asked.

He handed her the paper, and with ease, she read.

all i could see from where i stood
were distant mountains
and dying trees

leaves spinning to meet
their inglorious ends
snow-covered beneath the bitter sky

perfectly hidden in the frozen ground
unable to crack
its nostalgic shell

until the rain and her welcome warming wind
awakened the bees
who would not stop buzzing about it all

twirling between petal and plight
dancing in the arms
of these waving limbs

and the sweetness of honey
dripping from that same dying wood
onto my sun-soaked lips

was all i could see from where i stood

Cara slid the paper back into the book and turned her body to face Reid. She studied his pale blue eyes. "The past two and a half years have been so dark and bitter. After Adam's death, I thought it might stay that way forever. I often think of the first time I saw you—you read that Kierkegaard quote in class, the one about how a poet is an unhappy man whose lips are formed in such a way he can turn anguish into beautiful music. I identified with that so much. I felt that the only thing I could ever produce would be from my pain. But you brought a sweetness back into my life that I didn't think was possible and helped me re-shape my lips to write something beautiful from beauty."

Reid studied her as she reached behind his head and undid the rubber band holding back his hair. The dark curls fell around his face, and she combed her fingers through them. He placed one of his hands on the back of her neck and then brushed it along her exposed collarbone. He moved his fingers to her cheek and softly cupped her face with both hands.

"I am so in love with you," he whispered.

Cara wanted to tell him how much she loved him, too, but he was already pulling her towards him. Their chests pressed against each other so tightly their hearts seemed to be beating in the other one's body. Their lips grazed, and they both trembled a little at the touch. Then his lips pressed against hers with a gentle firmness. It was slow, and soft, and ethereal. With every exhale of his warm breath against hers, Cara thought she was going to fade into him.

Suddenly, Reid tore his lips away from hers and grabbed her hands—holding them against his chest. "I'm so sorry."

Addled, she pulled back. "Sorry?"

He rested his forehead against hers—eyes fixed on their hands as he took a deep breath. "I shouldn't have kissed you. I am so in love with you, Cara . . . but I can't let you be in love with me."

Her eyes darted back and forth across his face, trying to make sense of the words. "Reid, at this point, I don't think there's anything you can tell me that would keep me from loving you. I need to know why you're saying that."

Pain consumed his eyes, knowing that what he was about to say would likely end what he never wanted to end with Cara. "Because . . . I will never be able to grow old with you—"

She shook her head and cut him off. "What are you talking about?"

He closed his eyes as if dreading the words he needed to say. He said them softly and slowly. "The reason I need to be by the ocean water, why I have bad coughing spells, why I don't gain weight, why I always wear a shirt at the beach, why I couldn't be around you when you had the flu, why I'm gone every afternoon . . . Cara . . . I'm sick. I have cystic fibrosis."

Cystic fibrosis?

She knew she'd heard those words before but couldn't place what it was.

"Cys . . . cystic fibrosis? What, what is that?"

"It's a disease that affects the lungs. They basically fill up and get clogged with thick mucus that'll eventually get so bad I won't be able to breathe . . . I can never have kids . . . I will only live to be about thirty—at best. Realistically though, I probably have less than five years to live."

He paused and ran his hand through his hair.

"Cara, I didn't tell you sooner because my whole life I've been sick and out of school and known as 'that poor kid.' When I came to Wilmington, I wanted to start new, like you did. I didn't want anyone to label me or just associate me with my sickness. I just wanted people to see *me* . . . I've been thinking about how you've already lost Adam so young, and you'll lose me in an untimely way, too. It wouldn't be fair to you. Life with me will be full of dozens of pills a day, constant doctor visits, hospital stays, breathing treatments . . . until you eventually watch me drown in my own fluid on some sterile hospital bed. That's not the kind of life you deserve . . . That's why you can't be in love with me."

The silence between them, which had once been a source of ease, was now thick with angst. But her head wasn't spinning, as it should have been. When the weight of his words settled into her chest, she spoke as clearly as ever.

"No."

His eyes, red from tears, met hers.

"No," she repeated. "You don't get to tell me how I'm allowed to feel. I've never felt this way about anyone in my entire life. The past few months I've spent with you have been the best I've ever experienced. Reid, you taught me how to live! I don't know what tomorrow is going to bring, but I do know I want you by my side as long as you have. If I get hurt again, at least I will have loved well while I had the chance."

This time she wrapped her hand behind his neck to pull him toward her. He didn't resist, and they kissed until they faded into each other's embrace.

45

BRACELET

"So, what's the real reason that you can drink so many milkshakes and not gain weight?" Cara asked the next afternoon while they grabbed coffee at Madison's Cafe.

"Because cystic fibrosis doesn't just affect the lungs, it affects the pancreas, liver, digestive system, to name a few. It keeps me from being able to digest food properly."

"Why do you need to be by the ocean?"

"It's the saltwater. Inhaling the ocean air helps hydrate the lungs and loosen the mucus. That was pretty impossible to get out in Kansas." Cara realized he'd never told her where he was from before, just like he didn't know she was from Ohio.

"Why couldn't you be around me when I had the flu?"

"Because my immune system is weak. If I were to catch the flu from you, that could be fatal for me."

He started to laugh at her.

"What?" Cara asked.

"You sound like Trenna again."

"Whatever! Trenna asks like fifty-four questions in a row without giving you a chance to answer. I patiently await your response, and then I move on."

"You know who we should match her up with?"

"Will!" they said in unison.

Cara laughed so hard she had no sound coming out. She held onto the edge of the table as she regained her breath. "But they would do nothing but ask each other rapid-fire questions that neither would get a chance to answer."

"True," Reid said. "But he would stop to talk about *Walden*, too."

"Oh my gosh, we could never double date with them. I would lose my mind." She kept giggling at the thought. "I'm still going to introduce them, though."

After the laughter died down, she asked, "Where is it you go every afternoon?"

"Usually to my apartment. I have to take all my pills and wear 'the vest.'"

"'The vest?'"

"Yeah, it's a vest I have to wear that is attached to this machine. It vibrates at a high frequency to help break up all the gunk in my lungs."

Cara reached across the table and took his hand. "No running away from me this afternoon. I want to come with you."

～

IT WAS the first time Cara had been to Reid's apartment, and now she understood why they only spent time at hers. It would have been impossible to hide his illness in the small space. On the kitchen counter were dozens of bottles of pills. In the corner, a chair held a huge vest connected to a machine that looked like an old vacuum with giant tubes coming out of it. Reid showed her everything, explaining each bottle of pills and how the vest worked.

"I used to take over a hundred pills a day, but now I'm down to about sixty. For a while, I didn't even have to do the vest, but I had to start it back up about six months ago."

"Do you have to wear it now?"

Reid looked at the clock. "Yeah. You don't have to stay, though. It might be weird for you to watch."

"I want to stay if that's all right." She saw Reid consider this before answering. "Reid, if this is going to be a part of my life — I might as well start being around for it now."

"If I'm honest, I don't want you to see me this way." He lowered his eyes.

She grabbed his hand. "I won't even see the vest or the tubes. I'll only see you."

Reid kissed her forehead with a relieved sigh. "Okay. I have to have this nebulizer in my mouth most of the time, so I won't be able to talk or anything."

"Then I'll read to you," Cara said. "That way, I won't be staring and making you feel uncomfortable. Where are your poetry books?"

Reid pointed to a bookshelf in the corner of the living room. "I have some poetry over there."

Cara retrieved a copy of Lord Byron's poems while Reid hooked up his vest, put the medicine into his nebulizer, and turned everything on. Cara read to him above the noise. She glanced up every once-in-a-while and saw the vest shaking his thin frame, with mist emitting from the nebulizer. Every ten minutes, he stopped to do what he called a huff cough to clear the mucus from his lungs.

The treatment took about thirty minutes. As Reid signaled he was almost done, Cara found a good stopping point and put the Byron book back on the shelf. She wandered around the apartment to give him a little privacy. Other than the pills and machines, it looked like a typical bachelor pad, except it was so clean it was like her mother had been there. The whitewashed walls had minimal decorations, multiple shelves overflowed with books, and small piles of books were stashed in other places.

Reid started to unhook himself from the machine.

"Your apartment is so clean."

"It kind of has to be. I have to sanitize to keep away as many germs as possible."

Before she could respond, something caught her eye on a small shelf by the door. It was a brown leather bracelet that looked exactly like Adam's. She walked over and picked it up. Engraved in capital letters was the word.

AEGGERS

Her eyes had to be lying, but she kept staring at the bracelet and rubbed her fingers against the letters to make sure they were there.

"Is something wrong?" Reid asked.

She whirled around and held up the bracelet. "What the hell is this?"

"What? The bracelet?"

"Is this some kind of sick joke, Reid? Why do you have this?"

"Cara, what are you talking about?" He tilted his head, confused. "How do you know about that bracelet?"

"This was Adam's!" She tried to control herself from getting hysterical. "Aeggers was his nickname, and I had this made for him — he wore this bracelet every day and was wearing it when he had his accident. I made sure to take it off when he was on the field and gave it to his mom. So, please! Explain to me why the hell *you* have it in your apartment right now!"

"Oh, God," was all he could say. He ran his hand through his curls and stared in shock at the piece of leather.

"Reid. Tell me," she said through gritted teeth.

"I don't understand how this—" He fumbled for the words. "Cara, two and a half years ago, my lungs were so bad that I was going to die any day. I ended up having a double lung transplant in November of 1997. That's why I've been so healthy — relatively — and able to do things like surf that I never got to do before. About six months ago, my parents received a small package. It was through some company with a letter that didn't go into a lot of details, but the lady said her son had been adamant about being an organ donor, and I was the one who received her son's lungs. She sent me that bracelet — his bracelet — as a gift."

Cara shook her head. "No. No, that's not possible. Adam didn't want to be an organ donor. He told me himself when we took Driver's Ed. together."

"I can show you the letter."

Without waiting for a response, he opened the drawer of his end table and handed the envelope to Cara.

She unfolded the letter and skipped immediately to the signature: *Gloria Aether.*

She couldn't even focus on the rest of the letter. The words seemed to be jumbled in the air, but she made out a couple sentences:

When I took my son to get his driver's license, he told me he wanted to be an organ donor, something he initially didn't want to do. I asked if he was sure, and he said, "Yes, because I want to help people, even after I die. And besides, when I die, I won't need those organs where I'm going anyway."

That was a direct quote from her while they rode the bus

sophomore year. She had no idea he was really listening, or that she had changed his mind. She looked from the letter to Reid's chest, imagining Adam's lungs inside his body—keeping him alive. Pain and confusion and a million other emotions simultaneously filled her head.

Reid crouched on the ground. "Cara," he said, "I promise I had no idea. From what you told me, I never knew Adam's last name, where he was from, when he died. I didn't put any of this together. I'm so sorry . . . I understand if this is too much right now."

Cara glanced down at the bracelet, still in her hand. "I . . . I don't really know how I feel right now."

"I understand," Reid said. "I would understand if you were mad that Adam died and I'm the one who got to live. I know how much he meant to you and wouldn't blame you if you never wanted to see me again."

"I'm going to need some time to clear my head and think about all of this."

Reid stayed on the floor. He looked too emotionally weak to stand.

Cara started for the door but paused and turned around. "Reid?" Tears ran down her cheeks, and her voice trembled. "May I please listen to his lungs?"

He nodded, and she walked over and got down on her knees to be level with him. She wrapped her arms around Reid and placed her ear to his chest. The rising and falling that had so many times calmed all her anxieties was there.

But this time, as she listened, she gasped for her own breath as she wept.

46

THIEF

Back at her apartment, alone, Cara paced the floor and tried to make sense of all the thoughts and emotions exploding as little bursts inside her brain. In less than twenty-four hours, she'd told Reid she loved him, they'd kissed, she learned of his disease, and that he had Adam's lungs living inside him. It didn't all compute.

She reached for the phone to call Mrs. Aether when she noticed Adam's bracelet was still in her hand. She had taken it without realizing. It didn't belong to Reid anyway.

Adam's mom picked up after the third ring.

"Mrs. Aether?" Cara's voice shook.

"Cara? What's wrong?"

"I'm sorry to bother you, but there's something I need to know . . . about Adam." She paused. "Was he an organ donor?"

Mrs. Aether stayed silent for a moment. "He was."

Cara leaned back against the wall and rubbed her temples. "But that doesn't make sense. I specifically remember him telling me that he didn't want to be one."

"You're right, but he changed his mind right before he got his driver's license. He actually talked about it several times to me. That was one of the reasons we decided not to keep him on life support because we knew his organs would save other lives."

How did I not know any of this?

Cara struggled to ask the next question, not sure if she really

279

wanted to know the answer. "Have you had any contact with any of his recipients?"

"Well, you're not allowed to contact anyone for at least a year, and even then, you can't contact them directly. I had to go through a special organization. I didn't think about it much until the second anniversary of his death approached. I wrote a short note to all of the recipients I could find and sent them each something of Adam's as a memento."

"Did you send his leather bracelet? The one that says 'AEGGERS'?"

"I did." Cara started crying. "I know you gave him that bracelet, Cara. I am so sorry if—"

"You don't need to be sorry, Mrs. Aether. It's just...I saw his bracelet today."

Mrs. Aether breathed in a small gasp. "How? That was for his lung recipient. He's from Kansas."

"He's a student at UNCW . . . It's Reid."

There was a stunned quietness for a long time.

Mrs. Aether whispered, "The friend you told me about—"

Cara went on to explain the love interest, the kiss, the cystic fibrosis, the bracelet, how seeing Reid with it felt like a betrayal, how she left, and how she still desperately missed Adam. "I'm trying to make sense of it all. I don't know what to do."

Finally, Mrs. Aether asked, "Do you love him?"

Cara stared at the book of poetry on her coffee table, the one Reid read to her the night before, with her poem to him still tucked inside. "Yes . . . at least, I thought I did. I don't know. I wish someone could just tell me what to do."

"That's not anything I could possibly decide for you."

~

CARA'S exhausted body fell prostrate on her bed. She grabbed onto Adam's blanket and tried to rest, but her eyes stayed fixed on the wall as she weaved in and out of numbness. There she lay until darkness replaced the light through the windows.

She finally rolled over and grabbed a box of memories from Adam—a few stories he'd written as a kid, the Fisher-Price Sky Talkers, and the note he'd given her the morning of the accident. Having not read it in over two years, she'd almost forgotten what it said. She carefully unfolded it and smoothed out the creases.

Cara read it slowly and stopped to digest the lines that mentioned Angela's prophecy—that some way or another, the two of them were going to end up together, even though it may not be in a normal way. And then his ending which said:

I don't know what will happen in the future, but I hope I am always able to take care of you and offer you the comfort that you need.

She decided to step outside to take in some fresh air to help clear her thoughts. Her front door led to a small courtyard heavily lit by the moon. The night was warm with a mild breeze. She closed her eyes for a long time and slowed her breathing with deep inhales.

When she opened them, she saw the entire courtyard surrounded by a throng of ladybugs.

∼

IT WAS the last day for poetry readings before finals. When Cara arrived, she noticed Reid's seat was empty. They hadn't talked since Saturday afternoon—neither one sure what to say to the other.

Dr. Wilkes started class when the door opened, and Reid appeared. His dark, curly hair pulled back as usual. Cara observed his every step as he moved toward his seat across from her in the Circle of Comfort. She thought of the first time she saw him and how she watched him in the same way that day. He was a mystery then, and now, she knew everything she didn't want to know. Cara could see puffiness under his eyes like he had been crying for the past couple of days. He glanced at her briefly with a sad smile that kept his lips together. She returned a similar expression, and then they both looked away.

The floor opened for anyone to share their writing with the class. Hands went up to volunteer—Reid wasn't one of them. His eyes were absent as he stared at the floor during each reading, not even filling out Feedback Slips.

"Who wants to go next?" Dr. Wilkes asked.

"I'll go," Cara said.

She took slow steps to the front of the room and placed her paper on the podium with trembling hands. After a deep breath, she looked into Reid's sad, uncertain eyes then lowered hers to her poem. Then she let go of the words that had been swirling inside her the last three days.

you are a thief

the strangest kind of taker
slipping silently through the window
calmly gathering up the strangest things

you took nothing of value
but everything of worth

how did you find your way in here
thief
robbing me of the very gifts you had given
marauding my memories

you are like the wind
seeping through cracks in the glass
bleeding through fractures in the floorboards
scattering remains of sunlit days
glittering the ground beneath these bloody feet

why must you be such a thief
why such a taker
why give peace to these seas only to take it back
why take away emptiness only to give sorrow
why give me life only to take my breath

even now
looking into the windowless blue of your eyes
i can feel it slipping past my lips

why are you so
breathtaking

you of all people
and my breath of all things

you have stolen from this locked chest

Breathtaking

you have taken my heart into your hands
and have massaged it back to beating
you have taken words from dry lips
and drawn them out colorfully
into this wide landscape

you have ransacked the all of me
laid everything out on the ground
wide as the ocean is deep
you have touched all of it with your gentle fingers
you have plundered me
inhaled the whole of me
even with your half breath

you really are a thief
the strangest kind of taker

and willingly
i have been taken

As she walked back to her seat, she laid the leather bracelet on
Reid's desk.

47
_____

OUR STORY

W hen Adam died, a part of me died with him. But in a way, his death gave me life because it gave me Reid.

I took Reid to Ohio that summer to meet Adam's family. It was painfully beautiful. Reid, reverent that they lost their son for him to live. The Aethers, gaining closure through their heartache, knowing that Adam's organs saved someone else's life, and he didn't die in vain. When they placed a stethoscope to Reid's chest, it was hard to let go. A small part of Adam had come back to life for them.

Mrs. Aether told me it was as if Reid was Adam's way of taking care of me, continuing to offer me comfort, like he always wanted, during the most vulnerable years of my life.

Most double-lung recipients only live one more year after the transplant. But Adam's selfless decision to donate his organs gave Reid six more years of life, and four of those we had together.

We took full advantage of this miracle and tried to suck as much marrow out of life as possible. We both graduated from college with English degrees and got married that summer. We traveled the world, invited new experiences, learned new things, frequented the ocean, and spent so much time writing. We wrote down everything —immortalizing our philosophies, our fears, our love.

In 2004, Reid's cystic fibrosis worsened and took over the once healthy lungs of Adam inside him. It was like saying goodbye to both of them. Our last six months of marriage consisted of hospital stays, hundreds of pills a day, daily breathing treatments, feeding tubes, and constant oxygen—all that he predicted.

And I stayed by his side until his very last breath.

Reid left me a letter before his death like Adam did, but his was different—he knew he was going to die. He wrote it when he could no longer breathe on his own. The ventilator breathed for him, which hindered him from speaking. Even in his weakened state, it was beautifully simple.

Cara,

All I ever want to do in life is make you happy, yet I know that writing this letter does not come at a happy time because it means my short life on earth is about to end.

Since I was a kid, I have been insecure about the treatments, the oxygen tubes, and the scars. But you never saw those things. You just saw me. I never imagined I would get married or even experience love. Thank you for loving me and letting me love you back.

We all have a story—our reason to breathe. We don't get to choose how it begins, the people who enter, or the pain that comes along the way. You didn't, Adam didn't, and I didn't. But we get to choose the people we love, how we love them, and the stories we're going to tell. We had quite the love story, Cara Phoenix. And as I am about to leave your story, I beg you not to let my death prevent you from continuing to live your life or keep you from writing because the world needs to read your words. Please promise me that you will continue to breathe life into your words and always tell Adam's story, your story, my story . . . our story.

I love you more than anything,
  Reid

Adam was my first listener and encourager as a writer, and Reid got me back on the road I needed to travel with my craft. Just as Adam breathed new life into Reid, Reid breathed new life into my writing. My time with both of them allowed me to create and rekindle my desire to be an author.

Before Reid took his last breath, I lay next to him on his hospital bed and whispered in his ear, "I promise to do what you ask of me. To live. To write. To always share our story."

And that is why I wrote this book.

THE INSPIRATION BEHIND
BREATHTAKING

At the age of sixteen, Alex Lott decided to be an organ donor when he received his driver's license. During his senior year of high school, Alex was playing touch football with his baseball team when he had a freak accident that crushed his C5 vertebrae. Although it was initially believed that he would survive as a quadriplegic, complications occurred after a massive stroke, causing his brain function to cease. Alex's parents made the decision to take him off life support so he could donate his organs. Two days after his accident, Alex died on November 4th, 2012, but his unselfish decision to be an organ donor saved the lives of five other people.

Madison Taliaferro was diagnosed with cystic fibrosis at the age of two. When she was eleven, her lungs only functioned at eighteen percent, and she was in desperate need of a double lung transplant. On November 5th, 2012, just a few weeks after her twelfth birthday, a perfect match was found—they were the lungs of Alex Lott. Alex's lungs gave Madison six more years of life, and she took advantage of each day. During her senior year of high school, complications with cystic fibrosis took her life on December 15th, 2018. She was a close student of the author and knew she had inspired this book, but she never got the chance to read it.

TAKE ACTION

Please consider becoming an organ donor.
For more information, please visit
www.organdonor.gov/register

Help find a cure for cystic fibrosis.
To see how you can help, please visit
www.cff.org

A NOTE FROM THE AUTHOR

Thank you for reading my debut novel, *Breathtaking*. I have breathed so much of myself into this book so it could come to life.

I've wanted to write a novel since I was eight years old, but I never had an idea for a compelling storyline until I met Madison Taliaferro in 2015. At that time, she was a ninth grader where I teach who was too sick to come to school due to her cystic fibrosis. I was hired to be her homebound teacher, and for two years, I spent two-three nights a week in the Taliaferro home working with Madison. I quickly learned the compelling story behind the double lung transplant she'd received from her organ donor, Alex Lott. And I was mesmerized by this spunky girl who literally struggled through each breath to make the most of her second chance at life.

It was then that a concept for a plot finally clicked.

When I shared with Madison that she'd inspired the idea for my book, she was so excited. Sadly, she never got to read the novel because I was only a quarter of the way finished with it when she passed away from cystic fibrosis in 2018.

At first, I contemplated abandoning the book. I was so heartbroken by Madison's death and thought it would be too difficult to write with her gone. But I knew I couldn't not write it. I wanted a tool to help spread awareness about organ donation and cystic fibrosis research, and I needed to write this to honor Madison and Alex.

That is why a portion of the proceeds from this book will be used to help support the Madison Taliaferro Memorial Scholarship and the Alex Lott Memorial Scholarship.

The plan for my next project is to write the joint biography of Madison and Alex, so everyone can see the incredible connection between these two amazing kids who breathed with a purpose.

Stay tuned, sweet readers.

STAY CONNECTED
WITH COURTNEY TURCOTTE BOND

Website: www.courtneyturcottebond.com
Facebook: Facebook.com/courtneyturcottebond/
Instagram: @courtneyturcottebond
Twitter: @courtney_t_bond
Hashtag: #BreathtakingBook

If you sign up to be an organ donor after reading this book,

tag Courtney Turcotte Bond about it on your favorite social media platform.

IF YOU ENJOYED THIS BOOK:

Please leave an honest review on Goodreads, Amazon, or
wherever you purchased the novel.
Reviews are crucial to the success of a book.
Plus, it's good karma for you.

DISCUSSION QUESTIONS FOR BREATHTAKING

Are you reading *Breathtaking* with your book club?
Contact Courtney Turcotte Bond through
www.courtneyturcottebond.com, and she'll do an in-person or
virtual Q&A session with your club!

1. Do you think it was necessary for the setting of this book to take place when it did? How would it have been different if the setting was more modern?
2. Why do you think the plot opened with a flash-forward? What were your initial thoughts about the unnamed male?
3. Why do you think the plot starts when Cara and Adam are eight instead of high school?
4. Psychoanalyze the parents. Do you relate to or feel sorry for either of them? What do you think drove them to be the way they are? Which one do you think is more detrimental to how they raise Cara? Why do you think some of their actions are contradicting in the plot?
5. Do you feel Cara is justified in being upset with Adam in high school?
6. Do you think Adam and Cara were ever romantically in love? Just really good friends? How does this change the plot either way?

7. What do you think is the significance of the ladybug(s)?
8. Where did you notice foreshadowing in the plot? Or what was something you didn't realize was important or ironic until the end?
9. What are some symbols you discovered in the book?
10. After reading the novel, what is the significance of the title *Breathtaking*?

ACKNOWLEDGMENTS

This book would not have been possible without the following people:

To **Penny Lott** (Alex's mother) and **Desiree Taliaferro** (Madison's mother), I am eternally indebted to you and your husbands for raising such stellar and inspirational kids. Thank you both for your friendship, support, and openness to revisiting the beautiful and heartbreaking memories of your children to help me develop this story. I pray that, above everything else, this novel honors your precious son and daughter.

To **Jade Kitchens** (Alex's girlfriend at the time of his death) and **Ethan Teter** (Madison's boyfriend at the time of her death), getting a peek at your relationships with Alex and Madison was so special. I cannot thank you enough for sharing perspectives that only you hold and for also revisiting the devastating loss of this person you were so in love with. Both your real-life love stories are so touching and were instrumental for the inspiration behind much of this book.

To everyone who willingly let me interview them about their functioning alcoholic parents (all wishing to remain anonymous), "thank you" doesn't feel like the right phrase to use for digging up painful memories so that I could better characterize Mr. Ecrivain. I appreciate you all for your insight.

To **Hope Bolinger**, my editor, who gave me so much needed feedback in such a loving and gentle way. You have a great talent, and this story is much better because of your help.

To **Sarah (Rowan) VanValkenburg**, who graciously proofread the final copy before publication. Thank you for your extra set of grammatical eyes that have been helping me out since college.

To my campaign manager, **Arianne Gross**, who was essential in helping me launch this book. I cannot repay you for all the brainstorming and behind the scenes work you did. Your friendship, thoughtful consideration, and words of encouragement are such a gift.

To **Dr. Brian Reuhland**, thank you for your vast knowledge and for helping me make sure everything I included in the novel was medically accurate. Also, thank you for all your insider information about Wilmington and UNCW. It was the perfect setting for the last third of the book. I'm blessed to call you a family member and a friend.

To **Mr. Gary Soto**, thank you for your encouragement and for allowing me to use your poem "Oranges" in my novel. You've been one of my favorite poets since I was in college, and it was an honor to receive such a gift from you.

To **Paul Fredrickson**, who co-wrote three of the poems with me for this book. What a fun experience to go from a student-teacher relationship to co-creators. You have such a beautiful and powerful command over the English language. Thank you for sharing that talent with this project that is so dear to me.

To **Adam Boyd Stevens**, who wrote nine of the poems in this book, I thought the use of your poetry would be a nice addition to this novel. I was wrong. Your poetry *completes* this novel. I can never thank you enough for the gift of your words.

To **Mr. Greg Kurtz**, my senior English teacher in high school. I would not be who I am today without your class. Thank you for inspiring me to love the language arts and teaching me how to write well. I tried my best to eliminate as many weak verbs as I could in this novel, but sometimes, they are inevitable (like that one I just used). I hope you don't cringe after each one you see.

To my friend, **Jay Asher**, you've been such an inspiration and source of knowledge over the years. Thank you for your friendship and for always being available to answer my never-ending questions. You've been an invaluable asset to me on this writing journey.

To my beta readers: **Kaylie Arnold, Kinsley Bush, Kara Fortner-Bush, Joel Goodsell, Faith Maddox,** and **Holly Bierly Young**, thank you for believing in this project and for taking on such a significant role. You're all wicked smart and insightful, which I is why I specifically asked each of you be a beta reader. Your hours of reading, providing feedback, and answering all my questions helped this story develop so beautifully. It was a joy to have you all see this work in its early stages and then blossom. I value each of you.

To my children, **Katelyn and Jackson**, thank you for being my littlest biggest fans and for cheering me on the entire three years I worked on this book. A special thanks to Jackson for allowing me to use his story *Adventures in Food* that he wrote when he was eight.

To my parents, **Jack and Patricia Turcotte**, thank you for fueling my love for reading at a young age, for giving me the wind to fly, and for always believing in me. Your support means everything and making you proud is something I've always strived to do.

Finally, to my husband, **Randall Bond**, who probably knows every speck of this story better than I do. Thank you for being my first reader when this still needed so much work. Thank you for spending countless late nights agonizing over revisions and edits with me. Thank you for helping me punch up certain scenes to make them funnier and for your football knowledge so those scenes were accurate. Thank you for your patience and understanding as I poured so much of my life into this project. Thank you for wiping away my tears when I didn't think I was good enough. Thank you for believing in me and my writing. I love you.

A SPECIAL THANKS TO THE
LAUNCH TEAM

Collin and Kirstin Adams // Alex Who Hates to Lose (@alymakezukirai) // Ashlan Alexander // Aunt Allie (Madison's Aunt) // Aunt Andrea (Madison's Aunt) // Jamey Andrews // Erin Baker // Jill Bell // Jennifer Berges // Annika Bergsten // Julia Blair // Anissa G. Bloom // Clay and Emily Bond // Kevin Bost // Nahtanha Bourgeois // Shelly Boyd // Kodie Brady // Aunt Brandi (Alex's Aunt) // Kim Brown // Staci S. Brown // Angela Brown-Fraley // Yvonne, Gary and Ethan Brownell // Brooklyn Busdiecker // Harley Calhoon // Heidi Carlson // Traci Carson // James G. Cash // Kelly Catlin // Jessica Cowan // Gina Cremeen // Courtney Cruz // Susan B. Cunningham // Megan Quaney Davis // Karen Davis-Powers // Rachel Denning // Miranda Dessenberger // Jennifer Diaz-Reyes // Cindy J. Doerr // Mandy Doerr // David Dunn // Lauren Elwood // Vickie Enciso // Phoenix G. Entrikin // Katelyn Eshelman // Jill Evans // Allison Fedon // Peggy Fisher // Jessie Foster // Heather Fowler // Taige, Tuley, and Marley Gilliland // Melanie Gilliland // Carolyn Gonzales // Janine Gustafson // Porter Haddock // Sheila Hasenkamp // Robin Hartpence // Kimberly Haxton // Jennifer Haynes // Jimmieann Helmbold // Holly Sutherland Hoffer // Ashlie Hogan // L. D. Holmes // Shania Holston // George Huckabee // Andrew Humphreys // Deb Hundley // Kristen and Chloe Hunnicutt // Debbie Jackson // Kat Jamison // Kendra Jellison // Annalise Johansen // Lindsey Johnston // Kim C. Jones // Annabelle Jordan // Maegan Trafton Joy // Rachelle Kaur // Mary Kerr (Madison's Great Aunt) // Marion Key // Jennifer Klaus // Tennille Kress // Tamela Lake // Kayla LeDuc // Megan Leffler // Kathy Little // Kelly Livingston // LouAnne L. Maddox // Meredith Mannier // Traci Marcum // Betsy Martin // Kaitlin Toelke McCormick // Michelle Meddock // Niki Meerpohl // Kylie Miller // Matt Miller // Philip Miller // Rachel Mitchell // Laura Moore // Jess Morgan // Taylor M. Morrow // Madeline E. Murnahan // Allyson E. Myers // Andrea Norman // Hope Oswald // Tricia Parciak // Damon Parker // Tonya Phillips // Stacy Pinick // Emily Potter // Emily Prekopy // Katie Rannebeck // Amy Colonna Remillard // Bailey Renfro // Keri Revett // Julianne Richardson-Valentin // The Adam and Jenny Roberts Family // Alyssa Robinson // Rylie Rumsey // Hayley Rylander-Stevens // Israel Sanchez // Marcy V. Warren-Sandberg // Angelia Scholz // Debi Sherman // Marion Taylor Shute // Stacey

Sinkula // Andrew and Rebecca Sivils // Marilyn Skidmore // Rachel Vore Slabaugh // Pam Slack // Scott, Angie, Rylan and Bradyn Smith // Kitty Smith // Sydney Snyder // Lynn K. Spencer (retired Registered Respiratory Therapist) // Amy Sperske // Sarah Sproul // Bethany D. Staats // Keely D. Stark // Maria Steinbrock // Lincoln and Betsy Stevens // Taylor Stevens // Randi Stones // Susie Stringer // Emma Summers // Olivia Summers // Dena Swisher // Grandpa Don and Grandma Ruth Taliaferro // Tondra Taylor // Cynthia Teter // Abbie Towns // Lisa Towns // Becky Ann True // Emily Imperial Vaccar // Amanda Vanderbogart // Kortnee VanDonge // Meagan Vargas // Kasey Ventimiglia // Katy Wagner // Kathie Wallentine // Alexandra Wampfler // Emily Webb // Katie Welch // Michael White // Trenna Whitmore // Brandy Wilcke // Hollie Williams // Hannah Wilson // Samantha Wilson // Josh Yoho // Alexandra Young // Jamie McGraw Young //

The Winey Bookers Book Club: Tiffany Brubaker, Michelle Burdett, Catherine Craig, Tara Dimick, Debbie Gibson, Vicky Goodlove, Bridgette Hooper, Stephanie Konrade, Jenny Lang, and Laura Schwerdt